'Shepherd writes ... ... with wit. Some of the descriptive passages point to a striking lyrical talent, and a razor-sharp feel for female pain . . . readable, witty and poignant'
Time Out

'Enjoyable, witty . . . perfect for a wet Sunday afternoon'
Today

'Magazine agony aunt Dee thinks she has all the answers – and the perfect life . . . a hugely satisfying cautionary tale'
Woman's Journal

'A funny, fast-paced fairytale with a happy ending – for those who deserve it'
Living

'Sharp humour and a healthy helping of wit'
Prima

'Our sympathy is enlisted for this unlikely heroine, and there's plenty of fun along the way . . . a light-hearted, witty read'
Good Housekeeping

'Combines scathing observations with a highly readable style'
Bite

HAPPY EVER AFTER

———————— • ————————

'Dear Dee,' they would confide, 'I don't know where to turn.' And she would shed a tear over certain of their letters, she really would, she was not ashamed to confess it. But the great thing was that they had summoned the strength and courage to write to her. For, in so doing, they had taken that vital first step on the road to happiness and self-fulfilment. They had started to make their own luck.

Donning her half-moon spectacles, which she wore on a cord around her neck, and which she used both for reading and for waving about, for emphasis, she peered at the contents of the day's folder.

And here, as if to prove the point, was a communication from this little girl, Kayleigh, who related in a childish hand a harrowing tale of domestic violence, lovelessness, poverty and squalor, and who, in spite of all, had found within herself the firmness of purpose to sit down to put pen to paper, to address an envelope, to stamp it and send it off. The kid was not without gumption, then. Good! She would need to call on every ounce if she were to do as Dee intended to propose.

Rose Shepherd is a freelance journalist and has written for numerous publications, including the *Sunday Times*, *Independent*, *Woman's Journal*, *Good Housekeeping*, and the former *Honey* magazine, on which she was herself, for a time, an advice columnist. She has the dubious distinction of being listed in Stephen Pile's second *Book of Heroic Failures* as Worst Agony Aunt. She lives in London and has problems of her own.

ROSE SHEPHERD

Happy Ever After

———— • ————

ARROW

Published in the United Kingdom in 1994
by Mandarin Paperbacks

3 5 7 9 10 8 6 4 2

Copyright © Rose Shepherd 1993

The right of Rose Shepherd to be identified as the author
of this work has been asserted by him in accordance
with the Copyright, Designs and Patents Act, 1988

First published in the United Kingdom in 1993 by William Heinemann

Arrow Books
The Random House Group Limited
20 Vauxhall Bridge Road, London, SW1V 2SA

Random House Australia (Pty) Limited
20 Alfred Street, Milsons Point, Sydney,
New South Wales 2061, Australia

Random House New Zealand Limited
18 Poland Road, Glenfield
Auckland 10, New Zealand

Random House (Pty) Limited
Endulini, 5a Jubilee Road, Parktown 2193, South Africa

The Random House Group Limited Reg. No. 954009

www.randomhouse.co.uk

A CIP catalogue record for this book is available from the British Library

Papers used by Random House are natural, recyclable products made from
wood grown in sustainable forests. The manufacturing processes conform to
the environmental regulations of the country of origin

Printed and bound in Great Britain by
Bookmarque Ltd, Croydon, Surrey

ISBN 0 7493 1356 0

For Les Daly,
fierce and fabulous for ever

CHAPTER

———— • ————

I

The summer was over, you could smell it. The late September air, fogged now with petrol fumes, was damp and apricot and tainted. Sniffing, Eric fancied he detected that sour tang of seasons on the turn. Or was it just his own dyspepsia, an effect of chemical fall-out in the system, yesterday's nightcap, Old Bushmills turned to vinegar in his liver?

Spikes snatched at his sweater; fat, wet droplets showered him as he squeezed along the trimmed border, between the tall hawthorn hedge and the BMW, to mop the wing mirror, and to peel from the windscreen a sopping yellow leaf the size of a man's glove. The hems of his polyester trousers were stained with dew. Grass thatch, hayseed, trefoils of clover clumped on his tan suede shoes and clung tenaciously as he stamped about on the blistered tarmac. With sleep-scumbled eyes he peered at his watch. He puffed with irritation, whistled tunelessly in that way which irked his wife half to death, extruded a noxious outbreath through his teeth. Twenty-five past six. Madam was due at the television studios in a little over an hour. They ought to have been on the road by now. He detested early starts, still more detested running late, he loathed that sensation of swimming against the fast-flowing tide, retarded by some powerful undertow. But there might be no hurrying her ladyship. Oh, come *on* you silly old . . .

A big yellow Hiace van with an advanced case of impetigo

drew up alongside him, its engine running lumpily. The young man at the wheel was so nearly beautiful: but for a slight, not displeasing asymmetry, he would have been perfect. Still, they say that nobody's perfect. He might have been sculpted from clay, his cheeks thumbed in, his mouth stroked out, his upper lip nicely nipped. He had slate-grey, vagrant eyes which wandered hungrily, dark hair drawn back in an elastic band. When Eric Rawlings looked upon him, a small part of him withered and died.

Fine apparition! he thought moodily, picking at a paint scab on the van's nearside. My quaint Ariel.

'Lovely day,' the young man leaned across to shout to Eric through the passenger window, hanging on to the scruff of his lardy blonde labrador, Polly, wobbling the folds of doggy flesh till she drooled deliriously. And it was, of course, for Charlie Horscroft, it was *always* a lovely day.

'A bit fresh.' Eric ceased scritch-scratching at the van, to inspect his blue fingertips with paint shards under the nails. The cold had seeped into him as he stood about. The blood did not run warm in the Rawlings veins. He could not synthesise his own sunshine the way the Horscrofts appeared to do.

There were hundreds of them. Well, perhaps not hundreds, but their name was Legion, for they were many. They issued from Jubilee Terrace, the 1970s council houses by the village green which the newcomers, the commuters, the weekenders in their pristine Tudor cottages up the lane, had so vigorously resisted, and multiplication was the name of their game. Every year, it seemed, there were more of them – more dark-eyed Horscroft sprite children skipping hand in hand to school.

Charlie was the eldest boy. He worked for himself, was a carpenter, decorator, general handyman. He flew on the bat's back. He sucked where the bee sucked – or, at least, in the public bar at the Hare and Hounds. He lived merrily, merrily, free as the wind. And Eric, at that instant, envied him to the depths of his being.

'When are you coming to do our tiling, then?'

'Soon,' Charlie promised lightly.

'How soon is soon?'

'Two weeks. Ten days, maybe. The minute I finish with Mrs Venables. You're next on my list, I promise.'

'That's good, then. Because', Eric chaffed him matily, man to man, 'there'll be no peace for any of us till it's done, you realise?'

'Sure. Well, look, I'm on the case. I'll be seeing you.' Then Charlie gunned his engine and was gone.

Upstairs in the pretty-pretty front bedroom, Dee Rawlings inclined over the hand-painted pine chest of drawers, towards the elliptical mirror which, tilting up at her, emulsioned with amber light the tucks and folds of mature flesh, the much loved moonscape of her countenance. Someone, she thought, as the breeze caught the sounds of voices and swirled them about like fallen leaves, *someone* should have a word with the Horscroft family in the matter of contraception. Enough, after all, was enough.

She mangled her mouth to blot her lipstick, then wadded her lips into a tight rosebud, as she offered for inspection first one profile, then the other, primping her stiff, styled, swept-back, russet-rinsed hair.

Her plumpness – as she termed it – was not displeasing to her, to the extent that she scarcely saw it. She liked her ample form, her big, round face, with the dimply chin embossed upon it. To herself, she was absolutely fine. And she undoubtedly had presence, she could fill a room with herself, reaching into every corner.

Her fat did this much for her also: it lent an illusion of innate prettiness, a hint that underneath it all she was a looker. If she could only lose weight, people supposed, this quality would be consummate. Whereas in fact such prettiness as she possessed was purely superficial. It came *with* the fat, it was a constituent of it, and to lose it would be to lose it.

Not that she dwelt upon such matters. She had, at this moment, at the start of another working week, a sense of absolute sufficiency, of the extraordinary richness, the utter all-rightness of her life.

At fifty-two, she had done so many things so very well. She had never been crossed in love, never known the torment of jealousy; never had sex before or outside of marriage; never been accidentally pregnant – never had to face the dilemma which that can pose. She had not suffered from pre-menstrual tension, a recent invention which she tended to scorn. She had not been addicted

3

to drugs, tobacco, alcohol; or battered her babies; or been beaten or betrayed by her husband; or been heavily in debt, lived hand to mouth. She had never been homeless or helpless. Or fallen out with her parents. Or been caught, distrait, with her hair uncombed, with a wild look in her eyes, and with a pound of pork chipolatas or a pair of support tights unpaid for in her shopping bag.

She had carried her babies to term, working right up to the last minute, before being delivered of two thumping nine-pounders. Middle age became her. She had sailed through the menopause without hot flush or depression, palpitation, constipation, pins and needles, itching skin or flatulence. She could still keep her man happy in bed. She had sustained almost thirty years of blissful marriage. She had brought up her daughter, her son, to be model, useful citizens. Her career had flowered perennially, magnificently. She was gutsy and bouncy and – why not say it? – brilliant. She was *the* Dee Rawlings, journalist, author, media personality, pundit, and for some reason, this Monday morning, that realisation was peculiarly sweet to her. Her famed maternal bosom swelled with pride inside her brassière, testing to the limit the two-way stretch of the Elastane.

She became conscious then that the cottage was full of noise – the roaring of the boiler, the hiss of water in the cistern, the sob of the motor in the lane beneath the window, the answering throb of the walls. She thought it sounded not merely lived-in, but *alive*. And it pleased her to imagine how, the instant the studded oak front door closed behind her, a waiting silence would descend, pointed up by the fussy tick-tocking of the grandmother clock in the hall, measuring the minutes until her return.

In this mood of dreamy sentimentalism and self-absorption, she embarked upon a tour of inspection, checking that all was as it should be, that plugs had been pulled and switches switched.

The signs of human habitation, of a weekend's occupation, were all around. The cherrywood bed was unmade; the crisp, Graham and Greene lacy pillowcases bore the his-and-hers imprints of two heads.

In the bathroom, a tap dribbled into the basin; the towels were soaked and bundled, the wooden floor awash. The soap in the dish was beady with bubbles. The porcelain handle, with the polite exhortation in scrolly lettering to 'please pull', swung gently

4

on the lavatory chain; the water quivered in the bowl. The enamelled surface of the bathtub was warm still, and scurfy. Wisps of steam drifted, secretive and scented, out on to the landing, taking ghostly shape at the top of the stairs before dissipating.

Downstairs in the sitting-room the sofas needed plumping, their Osborne and Little fabrics were crumpled, their cushions collapsed. Pages of the *Observer*, of the *Sunday Times*, were strewn about. Footprints patterned the rugs, they flattened the pile of the washed Chinese carpets.

Beyond the French windows, the garden was bursting with life, it was blazing with glorious, last-gasp colour. Wine-dark Virginia creeper vied with showy gold climbing bittersweet, velvety mauve clematis, flaming torch lilies, old blush roses and tousled mophead hydrangeas.

Farming Today played to a deserted kitchen. Cut-out-and-keep recipe cards spilled out of the index-file and on to the counter. Dirty dishes were piled in the sink. Bistroware coffee-cups crowded the draining-board. There were Edinburgh crystal claret glasses, red with sediment, on the table; and, on the hob, a Le Creuset casserole with the remains of last night's lamb tajine, tarry, black-baked on to the cast iron.

As the concerns of agri-business gave way to daily prayer, Dee reached distractedly to switch off the radio. Such a mess! And yet, out of this chaos would come order. Magically, while they were up in London, all would be put to rights. She could rely upon it.

In truth, of course, there would be nothing magical about the transformation. Eminently capable though Mrs Burston might be, and thoroughly dependable, and largely invisible, she was no fairy godmother. She was merely the domestic help upon whom a career woman such as Dee Rawlings must rely. She was one of those stalwarts, the salt of the earth, who do for the doers.

This morning, Ivy Burston would strip the bed and parcel up the sheets for the laundry. She would swab the bathroom floor and scour the porcelain. She would fold the newspapers and stack them neatly in the pantry for later use (they would serve to line boxes when the apples were gathered in; or they could be rolled and plaited to make firelighters). She would wash the crocks and replace them in the Smallbone dresser. Then, twice daily, she would pop in to feed Oedipuss, to water plants, to keep a weather eye. And for this fair week's work she would receive a fair week's pay.

Their relationship, Dee was pleased to think, was wholly equitable. They had a happy arrangement based on mutual need and mutual regard. Certainly she had no end of admiration for the redoubtable Mrs B who, in turn, was surely tickled pink to keep house for a celebrity. Oh, yes, Dee had no doubt that Mrs B dined out on their association – inasmuch as Mrs B dined out at all.

Not that these things were ever articulated. On the few occasions when they actually met, their talk was of local matters, of village life, of family. And it was always reassuringly the same, as though, having once held a successful conversation, having hit upon a formula which worked for both of them, they saw no reason to vary it.

Otherwise, all communication was in the form of notes. 'Would you please . . . ?', Dee would write, before departing each Monday. And, 'Thank you so much.'

Then, when she returned on Friday evening, she might find on the hall table some cryptic message. 'Window-cleaner Tuesday.' 'Ajax 54p.' 'Hoover on blink again.' 'Wasps back in garage.'

Out in the lane, Eric leant on the horn, a long, angry blast. And at that instant Oedipuss banged in through the cat flap, all snazzy in black and white like a demon waiter slamming through the swing doors of hell's kitchens, with a blackbird in his jaws, a sorry, tattered thing, unzipped from throat to tail, spilling its slimy red insides.

'Put that down at once!', Dee seized the cat as he tried to ooze under the table. Holding him at arm's length, she shook him until, with a mew of protest, he released his prey. 'Right.' Breathing heavily, flushed with exertion, she shovelled him back through the flap and put the catch up.

As Oedipuss squatted, glaring citrine-eyed through his little Perspex window, Dee considered the mess on the Tuscan tiled floor. Feathers, entrails, a jaunty, songful yellow beak. She ought to fetch dustpan and brush, she ought to clear it away. But Eric was leaning on the horn again, and she had to dash. Then, why, after all, employ domestic help, if not to call upon it in time of crisis? One did not, frankly, keep a dog and bark oneself.

So, pausing only to toss a tartan throw about her sloping shoulders, she hurried out to greet the new day, and was away on a mission to set the world to rights.

———————— • ————————

Jamie Rawlings lay propped up in bed feeling ever so slightly queasy, and deeply, deeply disconsolate. He was not – oh, very much not – H, A, double P, Y.

He'd pranged the Porsche, hadn't he? Coming round the Wandsworth one-way system on the drive home last night. Whacked into another vehicle on his near side. Gouged the bodywork, scraped the paint.

It hadn't been his fault, of course. Not remotely. Some silly old sod in a white Transit van had come at him from nowhere.

He would have raised hell, he would have called in the fuzz, but he had had maybe one too many. He had, indeed, been wazzocked. Rat-arsed. Pissed as a newt. It would not have been prudent to make a fuss. His own best interests would not have been served – and the service of his own best interests was Jamie's life's study.

Sufficient unto the day, if his mother were to be believed, was the evil thereof. But that was to reckon without the repairs, the bill for which would be horrendous. Five hundred pounds at least down the toilet. The insurance would pay up, but then he'd lose his no claims, so he would be quids out whichever way you cut it, unless his doting mama could be moved to meet the expense.

He cleared his parched throat in a series of irritable little hacks, then got out of bed and went to the window, to stand there scratching his ribs, gazing testily down at the smart, tree-lined street.

The red Carrera looked just the job out there, it seemed to Jamie, who had an eye for these things. It was so in keeping, somehow, so much of a piece with the elegantly proportioned Victorian houses, with their gleaming brass door furniture, their tall bay windows, their imposing gables, their orderly front gardens.

There was much that Jamie was not. He was not, for instance, an athlete, or an artist, or an Einstein. He would never be a Nobel

7

Laureate or an Olympic gold medallist. But he was God's gift to estate agency. He knew about property, about bricks and mortar. And he knew about taste.

It was he who had chosen the house for his mother, when he was barely out of school uniform, before he found his metier, his niche, and when this road was still up and coming. Well, now look at it. It had upped, and it had come.

There had been a few frantic years of stripping down and tarting up and knocking through, as mean little flats and bedsits were dismantled, and as buildings reasserted their integrity. Low-level primrose bathroom suites had been ripped out like rotten teeth and replaced with old-fashioned, cast-iron jobs. Fitted carpets had been rolled, floorboards sanded, stained and sealed. Façades had sprouted cheery window-boxes, and burglar alarms with such heroic names as Magnum, Trojan, and Bastion. The yellow skips which used to line the kerb, lumbered with patterned lino, Formica wall units, kitchen counters and quilted headboards, had finally disappeared, to be replaced by Range Rovers, and by jolly little jeep affairs, wearing metal braces on their goofy grilles.

The process of unmodernising, of deconversion, of antiquification and up-marketing was thus complete. Today, number forty-nine was a beautifully presented period residence in a leafy road, in a much-sought-after location, in a conservation area, twixt the commons, within minutes of shops, restaurants, swimming, tennis, and with fast, regular services to City and West End. It had many original features, had been sympathetically – nay, *lovingly* – restored, and was in good decorative order throughout. It had a well-stocked, secluded, south-facing town garden and a traditional, hand-built conservatory. It was, in a word, *desirable*.

What was more, it was holding its own, it was keeping its price when all about were losing theirs, when in London the repossessed and dispossessed were everywhere under your feet, and when an agent's flagboard was a signal not so much of reckless optimism, or of upward mobility, as of sheer desperation or of private grief.

Jamie, in his twenty-seventh year, and still in residence, had no plans to move. Why should he when, for a very modest contribution to the household kitty, he had his own bedroom, his own *en suite* bathroom, when he enjoyed all home comforts, home cooking, could tap into a bottomless wine cellar, and when every weekend, in his parents' absence, he had the run of the place? If he bought a property it would be as an investment, or to make a killing, it would be for letting out or selling on. He was a wheeler, he was a dealer, and if in the course of his wheeling and dealing he ventured one toe – well, ever so slightly – across that fine line which divides the reputable from the disreputable, who *gave* a damn? You had to peculate to accumulate, he always said.

For several minutes he stood there, lost in introspection, holding hard to a creditable erection. He was a good-looking young man, if you liked that sort of thing, and he worked assiduously at his appearance.

He had a Knave of Hearts hairstyle, wavy, parted, a sunbed tan, a worked-out body which would blur with fat if he did not take it three times a week to the gym, there to put it through a punishing regime involving weights and pulleys, and oofs and ahs, and a – to him – abhorrent amount of sweat.

He was fastidious almost to the point of finicality. His complexion was smooth with a slight, plasticky sheen, and now that designer stubble was not quite the thing, he shaved it close before slapping on liberal handfuls of scent. His current favourite was Baryshnikov Pour Homme, which described itself as 'classic but a little crazy', and which was the only smell he would permit to emanate from his person.

He kept his nails short and pink and scrubbed. He avoided garlic, would go through fifty metres of floss in a fortnight, and was always in good odour with the dental hygienist. He was one of the very few Englishmen actually to use a bidet – to use it, indeed, *as* a bidet, not as a footbath.

Twice a week, his shirts were collected and returned to him professionally laundered; and he had never been known to leap on his girlfriend without first folding his trousers, hanging his jacket on the back of a chair, and pairing up his highly polished McAfee leather shoes, clunk-clunk, heel to heel, toe to toe, beside it.

He was physically squeamish, had no tolerance of pain, could not bear the sight of blood or the thought of what lay beneath the skin. He would have preferred to think of himself as hollow, like the tailor's dummy which he to some extent resembled.

He could be said to take after neither his father nor his mother, and yet, because there was in the synthesis something of the best of each of them, he had at times been likened to one or the other. He did actually look like his sister, though his features were somehow less crude, more refined. It was as if she had been fashioned for practice, in hasty preparation for his arrival two years later. And, of course, what is good for a man by way of features, is not always good for a woman.

His ears were small and lay very flat. His nose was a bit large – almost as broad, actually, at the bridge as at the tip – but it was none the worse for that. Big conk, big cock, he congratulated himself often.

He had the petulant mouth, the slightly squinty gaze which male models affect when they peer into the camera lens. He was outrageously attractive to women, despising of anyone who lacked sex appeal, and it was a matter of private regret to him that he had not been born Italian.

Turning from the window, from the sight of the damaged car, taking comfort from the knowledge that he was a sex god, a formidable fuck, he jousted over to the bed, where Lucinda lay sprawled on her back with one arm across her belly and the other flung up above her small blonde head.

Even in sleep she looked fearfully posh. There was something about the snarl of the lip, the supercilious tilt of her nose, the quality of her skin, her hair, the fan of dark lashes resting on her peachy cheek, her air of absolute repose. Flights of angels, one somehow felt, had sung her to her rest. Not by the flicker of an eyelid, or by the twitch of a cheek muscle, did she betray ill-ease. Wherever she went in her dreams, it must be to a very safe place. As safe as was the waking world for an adored, indulged and moneyed daughter of a Right Hon, who had no need of a proper job, but who had her own shop, selling the kind of frivolous, arty-farty stuff that few people could afford, and to which fewer yet would give house-room.

Lucinda sleeping, however, had nothing on Lucinda up and running, when her voice, her vocabulary, her body language, her whole demeanour spoke to him of class and privilege.

Consider yesterday night. They had popped in for drinks with Giles and Henrietta, had got mildly and pleasantly sloshed, then they had strolled down, all four of them, to Café Rouge, had walked in off the street, demanding to be fed and watered. And when the waiter had said sorry, there were absolutely no tables, Lucinda had raked at her fringe with her fingers so it stood up in tufts, she had glared around in exasperation, and in utter disbelief that the motley assortment of diners shovelling *escargots* into their silly faces should somehow have precedence over her.

The arrogance of her assumptions! Left to himself, Jamie would have phoned ahead, he would have made a reservation, and thus would he have felt secure. As it was, he had been mortified to find himself standing around with, as it had seemed to him, all eyes upon him, and with no choice but to melt away, to try another restaurant.

Lucinda hadn't been embarrassed, though. Nor had Giles or Hennie. Indignant, yes. Incredulous, certainly. Snooty, indeed. But embarrassed? Not on your life! Because they were, he had acknowledged to his acute chagrin, of a different ilk. He had so much still to learn about these people before he could move freely, unthinkingly among them and be one of them. Involuntarily, now, he dropped his head, he looked at his feet, and was half surprised to find that they were not made of clay.

Lowering himself on to the bed he gave Lucinda a tentative nudge. 'Luce.'

'Piss off.' She rolled away from him, clenched her fists under her chin, showed him her back, the knobs of her shoulders, her spine. She was always grouchy on first waking – had been grouchy, too, on the way back last night. Barely had she got into the car than she had gone out like a light. He had been talking to her about this and that, about his plans to set up in business of his own – a matter close to his heart – when the bump, bump of her head against the passenger window as they bounced over potholes had informed him that she was not hearing him.

If she hadn't nodded off, he thought suddenly, savagely, if she had been sitting up and taking notice, she might have alerted him to the danger as the van came alongside.

As it was she had slumbered peacefully through the scrape. Then, roused by the sound of an altercation, of raised voices, of some fairly fruity language, she had flung open the door and draped herself out of it, to call imperiously to him, practically commanding him to stop farting around for Christ's sake, because she was absolutely zonked, and had the most god-awful headache, and wanted to go to bed.

Not surprisingly, they had had a row, or as near to a row as it was possible to have with someone who frankly couldn't be fagged to argue, who yawned in one's face, who said 'Jamie, do be civilised', and 'This is utterly pointless'.

Most of her adjectives, it occurred to him, had a contemptuous 'less' tacked on the end. People, in particular, were hopeless, witless, dickless, chinless, worthless, spineless. They bored her shitless. On Lucinda's lips, less was a great deal more. It was her favourite suffix, delivered with a Roedean accent. Roedean, Brighton, Jamie told himself. Brighton, Suffix. Suffix by the sea.

The idea of making love to her was all at once unappealing. His sense of grievance was like indigestion burning in his chest. His heart blackened. Tushing, he got up, reached for a robe, and took himself off downstairs, where he flopped on to the sofa and snatched up the remote control.

When he switched on the television, his mother gushed into the room, holding forth as usual, talking – if you please, at this time in the a.m. – about genital warts.

There was something irresistibly awful about her performance. He sat forward in his seat, gritted his teeth, and watched with all the ambiguous emotion, the pride and shame, which the woman aroused in him.

She was frightfully up, this morning, she was round and rouged and jolly – a kind of poor man's Claire Rayner, he thought, an outsized Doctor Ruth, and he was instantly ashamed of his own disloyalty.

Fundamentally, he admired Dee. He even quite loved her. He had always considered her a good sort. She had energy, she had drive, she had initiative – qualities which Jamie esteemed, and which he found conspicuously lacking in his father.

Eric Rawlings was, in Jamie's view, a jerk. He was a joke. He was, if you got right down to it, quite hopeless. Witless, dickless, chinless, worthless, spineless. A failure at whatever he attempted, he bored his son shitless.

For as long as Jamie could remember, it had been Dee who had brought home the bacon; she who had kept a roof over their heads; she who had held the family together.

She had fought her way to the top in the competitive world

of women's magazines, she had earned both fame and fortune. She had come a long, long way since the early days, when she contributed the 'I, Me, Mine' column to the now-defunct and wonderfully quaint *Home Circle*. Those hilarious weekly jottings, tales of domestic chaos, of collapsing soufflés and leaky plumbing, of incompetent workmen and critical in-laws, confessions of a harassed young housewife and mother with a nest of robins in her hair, had brought her to the notice of the publisher, had earned her her first proper job, as assistant to the problems page editor on *Mia* – and the rest, of course, was history.

All the same, as he listened to her dishing out wise counsel, as she admonished some poor viewer who had rung in distressed – as she 'got to the bottom' of the problem, to the reason for the warts, the means by which the papillomavirus had entered the body – he felt not a little wretched.

'Silly girl,' Dee scolded, kind but stern.

And, Oh, God! thought Jamie. Oh, help!

He tried briefly to envisage how he might one day introduce his girlfriend to his family. He had managed thus far to keep them apart, by bringing Lucinda home only when his parents were out of town. But the twain must, he supposed, eventually meet.

'Mum', he would say. No, 'Mummy'. Or 'Mother'. 'Er, Mother, Father, this is . . . I should like you to . . .' Then, 'Hi,' Lucinda would respond insouciantly, offering a limp and dangly hand, her face the very picture of barely suppressed amusement. Dee, in her turn, would be effusive. She would solicit a kiss. Everyone, but *everyone*, was required to kiss Dee Rawlings.

It did not bear thinking about. Sighing, and with something like gratitude, half in love with easeful death, he gave himself over to a hangover, closed his eyes, closed his mind to the realisation that his mother was, for all her wealth and celebrity – and one really had to face the fact – more than a tiny bit low rent.

●

Sandra Rawlings was not at home in her Camberwell flat that Monday morning to watch the television. While her mother was favouring Diana from Dorking, or Gill from Gillingham, with her usual golden words of advice, Sandra was sinking lower and lower in a black plastic swivel chair, crossing and uncrossing her ankles, gazing at her reflection, adjusting her expectations, coming to terms, trading down emotionally from a wild and secret aspiration, through creeping doubt and trepidation, to bitter disappointment, to humble acceptance, to quiet despair. She blamed herself, of course. She should have known. She should have learnt her lesson. She had had enough experience, for heaven's sake!

This was how it always went: you arrived at the hairdresser's, breathless with your own daring, clutching a picture of Michelle Pfeiffer, and hoping against hope. Then one, two, three hours later, having paid a small fortune, you were turned out on to the street, smelling pervasively of perming lotion or of hydrogen peroxide, looking still so very much yourself but with your hair sitting stiff as a nylon wig on your stupid, stupid head.

And as you stepped into the unforgiving London sunlight, as you glimpsed your flitting figure in the gleaming window glass of Mayfair, you would be overtaken by the awful, ineluctable truth that you were not — nor would you ever be — Michelle Pfeiffer. And you would be sickened to your very soul by your own presumption.

Sandra Rawlings was no great beauty. This was not just her assessment, this was fact. She was nothing to write home about. The girl who stared bleakly back at her from the floor-to-ceiling mirror might most charitably be described as pleasant-looking. Her face above the yellow nylon cape was broad and white and open. Her hair, wound tightly now round rollers, sprigged with pins and topped off with a plastic bag, was mid-brown, wavy, shoulder length. She had a wide and trembly mouth, a heavy nose, milky cheeks which bloomed spontaneously with brilliant colour, and quite nice, light, expressive eyes, in which swam grey, gas-permeable contact lenses in the soup of her disillusion.

At five foot eight, she felt tall and awkward, and she had an unreasoning, defensive hostility towards small, feminine women, who made her feel gawky and whom she frequently felt like slapping. Her long hands and feet displeased her endlessly. Even her toenails were, in her estimation, too large, and she never wore sandals. But, then, so what?

Sandra was a pragmatist. She did not as a rule indulge in self-pity. 'Put up and shut up', her mother, at her most abrasive, was apt to advise, and these words were imprinted on her heart.

Not that she was hard-bitten or unsentimental. She had thought she might *die* crying over *Anna Karenina*, and *Goodbye Mr Chips*, and at the bit in *Death in Venice* where Dirk Bogarde's dark rinse runs. Tears started the instant she heard the strains of 'Danny Boy'. Or 'Shenandoah'. Or old Sheppy has gone where the good doggies go. She had only to think of donkey sanctuaries, of seal culls, of Save the Children, of man's inhumanity to man, or of some corner of a foreign field that is forever England, to be overwhelmed by ineffable sorrow. She could even, when she was pre-menstrual, find unbearable poignancy in the Yellow Pages ads, and in those ones for British Airways in which families were brought together from the far corners of the globe.

But in the matter of herself, and of her own private dissatisfaction, she kept a resolutely stiff upper lip. She looked on the bright side. She thanked God for her sturdy legs, for a full set of teeth, for her eyesight such as it was, and for health and vigour.

Appearances were not, after all – or not quite – everything. Good looks did not make you a better person; *au contraire*. And, as her mother always said, while her brother Jamie, two years her junior, had charm, while he had style, while he was impossibly handsome and popular and successful, Sandra too had been blessed. She had lovely, legible, rounded handwriting. She made beautifully light short pastry. She was a good listener, a powerful swimmer and an accomplished cook.

She was a worker, too, according to Dee; she applied herself and had the knack of passing exams. Her teachers had actually said she was clever, although at home this had been rather discounted. (Academic qualifications, high marks, prizes, distinctions were not the only measures of intelligence. Jamie was the bright one, really.)

It occurred to Sandra now, sitting there in the treatments room, in gloomy communion with her looking-glass self, that she might have been forgotten. Patrina, her stylist, having informed her that she needed maybe five more minutes, had disappeared down to the ground floor salon, oh, *ages* ago, leaving her quite alone and unsupervised.

Listlessly, she leafed through *Mia* magazine, pausing at the problem page, at 'Dear Dee', to consider her mother's picture by-line, a photograph of 'Britain's best-loved agony aunt', with her chin resting on her bunched fist, with a twinkle of flashlight in her eyes, and with a tell-me-about-it expression on her gently smiling face.

JW of Epping was wondering if you could get pregnant the first time you had intercourse – and what exactly was intercourse, anyway? PF from Ulverston had a passion for a man at work, but how could she be sure that it was mutual? KC of Colchester suspected that her friend's husband was having an affair with her friend's friend, so should she tell her friend? And Sandra Rawlings from London SE5, wanted to know what the hell was going on here with her hair.

She was starting to cook under the heated lamps. The perming lotion felt as if it were stripping her scalp. Fumes from the chemicals were beginning to fuddle her brain. Or perhaps it was just that the room was stuffy. Someone should open a window. She fretted and fiddled with a roller. No need to panic, she reassured herself. Any moment, Patrina would be back.

She smiled experimentally at her reflection. The smile did nothing for her face, so she let it slide. She looked absurd, she decided, and snouty, and spiky. She looked like Mrs Tiggywinkle.

What happened, actually, if you left the perm stuff on for too long? Was she crisping beneath the plastic bag? Should she call out for assistance? For first aid? For an ambulance? No, best not to make a fuss.

Perming solutions were supposed to soak through the cuticle, it was said, and to loosen the chain links of the hair so it could be reshaped. She closed her eyes and tried to visualise that process, to comprehend it, but could see nothing except phosphorescent amoebas, floating, shaping, reshaping, dividing and sub-dividing in the darkness behind her lowered lids.

'How are we doing?'

To her intense relief, at that instant, Patrina came bustling in, very brisk, very businesslike. She was a small, self-confident girl with a pertly pretty face framed by a perfect dark bob. She unclamped a roller, unwound a lock of hair, tested the curl.

'It's a bit springy, isn't it?' queried Sandra, and her voice seemed to scrape against her throat. Patrina bit her lip so it it blenched. 'It's grab on,' she pronounced ominously.

'The perm?'

'Your hair must be very porous, that's the thing.'

Well, naturally. It could not be that the hairdresser had left the solution on too long, or that she had used the wrong sort of stuff, that she didn't know her job. The fault had to lie with Sandra, with her hair, which was as porous, probably, as a sponge, and which would therefore positively drink in chemicals the moment they were applied.

'Will it be all right?'

'Oh, yeah. Come over and and we'll neutralise it.'

Ten minutes later, left alone once more with her thoughts, lying back against the washbasin, against the hard enamel rim, straining to swallow, with her neck muscles creaking and with neutralising foam fizzing in her ears, Sandra brooded glumly upon her predicament. It all came down, she supposed, to who you were. Or, indeed, to who you were *not*. It was all about being Sandra Rawlings, and, *ergo*, *not* being Michelle Pfeiffer. Because you could bet your boots that nobody had ever left Pfeiffer, forgotten for half an hour under the heated lamps. Nobody ever unwound *her* hair, bit their lip, and sighed and said 'It's grab on.'

'All right, Sandra?' Patrina, rematerialising at her shoulder, turned the taps, tested the spray on the back of her hand. And, 'Fabulous,' she said when Sandra grunted her response.

The water felt lovely, cleansing, cooling to the scalp. Patrina, working with her thumbs, soothed the itching. The scent of shampoo, of coconut, was wonderfully refreshing. Thank goodness the day's ordeal was almost over.

'It's took all right.'

'So you said.'

'Your hair takes a perm very well.'

'That's good.'

By tacit agreement, it seemed, they were making light of what had happened, pretending to each other that it had not all gone so horribly wrong. For Patrina it was a matter of brazening it out; for Sandra it was one of reticence. Simply, she could not handle being rude or angry. If ever she lost her temper she felt too big in her skin, and red like a baked tomato, and it probably upset her ten times more than it did the object of her ire.

With a towel wound turban-fashion around her head, she allowed herself to be led back to the mirror, there to be unswaddled, moussed and lacquered and blown dry.

It could have been worse. It could have been far, far worse. Okay, the perm was a little bit frizzy. In fact it was a fright. But it wasn't an unmitigated disaster. She had heard tales of women leaving the hairdresser's with green hair. Or with no hair. Or with hair the texture of cottonwool. There was always somebody worse off than oneself.

So she thanked Patrina humbly, and tipped her immoderately, hurried out into the late summer sunlight, and headed blindly for home.

———————— • ————————

'I'm not going back,' said Kayleigh.

'Well, you're not stopping here,' said Margaret.

'Just until I'm on my feet.'

'We haven't the room. Not for the boy as well. And your dad won't stand for it.'

It was a conversation quite without possibilities. It had nowhere to go but around and around in ever-decreasing circles. Kayleigh might have wondered aloud what kind of mother it was who would throw her own daughter out on to the street. Margaret might have remarked – and was almost moved to do so – that having made her bed Kayleigh must lie in it. But in the end neither of them could be bothered; speech seemed to demand too much of them, so they sat side by side, in separate, sullen silences, staring at the telly which flickered, soundless, in the corner.

The television camera is said to favour a spoon-shaped face, an upturned mouth, a small nose and well-defined chin; whereas stripes, curly hair, busy patterns, can cause dazzle and confusion. Yet the face of the woman who now filled the screen could not have been described as spoon-shaped – unless, by that, a soupspoon was implied. And her mouth, when it was not on duty, not worked up into a smile, or chewing over other people's problems with unseemly relish, had a definite downward tendency. Her chin had got lost somewhere; and her nose was not inconsiderable. And her hair sort of sizzled. And her blouse was a riot.

Margaret Roth liked to have the colour turned up very bright indeed, she liked it vivid. No one in real life would be so red of

18

hair, or wear so mauve a mauve, so green a green, so checky a check. Which was, in a way, what was wrong with real life – or at least with Margaret's life, which was one of unrelieved monotony.

Poverty is about the most tedious of conditions. It has nothing whatever to commend it. Time passes very slowly between Monday, when you have just a pound or two in your purse, and Thursday, when your Giro is due. And yet, she reflected, as she rummaged down the side of the sofa cushion for her Silk Cut, it made you old beyond your years, it stole your life from you, it stole your teeth, and turned your hair quite white.

Wealthy and self-satisfied types will sometimes pose the question why the most hard-pressed in our society spend money on cigarettes when they can so patently ill afford to do so. Surely these inadequate individuals could find a better use for their money? And was it to subsidise their filthy habit that the conscientious citizen must be taxed until the pips squeaked?

Well, Margaret Roth could have answered them. Margaret knew. The poor bought cigarettes *because* they could ill afford to do so. It was a small act of defiance, a tiny victory of the cussed human spirit over penury, a chance to blow smoke into the face of adversity. Besides, it was an addiction. And a comfort. And who the hell cared anyway? Let the health-obsessed middle classes, those with so much to live for, eschew tobacco if they must. Their bodies might be temples; hers was not.

She lit up, took a drag, coughed productively, waved the glowing fag around and said, 'It's that Dee Rawlings woman.'

'Mm.' Her daughter rested her chin, flower-like, in the calyx of her hand. She was fragile, with a wan face and dingy complexion. Her eyes were deeply blue, but dull with misery and stifled intellect. Beneath the left one, a purple bruise stained the cheekbone. She puffed out her lips, then pursed them as she sucked on her displeasure.

'Turn the volume up, eh?' Margaret urged. 'Might as well hear what Mrs Know-All has to say.'

'Okay.' Kayleigh got up and bent to jab at the button, before crossing to the window, where she stood with hands on hips, with one insolent buttock dropped, distractedly booting the skirting-board with the toe of a Niké trainer.

Her fair hair hung in ropes down her back. Her jeans fitted close to her tiny frame. She had almost no flesh on her, she was bone beneath her skimpy vest top. It was difficult to believe that she had a baby, a boy of nearly two, for she was built like a child herself still, though at eighteen she had grown in all the directions she was ever going to grow.

Silly cow, thought Margaret wrathfully, to have got herself knocked up before she had even finished school, and by such scum as Greg Harper, whose family were known villains, despised throughout the neighbourhood. She had warned her daughter often enough, she'd done her utmost. 'That one', she'd cautioned Kayleigh, 'has bad news written right through him like a stick of rock.' And, 'You be careful, you hear me?'

But Kayleigh had been headstrong, obstreperous, out of control. A little sexpot, she'd been in and out of bed with all the boys, and it had been, in retrospect, a question not of if but of *when* she would cop it.

'Mum.'

'Mm?'

'Oh, nothing,' said Kayleigh, in that husky voice which was a constant surprise, issuing as it did from someone so slight.

The view from the window was not uplifting. The flat was above the off-licence, down wind of the Kentucky Fried Chicken. It was approached by an iron fire-escape which rang under the officious feet of meter readers and debt collectors and the man about the drains. It looked on to the concreted square of back garden, where the refuse was stacked, and beyond to a strip of grass sick with dog shit, a playground for *Toxocara canis*, afflicted too, this summer, with serious alopecia.

All the same, the prospect was more pleasing than that from the eleventh floor of E block on the Wavertree Estate, from the flat which Kayleigh had been allocated, a familiar vista of wasteland and dereliction, outcrops of light industry, a car breaker's, shunting yards, the lazy curl of railway lines.

So Kayleigh went on standing there, worrying a loose front tooth with the tip of her tongue, and staring, staring, as though the answer to her troubles must be out there somewhere among the plastic rubbish sacks, and cardboard boxes marked 'Merlot' and 'Malibu', and the buddleia which barged through the brickwork by the rotting wooden gate.

She had been brought up to believe in external solutions, to put her faith in the very agencies which she most bitterly resented, and which she thought of, vaguely, collectively, as 'them'.

It worked, too, of course, up to a point. You *could* turn to your GP, to your MP, to the CAB, to the Social Services, to housing officers and health visitors, to the pest controller, to the family planning, and even, in the extreme, to the police. Why else would the whole panoply of public service and do-goodery exist? Why pay that vast army, if not to serve and to do good?

No one had ever suggested to Kayleigh that she might have her own resources, her own answers, and it had simply not occurred to her to enquire within.

She rested her hands on the sill. They were not very handy-looking hands, not very useful. They were small, and the nails were bitten right down, and the knuckles were red and scaly with eczema. They would not do at all for stroking piano keys, or for soothing a fevered brow, or for any kind of fine art, though the nippy little thumb and forefinger might be good for tightening small screws and for fastening safety-pins. Wretchedly, she scratched the rashes until the skin felt as if it were on fire.

The door flew open and her baby, her unplanned child, her Ben came reeling into the room wearing nothing but a T-shirt. As she turned to watch him, he tottered a few paces towards her, before his legs folded under him and he sat down heavily on the rug. His face was puffy with sleep, and there were snot scars running from his nostrils. He yawned, stoppered his mouth with his thumb, and traded with his mother and grandmother looks of blue-eyed insouciance.

'You should of put a nappy on him. He'll of wet the bed,' Margaret carped. 'Lisa's bed.'

'I didn't bring one, did I? I didn't have a chance. I done a runner. It doesn't matter, anyway.'

'To Lisa it will.'

'I'll do the sheets. I'll take them to the Wash Inn. And I'll turn the mattress.'

'So where will you get the money?'

'I can lend it from you.'

'Not if I haven't got it, you can't.'

'All right, I'll do them in the bath.'

'They'll never dry.'

'Yes they will. By tonight. They'll drip out.'

Kayleigh went and hauled her little boy off the floor, grasping him under the armpits. His legs swung loose as she whirled him on to a chair. 'I'll get him some cereal. Where is Lisa, actually?'

'She stayed over with Simone.'

'That's what *she* told *you*.'

'She's a good girl. Not like you.'

'Oh, yes, of course. Goody Two Shoes.'

She felt almost pure hatred for her sister, who had been a pain in the bum and a burden since the day she was born. Kayleigh had been charged, at the age of eight, with the care of the four-year-old Lisa, who had driven her round the bleeding bend, always tagging along, asking questions. Oh, she had had a use *then* for her pinchy fingers, with which she would grip the chubby flesh of cheek, of upper arm or bottom, and squeeze and twist. Then Lisa would scream, and run to tell tales, and Kayleigh would get a thump from her dad.

Belted by her old man. Belted by her boyfriend. Was it, she wondered morosely, her fate to be bashed up all her life by the men in it? She drew a deep breath. Tried once more, forlornly. 'Let me stay, Mum.'

'I told you, no.'

'But I can't go back.'

'You're going to have to. Be sensible, Kayleigh, we've not got the space. Not now you've got Ben.'

'He could sleep in with me. In Lisa's room.'

'I said no.'

'A fine sort of mother you are, putting me out on the street.'

'Not on the street. You have a home to go to.'

'Some home, with *him*.'

'You should have thought of that before you went and got yourself in the family way.'

'Well, I didn't *think*, did I? It just happened.'

'A baby can't "just happen". Thunder and lightning just happen. And earthquakes. And hurricanes. But not babies. Babies are caused.'

'It was an accident.'

Margaret extinguished her cigarette in the dregs of a cup of Nescafé. 'Some accident! You've made your bed, young lady, and you must lie in it.'

So there it was.

Kayleigh fetched cornflakes and sugar from the kitchen. She tied a towel around Ben's neck. When she brought her face down beside his, he smelt milky and faintly sour, arousing in her both love and disgust.

In the television studio, the presenters, on twin couches, were thanking viewers for ringing in, thanking their guest celebrity for taking the time to come along to deal with their calls. It had been, responded Dee Rawlings, a pleasure. Her smile was like the plop of a stone in the smooth centre of a millpond, sending ripples out and out.

'You could always write to her,' said Margaret sarcastically, gesturing towards the TV. 'Ask her what you should do. Look. Here.' And picking up a copy of *Mia* magazine, another of her extravagances, she sent it flapping through the air like some great, wounded bird, to land slap at her daughter's feet.

Kayleigh retrieved the magazine. She straightened up. She read through the cover lines, promises, promises; she considered for an instant. 'I might do that,' she said in earnest (for what had she to lose by it?). 'Yes, I might.'

———— • ————

As Charlie Horscroft took a chisel and prised off the metal lid, it crossed his mind to wonder why paint tins were round when they ought to be square. They would stack more neatly, for one thing, they would save a lot of space, and a straight edge would serve better for cleaning off your brushes.

On the other hand, he allowed, as he stirred the custardy emulsion, a square tin would have corners, and wherever you had corners, you had waste.

He whistled as he went creaking up the rickety step-ladder to stroke on the first coat, his head filling up with fancies. Polly, who was flopped out on the floorboards at the foot of the steps, with her nose between her paws, thumped her tail rhythmically and raised her brown eyes to him, to reveal tragic little milky

23

half-moons beneath.

It could be boring work, painting, and yet Charlie was not bored. Charlie was *never* bored. He was too fervently curious, too avidly alive, ever to find living less than gripping.

He had left school at sixteen with undistinguished O-level grades, not so much because he had failed his education, as because education had failed him. It had neglected to answer his most urgent questions. It had neglected to address the big issues. It had not fed his spirit.

It was all very well to learn that the air you breathed was seventy-eight per cent nitrogen, or that light travelled at more than a hundred and eighty-six thousand miles a second, or that water froze at zero degrees Centigrade, it was all very interesting. But what Charlie wanted to know was *why*. And he had somehow sensed he wasn't being told the half.

He would never be anything, his form teacher had warned, meaning he would not be a banker, or a doctor, or a town planning officer – as if it were not sufficient just to be.

Well, he was. He just was. He was Charlie Horscroft, handyman of this parish. And he was happy here, today, in the rectory dining-room, with his dog for company, and with the furniture looming, ghost-like, lumpen, under dust sheets. He liked his work, and applied himself to it.

He was utterly meticulous, he would not skimp, he would not tosh, but brought a craftsman's single-mindedness to bear upon a task. 'No job too small', announced the flyer which he pushed through people's letterboxes, and there was, indeed, no commission so trifling that he would not give it his best shot.

He liked drilling holes, erecting shelves, hanging pictures. He liked bevelling, dowelling and dovetailing, grouting and glazing. . . . He liked the resilient feel of putty, the pungent smells of wood-stain and shavings. He liked to watch as his saw chewed into a plank and spat out the sawdust. He liked instant cash payments, crumpled notes, which he stuffed in the back pocket of his jeans and then forgot, so that they sometimes went once, twice, three times through the hot wash cycle, giving a new meaning to laundered money. He was capable and independent; he lived alone, he shifted for himself. And, above all, he served no master.

24

Not that they did not try to boss him, the village ladies in their posh houses who summoned him to see to their leaks and damp patches, to sand their floors, to rag-roll their drawing-rooms, to hang their Laura Ashley paper. Not that they did not patronise him. They called him Charlie, always Charlie, in a false, familiar tone. They fed him tea and big, dry wodges of home-made fruitcake at their kitchen tables, having first put down sheets of the *Daily Telegraph* against his treading dirt into their shining floors.

They asked after his mother, Ann, and, with inappropriate concern, after his brothers and sisters, as though they had been born of hideous misadventure, and not according to his parents' plan. Even Peggy Vine, who had a sticker pasted on the rear window of her Cavalier declaring her to be on the side of life, seemed somehow to imply that you could take the thing too far, that there should be some moderation, some . . . continence.

They pressed upon him immaculate cast-offs, classic clothes with pleats and tucks and sailor collars, which their children and grandchildren had outgrown, and in which his fashion-conscious young siblings would not, of course, be seen dead. But he took no offence, he simply smiled acceptingly and went his own sweet way.

He knew them all, this was his strength. He knew inside their houses and inside their heads. They had a particular brand of self-confidence, they had an overbearing manner, an inability to listen, and thick skins under multiple layers of clothing. But they, too, had their problems, they had errant husbands, or wayward children. They were stoics, most of them, soldiering on in stout shoes, with stout hearts.

They needed their good works and their gossip, their moral outrage and their home-made marmalade. They sought solace in their sales of work, their bring-and-buys, in the gardens scheme, the steeple fund, the WI. Here was their choice: to get up a petition, a round robin against this ward closure, against that road widening – or to look into the abyss. Pragmatists, they imposed a structure, they filled their hours, and they lived within bounds.

Charlie, for whom labour and leisure flowed together, whose every moment brimmed, Charlie, who lived beyond the bounds, was actually rather sorry for them, with their sad, slack, querulous, disapproving mouths, their crackly nylon petticoats, their disciplined hair, the loose skin at their elbows.

He had a lot of time for the ladies – for the conceits of Mrs Vine, who would have him build a grotto by her lily pond, while her husband dallied with his girlfriend at the golf club; for the impossible Miss Chitty, who had been disappointed in love, who wrote epic poetry and had kippered hair and worm in her roof timbers; for Betty Prys-Jones, whose daughter was on a drugs rehabilitation programme, and whose spare room must be wallpapered; for Cecily Tait, two years widowed, not able even now to cope with the loss, to throw out Harold's old, crazed shaving mug, his Brylcreem, his Right Guard from the bathroom cabinet, or to stay off the sherry, and whose scullery walls were green with mould.

There was more trauma, more scandal, more *Sturm*, not to say more *Drang* among the twin-setted middle classes of Ashcombe, or so it seemed to Charlie, than he had ever known in Jubilee Terrace.

He was *Sturm*-free, himself, this morning, as he emulsioned the rectory dining-room. He was *Drang*-free. He had not – nor did he anticipate – a care in the whole wide world.

———————— • ————————

Eric Rawlings strolled up the tiled path of number forty-nine in a mood of high good humour. The sight of the Porsche Carrera parked out there with a nasty gash on its flank was somehow so very cheering, it filled him with infantile glee. The lark – it now came to his notice – was on the wing; the snail on the thorn. God was in his heaven, and all was right with the jolly old world. Wondrously, the acid in his gut seemed to have turned to treacle; it suffused his whole being with its sweetness. As he set down the luggage in the tiled porch and jiggled the key in the latch he began to whistle exuberantly. He whistled 'Crawling From the Wreckage'.

Trampling underfoot a flurry of circulars – the sort of coupons, come-ons, solicitations and free sheets which sick through a London letterbox every day of the week – he dumped the bags at the foot of the stairs and strolled into the long through-lounge, where he surprised Jamie stretched on the sofa, very languid, dozing in front of the TV, looking like a right little ponce in his blue silk

26

monogrammed dressing-gown, and evidently none too pleased to be disturbed.

Father and son exchanged glances – for an instant their eyes locked – then each, without a word, dismissed the other.

Eric flopped into an armchair, tossed the keys on to the Japanese lacquered table, kicked off his shoes, put his feet up, waggled his toes, laced his fingers behind his head, and, with a self-indulgent yawn, settled back to watch as Dee, his helpmeet and better half, did one of her cosy wrap-ups, delivering a homily on marital infidelity, of which no good had ever come or ever would. I lift up my finger, he told himself darkly, malevolently, and I say tweet tweet, hush hush, but now, come come.

He had never been able adequately to account for it, to explain to himself how it had come about that he had married this woman. He had been, so far as he recalled, a blithe spirit, his own man, drifting through life without a care, when he had met a big, demanding girl who had taken him, unasked, to her bosom. She had determined that they should be man and wife, and it would have been unchivalrous to demur.

She had tucked him up so thoroughly, she'd tucked him in tight. He'd not had the chance to put up a fight.

'What the hell time is it?' Lucinda drifted through the door, drowsy, docile, steering an uncertain course, tacking in the general direction of the sofa and of a dismayed Jamie. She was wrapped in a bedsheet, which she grasped at her breastbone, where the merest shadow hinted at the fleshy curves beneath. With her shapely shoulders bare, and her hair falling in her eyes, she appeared both deliciously tousled and sweetly acquiescent.

It was a stage she went through between the ill temper of waking and the brittleness which returned to her with full beta consciousness. It might be very brief, and was absolutely the best time to have her. When he saw her this way, Jamie wanted to seize the moment, to bounce all over her.

Sensing a similar response in his father, he shot him a warning glare, and got snarled up once more in his line of vision, snagged on the hook of his derisive regard. Then would have been the moment to introduce them formally ('Dad, this is Lucinda'), but Jamie was too sickened to contemplate it.

If, as Dee cheerily maintained, all boys fantasise about

27

killing their fathers (nothing to worry about, perfectly natural), Jamie Rawlings' fantasies were more vivid, more inventive, more thoroughly thought-through than most. And it wasn't Freudian; it was personal. He disliked the man profoundly.

'Is there any coffee?' Lucinda swayed slightly on her feet and blinked endearingly.

'Sit down. I'll make a pot,' Jamie offered. And then, because the idea of leaving her alone with Eric was simply too repellent, 'No, come through to the kitchen and keep me company. I'll do you some toast if you're good. Or would you like muesli?'

'Yuck, no, I hate the stuff!' she replied as she swished down the passageway after him. 'It's like eating scabs.'

'Well, I wouldn't know about that.'

She perched on a chrome stool. The sheet coiled around its legs. 'You remind me of a mermaid,' said Jamie, slicing granary bread. 'Shall I make some cappuccino?'

'Yes, do that.'

He put the bread slices in the pop-up toaster and jammed the knob down.

'What time is it?' she asked again.

'About twenty past eight.'

'You're late. You'll get the sack.'

'No, I won't,' he snapped. He was, after all, with his easy charm, his style, his ready smile, by far the most successful of the sales staff, he was surely indispensible. In any case, he was not expected in the office until noon. He had a couple of house calls to make in the meantime.

'I was only joking,' she said, which was probably the case. She might have a sense of fun, but a sense of humour lay somewhere beyond her.

'And what about *you*? What about the shop?'

'It'll keep.' she yawned. 'Monday's always a dead day. Anyway, I can't sack myself, can I?'

'I should be tempted to if I were you.'

'Well, thank goodness you're not me.'

She let the sheet fall, extricated herself with difficulty from its polycotton clutches, and opened her arms to him. He moved into her delicious, naked embrace at the moment that the toast popped up.

As Eric crossed the hall on his way to the bathroom, he caught a tantalising glimpse of his son's girlfriend, white-skinned and lissom, wedged between Jamie and the old apothecary's counter which had been such a find in a stripped pine warehouse in Stockwell.

'Ouch, it's sticking in me,' grumbled Lucinda, meaning, actually, the handle of a spice drawer.

Eric had to grasp the newel post, to haul himself up the first stair, for he was weighed down by the lead in his soul.

He saw himself, starkly, then, as a disappointed man.

He saw himself as worse than disappointed. He had, as it seemed to him, been cheated, he'd been robbed.

———————— • ————————

2

Attractive, airy, ample . . .

Jamie sat at his executive desk, at his computer, writing the weekly advertisement copy for the local paper, conjuring adjectives to sell a variety of very mediocre South London dwellings.

It was a job in which he normally took pride. He was pleased to think he had raised it almost to an art form, and would while away a happy hour or so each Wednesday morning, composing lyrical descriptions, honing his prose, searching for the precise words to sing of the properties in question, to put the merest gloss on the truth, striking a delicate balance between the need to captivate and the rigours of the impending Property Misdescriptions Act, before the twelve-thirty copy deadline.

Today, however, his heart was not in it. His mind was elsewhere. He had more important matters upon which to muse. And, as ranks of London stock brick, terraced houses marched endlessly and all the same through his imagination, he found himself drawing on old stores, on such standard phrases as 'architect-designed', as 'early viewing advised', and even 'deceptively spacious', albeit that he was never quite sure if that meant what he meant it to mean, and not, as he rather suspected, the precise opposite.

Gingerly, he picked out the characters l-a-i-d t-o l-a-w-n (like so many men, he was fascinated by machinery, by technology, and he fancied himself as dextrous, yet he had an aberrant dislike of typewriters, could not relate to a keyboard, and refused to bring more than two fingers to bear upon one). Then he sat for several minutes, staring unseeing at his PC screen, ignoring the winks and blandishments of the cursor. And even the sight of Francine, his secretary, flashing a plump thigh as she teetered on a chair to hang a poster, failed to rouse him from his reverie.

He had been called upon that morning to give a valuation, to size up Clovelly, a six-bedroomed 1920s oddity, a real one-off, which stood, sturdy and implacable, behind a high privet hedge, on the Streatham-Tooting borders, setting its face against progress, stolidly ignoring the passage of time.

Wearing his most professional frown, he had measured his way down from attic to cellar. He had gnawed his nether lip and tapped his pen in a considering manner before making copious, scratchy notes on his clipboard. And only once had he been compelled to turn away, to check his excitement, which threatened to ignite inside his head and to set his eyes ablaze.

The vendor, a Mrs Atkins, had hovered small and anxious at his elbow, tweaking his sleeve, now and then uttering a little 'Uh . . .', as the nerve to ask a question came and went.

They had no choice but to sell, she had explained, ushering him at last into the gloomy sitting-room, which had been bathed in a curious, watery green light, in wobbly sunshine filtered through a waving overgrowth of shrubs. The place (her late parents' house, God rest their souls) was getting too big for her with her knee. And then there was Cyril, her husband, who was 'very poorly'.

Yes, poorly, indeed. Cyril had sat in silence in a fireside chair, with his leather-slippered feet propped on the tiled hearth, in a world of his own, neither use nor ornament.

It *could* be a tricky one, Jamie had warned Mrs Atkins, shooting a wary sideways glance at the catatonic Cyril (was he even *alive*? would she notice if he weren't?). He had accepted from her trembly hand a stained mug which declared itself in capital letters to be the property of Dad, and, taking from his pocket a plastic dispenser, he had clicked in the tiny pellets of artificial sweetener that in his experience were the only thing to make palatable the kind of gnat's-piss tea which clients always pressed upon him.

He had sucked on his teeth – a habit of which he was not wholly conscious, and which, if he did but know it, he had inherited from his father. He had smiled in gentle sympathy, to reassure her that he was on her side, before lifting 'Dad' to his lips and taking a sip. Then with infinite patience he had explained to her how the recession was biting deepest into the middle market.

The biggest detached houses, real mansions, in prime locations were holding their price, and business at the top end was brisk. Why, he had a couple of customers actually racing to sign a contract on a property in Clapham Old Town, which would return them very small change out of half a million pounds. (The rich, he had joked, were always with us.) Then, at the bottom of the scale, you could match a modest maisonette with a first-time buyer for around fifty, sixty thousand. But between those two extremes the waters were stagnant.

She should talk to his competitors, talk to Winkworth, talk to Edwin Evans (although, of course, in so doing, she would forfeit the not inconsiderable benefits conferred by a sole agent), and they would tell her the same.

However, *nil desperandum*. One never quite knew. It was a funny old world. There was always hope. She should not – oh, no, *certainly* not – run away with the idea that Clovelly was a white elephant. *Somebody* would want it. There might be a customer back at the office, even as they spoke, with cash at the ready, and a dream of buying just such an unusual residence as this.

How much was she hoping to raise? Hmmm. That figure was maybe just a *teeny* bit optimistic, just a tidge on the high side, what with the damp in the back bedrooms, and the suspicion of dry rot under the stairs, and the regrettable state of the roof.

Then, of course, the decor, the chocolate gloss paint, while absolutely charming, would not be to everybody's taste. Neutral colours, plain whites, soft pastels might be lacking in character, they might make no statement, but they were what people seemed to go for.

Built-in kitchens, too, as she would no doubt be aware, were slightly outmoded, especially when the furniture was of such an age. People were getting away from this kind of formality, they were going for something less finished, for a mix-and-match, a farmhouse feel. While central heating, needless to say, was pretty well a must.

What she had to decide was how desperately she wanted to move, and how soon.

Here was the dilemma: to put Clovelly up at the price she had proposed, and to take the risk of finding oneself, in eighteen months' time, forced to make a substantial reduction; or to be, from the outset, that much more realistic, and to go for a quick sale.

He could find her a lovely, manageable apartment, with all modern conveniences and a bit of a garden, in a quiet, friendly neighbourhood, for well under a hundred thousand. She could let this place go for a hundred and twenty, with something on top for the fixtures and fittings (he had glanced again at Cyril, who might, he had felt, be among these). She would probably want to sell off one or two of her bits and bobs, her bric-à-brac (he could help her there if she wished, he had first-rate contacts in the trade). And she could be in her new home for Christmas, she could be sitting pretty with a nice little nest-egg in the bank. In which event, no one would be more gratified than Jamie Rawlings. Why else was he in the agency game, but to see people thus set up, and to know he had been of service?

'Sleep on it,' he had urged her, proffering his business card, as she followed him, still jibbing a bit, still fretful, to the door. 'Talk it over with Cyril. Then give me a call if I can help you in any way whatsoever. And let nobody pressure you into doing what you don't want to do, you hear? Now, cheerio. Take care of yourself. And thanks for the tea.' With which, he had prised her fingers off his arm, and with a gallant salute, and a devastating smile, a Jamie Rawlings special, he had strolled to his car.

'I'm going to the bank,' said Francine, leaning against him, deliberately jogging his shoulder with her hip as she peered at his screen. She was buxom, bustling and flirtatious, with the kind of little-girl mannerisms which essentially tough women often affect. She had a penchant for hair slides and appliqué teddies and Snoopy stationery, and she had a fiancé whom, unaccountably, she referred to as Wobert, and to whom her virginity was pledged. She described herself, often, as 'petite', and her bust must have been meant for

33

somebody taller. Behind her desk a printed notice advised that you did not have to be mad to work here, but it helped, and it occurred to Jamie now that she had a mission to send him off his head by contriving to arouse him sexually, even as she drove him to distraction with her idiocy.

'There are two Ss in repossession,' she chided. 'I should have thought you'd have known that by now. Do you want me to get you a sandwich?'

'Of course I know it. It's a typing error. Yes, please, if you will.'

'What sort?'

'What?' Jamie scowled as he lined up the cursor with repos . . .

'What filling?'

'Oh, *I* don't know. Whatever you're having.'

'I'm not having one. I've got Pot Noodles.'

'They're disgusting. Full of E numbers.'

'I like E numbers. At least I *know* what I like.' She thrust out her chin and combed back her glossy, mahogany hair with her fingers.

'So do I. I'll have chicken salad,' he told her. 'No mayo.' He would actually have preferred egg and onion, or sardine and tomato, but the foody, fishy smells would linger through the afternoon, while his favourite brie and walnut would be smellier yet, and far too calorific.

'How was it this morning?'

'How was what?' he asked testily.

'The place you went to see.'

'Oh, that.' His brow was furrowed as he typed the additional S. 'Building society repossession'. It was the latest, coded way of implying that a place was a steal, and it was guaranteed to pull in the punters.

People were all, in Jamie's experience, pig greedy. Few would admit it, they invariably dissembled, they put on a fine show, but deep down they were driven by avarice. 'Oh, we just couldn't, somehow,' they would scruple, when he showed them around one of these snatch-backs. And, as they poked about, peering into everything, yanking out drawers and opening doors, 'We would feel so dreadful,' they would agonise. 'It would be like living in somebody else's home.'

'You realise', he would reassure them smoothly, 'that it's costing

34

the poor chap an arm and a leg every day it remains on the market. He'll never clear his debts until it's sold. You'll be doing him a favour if you take it off the bank's hands. When his mortgage is paid off, he and his family can make a fresh start.'

Then, ah, well, they would say, if he put it like *that*. And the next thing you knew, they'd be haggling ruthlessly over the price, driving a hard bargain, demanding that curtains, carpets, lamps and all be included.

'*Well*?' Francine pressed him.

'Eh?'

'What was the house like?'

'Nothing special,' he lied, sitting back, yawning, stretching, wrapping his arms around his head. 'Fool's errand, actually. Nothing in it for us. Just a typical couple of time-wasters. You know the type. They've seen a bargain up the road in Wandsworth, they're crazed to get their hands on it, but they can't bear the thought of selling at a loss. Everyone wants to offload at eighties prices and to buy at nineties prices, that's the bugger of it. In the end, they're stuffed by their own tight-fistedness. I don't expect to hear from them again.'

———————— • ————————

Dee, too, had had a morning rich with promise. She had met with her agent at the publisher's in Bloomsbury to discuss the presentation and promotional package envisaged for her new book, *Searching For Mr Wrong*, a guide for love junkies, the fifth in the highly-acclaimed 'Lifelines' series.

There was a plan to maximise the in-store presence of this important text, to create a high profile for its distinctive and dynamic writer, with a full range of point of sale, including colour posters and dump-bins, to carry through the impact of the work, to achieve the appropriate level of sell-in. A five-city author tour, interviews on radio, television and in the national press were scheduled.

And (Dee had told herself, bestowing upon the marketing team, between sips of strong coffee, her most beneficent smile) you could not say fairer than that.

Thus, one way and another, it had been a jolly good meeting, it had bucked her up no end. But now she was experiencing the first stress of the day, as she was forced to make a choice from the menu at Joe Allen, where *Mia's* new editor, Clare Constantine, had been pressed into treating her to lunch.

The problem, as Dee identified it, was that in opting for this dish one necessarily deprived oneself of that one. It was a train of thought which led her rapidly on to some pretty profound reflections on the nature and meaning of life.

Because if you were to order, so to speak, from life's great bill of fare, the Cajun chicken with cheese sauce, you would have to deny yourself the spicy Italian sausages, you'd have to pass up on the pan-roasted lamb with grilled vegetables. And then, if the next person had the sausages, and they looked to be more delicious than the chicken, you would be disconsolate and sick with envy.

As a metaphor it was extremely telling. It had resonance. She would use it next week to head up her page, to deliver a little lecture (message: you can't have everything in this world; just make your selection, then *enjoy*).

'So . . .' said Clare, laying aside her menu without so much as a glance, making a dismissive little brushing gesture with the back of her hand, signalling her distaste for the whole enterprise. At the best of times, she was not one for hot lunches, preferring to spend the time at her desk, or at her health club, toning her muscles till they twanged.

She was twenty-eight years old, chic, spare and spiteful, with pale chartreuse eyes, a luscious scarlet mouth, and swishy auburn hair cut to just above her jaw line in an artful bob. She spoke in a dangerously soft, sweet voice and was rigid in her self-control. She was sharp rather than clever, past-mistress of the elegant put-down, and if she had a particular talent, it was for reducing subordinates to tears.

Since her appointment as editor three months ago, she had set out to steer *Mia* up-market. It must mirror her own preoccupations, must appeal to a younger, smarter readership – and to this end she had purged the staff, ridding herself of most of the 'dinosaurs', the older hands, whom she had replaced with ambitious, inexperienced college-leavers.

The icy winds of change had been blowing these past few weeks through the corridors of Magazines UK, but Dee and her department had survived. Clare Constantine could huff, she could puff, but she would not blow Dee Rawlings' house down. For one thing, Dee had the ear of Bob Tanner, the editorial director, in a way that Clare did not. (Other parts of his anatomy were, according to malicious rumour, on offer to her; but that organ was denied her.) For another thing, Dee was too great an asset, too hot a property, far too popular, too public a figure to be displaced. The irresistible force had met at last with the immovable object.

Clare rested one elbow on the table and propped her head, ramming her fist into her cheek, to make it plain how it pained her to find herself here at all. The lunch had been Bob's suggestion. He had conceived it as a treat for the 'girls'. They should discuss, he had said, the possibility of redesigning the 'Dear Dee ' page. She and Dee should talk about it, they should have an exchange of ideas in a relaxed, informal setting.

That it would be a fruitless exercise, neither woman doubted. But needs must when the directors drove.

'What will you have?' Clare asked coldly.

'You know, I honestly can't decide.' Dee drew a deep breath and expelled it. Her bosom rose and fell. 'And you?'

'Just a salad.'

'No starter?'

'Not for me.' Which, in Dee Rawlings' view, was typical of the jealous, joyless bitch. She was perfectly well aware, of course, of her editor's hostility towards her. Fortunately, Dee was an expert, an A-student on the subject of human nature; she was a happy, fulfilled individual, at peace with herself, and was thus able to show forbearance, to make allowances for a driven and desperate, anorexic control freak such as La Constantine.

Almost certainly, the girl was the product of a dysfunctional family, perhaps the only child of toxic parents – of a critical and competitive mother, of a cold and distant father, who would probably have preferred a boy. If only they had given her the approval she'd craved, if they had rewarded her in infancy and had loved her unconditionally, she would not now have this irrational need for power, for a high salary or for an androgynous body. One had to feel sorry for her really.

Beaming up at the waiter, Dee stabbed at the menu with her

finger, plumped for the sausages, and almost at once rued passing up the chicken.

'The spinach salad for me.' Clare sort of tossed her order at him. To Dee she said, 'Do you want wine?'

'*Rather!*'

Clare arched finely shaped eyebrows. 'A glass of white wine then. I shan't join you, if you don't mind. I'll stick to mineral water. I find if I have any booze at all at midday, I'm not fit for work in the afternoon.'

'Oh, really? I have no such difficulty.'

'Well, they do say one's tolerance of alcohol depends on one's body mass. Tell me, by the way, how is Derek?'

'You mean Eric?'

'I beg your pardon. *Eric.* Did he lose his business? I seem to think you said he was in trouble.' Surely Dee's husband was her Achilles heel? She was unassailable on most fronts. Her career was still, in spite of everything, in the ascendant. She was effective, prolific, prosperous, energetic. She might not be as famous as the stars of stage and screen whose black-and-white photographs adorned the restaurant's brick walls, but she was a name, she was a face, she was high profile. She was, indeed, distinctive and dynamic, whereas her husband was an abject failure, a nobody.

'Eric is very well,' Dee assured her serenely, raising her glass to her companion. 'Here's to a long and fruitful working relationship. Mm. Delicious. Yes, he is very resilient. Very resourceful. He has all sorts of plans and schemes. In any case, I don't suppose we'll starve.'

'No,' said Clare tartly, as a plate of sausages, peppers and garlic potatoes arrived at the table. And, as a little bubble of eager anticipation rushed up inside Dee and burst upon her face, 'No, I should think there was little imminent danger of that.'

———————— • ————————

At about one o'clock, the phones in the fifth-floor offices of *Mia* lit up with calls from readers and advertisers, from PRs and other professional nuisances. And at two o'clock they were still ringing. This was particularly vexing for the secretaries, who liked to seize the opportunity, while the senior editors were all out at important lunch meetings, of getting on with the routine business of producing a magazine.

In the 'Dear Dee' office, Nancy Wilkins scribbled a message on her pad, replaced the receiver with a sigh, and applied herself once more to the task of opening the mail.

She was a pretty nineteen-year-old with a ponytail that bobbed about as she bent earnestly over her paperwork, and with a disposition so sweet it aroused suspicion and mistrust in anyone who didn't properly know her.

Most of the time, she smiled. This was the expression she offered to the world – to the rest of humanity, who seemed to her at times to be in the grip of some great communal gloom – and already it was etching itself into the soft planes of her face, foreshadowing the kind, complaisant woman she would become in middle age.

On her tube journeys back and forth, racketing through sooty tunnels deep beneath the capital, Nancy would gaze around at the pinched faces of her fellow travellers, and would wonder at such manifest misery. What was the matter with them all? What did they *want*?

You could never catch another passenger's eye, exchange a grin or a nod or a friendly word. They were all too preoccupied, staring into space, or scowling into their newspapers, or twirling on straps and watching, hawk-like, poised to swoop on the first available seat.

Only when something went horribly wrong – when the signals got stuck on red, or the police had to be summoned to arrest a drunk, or someone fell under a train, and they were forced to sit there for minutes on end, with the engine intermittently going ticky-ticky-ticky – would the mood lighten. Only then would they become busy and animated, recalling other such disasters, practically telling each other their life stories.

Oy, oy, oy, thought Nancy, in the manner of Mrs Meyer next door. Oy, oy, oy, people's life stories!

Nancy felt extraordinarily fortunate and privileged to work at *Mia* magazine. She woke each morning, knotted up with eager anticipation. Every minute of the trip to the office, she looked forward to arriving. And the thrill of walking into reception, of seeing *Mia* covers displayed on the walls, and of knowing that she was here, really here, where it happened, was as exquisite after two years as it had been on her first day.

But more than that, and increasingly, she felt fortunate and privileged to have a big, loving, supportive family, and a devoted boyfriend, to have a perfectly delightful life, when, on the evidence of the postbag, for legions of others, young girls like herself, and middle-aged women, and little children, and grandmothers, all was pain and misery and strife.

As she pondered this, she relinquished her smile. And, as she sorted the post, a frown of perplexity stole in to take its place.

It was her responsibility to sort the letters into three unequal piles. A high proportion of them she could deal with herself, and merely put through for a signature. These were the least onerous of the lot, requiring a standard computed reply, an address, a phone number, and maybe one of Dee's upbeat, optimistic leaflets on infertility, or on infidelity, or on impotence, or on rekindling the romance in marriage. But any which required a fine judgement, or about which she was in doubt, she handed on to Dee's assistant, Edie. While the trickiest ones were slipped into a special folder marked 'priority', and passed immediately to Dee herself.

At the end of the day, they would all be returned to Nancy with handwritten answers clipped to them, and Nancy would type them up and get them signed and sent. Then, finally, Dee or Edie would select any suitable for publication.

It was an efficient system. It worked well enough. And, as Nancy would often remind herself, hers was not to . . . , hers was but to . . . Yet she could not help wondering, every now and then, as she rattled away at the keyboard, clapping out Dee's responses, how it was that X from Exeter was told in soothing tones to go ahead and have her baby, that everything would be just fine, when Y from Wymondham was given the address of a good clinic and strongly advised to take herself off there without delay. Or why Mrs A from Aberystwyth was exhorted to return to her unhappy marriage, to give it another go, when Mrs B from Bloxwich was counselled to make a clean break.

Because, try as she might, she could see no distinction between X's situation and Y's. Or between A's and B's. She would search in vain for a pattern, for logic, for coherence, and, when she failed to find them, she would suppose, with humility and a slight shrug, that she must be very dim indeed.

She was young, of course, and unworldly, she lacked experience. But Dee had a talent which Nancy had not (and which she despaired of acquiring if she lived to be a hundred), an almost mystical ability called Reading Between The Lines.

Nancy would spread the letters out on the desk and pore over them, tacking her bottom lip down with her teeth in the effort of concentration, but *still* she could not see that which was so evident to Dee, and which she had come to visualise, vaguely, as something actual and perceptible, like a watermark. And she would abandon hope of ever learning, ever knowing, ever being as wise or as sharp, or as perceptive or as certain as the estimable Dee Rawlings.

'Do you think . . . ?' she said now, ruminatively, to Edie.

'Not if I can help it,' Edie told her tersely.

'No, seriously. Do you ever wonder, when you send a letter, what the consequences will be?'

'Not a lot,' said Edie baldly. 'It will all be the same to thee and me, you know, a hundred years hence.'

She was a short, sturdy woman of perhaps forty-five, who peered at Nancy through no-nonsense spectacles. She lived on her own in a flat in Kentish Town, and every evening – for this was the kind of person she was – she laid out her clean, pressed clothes for the morning, and made her sandwiches, which she stored in the fridge, in an airtight polythene box, overnight.

Tonight, this being Wednesday, she would open a tin of sardines. And she would lay out the tartan skirt with the kilt pin, and the starchy white blouse with the high collar and a black velvet ribbon at the neck. She would buff up her shoes, and rinse out a pair of spectre-thin, pale tights and hang them over the bathroom rail to drip dry.

She was emotionally completely centred, as low-key and phlegmatic as Dee was ebullient. And while Dee dressed flamboyantly, in some kind of belated over-reaction to prevailing tastes, Edie had a straightforward relationship with fashion: she did not mess with it, and it did not mess with her.

'It would be nice to know, though, wouldn't it, if it really, really helped?'

41

'I doubt', Edie replied, taking off her glasses, huffing on the lenses, polishing them, holding them up to the window, polishing them some more, 'if it makes a deal of difference either way. They usually know what they're going to do before they so much as pick up the pen. We're just supposed to say "All right, bless you, go ahead".'

Without her specs she appeared, to Nancy, strangely unfinished. They seemed more a part of the furniture of her face than did her nose or ears, which might have been tacked on for no better purpose than to support them.

'But how can you *know* that?'

'Ah,' said Edie sagely (and here it came again), 'just reading between the lines.'

'I see,' said Nancy, not seeing at all. And she sighed as she bent over her work once more.

Take, for example, this scrawly, semi-literate letter before her now, from some poor little body. (Nancy flipped the page, read the signature.) A cry for help from Kayleigh from Bermondsey, an unmarried mum from a loveless home, with uncaring parents, a faithless, jealous, violent boyfriend, and nowhere in the world to go but down and out. There were times, Kayleigh swore, when she felt like topping herself. She just did not know where to turn. And, seeing how she was fixed, Nancy understood. But how to help her? What answer to give to a girl in such straits?

This was all way, way beyond her. She slipped the letter in the priority file and put it, as far as she was able, from her mind. It was one for Dee, without question.

And here, at last, *was* Dee. 'Hello, hello, hello.' She wafted into the room on the way to her own private office, to her inner sanctum, in a swirl of grey silk and a cloud of Estée Lauder's Knowing, bearing aloft an early copy of the October issue of *Mia*, as if it were a banner with the strange device, Excelsior!

She inclined over Nancy, breathing exuberance, alcohol and garlic, to place the magazine before her, to show off her latest minor triumph. This month, in the regular 'Town and Country' series (soon to be axed by the vengeful Clare along with Marianne, the homes editor), were featured her two lovely residences, supported by a thousand words of text, an interview with Dee herself on the joys and drawbacks of owning a second home.

In town, according to the text, in fashionable Clapham, Dee Rawlings had gone for a more plush 'designer' look, for a tasteful mix of old and new. While Foxholes, her enchanting cottage in the 'garden of England', the Weald of Kent, had been decorated and furnished more casually, in the style of yesteryear. It was her bolthole, her hideaway, her haven of peace. With a stroking finger, Dee pointed out to her secretary the finer detail, those all-important touches that make a house into a home.

'Fabulous,' said Nancy, awed, nodding so her ponytail danced about at the back of her head. 'Yes, really smashing.'

Then she picked up the file of letters, and placed in Dee Rawlings' capable hands, people's fates, their futures, their dreadful, dreadful lives.

———————— ● ————————

Sandra took a bunch of rocket, rinsed it under the cold tap and shook it vigorously. She was using a lot of the stuff lately. Everyone seemed to want it, while, for reasons which she did not understand, it had gone up not down in price; it had, well, rocketed.

Funny, because it tasted to her as it looked: like something to which a gardener would take his hoe, the kind of untidy and tenacious weed that gets a grip in some dank and sunless corner, then comes tramping up the borders to the back door.

Still, there was no accounting for fashion. And if her clients wanted to serve as a starter her delicate poached salmon fillet on a bed of *rucola* with a blob of lemon *aïoli*, she was happy to oblige.

For the twentieth time she glanced at the clock, to find that she was ahead of the game, she was winning. When, at the very last minute, Jenny had called to say she couldn't make it, Sandra had panicked momentarily, persuaded that she could not cope without a second pair of hands. But she was actually doing rather splendidly with no one to get under her feet, or to ask 'What do I do with this?' (a second intellect was not part of the deal, it did not come with the pair of hands in question).

It was just after seven o'clock. The fish was on the hob, on a halogen ring; the guinea fowl was in the eye-level oven. The vegetables were trimmed and prepared for blanching. She had made the *aïoli*, and the mango and cilantro vinaigrette. The blackberry fool was chilling under clingfilm. The dainty tarts of goat cheese, sun-dried tomatoes and thyme had been prettily arranged on a fine bone china plate, all ready to be handed with the aperitifs.

Sandra was peculiarly confident around a hot stove. It was where she seemed to belong. Ever since she was tiny she had been encouraged to lend a hand with the preparation of food. One of her earliest memories was of standing on a wooden box at the table, in the basement kitchen at the old house in Sydenham, with a teatowel tucked into her waistband, laboriously excising pastry stars.

Her mother loved to feed people, loved entertaining. It was a matter of honour that she kept a good table. And over the years, enthused by the cookery department, by the lavishly illustrated recipes in *Mia* magazine, Dee had indulged in ever more dizzy flights of gastronomic fantasy. She had given endless dinner parties, lunches, brunches, barbecues, beanfeasts, finger buffets, fork suppers, fondues, clam-bakes, chilli dips, pig roasts, tapas evenings and Arabian nights.

Always, Dee had expected her daughter to assist her. Always, she had praised her efforts to the skies. 'Alexandra made these,' she would proclaim to their guests, holding aloft a plate of canapés, as everybody oohed and aahed and said how simply brilliant. 'She has a great future in catering.'

Thus, gradually, it had been borne in upon her that cooking was her thing. It was what she did. She might have gone up to University – Oxford had been spoken of at school, and Cambridge – but instead she had found herself attending Mrs Palfrey's exclusive little classes in Kensington, where she had learned, in the company of a dozen rather dim and undirected gals, the secrets of boning a chicken, and of making the perfect béchamel.

Well, that was okay. She was accepting. She had enjoyed herself on the whole (it is hard *not* to enjoy something at which one excels). She had read all the cookery books, developed her own distinctive style. And she was happy running her own little business.

Besides, she fully understood, she had read the small print, she knew the deal. Jamie had not been destined to make the grade at school. It had been evident, almost from the start, that higher education would not be for him. And if higher education was to be out of the question for Jamie, it must be out of the question also for her.

We all have our limitations in life: Jamie Rawlings was Sandra's.

With everything now steaming or baking or cooling on schedule, she had nothing to do but to hand-write the twee little menu cards which were such a critical success at these soirées. She drew a stool up to the table, took a chewed biro from her bag, clamped it between her teeth, and considered.

Clients were usually most impressed by foreign words, by French or Italian as appropriate. But you could, in her opinion, take the thing too far. She liked to draw the line at *saumon d'Ecosse*, never mind at *boudin yorkais*. On the other hand, she sensed that the Clarkes were the sort of people who would feel more gratified to serve their guests with *saumon* than with plain old salmon, so she was in something of a quandary.

Another trick was to pepper the thing with adjectives. Words such as 'warm' and 'wild'. So was it to be warm, wild salmon? Or *saumon*? Or what?

To defer the decision, and by way of *divertissement*, she set about composing a politically correct translation, lettering it with inordinate care, biting on her tongue the way she always did when she was concentrating.

Dwarf beans would, of course, have to be vertically challenged. They would be beans of restricted growth.

Blackberries could not be black, they must be – what? – berries of colour.

Mango would be persongo. Or even, as the Rastafarians would have it, personcome.

Fool would obviously not do at all. It must be intellectually challenged.

Then what could you call a tart? A freelance sexual operative? A coitionist? A professional eroticist, psychosexual counsellor and climax facilitator?

At which, not unnaturally, her fancy lightly turned to thoughts of love.

Sandra was not a total novice in matters of the flesh, she was not a virgin. You didn't get to be twenty-eight years old in the 1990s without having some sex if you put yourself up for it – at

45

least, not unless you were very seriously aesthetically challenged. And it was absolutely wonderful, it was the best thing.

Yet, she had come to the dispiriting conclusion that it was a snare and a delusion. It was so good, it left you always wanting more – ideally with the same person. Then if, as was all too often the case, the same person did not want to have more with you, it was most awfully hurtful and unsettling and undermining. The pain went through you like a knife. It left you aching and aching. It left you heartsick, wondering what you were doing wrong – if indeed you could be said to *doing* anything. (She was usually too inhibited by self-doubt to play a very active role, preferring to lie there making all the right noises, passive but, she hoped, collaborative.)

Anyway, in the long run she had come to question if the game was worth the candle, and these days she avoided all temptation.

She missed it very much at moments, missed the intimacy, or the *illusion* of intimacy, someone's damp hair in her face and tickling her nose; a scratchy cheek against her breast, bringing her up in a furious rash; skin sucking at skin . . . But she had more or less made up her mind that she would wait for a steady relationship.

There was a catch in that as well, however. She knew it from her experience of friendship, and from having been engaged in her early twenties, for almost a year and for no good reason, to a self-obsessed emotional retard called Simon. Because when you first met people, you thought they were somehow other than mere mortals, you could find no flaw in them, and admired them utterly.

Then, as you became closer acquainted, you saw another side to them, and felt not necessarily worse but differently about them – a bit like going round the back of a house, where the dustbins are kept, and the washing hangs out.

She clicked her tongue, whistled through her teeth the way she knew her father did, and wrote 'salmon'.

'Hello there.' The young man who sauntered into the Clarkes' spacious, labour-saving, spick-and-span, wipe-clean kitchen was tall – at least six foot two, she reckoned – with a slight, accommodating stoop. He wore a striped shirt, which had been buttoned awry. His skin looked rough and crudely razored, and a faint scar on one cheek contributed to a vague impression that he had his face on inside-out. He had straw-blond hair, a pointy nose, eyes so round and brown they looked like holes. Something in his mien made her want to laugh out loud. She sensed in the upward curl of his mouth a self-deprecating and subversive humour, a sort of tragic clownishness, which was tremendously appealing to her.

What she did not at that moment know – how could she? – was how beautiful this slightly shambling character would become to her. He would never again appear to her as he did at the first blink, nor would she ever recapture the image, try though she might to do so. Close acquaintanceship, familiarity, do not, after all, invariably breed contempt.

'Hi,' he said.

And, 'Hi,' she replied.

'You must be the caterer. Dinah's Dinners.'

'That's me.'

'You're Dinah?'

'No, Sandra, in fact. It's short for Alexandra.'

'Colin,' he responded, extending his right hand. 'It's French for halibut.'

'Hake, actually,' she corrected, laughing, and it was as if a door flew open in her heart, and merriment came rushing in.

'Oh, really? Well, you would know, I dare say. Where is Dinah tonight?'

'There is no Dinah, since you ask. I just thought it was a good name for the biz.'

'I see. And you manage all on your own?'

'Well, there's Jenny, a student who helps me sometimes, but she couldn't make it this evening.'

'You seem very organised, anyway.' He raised his head and sniffed the air. 'I can smell thyme.'

'How very metaphysical,' she said, for her own amusement really, unaccustomed as she was to sparking with anyone, and she was surprised by his reaction.

When he grinned, his face seemed composed of curvy, smiley lines. 'Thyme the herb,' he said.

'It's the goat cheese tarts. Would you like to try one?'

'Oh, yes, I'm starving,' he enthused. And, with his mouth full, spraying pastry flakes, 'Oh, yum. Very good.'

Still chewing, he crossed to the stove, lifted a pan lid, peered in at the contents, then turned to her a face dewy with steam. 'Salmon?'

'Yes, salmon. It ought to come off the heat now. Can you turn the light out under it?'

'Sure thing.'

'Who *are* you, though?' she wanted to know, pulling on an oven glove, waggling it like a puppet, bustling him out of the way so she could attend to the cooking. 'I mean, as well as being Colin.'

'Colin Clarke.'

'The Clarkes' son?'

'Their one and only. Now, I know what you're thinking.'

'You do?'

'Yup. That I don't take after either of my parents.'

He was right. Mrs Clarke was a prissy, diminutive woman with neat, bobbed hair and a prim mouth, red and glossy as a glacé cherry. She was an inattentive listener: for as long as anyone else was speaking, she was constantly ticking over, going 'yes, yes, ye-es', impatient to be off again, to have another say. She evidently did not smile without prior arrangement, and would probably require five minutes' notice of an oncoming joke. The skirt and blouse she wore were made of some kind of ungiving, inorganic fibre, and they might have been brand new, straight out of their cellophane, so pristine did they appear.

Mr Clarke, whom Sandra had met only briefly, was not an inch taller than his wife, had an Errol Flynn moustache, and looked, she had thought, the way a brush salesman would look, if there were such things as brush salesmen any more. He was 'in the office stationery game' and seemed very jolly and not a little pleased with himself.

Truly, it was difficult to imagine that the gawky Colin was the issue with which this union had been blessed – still more to imagine how he might have been conceived, to visualise Mr and Mrs C, Roy and Shirley, in the act of procreation. About once a month, they might get down and do it. Or less often than that: just Christmas and birthdays, for a minute or two, in the dark.

Shirley came across as uptight and prudish (she had spoken of 'white meat', in reference to the guinea fowl, because she could not bring herself to say 'breast', and then, by a gesture, by the cupping of her two hands in front of her, she had betrayed her subconscious, she had given herself away).

48

Intellectually, as well as physically, their son Colin was so strikingly other, he seemed not to have so much as a chromosome in common with either of them.

Still, 'I wasn't at all,' Sandra quickly denied, since this was a conversation which she could not really have. And, 'Can I help you to find whatever it is?' she offered briskly as he began to tour the room in an aimless search for something.

'Oh,' he told her vaguely, 'I just hoped there might be a needle and thread lying around.'

'I rather doubt it,' she said frankly. This was the kind of house where the sugar was kept in a jar marked 'sugar', the flour in a matching jar marked 'flour', where the spaghetti lived in a tall perspex tube. It was not the kind of house in which things just lay around. 'I mean, the kitchen's not really the ideal place . . .'

'Well, you know, I haven't a clue where these things live.'

'I might have one, as it happens.' She usually carried an emergency repair kit in case she should fall apart. 'What did you want to sew?'

He held out his left fist at arm's length, turned it over, unfurled his fingers. A pearly white button lay winking in his palm. 'It's the top one off this shirt,' he explained in apparent seriousness. 'I thought it might be all right if I did it up differently so the spare hole was at the bottom and I could tuck it in my trousers. But it's all kind of wonky, isn't it?'

'Well, of course it is. How could you expect . . . ? Look, hang on.' She went to her bag and dipped in it. 'Ah-*hah*. Yes. Good. *Et voilà*. One needle. Some thread.'

'Oh, terrific! Ta.'

Then she could not bear to watch him, could not endure to stand by and be a witness, as he tried, the way men do, to force the needle down on to the thread. 'Look, let me. Give it here. It won't take me a mo.' Moving into the light, squinting, she poked the cotton through the needle's eye. 'Now, come.' She pointed to a spot a few inches from her feet.

So there he stood, with his head tipped back, as deftly she re-attached the button.

'Do you like to dance?' he enquired, his Adam's apple dipping.

'Not just now.'

'I don't mean now. Do you ever?'

49

'Not much, to be frank,' she confessed, addressing her reply to his throat, 'I have no sense of rhythm. Why?'

'I was just wondering . . .'

'What?'

'I thought you might come with me to the firm's do tomorrow week.'

'What firm?'

'The family business, you know. Of which I am part.'

'Stationery and stuff?'

'Stationery and stuff.'

'Well, I'm not sure . . .' She wound the cotton round her index finger and snapped it. 'There. You're done.'

'Marvellous.' He stepped back, brought his chin down and held her in his gaze. 'Thank you. I'm talking about a dinner dance. That's a bit different, isn't it? I mean, it's not *dancing* dancing? No hip-swivelling or pelvis-thrusting. We could just jig around a bit. Or sit it out if you preferred.'

'How old are you?' she asked, curious.

'Twenty-four.'

'I'm four years older than you.'

'So?'

'So nothing. Why me?'

'Eh?'

'Why do you want *my* company?'

'You seem very practical. Perhaps you were a Girl Guide? I can picture you with proficiency badges all up your arm. I imagine you would be good in a crisis.'

'You anticipate a crisis? You have many in your life?'

'One can never be too careful. So what d'you say?'

She hesitated an instant. She asked herself, why would I? Then she asked herself, why wouldn't I? He was harmless enough. He was better than harmless. And besides . . . Men had on rare occasion paid her compliments, they had said flattering things, but none had rung so true as this one. She was indeed practical, she was proficient. 'If you really want me to, then', she told him, 'yes, I will.'

———————— • ————————

Charlie Horscroft turned the key in his front door and was almost skittled by Polly barging through it. He stepped in after her, snapped on the light and scuffed his feet on the coconut mat to knock off the debris, to dislodge the day from his tired boots, while his dog scuttled up and down the hallway, nosing excitedly under the doors, sneezing as she snuffled up the fluff.

Providence Cottage was a boxy, red-brick Victorian building with a steep pitched roof, and with disobliging chimneys that coughed the smoke back at you if you tried to light a fire. The front door opened directly on to the pavement and looked across the road to the village shop; the back door opened on to a strip of garden, which trickled down to the fields of wind-blown grass, with a distant view of ancient deciduous woodland.

The place had belonged to Tom Jenner, who had moved away nine months ago to eke out a kind of Jack Spratt existence with his sister in Groombridge.

Tom had been a bachelor for all of his seventy-four years. His intended, Doris, a great big girl as he told it, had run off with his first cousin while Tom was fighting for King and country in the Western Desert. Fortunately, his sergeant major had taught him to cook, so Tom had had no need of a wife after all, and there had been nothing lost and no hard feelings. He had survived alone until last winter, on a stew which he would make each week from mutton bones and home-grown veg, an ideal culture medium which sat on the stove and grew a pelt.

He had done his own housework, redistributing the dust with a rag, and had washed his own combinations, which used to hang on a wooden airer, from the ceiling, like knitted semolina, making milky puddles on the brick floor beneath. Now, while his sister cooked and cleaned for him and scolded him without mercy, Tom shut his hearing-aid in the drawer and went outside to dig her spuds for her. It was an arrangement which reportedly suited them both.

'You can't be serious,' Ann Horscroft had wailed, when Charlie had announced his intention to buy the cottage. 'It's a hovel. It's a health hazard. It ought to be condemned.'

'It will be all right, you'll see. When I've fixed it up.'

'And where will the money come from? To buy it? To fix it?'

'From the bank.'

'You think so?'

'I do. It's dirt cheap, after all.'

'"Dirt" is right.'

'It's a bargain. I'd never find another house at the price.'

'And the cost of the repairs . . . ?'

'I'll do them myself, won't I?'

'You want your head seeing to, Charlie Horscroft.'

'I know what I'm doing, Mum.'

'You do?'

'Of course I do.'

And of course he did. He could close his eyes and see how it would be when it was finished. He could see the front sitting-room, with a mirror over the tiled fireplace, and with a fringed lamp on a table, and the carpet buttered with light.

He could see the bright little kitchen with the door standing open on to the garden, and with everything functional, built in or built under.

He could see his bedroom (for the first time in living memory, a bedroom of his own), at the back of the house, where the morning would find him, where the sun could wake him. He could see the curtains blowing, see them fluttering like flags. This was all, of course, a way off yet, it was all some months in the future. He was more-or-less camping in the meantime, but much had already been achieved.

He had had to rip out floorboards, to renew the lacy joists. The very fabric of the house had been replaced. He had done the electrics. He had installed a boiler and had run pipes off it; he could lie back in the bath and turn the tap with his toe, and know that the water would stream forth hot, hot, hot, that his sisters would not, *could* not have used up every drop.

He had a fridge, he had a washing-machine, and a nearly-new electric cooker. But more than that, he had his own space. Much as he loved his family, and missed them, there were times these days when Charlie Horscroft thought he'd died and gone to heaven.

'Come on Pol, let's get you fed.' He opened a tin of Meaty Chunks and spooned a pile on to her dish. Then, while she had her face in her dinner, he went upstairs to wash and change.

Using the spray attachment, he rinsed away the alluvium, yesterday's silt, from around the tub, then sat in it and showered, gazing impassively down at his body, which was hard and strong and serviceable, and suntanned to the waist.

He wondered idly about Tom Jenner's Doris who, Tom had recalled without rancour, had been a strapping girl with thighs like tree-trunks. Had she found happiness with cousin Alf?

For half a century, Providence Cottage had had a single male occupant. It was – and the notion amused him hugely – a bachelor pad. He was thoroughly enjoying living in it, he had no plans to share it. There was silence here, there was stillness, and, out the back among the drills of Maris Piper, and the shrubby kale, and the turnips big as tennis balls, a sense of being connected to the earth.

When he thought of marriage, he thought of children. Lots of them. And nappies. And noise. And it made him screw his eyes shut. But he liked to think sometimes of girls, to flirt with notions of them. Not of big old sorts like the famous, faithless Doris, not of tree-trunk thighs, but of warm and wispy creatures with clouds of hair, who wrapped their legs about him and breathed raspingly in his ear.

He could have been, if he'd wanted, a bit of a boy. He could have put himself about, he could have had his evil way with half of Kent. But that was not how Charlie chose to play it. He was, in his heart, a perfectionist. He, who would not botch a job, who was never slipshod or slapdash, would not botch up on human relationships, he would never be slapdash in love.

———— • ————

Dee Rawlings sat at her desk, in her long, narrow office, which had recently, at her behest, been painted a soft powder blue to promote deliberation, introspection and duty, while creating the state of serenity, emotional control, repose, calm and compassion which were so essential in her job.

She had, as she would laughingly admit, a bit of a bee in her bonnet about colour. Employers must be encouraged to appreciate its influence in the workplace. She had a thoroughgoing knowledge and understanding of the theory, which she applied with great rigour in her home environment and in her wardrobe.

Across the room, by the door, on top of a filing cabinet, an ioniser went silently about the business of regenerating the air, negatively charging microscopic particles, molecular pollutants. And, in eager response, her body stepped up its production of seratonin, with a consequent invigorating, tonic effect upon her whole being.

Or was it just those three glasses of wine from lunchtime, still coursing through her system like liquid bliss and fuelling her mood of sublime contentment?

We all make our own luck in this life. This was one of Dee's tenets. She, at any rate, had made her own luck; she had made enough of it for four. And how? By being *pro-active*.

But she was forced to allow, as she leafed through her correspondence, that some people did start at the most fearful disadvantage, and her heart went out to each and every one of them.

'Dear Dee,' they would confide, 'I don't know where to turn.' And she would shed a tear over certain of their letters, she really would, she was not ashamed to confess it. But the great thing was that they had summoned the strength and courage to write to her. For, in so doing, they had taken that vital first step on the road to happiness and self-fulfilment. They had started to make their own luck.

Donning her half-moon spectacles, which she wore on a cord around her neck, and which she used both for reading and for waving about, for emphasis, she peered through a dried-on spurt of sausage fat at the contents of the day's folder.

And here, as if to prove the point, was a communication from this little girl, Kayleigh, who related in a childish hand a harrowing tale of domestic violence, lovelessness, poverty and squalor, and who, in spite of all, had found within herself the firmness of purpose to sit down to put pen to paper, to address an envelope, to stamp it and send it off. The kid was not without gumption, then. Good! She would need to call on every ounce if she were to do as Dee intended to propose.

There was no doubt in Dee's mind as to how she should respond. It was clear to her that Kayleigh must take hold of her situation. She must leave her no-good boyfriend, remove herself and her baby from their pitiful circumstances. She must find a well-paid job, another flat – perhaps share with a jolly group of working girls. Certainly, she must meet new people, make new friends, develop new interests. She must learn the meaning of freedom and independence, discover the joys of standing on her own two feet.

But first, some words of sympathy and understanding. . . 'Poor you,' Dee began, the emotion running so rich in her it almost choked her. She was brimming now with the milk of human kindness. And, 'You *have* been in the wars, my darling, haven't you?' she continued, as the afternoon sun, streaming through her window, sparked off her darting nib and smiled on her endeavours. 'I should like to take you in my arms and give you a big hug. I should like to show you the kind of love of which you've been deprived, to meet you face to face, to look into your eyes and tell you that it doesn't have to be this way.'

And only later, much later, in the middle of that night, when the spicy sausages came back to haunt her, and she woke up and went downstairs for a glass of water, did she wonder, fleetingly, if she had not gone, in this one case, in an access of compassion – well, ever so slightly – over the top.

CHAPTER

•

3

Jamie sat on a wide terrace, under an awning, beside the river Thames at high tide, on what was to be the last truly glorious day of the year, wearing his Oliver Peoples sunglasses against the whiteness of the napery, and watching idly as the River Bus went gliding under Tower Bridge. Only by the depth of the shadows – great pools of black – could one have told that this was not July, and a larky summer atmosphere prevailed.

It had been Giles who had suggested the venue for their meeting. He had telephoned the office and left a message. Francine had taken it, she had jotted it on her special pad – the one with the amusing injunction to 'Read this, stupid!' printed at the top of every page. The two of them were at this moment, if she were to be believed, lunching in a restaurant called Pong de la Tour.

It was Friday, the end of the working week, it was sunny, so the place was thronged. The waitresses, who wore waistcoats and long, starched aprons and professional smiles, were rushed off their feet.

Jamie glanced around for someone to take their food order. Then, when he failed to make eye contact, he reached for the Bollinger, drew it carefully out of the bucket, tapped the droplets of ice water off the weighty green bottle, and topped up their glasses. 'How's Hennie?' he enquired in what he hoped was a laid-back, urbane sort of way, without a trace of edginess.

Giles unaccompanied was more hard work, somehow, and more intimidating than Giles with Henrietta. Jamie almost wished that she might be here, holding Giles's hand, kissing him on the tip of his aquiline nose, calling him Munchkin and Mr Cuddlebum and Uncle Oojah, and generally providing some form of distraction.

Giles tore with his teeth into a hunk of French bread, chased the mouthful with a swig of champagne, then responded through the resulting mish-mash, 'Oh, in the pink.' He would certainly have been taught social graces, and must have decided at some point to dispense with them. He seemed to get by perfectly well without them.

Jamie reviewed his own upbringing; he recalled his mother's insistence on ladies first, on pardon me, and please and thank you nicely. How picky, how petty, how bourgeois, it appeared to him now! And how he longed for the aplomb to eat peas off his knife!

'Where is the girl?' wondered Giles aloud, creaking back precariously on his chair to signal for service. 'Oysters for me. A dozen Colchesters,' he declared, slapping the tabletop with the flat of his hand. 'How about you?'

'Ah, no, well, uhm . . . I like oysters, but they don't like me.'

'Story of your life,' Giles joked (at least, Jamie *hoped* it was a joke and obliged with a laugh). 'Had a bad one, once, did you?'

'Yes. Yes, I did, as a matter of fact. I've never been able to look them in the eye since.'

In truth, he·had never so much as tasted an oyster; the mere thought of swallowing one made him queasy. It would, he envisaged, be something like oral sex, about which he was equally squeamish. He smiled up at the waitress. 'A salad niçoise *pour moi.*'

When she had left them, he inclined across the table, clasped his hands in front of him, and prepared to talk turkey. He felt his pulse quicken. He moistened his lips. He said, 'I have a little proposition to put to you . . .'

Giles de Lannoy-Hunt was a wealthy man, he had more money than you could shake a stick at, but he was always delighted to add a few noughts to his bank balance. For no other reason did he run his highly successful antiques business. It was his proud boast that he was able, with what wit and style, to come between old ladies and their prized possessions, *and* to leave them with the impression that he was a prince among men.

Mrs Atkins (or Audrey as Jamie planned to call her once he gained her full confidence) would be putty in those smooth, white de Lannoy-Hunt hands.

In a hushed voice, with barely suppressed excitement, Jamie began to describe Clovelly, to evoke the extraordinary property, which was like a living museum, and which both enthralled and revolted him.

He could visualise it so clearly, from the distempered ceilings of the bedrooms to the parquet-pattern lino in the hall. He could see the crazy-paved path leading to the stained-glass door with the galleon in full sail. The brown-glossed woodwork. The small, tiled fireplaces with stove-enamelled cast iron grates and wooden mantels. The moss-green, moquette three-piece suite, the bouclé-upholstered fireside chairs, the walnut veneer gramophone cabinet, the painting of the donkeys at Clovelly, a reminder of some long-ago family trip to the Cornish Riviera from which, presumably, the house took its sentimental name.

He could see the stone sink in the scullery, with its tiled splashback. The dining-room with its double-doored serving hatch, and with its heavy furniture, the draw-leaf table draped with a crimson cloth, the Tudor-oak-finish sideboard.

He could see the stairs leading treacherously up, with a narrow strip of mothy carpet breaking loose here and there from the rods. He could see the big, beige front bedroom, with the porridge wallpaper, the twin beds frigidly paired under slippery satin counter-panes. The ugly dressing-table and stool, the faintly hideous wardrobes. . .

'I promise you, you would not believe it.'

'Uh-huh,' responded Giles in a go-on, an I'm-listening, a quite encouraging tone, lifting to his puffy, slightly feminine lips, a flounced oyster shell, and slurping the juice, which trickled down his chin.

Jamie remembered reading somewhere that oysters taste as if your nose has run straight into your mouth. He felt faintly nauseated. 'And then . . .' He speared an olive with his fork, held it up consideringly. 'Then there's all her stuff.'

Her stuff? 'Bric-à-brac', he'd called it, dismissing it lightly. Her 'bits and bobs'. And, he had first-rate contacts, he had assured her. He could put her in touch with the best people. He could put her on to just the man.

Now, Jamie Rawlings might not know what he liked, but he knew what was good. And he had made, as far as he'd been able, a mental inventory of the various pieces for which Audrey Atkins would not have space in the compact flat he meant to find for her.

There would be no place, of course, for the Bechstein piano, from the top of which long-dead relatives peered wanly out of silver frames.

Nor could she hope to squeeze in an amboyna wood cocktail cabinet, nor the Art Deco decanter and glasses that lived within.

As for the huge silver chafing dish on the sideboard: surely she would not give it house-room?

The carved pearwood corner cupboard would presumably have to go, along with the oddments of Clarice Cliff that it contained.

Then what of the assortment of hand-painted Poole vases, lustre jars, *pâte de verre* figures, iridescent glass dishes, dressing-table sets and thingamies? Who needed all those ornaments around to gather dust?

'The house has *got* to be three hundred grand's worth of bricks and mortar alone,' said Jamie, *sotto voce*, 'never mind it's *character*. As for the rest, that's your department.'

'So the idea is . . . ?'

'Precisely.'

'Mrs Atkins, this is Mr de Lannoy-Hunt . . .'

'Mr and *Mrs* de Lannoy-Hunt. Who need a house large enough for themselves and their four children.'

'And his sick mother, who will be coming from Chichester to live with them in her twilight years.'

'Such a charming family.'

'But on a very tight budget.'

'Still, willing to take some of your knick-knacks off you.'

'I think we understand each other, Jamie.'

'I think we do, Giles.'

'And the deal?'

'Fifty-fifty off the back end,' said Jamie, because, whatever it meant, it sounded both equitable and assured.

'Fair enough.'

'You're in then?'

'I might be.' Giles, dabbed at the corners of his mouth. And over the top of the folded napkin he gave Jamie a mischievous, conspiratorial wink. 'I might well be.'

Half an hour later, Jamie parked outside the gym, on a double yellow line, careless of the clampers and tow-away trucks that preyed on the surrounding streets (this was, after all, an auspicious day), and for several minutes he just sat taking stock.

It had all gone far better than he had dared to hope, he reflected, pushing buttons, flicking switches, squirting the washers, giving the windscreen a wipe. Giles had been impressed, he was convinced of it. He had listened intently, which was rare in itself, raising his eyebrows and nodding, saying yes, yes, go on, without a trace of his usual superciliousness, and without ever once looking down his nose, shaped though it was for the looking down of. Finally, he had agreed that he was in, he had said they had a deal, and by that wink of complicity he had set the seal upon it.

Jamie ought then to have gone straight back to the office, but he was too wrought up, he would have to work off some of his tension before he could settle at his desk. A quick circuit of the exercise machines, he told himself, an invigorating cold shower, and he would be refreshed and ready for anything.

He snapped open his briefcase, drew out his mobile phone and punched in the agency number.

'Good-afternoon. Mabey Estates, ' his secretary responded in sing-song tones, as he had schooled her to do. 'Thank you for calling. Francine speaking. How may I help you?'

'Ah, well, now,' Jamie said, considering, 'you could start with a blow job.'

'Ooh, you should be so lucky!'

'Shouldn't I just!'

'Where are you, anyway?'

'I'm running a bit late. You know how it is.'

'No I don't.'

'Yes you do. Cover for me, there's a good girl?'

'It's been total bedlam in here while you've been out,' she grumbled mildly.

'You can't manage without me,' he boasted, not unduly concerned ('bedlam', in Francine's book, meant a couple of casual enquiries and one wrong number; it meant being called upon to take dictation before she had read her stars).

'You flatter yourself,' she said, giggling, coquettish (poor bitch, she really believed she had a chance with him!).

'Any urgent messages? Any new instructions?'

'Nothing that won't keep.'

'Ah, right. No word from that Atkins mob in Streatham, for example?'

'Not a dickie-bird. In any case, I thought you said they were time-wasters.'

'I rest my case.'

'You know, Jamie Rawlings,' she told him, 'you're mental.'

'If you say so. Now make my excuses, there's a poppet. Tell the old man I'm tied up with a client if he asks.'

'The things I do for you!'

'You're a saint. What are you?'

'I'm a saint.'

He blew a loud, squelchy kiss down the phone to her, and switched off.

The girls at club reception greeted him warmly and nodded him through without checking his membership card. Well, they knew him, of course, and fancied him like mad. *Everybody*, on that glorious autumn afternoon, had the hots for Jamie Rawlings.

He changed quickly into skintight black bermudas, a T-shirt and snowy white trainers, smoothed his hair with his two hands in front of the mirror, tipped a wicked wink to his reflection in the manner of Giles de Lannoy-Hunt, and hurried through to the gym.

Ten minutes on the exercise bike; ten on the arm bike. A further ten on the rower, then on to the step machine. He punched in his weight (a respectable seventy-five kilos), opted for a moderate effort level, and set himself to climb a dozen flights.

With every 'floor' attained, a bell dinged. A digital message flashed up to congratulate him, to urge him ever onwards. There was nothing like stairs to build stamina.

Ding. He passed the purely notional fifth floor and headed

61

manfully for the sixth. And he gritted his teeth and smiled grimly to himself.

'Well done,' said the digital display. And, 'Keep going,' it encouraged.

There could be no denying now, that Jamie Rawlings was, in a figurative sense, on the up and up.

———————— • ————————

Bloody stairs! For the second time that day, Kayleigh was forced to bump the buggy down eleven flights, heedless of Ben, who was rudely jolted in the chair with every step, his big, round head rocking on the frail stalk of his neck.

Between the sixth floor and the fifth she paused a moment on the dingy landing, waited for her breath to slow, and for her rancour to abate, for the sense of grievance to subside. But it didn't, of course. If anything, it got worse, she was seething with it. So she swung her canvas bag from one shoulder to the other, and – heavy with the knowledge that what went down must all too soon come up – she carried on, bump, bump, bump, right the way to the ground.

Illegible, spray-can graffiti disfigured the walls of the lobby. One of the double doors was off its hinges, and a flurry of litter – cigarette packets, lager cans, fast-food wrappers – had blown in. The lifts had been vandalised, they were, inevitably, not in service (a printed notice apologised to residents: Mr Otis regrets). And, as she trundled the pushchair towards the daylight, the stench of urine made her retch.

Nobody should be forced to endure this sort of half-life. It wasn't right, she told herself, it wasn't just. Then – although this thought was with her always, and never far from the tip of her tongue – as she stepped out of the shadows into shimmering sunshine, she was momentarily dazzled by the truth of it, which came to her with all the force of revelation.

It *wasn't* fair, it really wasn't, that some people were condemned to such conditions, while others had the lot, they had the works.

She realised, also, with a rare flash of insight, that there was a pattern to it – that it must suit the purposes of some-body somewhere, for her to be down here in the shit, while they were up there in bleeding clover. Then all the vague, instinctive, unconsidered, generalised, received resentment which she had nurtured for so many years towards 'them', coalesced and hardened to conviction within her; she saw how comprehensively she'd been dumped upon, and in a small but crucial way this changed her.

She had been this morning to the so-called health centre: eleven floors down; twenty minutes at the bus stop; another twenty-five minutes in the waiting-room, where Ben had cried fractiously till she gave him the *Reader's Digest* to chew; two-and-a-half minutes with the doctor; fifteen more minutes at the bus stop; eleven floors back up to the flat.

'What kept you?' Greg had demanded, the moment she struggled through the door. He had been stretched out on the sofa in his boxer shorts, doing a spot-the-difference puzzle in yesterday's paper, putting a cross to mark where a monkey was missing an ear, in the remote hope of winning a CD player. Seeing him there, she had felt like punching him.

'What's it to you? In any case, you're meant to be at work.'

'I'm off sick, aren't I?'

Yet there was nothing wrong with him – unless you could describe as a sickness his obsessive jealousy and mistrust of her which, at its worst, was enough to keep him at home for days on end lest there be any hanky-panky while his back was turned. It was all right for him, apparently, to have his flings. It was all right for her to come back from her mum's, as she had done the other week, and to find him there bollock naked, getting his end away with Pat from the Piano Bar. That was just a laugh, wasn't it? It was down to the drink, to one tequila slammer too many. No need for her to do her nut about it. But Kayleigh had only to smile at another guy, she had only to pass the time of day, for Greg to go didloe, to call her all the whores under the sun.

He had a casual job as a messenger, for which he was paid up front. He had a gentleman's agreement with his employers: they pissed all over him, and he pissed all over them. The way he looked at it, when you were on the suck, drawing benefit, the gaffers felt they had you over a barrel and took diabolical liberties. So you had to get back at them to show them what was what; you couldn't let them trot you.

'You should of come with me, then,' Kayleigh had told him, dead sarcastic. 'If you're sick, you should of come to see the doctor too.'

'What did he say, anyway?'

'Not a lot.'

Dr Flowers was a formerly conscientious GP, whose youthful ideals had gone the way of most youthful ideals. He had seen too much of the suffering born of hard labour – or of the want of it. His reserves of caring and compassion had simply been exhausted (it would take more than a lick of soft blue paint on the surgery walls to restore them to him). He was tall and thin and pale as a candle; and, like a candle, he had just burned out.

He had glanced across his desk at this *gamine*, this waifish young woman whose frustration was bringing her out in blisters, and at her child who was so signally failing to thrive. Then, knowing he was unequal to their suffering – that medicine had no solutions for the contamination of the human spirit – he had scribbled the expected prescription for corticosteroid cream, had said 'Mind how you go', and 'Try not to scratch', and had buzzed the next patient in.

Thus Kayleigh had been left, as always, with a sense that he had in some way failed her, that as usual she had been granted less than was her due.

'Lend us a couple of quid,' she had said to Greg when she had cooked some chicken nuggets for their lunch. 'I have to go out for some ointment. To the chemist. And we need teabags. And some sugar.'

'Yeah?' Greg had peered at her through narrow slits of disbelief. She played a funny game, his expression seemed to say. Who knew what she might get up to? He had half a mind to ground her, to confine her here where he could keep tabs on her.

'Some cream for my hands.'

'Oh, yeah?'

But she had refused to rise to provocation, to be drawn into a fight. She hadn't the energy, and, anyway, she couldn't risk another slapping. 'You want me to bring you something?'

'Such as?'

'Well, I don't know, do I? Is there something you need?'

'Can't think of nothing.'

'That's all right then.'

'What will it rush you? For the tea and that.'

'Three quid, maybe.'

'Don't ask much, do you?' He thrust his hand into his pocket, pulled out a folded fiver and threw it at her. 'I'll expect change.'

'You'll get it.'

Once upon a time she had loved him. She must have done, she reasoned, or why would she be with him? Why else would she have stuck by him, stuck up for him, when her parents dismissed him as scum?

He had dark, close-cropped hair, fine, pale eyebrows, an oddly stunted nose with small, pinched nostrils. He led with his shoulders, with the backs of his hands, when he walked. A tattoo on one bicep proclaimed his devotion to his mother; on the other, the conviction that death was any day to be desired above dishonour. She had though him, at the outset, both handsome and macho, and she had had no inkling of the loathing he would inspire in her when she was in too deep with him.

'Bastard,' she muttered, as she turned her back on E block and rattled the buggy up the hill to the valiant little parade of shops – a newsagent, an off licence, a late-night grocer, a video store, a chemist, a chippie, all with wire-meshed windows and security grilles.

In the newsagent's, where a German shepherd dog with topaz eyes reared up at the counter and menaced her, she bought some smoky bacon crisps to keep Ben quiet, and for herself twenty Silk Cut and the new issue of *Mia* magazine, which she determined to read right now, outside, sitting on the bench on the sun-baked concrete.

Her hand was trembling as she tore open the crisps for Ben, fending off with her elbow his grasping hand. Then, 'Here,' she said curtly, thrusting the bag at him.

Suppose her letter had been picked? Suppose it had been printed? Her own problem, there on the page, in heavy type, with an answer all to itself? Her life dignified by serious debate? It would confer a certain status upon her. It would be – well, almost – like appearing on television. It would send a message to the world that she was somebody.

Frantically she turned the pages, found the agony column,

scanned the text, reading aloud under her breath, 'Dear Dee
. . .', 'Dear Dee . . .'.

But it wasn't there. She checked each entry a second time, more
slowly, to be absolutely sure, and it absolutely wasn't. Shyness,
body odour, irregular periods, loss of libido were all apparently
more fascinating, more worthy of discussion than her own measly
existence. Well, she might have guessed! She felt utterly piqued,
slighted, insulted to have been so disregarded.

'Wouldn't you know it?' she said to Ben, watching without
seeing, as he rummaged with his tiny fist in the crackling cellophane packet. 'Wouldn't you just bloody well know it?'

She was sorely tempted to chuck the stupid book in the bin. But
she had paid good money for it, and it smelt inky and inviting, so
she might as well read some of the articles.

This one, for instance, about people with a second home.
Dee Rawlings, it showed, had both a sodding great house in
town and an old-fashioned country retreat with creepers running
riot up the walls. She was loaded, was she, then, Mrs Fatty Fucking
Rawlings? And, when you came to consider it, it was all thanks
to other people's hardship. You *could* look at it that she had got
where she was today on the backs of the poor and deprived. This,
at any rate, was how Kayleigh Roth, in high dudgeon, elected to
look at it.

'Come on,' she said suddenly, decisively, rolling the magazine
like a truncheon and hammering it against her palm, before shoving
it into her bag. Then she tipped up the buggy, took the brake off
with her toe, and was on the move again. 'Let's go and see Nanny,
shall we?'

That afternoon, on the last Friday in September, while most
of London sizzled in the aberrant, unseasonable heat, on the
seventh floor of the Magazines UK building, in the air-conditioned
conference room, remote from the roar of traffic, *Mia*'s senior editorial team was planning to ring in the New Year on an uplifting
and an inspirational note.

It is a curious fact of magazine life, determined by colour-
printing schedules, by the logistics of production, that one is

always about three months ahead of oneself. Easter is a major preoccupation in December, Christmas in August. It is thus a forlorn hope that a letter sent on Wednesday will be printed on Friday.

Not a lot of people know this. Most imagine, vaguely, that magazines are like daily papers, that they deal with stories almost as they happen. Still, to the initiates, the members of the magazine staff around the long oval table, it was not remotely odd that January should be on the day's agenda.

'Come The Resolution!' declared Clare Constantine. 'That will be our lead cover line. Now . . .' She slapped the latest printing schedule down like a gauntlet. 'What do you lot have for me?'

There was an audible shuffling; people shifted edgily in their seats, or frowned as they doodled in their shorthand pads. Clare was a great one for these meetings, at which she fomented dislike, rivalry and suspicion, picking on individuals, subjecting them to ridicule, setting this person against that one, to her own despicable ends.

She played a game with the unfortunates of whom she would be rid – a sort of musical chairs, in which they found, by and by, after so much ritual humiliation and unseemly scrambling, that there was no longer any place for them at *Mia*. Their powers would be eroded, their secretaries seconded to other departments. New job titles would be created; new people brought in over them. Office redesigns, the artful encroachment of partitions, would leave them cramped for space and starved of daylight. And the conference room was the theatre in which their tragedies were publicly played out. Too demoralised to plead constructive dismissal, most eventually retired hurt.

'Uhm . . .' said Kristina, the beauty editor, who, as a favoured one, had the nerve to speak. 'The Cutting Edge. The latest looks from London's top hair stylists.'

'Excellent. Yes, that's very much in the spirit.' Clare made a note. 'Right, who's next?'

'Put A Step In Your Spring,' offered Yasmin, another of the blue-eyed girls, the chosen few, who was in charge of health and fitness. 'Step aerobics. To tie in with a readers' offer.'

'Very good.' Clare poured herself a glass of Abbey Well and took a contemplative sip.

'Plus our own indispensable food plan,' tendered Chloë, the cookery editor, 'based on the latest nutritional wisdom, designed to target the parts that other food plans cannot reach – tums, bums and thighs.'

'Oh, Bottom, Thou Art Translated!' intoned Clare, and took another sip of water to disguise a simper, before jotting down her *idée*.

'Leaner Cucina,' Chloë continued. 'A week's low-fat recipes from the Italian chef Carlo Ciccone, one of the young Turks of the London restaurant scene.'

'Turkish Italian?' Clare raised a mocking eyebrow.

'I meant *enfant terrible*,' said Chloë defensively, compounding the solecism, wondering if her star was on the wane.

'And the recipes are tested by us, I trust? You know these chefs' recipes are notoriously half-baked.'

'Oh, they're fine. Yes, we've tried them.'

'And we're confident that they promote weight loss?' Clare pressed her. This was another of her little ways: she liked to push and push.

'Well . . .'

'We have to check that out. We can't simply give our readers a food plan. We have to know how it works. We need a guinea pig to follow it for a week or two. Right, who is going to volunteer?' She gazed around her, seeming to assess each member of her staff, mentally to weigh them all up. 'Step forward, Juliet Smart. You could do yourself a favour and come down a dress size. Stick to the diet for a fortnight. We'll pay the expenses.'

Bitch, thought Juliet, the fiction editor, enraged and mortified, biting her lip, dropping her head to hide a crimson blush. Clare has no right. Okay, I need to lose a few pounds, but it's no business of hers.

Clare, watching for a response, and sensing pure loathing, began to wonder if the magazine needed to carry quite as much fiction as it had in the past. She began to wonder if it needed to carry fiction at all. Personally, she had no time for it. When she went to make another note, her pencil lead snapped and the point went skidding across the polished surface of the table.

'I'll tell you what,' suggested Kristina, swapping smirk for smirk with Yasmin opposite, 'we could maybe ask half a dozen members of our readers' forum to give it a go.'

'The unspeakable in pursuit of the uneatable,' muttered Edie, removing her spectacles and polishing them on her tweedy Friday skirt. She gatecrashed these meetings to be bloody, and because they appealed to her highly developed sense of the absurd. It was particularly rich, she thought, the way the magazine, under Clare Constantine, colluded with its core readership in the pretence that it was not, as the surveys consistently suggested, fair, fat and forty, but an eternal, youthful twenty-one.

Edie knew she was not, theoretically, sufficiently senior, she was not high enough in the pecking order to attend editorial conferences. But she, like Dee, was a survivor, she had been on the magazine for longer than anyone. And she knew also that, while she enjoyed Dee's patronage, Clare would not care to challenge her, or to seek from her some positive contribution as she sat there scribbling on her ring-bound notepad, drawing up an alternative list of contents (an opening section entitled 'Middle-Age Spread', a cookery feature, 'Mutton Got Up as Lamb'. . . .)

Nobody, in these highly charged few moments, so much as glanced at Dee, who was positioned, as always, at the top of the table, at Clare's right hand, in the comfy swivel chair, much as if she were the editor's lieutenant, and who smiled serenely, conveying the impression that none of this had anything whatever to do with her.

Everyone knew that the flame-haired editor had met her match in the magazine's red-rinsed agony aunt ('The clash of the Titians', Edie had dubbed their conflict), but it would not have been politic to show it, so they all affected not to notice anything afoot.

For her own part, Dee was not even listening. She was miles away, mulling over her latest triumph. She had been approached by Eye See TV, a small independent film company, who were making a series with the working title of *Superwomen*, and who were most eager to include her. The producer would be coming in at five-fifteen to see her, to talk the thing through.

The programme would shadow her through her working day and into the evening, to see how she juggled her responsibilities, holding down a high-powered job while still finding time for leisure, for home and family, as well as for her writing and broadcasting. Much of the commentary would be provided by Dee herself, either speaking to camera, or as a voice-over. And thus would the great British public see the full extent of her warmth, her caring, her compassion, her protean talents, her extraordinary strength and humanity.

Dreamily, unknowingly, Dee folded her bulging arms across the soft cushion of her belly and gave herself a big, fat hug.

———————— • ————————

'Where's Mum?'

When Kayleigh let herself into her parents' flat, she found no one there but Lisa, who was standing in front of the television, ironing.

'Gone out.' Lisa peeled a pressed blouse off the ironing-board and held it, snapping with static, up to the window, to the light, so that she might inspect it for creases. She was not yet as potentially pretty as her sister. She might one day be, but her adult face had still to form. She was very neat, very protective of her beliefs, her thoughts, her clothes and possessions: as far as possible she kept everything folded away. She had made up her mind that, when she was sixteen, she would train as a beautician. In the meantime, she tolerated school and attended more regularly than Kayleigh had ever done.

'Out where?'

'Round at Auntie Maureen's.' Lisa twiddled a sleeper in her earlobe, which was sore and weeping. 'These are supposed to be gold, if you can believe it,' she grumbled, grimacing, gritting her teeth and sucking through them.

'Oh.'

Kayleigh bent to unstrap Ben from his harness, to lift him on to the floor. His front was speckled with crisp crumbs. When he grasped her T-shirt with one tiny hand, squeezing the flesh of her breast beneath in a way that maddened her, he left greasy fingerprints. 'What are you doing here?'

'What are *you* doing here?' Lisa echoed infuriatingly, so that her sister, even now, wanted to pinch and punch her and to pull her hair.

'I'm visiting, aren't I? How come you're skiving? Got no lessons, or what?'

'I've got the curse,' Lisa confided, leaking the words out of the corner of her mouth.

Margaret Roth and her two daughters went in for frank speaking, for Anglo-Saxon epithets, they were fearless in dialogue, they were free with the expletives, with the F and the C word. Yet, in the matter of menstruation, they were uncharacteristically coy. A caller at the Roth residence at *that time of the month*, might have been alarmed to hear that one or other of them had fallen off the roof, that she was therefore feeling *that way*, she was not quite herself. Then, who was this Auntie Ruby who had reportedly come to stay? And, most perplexingly, what would a young girl be wanting with a manhole cover?

Periods were regarded by the family rather as some unmentionable illness, and Kayleigh had learned early in her school career that she need do no more than hint at the imminence of one to be allowed to spend the day in bed. To take time off in such a condition was perfectly acceptable.

'Yes, ta, I will have some tea if you're making it,' she said now, plonking herself on the sofa and hauling her child on to her knee. (Thus encumbered, she could not reasonably be expected to put the kettle on.)

'He wet my bed,' grumbled Lisa. 'It was disgusting.'

But she did go, albeit ungraciously, into the small galley kitchen, where she banged the cups about. She turned on the tap and let it run for two minutes, because, as Nanny Roth always told them, there were maggots in the first lot. She yanked open the fridge then slammed it.

'Oh, by the way,' she shouted, sliding cupboard doors back and forth in a vain search for biscuits, 'a letter come first class for you. It's on the table. See it?'

———————— • ————————

Sandra threw open her wardrobe and scowled at the contents. She had seen more stylish collections of garments hanging on the rails at church jumbles, she told herself crossly, much as if she had had no part in their selection, as if they had marched upon her home, invading the bedroom of her third-floor attic flat when she was not even looking.

Almost every item of her clothing was black. Her mother maintained that, by wearing this non-colour, she was signalling a desire to suppress or negate, that it meant she lacked confidence and had put her life on hold. ('Colour, my dear girl, is a means of self-expression. So what are you saying to the world? Hm? Hm? You're saying, "Don't mind me." You're saying "Pardon me for breathing."') But Sandra had, she believed, purely practical reasons for favouring black: it didn't show the food splashes, and was ideal for waiting at people's tables.

Was it, however, so suitable for a dinner dance? She had a somewhat hazy notion of what happened at these affairs – a vague picture of women with pinned-up hair and flouncy frocks, swirling around as a live band played 'Blame It On The Bossanova'. In which case, she was in trouble, since her hair was way out of control, and she hadn't a flounce to call her own.

She did possess, it was true, one long dress in T-shirt material, in palest pink (very aptly the colour of indecision and of errors of judgement, since it was embarrassingly clinging, and inches too long: the hem was grimy and scalloped where she had hobbled up the inside of it). In opting, after much painful deliberation, to buy it, she had made a rare concession to frivolity, and she was not sure she was ready to make another.

In sour mood, she began to tug things off their hangers, to bundle them into her zip-up hold-all. She was going to spend the weekend with her parents at Foxholes ('We never see you,' Dee had chided, when last they spoke, her tone, as usual when addressing her daughter, one of faint exasperation.) It was half-past five. Eric would be stopping by for her at any minute, on the way to collect Dee from the office. He would sit outside and honk his horn until Sandra ran down.

When the phone trilled, Sandie went at once to her little sitting-room to pick it up, searching through the clutter on her work table, under the slanting ceiling, for her appointments diary, her felt-tip pen, in case somebody wanted to engage her.

'Dinah's Dinners,' she said in her special, crisp, posh, put-on telephone voice, as a pile of recipe books, bristling with paper page markers, teetered, then toppled on to the polished wood floor.

'Sandra? It's Colin.' He sounded morose. She supposed he was ringing to cancel their date, to cry off on some flimsy pretext, and in that instant she felt only relief. (This was her customary response to bad news or a rebuff. She could always find some compensation. Faced with the possibility of her own imminent demise, it would flash through her mind that at least now she would not have to bother about getting the loose covers dry cleaned.)

'Hello,' she replied guardedly. 'How are you?'

'I'm all right. You?'

'Fine, thanks.'

There was a moment's pause, in which she imagined him summoning the courage to bleat his excuses. Scornful, with hand on hip, she waited.

'What does it mean when you get a sort of ticking in your eye?' he asked eventually.

'What?'

'In your eye. When it goes sort of tick, tick, tick. What's going on there?'

'A kind of pulsing sensation?'

'Yes.'

'Oh, I don't know. Everybody gets that sometimes. When they're tired or whatever.'

'It's not life-threatening, then?'

'I shouldn't imagine so,' she reassured him.

'Not a brain tumour?'

'Definitely not.'

'Nothing that a good night's sleep won't cure?'

'I'm sure.'

'Eight hours in the arms of Morpheus?'

'Probably.'

There was another pause. Then, 'What do you call a deer with no eyes?' he asked.

'No idea.'

'That's right.'

'What is?'

'No-eye deer.'

'Ah. I see. Very droll.' She wasn't in a laughing mood. In some agitation she bandaged her hand with the curly telephone flex. She wished he would come to the point. If he was proposing to let her down, he should do it smartly then get off the line.

'Uhm, about Thursday . . .'

'Yes?' she prompted. And, turning her face, holding the receiver away from her ear, playing to an imaginary audience, grimacing at the empty room, 'Here it comes,' she mouthed.

Crackle, crackle, crackle went his voice. Then there was silence.

'That's all right, don't worry about it.' She spoke briskly into the mouthpiece. What did she care, after all, for this Colin, this halibut? There were plenty more fish in the sea.

'But I'd *like* to.'

'Like to what?'

'Come and get you. Now the car's fixed.'

'Which car?'

'I just told you. My Midget. It was the plugs. Or the piston rings. Or the alternating flange sprockets.'

'Ah.'

'I'm afraid I'm not very mechanically minded.'

'No.'

'Nor am I any sort of carpenter. Never ask me to put up a shelf.'

'I shan't,' she promised.

'Or to change a washer.'

'No.'

'Or to install sliding patio doors.'

'It's a deal.'

'I can nail one piece of wood on to another, but that's as far as it goes. If I then have to nail a third piece on to the second, you can lay any odds that pieces one and two will come apart.'

'I see.'

'And you don't mind?'

'Why would I mind?'

'I don't know. You might be looking for someone who's nifty with an orbital sander.'

'I'm not looking for anyone, as it happens.'

'You've not set your heart on marrying me?'

'Not as yet.'

'Well, I'll have you know I'm quite a catch. I'm very big in paperclips.'

'I'll bear that in mind.'

'Kindly do. Now give me the address, and I'll collect you on Thursday night.'

'You still want me to come, then?'

'Well, of course.'

'But I don't have anything to wear.'

'*You* don't want to come,' he accused.

'I do. I really do. It's just . . . what I said.'

'Wear any old thing. It won't matter.'

'It will. Don't be absurd.'

'Well, make yourself something. Run something up. You're a whizz with a needle, as we know.'

'There isn't time.'

'Cut up a lace tablecloth. I saw a play on television once where a woman did just that. It took her no more than half an hour and she was the belle of the ball.'

'I don't have a lace tablecloth,' she objected, as though the suggestion had otherwise much to commend it.

'A curtain, then.'

'I have Venetian blinds.'

'How do you make a Venetian blind?'

'Poke him in the eye with a gondola pole.'

'You've heard it.'

'Hasn't everyone?'

'Couldn't you buy a little number? *I'll* buy you one with pleasure. Whatever your heart desires.'

'No, no, that won't be necessary.' She would borrow, she decided, from her friend Alison, who was of roughly similar build and had a penchant for frills. 'I'll sort myself out.'

'I know you will. I have every confidence in you. You're very resourceful. Now, the address?'

She dictated it slowly. 'Flat four,' she told him finally. 'Top bell.'

'I'll be there at a quarter to seven. That way we'll have time to nip into the pub for a sharpener before we trip the light fantastic.'

'Aren't we supposed to be done up to the nines?'

'If not, indeed, the tens.'

'So much for "wear any old thing", then. And surely we'll be too dressy for a pub?'

'Not for our local, we won't.'

'I guess not,' she conceded, envisaging some plush, carpeted hostelry, with piped music and pink velour upholstery, somewhere in stockbrokers' Surrey.

'The actual dinner . . .' he ventured.

'Mm?'

'It won't be a patch on the food you do.'

'I shan't mind. It will be a treat to have someone else do the catering.'

'That's grand. So it's a quarter to seven on Thursday. Flat bell. Top four.'

'Top bell.'

'Flat four. I'll be there. Cheerio.'

'Bye-bye.'

When she had replaced the receiver in its cradle, she stood for several moments staring in an unfocused way at the wall, and smiling, smiling, smiling.

———————— • ————————

'All right, then?' said Charlie, setting the cardboard box of vegetables on his mother's work top. Whiskery onions from his garden, muddy swede and salsify, nubbly parsnips and bullet-hard brussels sprouts.

'All right, Charlie?' Ann Horscroft countered, standing at the sink, very glamorous in her high heels, doing the dishes.

'The parsnips will be better when the frost has got to them,' he told her, picking one out to examine it in the cold, blue, modern, kitcheny light of a fluorescent tube. 'Sprouts, too.'

'That's what they always say: they need the frost.'

'I'll bring you some mushrooms Sunday, in time for breakfast, if I find any.'

'Are there many?'

'The woods were stiff with them the other day. Anyway, how's it going, Mum?'

'Just fine. How about you ?'

'Really good. Great.'

'Not fed up, then, in that gloomy old house on your own?'

'Not a bit. And I'm not on my own. I've got Pol.'

He went to stand beside his mother, placed his hands upon her shoulders, stooped to kiss the smooth and scented cheek which, with a twitch of her mouth, she offered him. His dark looks were his father's, but his good and giving nature and his inner calm he owed in no small way to her.

She was a pretty woman of forty-three who took pride in her appearance. From morning till night she wore make-up, which she removed in front of the bathroom mirror, with cleansing milk and wads of cotton wool. Her light brown hair hung to her shoulder-blades, clean and combed and occasionally plaited. And she never, ever, ever set foot outside her own front door without her earrings.

She had given birth to her first four children in hospital, setting off in a taxi when the contractions came on strong, clutching a small overnight bag in which she'd packed her broderie-anglaise nightie, an eau de toilette spray, a pair of tweezers, a nail file, hand lotion and other absolute essentials for confinement.

She had been delivered of the youngest three at home in bed, from which position she could direct the running of the household, and could supervise the serving of family tea.

She had a slim and girlish figure because she walked a lot, cycled, went to cardio funk each Tuesday evening in the village hall – and because motherhood can be so very physical. Men at the wheels of trucks and tankers tooted when they saw her walking with a teenager's light tread, and then, turning to leer at her as they passed, they would be ever so slightly disconcerted by her mature and womanly face.

Still, to her husband Bill, who was no bad judge, she was but a girl, the loveliest on the planet, which went some way to explaining the Horscrofts' embarrassment of offspring.

'Are you staying for a bite to eat?'

'Have the little ones had theirs?'

'Just now, yes.'

He followed her through to the lounge, where Thomas, aged nine, sat stopped up with his Walkman, too cool to do more than raise a hand in greeting and mouth 'Hi', as Madonna seeped into his head and addled his brain. Ann sank down and took up her knitting, Charlie swiped an apple from the sideboard and bit into it with strong, white teeth innocent of fillings.

77

The boom of the boiler, the hiss of the plumbing, sounds of running water suggested that one of his sisters – Janine, probably, or Lucy – was up in the bathroom, washing her hair. The periodic crashing overhead, the jarring of floorboards, the shuddering of the ceiling, gave him to suppose that the littlest ones, Mark and Kelly, were playing Terminator, jumping on and off their beds. Apart from this, and the irritating ting-ting-ta-ting sound from Thomas's personal stereo, the house was relatively peaceful.

'What have you been doing with yourself, huh?' asked Ann comfortably, squinting at her needles, counting stitches.

'I've been up at the rectory. Decorating, you know.'

'Ah-hah.'

'Doing the dining-room.'

'Nice is it?'

'All right.'

Charlie removed Barbie and Ken from the sofa, sat down in their place and began idly to couple them, grinding them together, pelvis to pelvis. 'Not your taste,' he added, 'or mine.'

'Meaning what?'

'Meaning Regency stripes.'

'I see. Well, there's no accounting for it.'

'No, there isn't.' He hoisted Barbie's skirt and, in a spirit of genuine enquiry, inspected her moulded plastic nether regions. 'Then, when I'm through there,' he said, smoothing Barbie's skirt down, making her decent once more, 'I'm working at the Rawlingses'.'

'Ah, hah. So you're rubbing shoulders with the rich and famous these days, are you, Charlie Farley?'

'I wouldn't say that.'

'But she's pretty well known, Dee Rawlings. She's on the box and everything.'

'She is?'

'Sure she is. From time to time, at least. And in my magazine. I heard they were thinking of getting her to open the new Safeway.' Ann finished a row, whipped out a needle and used it to scratch down the back of her T-shirt. 'Ooh, lovely.'

'So what happened?'

'About what?'

'About Safeway.'

'Oh . . .' She looped the wool around her index finger, jabbed the needle in once more, and resumed her knitting, glancing now and then at the pattern, the instructions on her knee. 'I think they got Gloria Hunniford or someone instead.'

'Do you know her to talk to? Dee Rawlings?'

'To pass the time of day, perhaps. No more than that.'

'It was the husband asked me to do the job.'

'Derek?'

'Eric. He seemed nice enough.'

'So I understand from Ivy. You know she does for them? She says the old man's not so bad, but madam's a bit hard to take.'

'She won't bother me,' said Charlie easily. 'If I can cope with Mary Venables, if I can hold my own with Ellen Chitty, I dare say I can manage Mrs Rawlings.'

'Ah, yes,' agreed Ann tranquilly, pausing an instant, resting her knitting in her lap, and turning to consider her handsome eldest son, to indulge her own fierce pride. 'I dare say you can do that, Charlie boy.'

———————— • ————————

'Super,' said Jennie Gosling, the woman from Eye See TV, who was probably forty-something and had aubergine hair under a velvet turban. 'Smashing.'

She was sitting across from Dee, with one spotty-stockinged leg wrapped intriguingly around the other to show that she was complicated. She smoked continually, screwing up her eyes, dropping Gauloise ash all over the pages of her personal organiser, in which she scrawled her thoughts as they popped into her head.

The two of them were having a little getting-to-know-you session in Dee's workplace, imagineering, setting the objectives, creating a simplified overview vis-à-vis the projected television programme, throwing out ideas and then cherry-picking the best of them.

At the end of the day, the series as envisaged was to be about top-notch women and the strategies they employed to balance their lives, to exploit talent and opportunity, to remain in the fast track while still enjoying quality time in the home environment.

Dee and Jennie, both working women, wives and mothers, were in wholehearted agreement that it was very much a question of prioritising, that every life decision was basically a risk-reward calculation filtered through the clock. They were further agreed that Dee Rawlings was a phenomenon, a paragon, that she was Mrs One Hundred And One Per Cent.

'You see,' said Dee, in summary, 'I am a giver.' And, clasping her hands on the desk in front of her, she favoured her visitor, free, gratis and for nothing, with one of her caring, sharing smiles.

'Coffee,' said Nancy shyly, backing into the room with a tray of chinking china which she set down on the side table. As she picked up the cafetière to pour, she glanced at her watch, saw that it was five to six, and relinquished all hope of leaving the office within the next hour. Dee had yet to hand over to her the priority file containing her responses to half a dozen letters, which Nancy must type, and – since the post room would now be closed – stamp and drop into the pillarbox on her way to the station. At a pinch they would keep until Monday, but she could not endure to think of those poor, desperate souls hanging on a moment longer than they had to, for words of comfort and counsel.

'How lovely!' said Jennie Gosling as a cup was set before her, and she tossed her cigarette into the wastepaper bin where it started a small fire among the discarded press releases. 'No, no sugar for me.'

'You're quite sweet enough as you are, I've no doubt,' offered Dee. 'Thank you, Nancy, my dear, what an absolute treasure you are!'

'Of course,' she went on to say, as her secretary quietly withdrew to the outer office, 'one learns not merely to delegate, but to *motivate*.' (And, again of course, she added ruefully, philosophically, spreading her hands, turning them palm-upwards, as the door closed upon her words, though one might delegate some of one's work, one simply could not delegate the responsibility for it.)

'Well, I don't know about you,' announced Edie, shuffling papers, sliding them into drawers out of sight, out of mind, 'but I'm for home.'

'Er, I'll hang on here for a bit,' said Nancy, aborting a sigh. It couldn't be helped, she told herself. It was nobody's fault.

The weekly editorial meeting always made a big hole in the day. And the lady from Eye See TV had obviously to be accommodated. 'I really ought to get those letters out tonight.'

'I don't know why you worry,' Edie admonished her briskly, buttoning her camel coat right up to the neck. 'We're none of us going to get out of this world alive.'

Then, as she picked up her bag and her creaking wicker basket, 'Life is just a bowl of toenails, after all.'

'Oh, Edie, you're such a cynic!'

'I'm not, I'm a realist. So will *you* be, when you get to my age.'

'I shan't be. I *hope* I shan't.'

'Ach, it's the only way to be. Now, have a lovely weekend, won't you, toots? And don't stay here all night at her ladyship's beck and call. Cheeri-bye.'

Alone in the office, Nancy gave herself over for an instant to her mood of self-pity, to a feeling of being put-upon. Then she made a supreme effort to snap out of it, she tushed and tossed her ponytail and gave herself a stern talking-to, she reminded herself that she was privileged to be here, and she asked herself what mattered most, when all was said and done. She could be home in time to sit down for a meal with her family, in the cosy, nurturing atmosphere of the Wilkins household, to exchange with Mum and Dad, with her sister Larraine and her brother Michael, news and gossip about their day. Or she could put in that little extra effort, in order that a young girl abused by a neighbour, and with nowhere else to turn, should receive advice and solace as soon as was humanly possible from the dedicated people at *Mia* magazine.

She made, in other words, a risk–reward calculation. Then she filtered it through the clock.

She was doodling on her shorthand pad, drawing a mouse with long, droopy whiskers, when the telephone rang – a monotonous burr-burr, signalling an internal call.

'Dee Rawlings' office,' said Nancy with something like her usual chirpiness.

'There's a young lady in reception to see Miss Rawlings,' the night security man informed her, 'says she'll know who she is.' He took over from the receptionist at six and, as his tone implied, neither knew nor cared that Dee Rawlings was a Mrs. He wore a brown-and-beige uniform with a badge and cap and tie, with numbered epaulettes on the shirt. It was his job to patrol the building, speaking into a spluttering walkie-talkie, not to mess about with visitors who wanted to play silly beggars.

'A young lady?' It would be Sandra, Nancy supposed (hadn't Dee said that she was expected?) She swivelled in her typist's chair and peered over her shoulder at Dee's occluded office. Every door has a right and a wrong side, and she was acutely conscious of being on the wrong side of this one, of being shut out.

She *could* knock and poke her head in, and say 'Sorry to disturb you, but . . .' Only they'd seemed so involved, the two women, and so intense. She had had a strong sense, when she took them coffee, of her own superfluity.

'Will I send her up?' asked the security man testily. A tight ship he was running here, not a Tupperware party.

'Uhm, well, yes, I think so. Yes please.'

It would be nice to see Sandie Rawlings, Nancy told herself, cheered by the prospect, as she went out on to the landing, preparing to greet her when she stepped out of the lift. She had met Dee's daughter only two or three times, but she had really liked her. She was so friendly and easy and straightforward. The two of them could have a chat until Dee emerged, and the minutes would fly by.

So precisely did Nancy preconceive the moment of her meeting with Sandra, that she barely checked a 'Hi, how are you?' as the lift jaws parted to reveal a complete stranger, a young girl, with a sleeping baby keeled over in his pushchair.

'I'm here to see Dee Rawlings,' said the girl, in a surprisingly gruff voice, bucketing baby and buggy out of the lift car. 'I was afraid she'd of gone. It's taken me for bleeding ever to get here.' She looked weary and wan and sullen, and was slung about with bags. A sulphurous bruise showed faintly through the skin of her cheek. She did not return Nancy's tentative smile, but stood her ground and stared opaquely, working at a loose front tooth, wobbling it with the tip of her tongue.

'I'm Dee's secretary.' Nancy made as if to offer her hand, then withdrew it uncertainly. 'Can I help you?'

'It's *her* I've come to see,' the girl responded without grace. (She would not be fobbed off, her tone implied – she would speak to the engineer, not the oily rag.)

'I'm afraid she's in a meeting. And I don't think, unless

you have an appointment –'

'I'm Kayleigh Roth.'

'Ah, yes, I remember you,' Nancy assured her, because, naturally, she did. So many of the problem letters stayed with her. Their authors peopled her imagination. 'I know, you're from Bermondsey. You have boyfriend trouble.'

'Is that what you'd call it?'

'Well, sort of.' Nancy blushed. She felt foolish and inadequate and affronted. 'Why have you come?' she ventured.

Without a word, Kayleigh Roth reached into her jeans pocket and drew out two crumpled sheets of paper. 'This came for me today. It came first class.' She thrust it at Nancy, who, though she knew its contents well enough, took it appeasingly and ran her eye over it.

'She says,' prompted Kayleigh tonelessly, 'that she'd like to meet me face to face.'

'Yes.'

'She says she'd like to show me the love of which I've been deprived.'

'She does.'

'Because I've been in the wars, she says.'

'Yes. I see.'

'And it doesn't have to be this way, she says. I've got to leave Greg. I've got to leave him at once, not delay another day, because he's no good for me and will do me harm.'

'She does.'

'Well,' said Kayleigh, 'I left him.' And she folded her arms across her chest, as if there were no more to be said.

Nancy felt almost dizzy with panic. How should she proceed? She just wasn't up to this. Nothing had prepared her for such a contingency. 'I think', she said at last, with an audible tremor, 'you had better come into my office and wait for Dee. Yes, I think that would be best. Dee will know what to do.'

So everything was settled to their complete satisfaction. Dee Rawlings liked Jennie Gosling enormously. Jennie Gosling thought Dee Rawlings was extremely good news. The programme would, they had agreed, be a major triumph. They were both tremendously enthused, they could not *wait*.

They had sat a few moments basking in the glow of their mutual regard. Then the air-conditioning which blew through the building like the mistral and made everyone feel cranky and ever so slightly deranged, had shut off with a clunk and a hiss, recalling them to the room, to the business in hand.

Now, 'My job', said Dee in conclusion, breathless, throbbing with emotion, 'is to reach out and touch people, whoever and wherever they are.'

'It must be very satisfying.' Jennie, having smoked her last cigarette, was now reduced to dragging on a biro. 'I mean, to be able to do something for one's fellows.'

'We-ell,' Dee disparaged, puffing her lips out, flapping her hand in a modest gesture of dismissal. 'When I say "touch", I am speaking figuratively. One does, necessarily, operate at long range. One does not, you know, get involved.'

'Well, nevertheless . . .' Jennie got up to leave. She ducked into her purple wool poncho and emerged flushed and smiling. 'It is still so worthwhile.'

'Yes, indeed.' All the same, Dee experienced a teeny-weeny, wholly unexpected twinge of chagrin. What a shame that her work was not more hands-on! She felt somehow thwarted in her life's endeavour. People wrote to her, they said 'Help me, Dee', and she did, she truly helped. But it was all rather remote. How much more powerful would be her influence upon their lives if she could take them properly under her wing. And what good television it would make. It would be that much more compelling to watch her in action, dispensing tender, loving care in a personal, one-to-one situation.

'I'll give you a bell,' promised Jennie, as Dee ushered her out. 'We'll speak soon.'

'I shall look forward to it. Ah, Nancy. Still here?'

'Er, yes,' said Nancy, hopping about, flustered, and she made a distraught little gesture, flapping her hand, drawing attention to a slummocky young girl flopped out in a chair with a child clinging to her knee, grizzling up at her. 'Uhm, there's someone here wants to speak to you.'

'I say!' Dee raised her eyebrows. 'What is this?'

'I'm Kayleigh,' said the girl.

'She wrote.' supplied Nancy.

'She did?'

'And you wrote to her.'

'You said to leave Greg,' Kayleigh informed her. 'So I did. I walked out.'

'And now she's wondering . . .' Nancy looked wretchedly from Dee to Kayleigh then back to Dee again. It was all her fault, she reproached herself. The girl would never have got past reception if she hadn't been so lackadaisical.

'The point is,' put in Kayleigh truculently, 'where am I supposed to go now? I can't stop at Mum's. And I can't go back. Not at this time of day, without the teabags. He'll beat seven kinds of shit out of me if I do.'

'Well . . .' Dee's first impulse was to be angry, to scold her secretary, to send the girl Kayleigh packing. (The infernal cheek of it! The imposition!) But the next instant she remembered Jennie Gosling. And she remembered herself. She remembered that she was Dee Rawlings, she was Mrs One Hundred And One Per Cent.

'Well,' she said a second time, and her pulse quickened. 'I'm sure we'll think of something if we put our heads together. But, look, it's the weekend. This will keep until Monday. I think, in the meantime, my dear, you had better come home with me.'

—————— • ——————

4

Kayleigh awoke the next morning to the aroma of frying bacon and did not for one instant wonder where she was. The boxy little room with the insistent, spriggy paper all up the walls and over the ceiling, had pursued her in and out of her dreams. She had drawn in with every shallow breath the lavender scent of the creaking cotton sheets. The silence had pressed in on her subconscious.

Her sleep had been so ragged, she was thoroughly unrested and, without any of the usual indicators, she had simply no notion of the time. A glance at the little alarm clock on the bedside cabinet, however, told her it was a quarter to nine. Were they expecting her to get up, to make her own way downstairs? Or was she supposed to wait in her room till they summoned her?

Beyond the small window under the eaves, the morning sky was slate grey and empty of promise. A climbing plant tapped at the pane; a stiff wind harried the mad, red leaves. There seemed nothing to get out of bed for.

She didn't want to be here. This was not at all what she had planned. Everything was so very alien, so unlike what she knew. She had a sense of having been somehow compromised. Worse, of having been hijacked. Or kidnapped. They had bundled her into the back of a car and driven away with her at speed.

Her permanent feeling of disadvantage was heightened almost beyond bearing. She was totally helpless now, and dependent.

She had only the faintest idea where she was, and, indeed, how she came to be there. Events had been set in train so fast, there'd been no time to think, and it had obviously occurred to no one to consult her. 'You're coming with me,' Dee had said, and she had held up one hand, palm outwards, like a policeman, to halt the traffic of conversation.

Thus had Kayleigh come to find herself way out in the sticks, in a rambling cottage with, no doubt quite literally, roses round the door. She had visited such a place before, in her imagination. She had hankered after it. She had even bought from her mum's catalogue the flowered teacosy, the rustic bread board, and the harvest pattern stoneware mugs, which were fragments of the daydream. But in reality, of course, she did not and could not belong. She was, as her grandad would express it, fucked and far from home.

She supposed she could hack it for a day or two, she could hang on in and endure all the excruciating cosiness, the cloying kindness, the ordeal of being among the strangest of strangers, the object of their pity. But some more suitable arrangements must be made for her shortly. She couldn't just stay around for ever.

What she really needed, far more than this meaningless spoiling, was someone to speak up for her, to put her case, to have a word in the right ears. And Dee Rawlings, as it had seemed to her, would be the ideal advocate. She was bound to have some influence with the powers that be, to have contacts. She had a strong, bold voice and a bossy manner; she would be able to lay down the law, to pull strings.

Kayleigh saw some things very clearly. She saw, for example, where she stood. *She* could not walk into the benefits office, thump the desk and say 'Give me this, give me that, I need it now.' Dee Rawlings, however, would have none of the same difficulties. No one would ever keep *her* waiting four or five hours for an interview, then face her down with impossible questions, or force her to fill in impenetrable forms. No one would speak to *her* judgmentally through a hygienic sheet of glass, reduce her to tears of impotent fury, then send her away empty-handed.

Dee's type could command things. They would always insist upon their due. They had their own way of dealing with people, they behaved as if others existed for no higher purpose than to serve them, they spoke of them as if they owned them, said 'my accountant', 'my solicitor', 'my gynaecologist', and even 'my butcher'.

Well, no one on the Wavertree Estate, or very seldom, referred in such casual terms to 'my social worker', or 'my bookmaker', or 'my probation officer'. It was always *the* – the social, the bookies, or what have you.

Wavertree was a dustbin to which Kayleigh and her sort had been consigned, not, as was now so evident to her, by God, or by Fate, or through any fault of their own, but by the system. They were victims of simple arithmetic. Some smart-arse git, somewhere, had made this monstrous calculation, a great big sum of long division, and the likes of her had been a kind of human remainder.

And, you know the cleverest part about it? (Because it was, when you came to think of it, quite gobsmacking in its cunning.) When your life was one of endless struggle, and all your days, all your energies, all your emotions were absorbed by living it, you had nothing left with which to fight. You were completely and utterly stuffed. Kayleigh didn't know the word expediency, but expediency was what she had in mind.

Beyond the foot of the bed, Ben began to stir. She heard him burbling to himself, making nearly-talking noises, so she got up grudgingly to go to him. Bending, she stripped him off the undersheet and hauled him out of the old-fashioned cot. (It had been loaned last night by a tight-lipped old bag called Ivy Burston, who had muttered that she did not know, she really didn't, and such a carry-on she'd never seen.) He smelt almost sweetly, pungently of urine. When he butted against her he slobbered on her shoulder. Ugh. Babies were just so *wet*.

There was a diffident knock at the door, and, after a moment's hesitation, it opened and Sandie's head, her kind, open, anxious face, appeared around it. 'Hello,' she said. 'Would you like some breakfast?'

'I don't mind,' said Kayleigh, because she didn't much, one way or the other. She dumped Ben down on the floor and wiped her hands on the oversize T-shirt she slept in. 'I have to get him sorted out.'

'Well, use the green bathroom, it's all yours,' offered Sandie, in tones of strained cheeriness. 'Brekkie will be ready in about ten minutes. A proper fry-up. Not to be missed.'

'Okay,' Kayleigh capitulated.

They were a peculiar bunch, the Rawlingses, but the big-boned, frothy-haired daughter was at least less peculiar than her mum and dad. They had sat together on the rear seat of the BMW last night, with Ben silent and withdrawn between them, with Dee riding up front, and with a swearing, cursing Eric at the wheel.

Every so often, as the miles of shadowy countryside flew out behind them, Dee had turned to them, her face floating like a full moon in the darkened interior, to offer 'sucky sweets' and to enquire solicitously how the girls were doing back there.

Then the girls, peering out of the passenger windows, Kayleigh to the left, Sandra to the right, had duly replied that they were fine, and had continued staring out.

But once, when she'd sneaked a sideways glance at her travelling companion, Kayleigh had caught her doing the same. And, as they splashed through a pool of light from a street-lamp, Sandra had smiled a smile of complicity and of profound misgiving; she had looked as if she half-way understood.

'Perhaps', said Kayleigh to Ben, in an effort to dispel her mood of loneliness, 'I ought to have a quiet talk with that Sandra. After breakfast I shall try to get her on her own.'

She took him into the bath with her, into water laced with perfumed oil. Beside the tub, on an antique washstand, there was a little dish of scalloped soaps, like seashells, in different candy colours, and a jar of fluffed-up cotton wool. Such luxury! It was like being in a hotel. She picked one of the soaps, sniffed it, put it back, picked another and began to lather her baby's back.

She would have availed herself of shampoo, as well, only she was due to have, you know, her *friend at home*, and you could catch a chill washing your hair at that time of the month.

Dressing, with a child, is never a quick or painless operation. Kayleigh would want to scream sometimes with the sheer frustration of it. And today was especially bad.

Sandie had said ten minutes, and ten minutes wasn't nearly long enough, so she dragged her jeans on before she was dry, and the coarse denim grabbed at the flesh of her thighs, making her feel physically got at. She had brought so few things with her: only such oddments as could be gathered up at her mother's flat, items of clothing, hers, Ben's, Lisa's.

She bundled Ben up in a clean, fleecy terry nappy from the stack which Ivy Burston had supplied, and because she was used to disposables, to sticky tapes, not to this outdated fiddle-faddle, she made a proper pig's ear of it. When she spiked him with a pin, Ben turned puce and bellowed.

Ignoring his protests, she bullied him into his hooded jogging suit and zipped it up to the neck. She moistened her fingers with saliva and flattened his hair, which stuck up like pin feathers at the back where he had lain on it. Then she tucked him under her arm, supporting him on the sharp angle of her pelvis, with his chubby legs clamped to her waist, and thus burdened, she made for the stairs.

The landing was long and narrow. She counted eight doors off it (bedrooms, bathrooms). Two, at the far end, stood open so that bleak daylight spilled out on to the long strip of pale carpet, and she was afforded a glimpse of unmade bed.

The original building had been extended; a double garage had been added, with rooms above. The marriage of ancient and modern was about as successful as a marriage can be, it was somewhere short of perfection.

Muffled voices could be heard below.

'Hup,' said Kayleigh to Ben, hitching him up with a jerk of the hip. And, trailing the fingers of her left hand along the white, plastered wall – which habit, over time, would leave a faint black trace – she started uncertainly down.

'Ah, here she is!' said Dee as Kayleigh peeked into the kitchen. 'Come in, come in. Did you sleep well? Yes? I am so glad.'

She was presiding over the long pine table, where last night they had eaten a meal called supper with rice and lots of garlic, which repeated on you something rotten. She was dressed in a garment reminiscent of a small marquee, which might have been night or day wear, and smiling a smile familiar from the pages of *Mia*. Eric sat across from her, tangling with the *Independent*. Sandra, at the stove, waved a spatula in distracted greeting.

'Pour yourself a cup of coffee.' Dee indicated the Bistroware jug. 'That's a good girl. And sit yourself here beside me. This morning, you know, we must have a real heart-to-heart. We must decide what's to be done about you.'

———————— • ————————

'With a baby, if you can believe it,' said Mrs Burston to her daughter, and, as the ripples of indignation ran through her, she was forced to put down the biscuit tin, off which she had been attempting to prise the lid.

'Oh, *I* can believe it,' said Angie placidly. With a show of white knickers she hauled herself half out of her deep armchair, hooked the tin on to her lap, thumbed off the lid, and dipped in for a custard cream.

'A little boy. Not even two years old.'

'I *say*.' Angela made sympathetic clucking noises, then wedged the biscuit in her mouth as she replaced the tin on the coffee table.

'Well, we got your old cot down from the loft. And we asked the Horscrofts for a . . . Just a minute.' Ivy crossed smartly to the window, drew back the lace curtain and rapped on the glass. 'Stop that at once, Nicola, you naughty girl,' she called out. 'That frock was clean on this morning. You'll get it filthy. Angela, she'll get filthy. You should tell her.'

'I will,' said Angie easily, dunking the custard cream in her mug of Nescafé. She liked to do all four corners, to make them nice and soggy, then to nibble them one by one. It was a ritual that demanded her concentration (if she didn't pay close attention, the confection might disintegrate, then she'd be reduced to fishing for the bits with a teaspoon). It didn't awfully matter to her if her little girl got dirty. It would all come out in the wash, she reasoned, she could simply chuck the dress in the machine.

Angela Burston was as indolent as her mother was industrious, yet neither ever seemed to mark the difference – although Ivy would now and then privately ask herself if it might be thyroid. When her daughter dropped in, she would dust around her as if she were part of the furniture, holding forth all the while, going off alarming, as Angie tendered suitable responses.

In consequence, Ivy was thin and bony and birdlike, whereas no one would have compared Angie to a bird, unless they had in mind the Michaelmas goose. Both women had similar dark hair, though, and similar small, bright eyes, and were today wearing matching mushroom-coloured, brioche-rib-and-bobble sweaters, commissioned by Ivy from Ann Horscroft, who did home knitting for pin money.

'I'll stand for no nonsense,' she declared, squirting the sideboard with Mr Sheen, then buffing away with such vigour that she set the best china chattering hysterically within.

'No more you should.'

'I have enough on my plate, thank you very much.'

'Of course.' Angie went to work on the third corner of the biscuit.

'Well, she isn't going to – because she would, you know – get me running around after some delinquent little cockney.'

'If she could, she would, I'll bet.'

'She takes advantage.'

'Always did.' Angie ventured on the fourth corner.

Ivy took a few moments to recharge her batteries, then, 'Like I said to Ann, why not go the whole hog and open up a hostel? Turn the place into a refuge for lame ducks. Take in a load of drunks and drug addicts and down-and-outs.'

'It's the thin end of the wedge,' offered Angie darkly (having disposed of the biscuit, she was able to make this more positive contribution). And with some satisfaction she sucked clean her first and second fingers, then her thumb.

'I've a good mind to give in my notice.'

Ivy's resignation was far more to her than mere abstraction. It was like the atom bomb, and no less actual. She might never drop it on anybody, but it existed as a possibility and gave her strength. Any time she wanted she could blow the rotten job, which alone made the rotten job tolerable.

Then, 'Yes,' she decided, as four-year-old Nicola came running in, treading mud into the carpet, shedding grass mowings everywhere. 'I've a good mind to tell her ladyship to stick it. That girl had better be gone by Monday, or I quit.'

———————— • ————————

He couldn't resist it, he had to drive past. Round the block, then round again, just to make sure it was still standing. And it was, of course, the big, ugly, awesome beast of a house, grazing behind the giant hedge amid the weeds and grasses and gnarled fruit trees of its neglected gardens.

He felt almost faint with excitement and fear; he even fumbled a gear change. The first time he'd turned into the road, it had been in the sick expectation of seeing a flagboard, of learning that Roy Brooks or Raymond Bushell or Barnard Marcus had got in ahead of him – and that thus Audrey Atkins had been apprised of the true value of her property. But if his competitors had done, and if she had been, the house was giving no sign of it.

On the second circuit, he slowed right down, crawled along the kerb and, peering through the driver's window, saw to his dismay Audrey Atkins herself, making uncertain homeward progress behind a refractory wicker wheely basket laden with the weekly shopping.

What else was he to do? He waited until she had reached her front gate and was tangling with it, then hooted, waved, and whooshed on by, watching in the rear-view mirror as, doddering in confusion, she returned the salutation.

Had she recognised him? Probably not. Or his car? Again, he doubted it. The poor old duck was hopelessly bewildered. He remembered the way she had fluttered at his elbow as he made his tour of inspection, pecking at his sleeve with thumb and forefinger, unable even to formulate a question.

Then, so what if she *had* identified him? There was no reason why he should not be in this neck of the woods. It might actually be all to the good, it would bring him very forcefully to her mind. And the cheery hoot, the merry wave, had been, in hindsight, masterly. Toot-toot. Can't stop. I'm a busy man. I have places to sell and people to see. Call me if you want me. Make an appointment. Hey, we might do some business.

He was all at once as sure as he could be that she would be in touch. He knew she would instruct him, that she'd give him sole agency, there was simply no question about it. She would have been impressed with his easy, open manner, his patent sincerity, his obvious professionalism, not to mention his good looks and charm, to which, he had learned, even half-daft old wrinklies were not always immune.

As he headed north towards home, a battle royal was joined

93

within him by numbers of warring emotions: rapacity engaged with pusillanimity, avarice with abject terror.

On Tooting Bec he pulled up so sharply that the Citroën which had been panting up his arse for the past half mile was forced to swerve to avoid him. 'If you want to commit suicide,' shouted the driver, screeching to a halt alongside him, looking ugly as sin, 'take pills.'

'Go fuck yourself,' Jamie muttered, showing the finger that says more than words ever can. He leapt out of the Porsche, stumbled around to the nearside, then on to the verge, vomited violently behind a tree, and felt calmer.

He had always had what Dee termed a 'poorly tum'. Often, as a child, he'd been kept home from school because of it. He used to lie on the sofa under an eiderdown, while his mother smoothed his fevered brow and brought him chicken soup. Or she would sit in the small bay window of the Sydenham house, typing her weekly column for *Home Circle*, and an atmosphere of pure calm and timeless intimacy would settle upon them, enduring until Sandie came crashing in on them, all white socks and satchel, to shatter it.

After a time he had been able to bring on a bout of sickliness at will. He had only to think an anxious thought for the colour to drain from his cheeks. He had become an expert at the deathly pallor. Only, then it had all got out of hand, as anxious thoughts, popping unbidden into his mind, brought the bile to his throat.

In a small, shrivelled part of himself, now, he wished he had never set eyes on Clovelly, never dreamed up so hairy a scheme. For, having dreamed it, it seemed he had no option but to follow through. He had seen too vividly in his imagination all that would flow from the successful execution of it. It would bring him lots and lots of lovely crispies. But more than that, it would get him in really thick with Giles de Lannoy-Hunt, their destinies one and inextricable. He perceived it as a kind of rite of passage, a baptism of fire, a means to a most glorious end. He would thenceforth be a fully paid-up member of the *beau monde*.

'That Jamie's a boy,' said a voice in his head, admiring, affectionate, frightfully upper-class.

Then, 'Yes, isn't he brill?' concurred another, a breathy, female voice. 'I think he's just divine.'

Of course, if he were ever found out. . .

But, why should he be? How could he be?

Still, *if* . . . If the old man, the boss, got wind of the scam, James Rawlings could kiss goodbye to his career. He would bring shame and disgrace on himself and his family. He would be a social outcast, sacked without references, rendered unemployable, down on his beam end. The spectre of the Office of Fair Trading loomed suddenly horribly large. He might even . . . But that did not bear consideration.

Steadying himself with one hand against his new friend the tree, deriving obscure reassurance from the masculine roughness of the bark, he gazed pinkly, moistly, across the windswept grass to a distant row of redbrick houses under a glowering sky.

None of this need have arisen, he told himself bitterly. It was, in fact, wholly unnecessary. And it was all Richard Mabey's fault. Richard, who headed up the agency, was a man of fifty-seven with an amiable, almost other-worldly approach to business. Jamie had tried his utmost to urge upon him a more dynamic *modus operandi*. They could do this; they could do that. They could advertise more widely and with far greater oomph (heaven knows, he did his best to inject into their weekly small ads something of the style he felt they needed). They could work later at night, they could open on Sundays, do special deals, offer one-stop shopping, with a full range of services under a single roof.

He would sit across from Richard and thump the desk in his enthusiasm. And Richard would puff his pipe alight, and rock back in his chair, in a cloud of blue smoke, and say 'Hmm, you have a point. Leave it with me. Let me think it over.' Then, unless Jamie pressed him, it would never be mentioned again.

It had been the same story the last time he had asked for the pay rise, the reward for talent and enterprise, which he so richly deserved. 'Hmm, well, I'll think about it', and then not another word.

Bastard! Jamie sniffed contemptuously. Stupid, equivocating bastard! Richard May Be, he would call him from this day forth. He'd say, 'Yes, Mr May Be. No, Mr May Be. Three bags full, Mr May Be.' Oh, the bugger was well named, all right!

The up side of this (and wasn't it jolly, the way everything in life had an up side?), was that woolly-minded Mr May Be could be guaranteed not to tumble to his wheeze. Clovelly would go smoothly through the agency's books, in one month, out the next, with no awkward questions asked, and not a whiff of impropriety. On paper, at least, it would be completely kosher. He might even earn himself some additional brownie points – for what little they were worth – by fixing up the dotty Atkins characters with a flat from their files.

It was poetry, when you came to think of it, pure poetry.

Returning to his lovely red Carrera (and how was he supposed to run her on his niggardly salary?), he was affronted by the sight of the scraped paintwork. He had intended to mention it to Dee, to drop a broad hint in the hope of a handout, but all week she'd had her head in the clouds, she'd been taken up with other things – with publishing deals and TV appearances and heaven alone knew what – and the moment had never seemed quite right to approach her.

Tomorrow, perhaps? Or this very afternoon? He could nip back to Clapham for a shower and a spot of lunch, then motor down to Kent, be there in time for tea. It would be a surprise and a thrill for his doting parent. She would kill the fatted calf in his honour, and think nothing of stumping up the necessary to take care of the repairs.

Lucinda was away for the weekend in Wiltshire, on a duty visit to her granny, whom she hadn't seen for absolutely yonks. He had time to kill. He was feverish and jittery, with an energy that refused to be subdued.

He was shivering uncontrollably as he got back into the car. The day, though bleak, was not cold, yet his teeth chattered. He huffed into his cupped hands to warm them, and breathed the pear-drop smell of a nervous stomach.

And, in that instant he knew what he wanted. In that instant he wanted his mummy.

———————— • ————————

After lunch, Eric took himself out into the garden to be away from the women, to get some air, perhaps also to get his head together. He left Sandie stacking the dishwasher, while Dee had another go at their unkempt, surly little guest, lecturing her gently,

but in tones that brooked no argument, across the kitchen table.
*I lift up my finger and I say tweet tweet, hush hush, but now,
come come.*

She had surely gone too far this time, that megalomaniac
wife of his. She must finally be losing the plot.

They had been sitting in the car yesterday evening, he at the
wheel, Sandie behind, waiting for Dee to emerge at her leisure
from the Magazines UK building. They had been having the
kind of conversation that they both found soothing, as desultory
and undemanding as a game of I-spy. Then, 'Look sharp,' he had
said, '*cave* chaps, here comes matron.'

And, 'She's got someone with her,' Sandie had observed,
close to his ear, inclining forward, hugging the back of the
passenger seat, propping her chin, the better to peer through the
windscreen.

'So she has. Who is that?'

'Cripes, I haven't a clue. A girl with a baby.'

'Well, evidently.'

'She's bringing her over.'

'What the hell is she up to?'

'I honestly cannot imagine.'

Then, 'This', Dee had announced, tugging open the door and
bending to beam in at her husband and daughter, 'is Kayleigh
Roth. With her little boy, Ben. Kayleigh has been having a few
problems lately. She's going to stay with us for a while, until she
gets on her feet. Now, I know you'll do everything you can to
make her welcome.'

So, 'Hello, Kayleigh,' they had said on cue, exchanging with
each other, via the driving mirror, looks of sheer bemusement.

But the girl had declined to answer as she bundled her baby
in through the rear door and climbed in after him. And when
Sandie had said encouragingly, 'Hello, there, Benjie', the child
had betrayed not so much as a flicker of response.

'Bringing our work home with us, are we dearest?' Eric had
asked Dee with forced jocularity, lurching sideways to plant a loud,
derisive kiss on her cheek, although inwardly he had boiled. (The
damned impertinence of it to foist upon them a perfect – well, a
not so perfect – stranger!)

'Manners, Eric, please,' Dee had chided him, shooting him a

warning glance and slamming the door on the hem of her coat, which would hang out like washing all the way to Kent.

They had driven in a speaking silence to the cottage, each with his or her own very different thoughts.

She's gone clean off her head, he decided now, as he put his shoulder to the warped shed door and went busting in. It smelt of wood in there, and creosote and damp sacking. The air around him seemed very active; it shimmered with a life of its own. He peered in the half-light along the racks of tools, in search of purpose, of something to make sense of the day. If she gets any worse, he told himself, they'll have to lock her up.

He was charmed and diverted by this notion. He visualised Dee in a secure ward, in a dressing-gown, pumped full of Largactil, lost in her own private world, listlessly picking at the candlewick.

His duties as a husband would be drastically scaled down in consequence. He might be expected to visit her weekly, with grapes. But he would be let off PT, he would be excused games indefinitely.

No more servicing her ladyship; no more of that with-my-body-I-thee-worship nonsense; no need, any longer, to fulfil those functions to which marriage had condemned him. Free at last, free at last, from the tyranny of the wedding vows!

Not that he wasn't sexual. He was, as he put it to himself, a normal, red-blooded male, he was hot and lecherous as a sparrow. He had a riotous fantasy life, his imagination teemed with nubile lovelies, all of whom, by happy coincidence, had long, silken hair, and tiny waists, and big, heavy breasts, and soft, caressing voices, and wide, adoring eyes.

But sex with one's wife was another matter altogether – especially with such a wife as Dee. If he were to die tomorrow, it would be with a sense of profound regret that he had never in real life known (and by 'known' he meant, well, *known*) a truly beautiful woman. Like so many men, he nurtured a vague, irrational belief that such was his entitlement; and a strong suspicion was with him always that he had somehow been denied his due.

Rewriting history more than slightly, he recollected being, in the springtime of his youth, something of a wow with the girls. Even now, at fifty-four, he was not at all bad looking if his mirror told him true. He still had most of his hair, a trim little beard with no trace of grey, and perfectly regular features. It was a constant puzzle to him – misunderstanding, as he did, the true nature of physical attraction – that far more unsightly chaps than he were able to pull the birds.

He blamed Dee for his lack of success. It was all her doing. She had coupled her name to his – they had become known to all as a pair, not Eric-and-Dee, but Dee-and-Eric. Then, with her wealth and fame, she had subsumed him.

The process of emasculation was more or less complete now. He had manifestly failed as a breadwinner. His various enterprises, over the years, had gone down the pan. From the first it had been she who earned the real money, who kept the Rawlings show on the road.

He had been reduced, finally, to the status of bored housewife. On a Friday morning you could find him touring the aisles of the yuppies' Sainsbury's at Nine Elms, making informed choices between one brand of soap powder and another; or squinting at lists of ingredients, at nutritional information, checking out the additives; or shopping around for a penny off this or that.

They had domestic help, of course, both in Kent and in town. They had women in to clean. But he haunted the London house throughout the long week, doing useful little chores, loading and unloading the Indesit, venting the radiators, rinsing the milk bottles, watering the pot plants, defrosting the fridge, peeling the potatoes for the evening meal, or just skulking upstairs, out of sight of Pat-the-cleaner, on her three mornings.

And increasingly he occupied himself outdoors, not because he enjoyed it (he found the work messy and arduous), but because it offered some small salve to his *amour propre*. Gardening was man's work, at least as much as it was woman's. There was dignity in the tilling of God's good earth.

In the spring he had put in some creeping wintergreen, and he was as pleased as punch now to see, nestling amid the dark foliage, a ripe and fruity crop of berries. It was like magic, really; he could hardly believe it had actually happened. It gave him a thrill. He thought, *I* did that!

Getting in amongst the roses, he set about deadheading them, snipping off the frowsy flowers, whistling to himself about the last rose of summer which was blooming alone.

A dishevelled blossom dropped into the palm of his hand, and he stood for a moment, studying it.

The girl, this Kayleigh person, was similarly dishevelled. But he detected in her, as in a rose, an essential underlying beauty.

She had long hair, and an inviting, husky voice. And a tiny waist. And her breasts looked full and heavy.

Eric closed his eyes. He closed his fingers around the flower head. And he squeezed it and squeezed it till it was mulch.

———————— • ————————

'Would you like to come for a walk?' asked Sandra, standing framed in the sitting-room doorway. She spoke with some apprehension, since there was about their house guest a spikiness which neither encouraged nor endeared, and she held fast to the handle, as if she might at any moment slam out. 'Blow the cobwebs away, you know,' she added feebly. 'Work up an appetite for tea.'

But her suggestion was met not so much with antagonism as with a kind of non-response. Kayleigh merely stared at her from the sofa, where she had been sitting with Ben for the past hour and a half, ostensibly glued to the Saturday movie, though she had evinced neither interest nor emotion as the weepy plot unfolded. Now the final credits were rolling, and Sandra, who had been dutifully looking in on her at intervals, supposed that some other entertainment should be offered, some further hospitality extended.

Dee was closeted in her study, working up a new book proposal, and her muse must be with her this afternoon, to judge by the businesslike clatter of typewriter keys. (She favoured an obsolete Adler, about which she was theatrically superstitious and sentimental; of new technology she would have no part.) Eric was in the garden, giving the lawn its last short back and sides of the year (the green sap scent of cut grass was borne in on the stiff breeze). So Sandra, who naturally took such things upon herself, had assumed the role of hostess.

'Good film?' she enquired chummily.

'Not bad,' Kayleigh told her. 'But I've seen it before. I've seen it three times.'

'It's not so dreadful outdoors,' Sandra then persisted, pulling the door towards her, bouncing it on the rubber toe of her plimsoll, leaving faint black scuff marks on the white satin-gloss paintwork. 'I mean, it's not wildly sunny or anything, but it's perfectly warm and nice.'

She never, herself, paid much attention to the weather, she just took it as it came. She wasn't one of those types who, for sheer bravado, break the ice on the Serpentine and take a Boxing Day dip, or who labour obstinately over a smoking barbecue in drenching rain rather than admit defeat, but nor would she be dictated to out of all reason by the elements, and she took the view that a little wind and wet did no one any harm.

She understood, however, that most people did mind these things – that they minded very much. Some, indeed, were apparently so affected by a lack of sunlight, that they felt tired and listless from autumn right through to spring, becoming clinically depressed, even suicidal, in the depths of winter. Kayleigh might, for all she knew, be such an ill-adapted person. As the days drew in, her body chemistry could go all to pot.

In fact, Kayleigh wasn't, and it didn't. Like Sandra, she was more or less indifferent to the climate. She welcomed the sunshine when it reached her, mediated though it might be by London pollution. And she hated the winter cold, which curled her fingers and crinkled her papery skin, and trapped her so utterly inside herself. But there was, for her, nothing between these two extremes; she simply did not see or feel a thing.

She had a problem with Sandra's invitation, only because she had no concept of walking as recreation. Legs were for carrying you from A to B. A leisurely stroll in rural Kent lay somewhere outside her experience. And as for working up an appetite, what on earth was the point of that? Faced with such curious propositions, she did not know what to say, so she said nothing.

'We could go to Stott's farm and see the horses. Ben would like that, wouldn't he?'

'I guess so.' With unconcealed reluctance and a stifled yawn, Kayleigh got to her feet. If she was expected to walk, her manner implied, then walk she would. It made no odds to her. There would be nothing on the box but sport from now till five o'clock.

Sandra, witnessing this show of long-suffering, began seriously to wish she hadn't bothered. But, 'You'll enjoy it,' she said bravely, heartily. 'The countryside is at its loveliest, in some ways, at this time of year.'

'Hm,' replied Kayleigh, very noncommittal.

They went Indian file along Brocks Lane, which ran past the flank of the house and away from the village. Sandra took the lead, keeping tight to the verge; Kayleigh brought up the rear with the squeaking buggy. Whenever a vehicle swished by, the squeaking would stop, and Sandra would turn back to check that all was well.

'We have pavements where I live,' grumbled Kayleigh, quite without irony. 'They're a safety feature. You know where you stand with a pavement.'

'Well, of course. But so little traffic uses this road; there's not really any need for one.'

'Maybe not.' Kayleigh sounded unconvinced.

'Anyway, we can turn off just up ahead and follow the footpath to the farm. It's not too rough for a buggy, I don't believe, and at least we'll be away from the cars.'

'All right. If you say so.'

'I do. Look, we're here.'

As Sandra hesitated, glancing back, a young man with gypsy hair and lascivious gaze appeared through a gap in the hedge. He wore faded jeans, a scruffy sweater, and a wide, unabashed smile. A big, pale dog butted at his calf, till he laid a hand upon its head to soothe it. 'Hello there,' he said, the saucy git, giving them, as Kayleigh thought, the glad eye, looking them over in a strange, unsettling manner.

She was about to ask him if he'd had his flipping eyeful, when, 'Hello,' said Sandra to him, bold as brass.

'You know him?' enquired Kayleigh when he'd gone whistling on his way.

'Not really. Well, I mean, yes, slightly. He's called Charlie something.'

'Bit forward, wasn't he?'

'Oh, no, not really. That's how it is in a village, you see. Quite unlike London. Everyone says hello to everyone. It's nice, don't you think?'

'I don't know. Maybe.'

The stony track was wide enough – just – for the two of

them to walk side by side. It went very gradually up, between fields which in summer would be covered by blue drifts of linseed, or suffocated by rape, yellow, yellow, yellow, as far as the eye could see.

'Let me take over for a bit,' urged Sandra.

'If you want,' Kayleigh acquiesced, thankfully relinquishing her hold on the pushchair.

There was something oddly touching, Sandra found, about the weight of the conveyance, of its small and helpless human cargo. She ran the chair back and forth to see how it would ride on the uneven terrain, gazing down all the while at the funny little chap, whose ears stuck out like wing-nuts to right and left of his wobbly head. He was so tiny, so defenceless, and above all so compact. The makings of a full-grown human being were compressed within him. This notion tore at her.

The action of propelling him appealed to some deep and secret part of her. It was a keen and not altogether agreeable sensation. And it set her wondering, as so often before, if she could ever bear to have a child of her own. At worst, it would be one more thing to worry about.

How deeply did Kayleigh feel for Ben? Did fears for him come between her and her sleep? Did he drag and drag on her heartstrings? She appeared unconcerned, but it was unfair to judge her – at least by the standards of Sandra's friends, who behaved as if they were uniquely clever to have reproduced themselves, and who demanded that others endlessly celebrate their achievement, that they continually fête their wretched offspring.

In Kayleigh Roth's world, the merits of Montessori and the importance of appropriate work–play ratios were presumably not real issues. It was all very well for the chattering classes to expend time and energy developing no-lose strategies for achieving high-quality resolutions of parent–child conflicts. It was fine for them to boast of their little darlings' bodily-kinesthetic aptitude as they drove them round to Tumble Tots. But the more hard-up and put-down members of society could not be blamed if, in their desperation, they merely gave their kids a clip round the ear, then pacified them with Smarties.

Just the same, Ben's almost unnatural docility bothered Sandra. She thought he was probably backward for his age. Should he not have started talking by now? He must want desperately for stimulation.

'Does he say any words yet?' she asked.

'Just muh-muh,' Kayleigh reported without a flicker of a smile. 'He's very slow. Well, boys always are, so my mum says. It's only later that they get to be fast.'

'It's a start, anyway,' Sandra told her. Then, 'What do you do?' she enquired conversationally, to change the subject, and immediately wished that she hadn't. The question sounded somehow terribly crass and condescending.

'Do?'

'For a job, I mean. Do you have a job?'

'No,' Kayleigh told her tonelessly. 'I was still at school when I fell for him.' She nodded impersonally towards her little boy. 'Greg works sometimes,' she added rather as an afterthought. 'He does the double.'

'The double?'

'Oh, *you* know. He's on the dole, but he gets some days' work. He's on the bikes. I mean, he's a motorcycle courier,' she amended grandly.

'That must be fun, getting out and about,' said Sandra, secretly shocked, less by the thought of such duplicity than by Kayleigh's bland, bare-faced acceptance of it. The words 'dole scroungers' popped up through some trapdoor in her mind, from below stage, in which dark, airless space lurked her most judgmental, least tolerant, least generous attitudes.

'Yes.'

'Not being tied to an office.'

'No.' Kayleigh pondered this. '*I* couldn't work in an office,' she said with exaggerated distaste, rather as if for 'office' you might read 'orifice'.

'I can't say I've ever tried it.'

'No?'

'No. I'm always slaving over a hot stove, me. I do catering, you see. Directors' lunches, dinner parties, that sort of thing.'

Kayleigh sniffed, fished from her pocket some green festoons of tissue, and dabbed at her nose. 'That must be boring,' she said.

Sandra shot her a look, recognised the toilet paper from the spare bathroom, and retorted sharply, '*I* like it.'

'Ah well, it wouldn't suit me,' ventured Kayleigh more kindly, humouring her. 'But it would never do, I suppose, for us all to be the same.'

'Anyway, I understood that you'd left Greg,' Sandra reminded her. Hurt invariably made her angry. But then, doesn't all anger grow out of hurt? Self-esteem, like a grow-bag, splits open, and things shoot out in all directions from the fertile compost of degraded emotions. 'I thought that was why you were here, to get away from him.'

'I have left him,' said Kayleigh flatly. 'But. . .'

'But?'

'But he's still Ben's dad. And he still works on the bikes.'

At the top of the small hill they paused for breath, and to gaze out over the gentle, well-ordered landscape. 'Look,' said Sandra, 'this is Stott's farm.' Then, as two handsome chestnuts came nodding towards them, to snicker at them over the fence, 'These are Chester and Dylan,' she added. 'They're Annabel Stott's.'

Without seeking permission, she bent to unstrap Ben from his pushchair and hauled him up. He leaned heavily out of her arms and pointed with a tiny doll's finger.

'Horses,' urged Sandra hopefully. 'Say "horses".'

But the little boy's mouth was slack and drooling; it did not take a shape.

'It's good here,' said Kayleigh, gazing around. 'It's like a picture.'

'Isn't it lovely?' Sandra could not have felt more gratified if she'd owned the scenery; or if she'd made it herself.

'Just like in *The Darling Buds of May*.'

'Yes, it is. It really *is*.'

'I quite reckoned that programme.'

'Oh, so did I!' concurred Sandra, who loved H.E. Bates, and had been charmed by the character of Pop Larkin, never mind his tax evasion or his dealings in the black economy. (So what if he did, so to speak, 'do the double'?)

'You know . . .' Kayleigh rummaged around in the buggy, under the blanket, and pulled out a pack of cigarettes. 'Want one of these?'

'I don't smoke, thanks.'

'You know, they've only gone and made a book of it.'

'A book of what?'

'About them darling buds, with David Jason. I saw it in Smith's the other day.'

How absolutely brilliant! What a triumph! Humming with self-congratulation, Dee typed the word 'endit' – a printer's term, a little conceit – and yanked the page out of her typewriter so the ratchets screamed in protest.

In the space of a couple of hours, she had come up with an entire synopsis for her next book, another for her 'Lifelines' *oeuvre*, some words of wisdom on the modern marriage, on keeping love alive, on guarding one's female mystery, on sustaining the magic into the autumn years.

Now, tea, she thought, and crumpets. Meals were part of the ritual of country life, they were a tradition and might not therefore be skipped. Good gracious, was that the time? She had been too immersed in her writing to notice its passing. Where was her other half, her lord and master? Where, too, were the girls? Where Sandra? Where Kayleigh?

She must try to have another chat with their visitor, to see if they could make some headway. She had not for one minute regretted the impulse that had moved her to bring the child here. She would do the same again without a qualm. She had a Samaritan's instincts; she could not simply pass by on the other side. And she didn't look for gratitude, heaven knows!

Just the same, Kayleigh's attitude confounded her. She was so . . . fractious. So awkward. So belligerent, and so unbiddable. She plainly believed the world owed her a living.

She could go to a refuge, Dee had ventured to suggest. They were warm and nurturing institutions, run *by* women *for* women, with everybody rallying round to support one another in a spirit of genuine community.

'I'm not going in no hostel,' Kayleigh had retorted, and she had rammed her fists into her hips, and thrown her hair around, and fixed Dee with a glare of pure defiance.

'Not a hostel, my sweet. That's not what I'm saying.'

'Nor in B and B. So you can forget that and all.'

They were talking, Dee had been at pains to explain, of temporary solutions, of half-way houses (and when she'd said 'half-way house', she had not of course meant it as Kayleigh had construed it; she hadn't intended to evoke the Sally Army).

But, she wanted a flat, Kayleigh, the little madam, had insisted. A place of her own where she could bring up her child safe and unmolested. Was that too much to ask in a so-called civilised country. Well, *was* it?

Beggars, Dee might have told her then, in sheer exasperation, could not be choosers. But she had bitten her tongue and said nothing.

This evening, however, she was determined to progress this thing, to force it to a firm conclusion, to come up with an acceptable compromise. If Kayleigh would go, in the short term, to a refuge, then she, Dee Rawlings, would move heaven and earth to find her a place of her own. Or a house share? What was wrong with sharing? It could be the jolliest thing, with all girls together.

On her way to the kitchen to fix tea and crumpets, she looked into the sitting-room, where *Barrymore* played to an absent audience. Sighing, she went to switch off the television. It was a corner room, with French windows overlooking the garden, with a small side window giving on to the lane. Through this Dee watched as a red Porsche drew up, reversed, nosed forward, reversed, nosed forward once more.

'Jamie!' she cried aloud in delight, and she clasped her hands to her breast. Her baby, her boy, had come to see her. What a wonderful, wonderful surprise!

'Flash,' said Kayleigh, pointing to the sporty car which was going through the elaborate performance of parking as they approached the cottage. And, 'Who the fuck is that?' she wanted to know, as a tall, tanned, handsome man sprang out on to the road.

'Oh, him,' said Sandra, with a little moue. 'That's the Great Jamie Rawlings. He's my younger brother.'

'Yeah? Go on!' Kayleigh gave an appreciative whistle. For once she showed a flicker of animation. She glanced for an instant at Sandra, then again at Jamie, as though she were making some odious comparisons. 'A bit of all right, though, isn't he? A bit of bleeding all right.'

'I guess he is,' Sandra conceded dully. 'I suppose you could say that, yes.'

•

5

He simply could not get to grips with it. Words failed him. He was – not to put too fine a point on it – appalled. He had arrived at Foxholes yesterday afternoon, in time for tea, to find the place infested by strangers. A ghastly, slovenly girl with ratty hair and scaly hands and no grace or style or conversation, had got her feet under the proverbial table. And, as if this were not enough, she was burdened with a sickly infant who looked as if he had been grown in a damp, dark cellar, from a spore.

Jamie, who, at the best of times, could not abide children around food, had withdrawn from the family circle to the far corner, where he had sat, stiff and aloof, inhaling through his mouth, through a silk handkerchief, rather than breathe in the smell of baby, and had affronted his mother by refusing toasted crumpets.

'Who . . . ?' he had hissed at Sandie, pursuing her to the kitchen as she carried out the tea things. 'What in heaven's name . . . ?'

'She's called Kayleigh,' Sandra had informed him over her shoulder as she dumped the tray on the draining-board. 'And', she had added, running hot water, squeezing in a viscous glob of Ecover, 'the little fellow is Ben.'

She had seemed, unaccountably, to find some humour in the situation. She had turned from the sink, brandishing a plastic scouring brush, and though she had pasted her top lip over the lower one to envelop a laugh, sheer hilarity had shone out of her eyes. 'She's mum's latest project. Quite a challenge, I would hazard.'

'I don't see what's so amusing,' Jamie had told her, with all the distance, chill and strain which increasingly characterised their relationship.

Twenty years ago they had been very close. Sandie, at any rate, had loved her younger brother almost more than life. She had led him by the hand to school each day. And she had defended him with ferocity and naked fists against the classroom bullies who had found it great sport to torment such a spoilt, awkward, unconformable, tell-tale, tearful mummy's boy.

Time, however, had coloured their personal recollections of those days. The same memories which Sandie cherished, and which warmed her right through, left Jamie decidedly cold. And there was scant residual understanding between them. They had grown so very far apart.

'They're as common as muck,' he had sneered at her, 'the girl and the kid, they're a blight.'

'It won't be for long, after all,' she had soothed, with nothing like the appropriate concern.

'I cannot imagine what Mother was thinking of. What came over her, d'you suppose?'

'As far as I can gather, Kayleigh sort of wished herself upon her – turned up at the office late on Friday. It was a whim, I guess, on Mum's part, to bring her down for the weekend.'

'But it's crazy. It's outrageous.'

'Yes, it is a bit potty.'

'I mean, what are we running here, a refuge for any old wino or bag lady who wants to come knocking at our door?'

'That was pretty much Dad's reaction.'

'For once, then, he and I are of the same mind.'

'Look, it's just until Monday. Something will be sorted out then. Surely you can make the best of it meanwhile? Kayleigh's not a bad person,' Sandie had pointed out (and he could have done without the sermon, thank you very much, he could have done without the sanctimony). 'She's not had our advantages, that's the thing. We can't know what it's like to come from where she comes from.

Thank God we've not had to subsist on state handouts and the few quid you can earn on the side.'

'Dole scroungers.'

'Jamie, you shock me! You don't know you're born. You've had the kind of privileges that Kayleigh can only dream of.'

'My point precisely,' he had argued in triumph, with right entirely on his side. 'She doesn't belong among us. We can do nothing for her. She should be with her own kind.'

'You're a snob, Jimmy James.'

'I have taste and discrimination, if that's what you mean. And please call me Jamie, I prefer it.'

'Snobbish. Discriminating. It comes to the same thing.' Then she had apparently been unable to resist a tease. 'She's taken quite a shine to you, you realise? She thinks you're God's gift to womankind.'

'I wouldn't touch her with a barge pole,' he had responded feelingly. He had closed his eyes, and been visited by the image of a grubby bra strap chafing pasty flesh. An involuntary shudder had slightly unbalanced him. 'I hope I should never be that desperate.'

Well, needless to say, his weekend was ruined. He had come in search of respite. He had hoped for peace, quiet, a chance to relax, to escape from the pressures of the city, and to reflect upon his game plan. But the air had been tainted by this alien presence.

At supper, and again today at lunchtime, he had sensed the girl staring at him in the most disconcerting manner. And his eyes had been drawn in her direction, just in time to witness the disgusting spectacle of the baby gobbing a mouthful of mash and carrots down his front. (Jamie, who was all smiling indulgence around bread-roll-throwing hoorays, had none the less felt his gorge rise at such grossness.)

Now it was Sunday afternoon and, in spite of Sandra's blithe assurances, there was no sign that the matter would be resolved. Yet, perplexingly, Jamie's only true ally, the only other member of the household who seemed to share his sense of abhorrence with any wholeness of heart, was Oedipuss. The grumpy, neutered tom had made himself extremely scarce since the child arrived, coming in only for meals, which he ate quickly and furtively, with his ears flat, before crashing out through his flap-door to lie low in the forsythia.

In an irrational way, now, Jamie directed his anger, not at his mother, whose wheeze this had been, but at his sister, who had appeared so lightminded, so uncaring about the whole sorry state of affairs. She annoyed him beyond endurance. She was, in his estimation, stubborn, solid, wilfully plain. (And what could have possessed her to have such a perm, to go for the *frisée* look? Christ, that hair-do was actionable! She should get herself a shit-hot lawyer. She'd clean up.)

He watched her now despisingly through the French windows. She was walking in the garden with Kayleigh, pointing out various late-blooming flowers, to the stupid girl's manifest lack of interest.

His mother was shut up once again in her study and would not be disturbed. (So much for his plan to get her on her own, to touch her for a few hundred quid!) His father was sleeping in an armchair (by the occasional snore he signalled his presence). The brat had been dumped on the floor, on a blanket in front of the TV, and was apparently glued to a Western.

This was one explanation, if you liked, for the malaise of the underclass. This was what was wrong with the great unwashed. They were addicted to television. Their income went on booze and fags and the box. Their homes sprouted satellite dishes like ears. Late-night video shops sprang up on their streets.

You would have thought – Jamie, at any rate, would have thought – that they might find some better use for their dole money. And was it to subsidise their filthy habits that conscientious citizens such as he must be taxed until the pips squeaked?

Consider this child, this Ben. He would almost certainly have been damaged *in utero* by his mother's addiction to tobacco and alcohol. He has a head like a giant puffball. He was unquestionably a late-developer, if not actually moronic. And could one wonder at it, when his only stimulation was beamed in on him via the cathode-ray tube?

At that instant, as though he sensed he was the object of malign attention, Ben twisted his squat little body and gazed up at Jamie, his wispy eyebrows tilting worriedly, his mouth working. He lifted his hand and pointed waveringly at the screen. 'Horsy,' he said, in an earnest appeal to the better nature of this strange, glowering man. And, a second time, winningly, with a smile of sorts, 'Horsy.'

But Jamie Rawlings was not to be drawn. He set his face against the boy. Studiously, unsmilingly, he stared into the middle distance and ignored him. If he gave the little yoblet the slightest encouragement, he would be bound to come crawling all over him, demanding to be dandled on his knee.

'My mum had a ponsy-etta,' said Kayleigh, really just to make a contribution, to give something of her own to the conversation, which so far had been pretty one-sided.

'A . . . ?' Sandra ran her fingers through her hair, which felt unnaturally coarse, like man-made fibre, and she frowned, uncomprehending.

'You could brush it out, you know,' Kayleigh advised her, glancing up at her and then immediately, shiftily, away. 'The curl would drop a bit, and it might look all right.'

'D'you reckon?'

'Well, at any rate, it would be worth a try.'

'I shall give it a go, then.'

'I'll do it for you, if you want. You can wash it and I'll dry it straight. I'm good at hair.'

'Oh, *would* you?'

'I don't mind.' Kayleigh paused. 'She made a bit of a balls-up, whoever permed it.'

'She did, didn't she? It's a horror story.'

'Still, we'll see if we can fix it.'

'That would be great.'

'Anyway, my Auntie Maureen bought it for my mum.'

'Bought . . . ?'

'This ponsy-etta.'

'I'm not sure if I've ever heard . . . '

'No, mum hadn't either. My Auntie Maureen said to her, "I've got you this plant, which won't be familiar with you." She give it her for Christmas. It had, like, bright red leaves at the top.'

'Ah, a poinsettia.'

'A ponsy-etta,' Kayleigh corrected her firmly.

'They're called "bracts" those red bits.'

'Why?'

'I'm not sure.' It was, after all, just one of those useless scraps of half-knowledge which Sandra seemed to collect in the same desultory manner as one might collect petrol tokens, without ever going for the full set of highball glasses or the melamine tray.

'Anyway, it died.'

'Well, that happens sometimes. Plants aren't easy.'

'They're a waste of money, if you want my honest opinion.'

'But they look so lovely. And, you know, I was reading, it's been scientifically established that common house plants can improve the atmosphere.'

'You'd need a fair few plants to improve the atmosphere at *our* place,' Kayleigh commented. And she wasn't kidding.

'Bad, is it?'

'Sometimes.' Kayleigh sniffed. She brought out the inevitable festoons of green tissue and swabbed her nose.

She seemed generally poorly, Sandra thought, with a sudden excruciating pang of sympathy. Poor kid! She had probably never had the merest inkling of rude health. 'They remove toxins from the air,' she plodded on, although she had herself, by now, lost interest in her theme, in the findings of NASA researchers, as distilled by Yasmin Woods for *Mia* magazine. 'And doesn't it lift your spirits to watch things grow?'

But Kayleigh merely sniffed again.

'Are you frozen?'

'A bit.'

'Shall we go inside?'

'I don't mind.'

'All right, let's. We should relieve Dad, anyway.' For Eric had been deputised to mind the baby. He had consented to watch over him. Yet, when they walked into the sitting-room, they found him stretched out in a chair, dozing at his post.

'Has he been good?' Sandra enquired of her brother, scooping the child up in an exuberant embrace.

'Who?' asked Jamie, deliberately obtuse.

'Oh, *you*,' Sandra chided him. 'You're a pain, Jimmy James.'

And Kayleigh shot him one of her maddening looks.

They stood a while, taking in the movie.

'Cowboys and Indians,' said Kayleigh.

'Cowboys and native Americans,' corrected Sandra, and giggled idiotically.

113

Then the two of them took Ben and disappeared upstairs together – as thick as thieves, thought Jamie dourly.

'Yes, all right, all right,' said Eric fretfully, a few moments later, waking with a start to find the sitting-room deserted.

Everyone had gone. Jamie, Sandra, Dee, Kayleigh and her baby, the lot of them. Through the thin partition wall that separates the conscious from the unconscious, he had heard, while he slept, the sound of raised voices, of people close by. But, after all, it was just a film; General Custer and his gallant six hundred had intruded on his slumber.

It was at first faintly shocking, and then a relief, to realise that he was quite alone. He was particularly thankful that the girl was not around. In his dream he had done such things to her, he shrank inwardly to recall them. It would have been mortifying for him to open his eyes and to look straight into her face.

He felt so vulnerable, in the instant of waking, he felt utterly transparent (people would be able to peer into his head, through the skin, through the skull, and see the works).

His brain was fuddled, his whole body creaked, he had a crick in his neck, which he massaged with the flat of his hand as he sucked on his teeth. Weekends in the country were always the same: eat, sleep, eat, drink, sleep, eat drink. . . Once upon a time he had found pleasure in it, but he simply couldn't take it the way he used to do. The protein-rich food which his wife served him seemed to lie in his stomach, marinating in a pool of alcohol, and to go nowhere. Every now and then, and even after a back-breaking hour in the garden, he would have an intimation of it, still with him, still around.

He wondered if he had an ulcer. He rather hoped he might. It would be a something in place of his nothing; it would provide a focus for his discontent; a centre for his being where before was just a hole.

He yawned, got to his feet, stumbled to the door, out into the hall, and thence to the downstairs cloakroom, a cosy little bolt-hole with a macramé plant-pot holder, and a shelf of old Penguins in white and orange covers, and a polite notice, purportedly genuine, from a golf club, requesting that members refrain from washing their balls in the basin.

He braced himself against the wall with one hand as he emptied his bladder into the bowl. Then he stood for a while, thus, peering down into the water, watching the bubbles winking beadily at him.

He had a sense of utter, utter futility; he could have wept, had he any tears.

Instead, he shook his poor, deprived penis, flushed the loo, and soaped his hands, and dried them on the little square of cloth which Dee referred to as a guest towel (as though guests were a race apart; as though they had more modest needs than the rest of humanity, as though they never got thoroughly wet). The small looking-glass returned to him an image of a deeply ordinary man.

When he went out again into the hall, he heard laughter, girlish laughter, from upstairs. Sandra, at any rate, was having a good time.

'I told you it would help,' said Kayleigh with the merest smile of satisfaction. 'Pity you didn't do it sooner. You should have shampooed it the minute you got back from the hairdresser's, and brushed it hard, like this, see?'

'Ouch! I didn't realise,' Sandra's hand flew to her stinging ear. 'Sorry.'

'That's OK. I simply hadn't a clue. I thought a perm was more, you know, *permanent*. I figured the damage was done.' Apprehensively, she checked her reflection in the dressing-table mirror. Her hair was no longer fuzzy, but full and bouncy. It framed her face nicely. 'It looks a thousand times better, anyway. Not nearly so tight. Thanks awfully.'

She was sitting at the foot of her bed, with Ben on her lap, jigging him about, dee-dum, dee-dum, dee-dum, dee-dum, doing the galloping major, as Kayleigh moved around her with brush and drier. Since yesterday, the mood between them was subtly altered; it was easy now, and matey, and even – Sandra dared to tell herself – quite sisterly. She had always longed for a sister, and had, at one stage, gone so far as to invent one, a girl called Samantha who had been extraordinarily willing and tractable and generous in the matter of who had the last biscuit. Kayleigh would not be so easygoing.

'I've got a date on Thursday night,' she disclosed coyly.

'Yeah?'

'Yes. I'm going to a posh do.' Then she could not resist a touch of self-mockery. 'I have to get all dolled up for the occasion. I shall be in fine fig.'

'A nice long pair of dangly earrings,' Kayleigh pronounced, bending at the knee, swaying back to admire her handiwork. 'That's what you'll want. Big sparkly ones.'

'I don't have any, unfortunately,' Sandra admitted, resting her chin on Ben's warm head and blowing gently through his fine, fair hair to make him squiggle and squirm. 'I'm afraid I'm a bit of a plain Jane.'

'Yes,' endorsed Kayleigh, who evidently saw no point in prevaricating, 'you are. You don't do yourself any favours.'

Sandra was more and more taken with such candour. Kayleigh was a strange, inert sort of person; she didn't give a great deal, but what she did give was truth. Like a cold shower, it was shocking at first; it took your breath away. But when you were used to it, it could be extremely refreshing.

No one else of Sandra's acquaintance dealt so readily in ruthless honesty. 'It looks lovely,' her friends would tell her, of her disastrous hair-do. Or, 'It suits you,' they would say of an ill-chosen garment. Then, later, much later, when the hair had grown out, or the unfortunate blouse had been cut up for dusters, they would finally come clean. 'I never really liked it blonde,' they would say at last. Or 'That lacy collar really wasn't you.'

'I could lend you some of mine,' Kayleigh persisted, 'only they're all for pierced, see, and you'd need clip-ons.'

'Yes, I would. You know,' Sandra confided, 'I always wanted to have my ears done, actually. I remember going on and on about it when I was twelve or thirteen. I wanted nothing more on earth than gold sleepers. But Mum would never let me, she said pierced ears were common. Oh!' She clapped her hand to her mouth. 'I'm sorry, Kayleigh. I didn't mean . . .'

'Don't worry about it,' Kayleigh told her dismissively. 'I couldn't give a toss.'

Which probably she couldn't. It was only mealy-mouthed, pussyfooting, hypocritical, so-called liberals like herself, Sandra thought humbly, who could not cope with labels, who would deny the evidence of their eyes, and got in terrible twists over their own unconscious prejudices. She had been friends for five whole years at school, with a girl called Marjorie Richards, without ever once letting on that she'd noticed she was black. She wondered now, sheepishly, what Marjorie must have made of that.

'What does Jamie do for his work?' asked Kayleigh, craning towards the mirror to probe a pimple on her chin. Her mirror image addressed Sandra disingenuously from the glass.

'He works for an estate agent.'

'That must be interesting,' was Kayleigh's curiously arbitrary response.

'I guess it has its moments,' Sandra allowed, ever so slightly piqued. (Estate agency was interesting, was it? And catering dull?)

'Selling houses and that?'

'Yes. And flats. And shops and offices.'

'A good job.'

'Not bad.'

'Does he have a girlfriend?'

'I'm not sure. I mean, yes, there is someone, but I have no idea how serious he is about her. I've never met her or anything.'

'He's nice, isn't he?'

'Nice?' Sandra raised her eyebrows. This would not – she conveyed by her expression – have been her first choice of epithet. She still loved Jamie with a painful intensity, but she could no longer say, with her hand on her heart, that she liked him.

Kayleigh damped her fingertips on her tongue and patted her fringe. 'Shame for you', she said, still communicating through the glass, 'that he was the one who got the looks.'

Dee Rawlings had passed a sleepless Saturday night. She had found herself, for once, to her acute discomfort, on the horns of a dilemma, and had been able to bring none of her usual moral certainty to bear on the problem.

She had not even been sure that it *was* a problem: she'd had half a mind to reclassify it, to label it 'positive opportunity'. For, if the present situation was fraught with the one, it was also charged with the other.

There, if you like, had been the rub. And she had decided

in the wee small hours to solve the thing the way she would urge readers to do, by drawing up a profit-and-loss account. She would not, of course, actually head up a page with the words 'For' and 'Against', she would not sit there slavishly listing the pros and cons, she was somewhat too advanced for that. But she would make a mental inventory of all the relevant considerations.

On the pro side, she had been able to muster some compelling arguments why Kayleigh should remain, for a limited period, under this roof.

To begin with, the most tedious and pressing question of where to send the girl would simply, if temporarily, be answered. There need be no more talk of a refuge, of a hostel or what have you, with Kayleigh digging her heels in and sulking, saying 'Shan't', and 'You can't make me'. There need be no bad blood, no embarrassing scene. They could look, at their leisure, for some suitable, permanent accommodation in which she might, in the fullness of time, be installed.

Against this she must balance the needs and sensibilities of her husband and children, whose co-operation would be as crucial to the undertaking as their opposition would be counter to it. Could they be persuaded to support her?

Eric had signalled his disapproval, but that was no great worry, she could always handle Eric. And Sandie wasn't any bother, bless her; Sandie would be easy. Jamie, though, was another matter. With what manifest distaste had he eyed their visitors yesterday from his self-imposed exile in the corner, flurrying a crimson hankie, covering his face. Then, with what unconcealed disgust had he averted his gaze at the dinner table as he pushed aside the plate of food which Dee had so lovingly prepared.

However, if Kayleigh were installed in Kent, rather than in Clapham, Jamie's path and hers would scarcely cross. And, of course, dear Ivy Burston would be only too happy to keep an eye on the girl (of that, at least, Dee was confident). This was surely a neat, a most satisfactory short-term solution.

But then again. . . Though she could not see what harm could come of such an enterprise – she was mindful of the golden rule of agony columnists everywhere, that *one does not get involved*.

These thoughts had been very much on her mind and unresolved as she sat down an hour ago to write. Now, in the clapped-out Adler before her was a sheet of bond paper, on which she had typed the word PLAN, while beneath, a horrible tangle of metal sticks like spillikins bore eloquent witness to events. For she had barely set to work when she'd experienced a sort of power surge, a rush of blood to the brain. She had laid into the keys in a creative frenzy, so they'd all jammed up. Then she had suffered a short-circuit. And now she was stuck. She was lost in introspection.

Kayleigh Roth had grown up on the mean streets. Hers had been a childhood without spiritual nurture, without promise. But she had come at last among people of a better – no, a *different* – class. Who could deny the benefits to the girl, if she were allowed this respite in a healthy, happy environment? Who could deny the benefits to the subdued and snuffling Ben?

It was surely not mere whimsy to suppose that six months of tender loving care *chez* Rawlings, would engender in Kayleigh profound and positive change. And while just to see it would be reward enough for Dee, there would be handsome collateral payments, she would be personally and professionally enriched.

She saw how her writing would be endowed, her work informed, her experience rounded by the goodness of her gesture. She saw the book she would write about the exercise, the publicity, the interviews, the articles which would flow from it, the appearances on prime-time telly. And it was as she came to contemplate this, that Dee had been seized by a sense of exalted purpose. It was an epiphany, a rising-up before her eyes, a quasi-religious experience. Trumpets sounded in her ears and the room seemed bathed in unearthly light.

So now we know for certain that there is a God. Or, if not, then someone calling himself God. We know because He revealed Himself to Dee Rawlings on that dull September afternoon.

Or else it was just temporal lobe epilepsy, to which we are all apparently prone, and which is presaged by an 'aura', visual, aural or olfactory hallucinations, and is frequently coloured by mystic and grandiose delusions.

Either way, it brought on a sick headache. She had to go to lie down until Sandie came up to call her, to tell her that supper was almost on the table. And thus was Kayleigh Roth's fate decided.

If this was how the other half lived, thought Kayleigh that night, lying sleepless under a duckdown duvet, seeing hideous faces in the floral-pattern wallpaper, then she wasn't sure she wanted any part of it.

It was so dull, for one thing. Nothing happened. There was no edge, no excitement. And it was very weird the way everyone sat down to eat together round a big table, making hoity-toity conversation, saying 'More roast beef for anyone' and 'Please pass the broccoli'. It was dead embarrassing, all that side of things.

And yet she would stay. She had made up her mind to do so. She had made a choice. And she had her reasons.

It would have been difficult, of course, to refuse Dee's offer, made as it had been with open arms, in words that brooked no argument, in a voice that bellowed out from Dee's heaving chest and made the crystal glasses ting. But Kayleigh would have said no had she wished to; she would have said stuff it – especially since she had detected more than a whiff of rat. Exploitation, like expediency, was not part of her vocabulary, but she had a shrewd idea when she was being used, and the only question was: for what?

Then, though Sandra was a mate, she could take her or leave her. She would not have stayed for Sandra's sake.

Nor would she have stayed for Ben, for the good that it might do him. She could not put his interests before her own, when in her mind he had none but those he held in common with her.

She liked the creature comforts which were part of the deal; the huge, comfy house and its lavish furnishings. She liked deep, hot baths, and clean linen, and warm radiators, and freshly squeezed orange juice and bacon for breakfast. Yet she felt about this much as the homesick business traveller feels about a four-star hotel. She had come to the conclusion that there was no place in the world like your own bed.

She had nowhere else to go, of course, but back to Wavertree, to Greg, or onwards and possibly downwards, to a refuge, or a half-way house. This, also, had to be borne in mind.

But none of these figured in her final reckoning. She had one single motive for hanging on in here, when her every instinct told her to get the hell out. Because, for the first time in her life – and all else paled beside it – she had fallen completely and hopelessly in love.

•

6

Lucinda was an absolute star that Thursday morning. She was brilliant. A natural.

It ought to have been Hennie, of course; she was the obvious choice. But then there had been a lurking suspicion that she'd screw up. She was not, after all, poor poppet – as Giles had put it – the brightest girl in school. In rehearsals she had fluffed her lines, she had forgotten the stage directions, and finally she had agreed to step aside, confessing that it wasn't, anyway, her sort of thing, and adding something under her breath, which Jamie had not quite caught, though he had thought he heard the word 'stinky'.

So, for one day only, Lucinda Blackstock had been deputed to pass herself off as nice Mrs de Lannoy-Hunt, a well-meaning if faintly imperious young woman, who drove a Volvo, who did the daily school run, and the flowers for the church, and numerous good works, and who was plainly a splendid sort.

She had dressed down for the part, in a plaid skirt, a cable-knit sweater and sensible flatties. Her face was bare of make-up, and an Alice band subdued her wayward hair. She was, thought Jamie, extraordinary in her conviction; she was terrifyingly real. Incredibly, she had transformed herself into her own mother. And if, in her old persona, she had intimidated him, in the new one she scared him rigid.

He had talked the two of them, Giles and Lucinda, through

the rigmarole, the buying ritual, and they had listened well. They were doing everything – or, almost – as he'd instructed them. Giles had gone straight out through the back door of the house, to the ramshackle shed at the bottom of the garden, where (typical man!) he could be seen from the upper storey, standing, staring, in deeply serious contemplation of its possibilities.

He would be planning a pool room, Jamie had murmured conspiratorially to Mrs A, turning from the window, letting the curtain swing back. No, not *that* sort of pool, not a swimming-pool. Pool as in snooker. Or a rumpus room for the kids, of whom the de Lannoy-Hunts had either three or four (there had been a small but sticky discrepancy in their accounting).

Lucinda, meanwhile, had made a beeline for the kitchen, for the bathroom, and for the master bedroom, poking about, sizing up the cupboard space, making disapproving clucking noises, saying 'This could be nice', for all the world as if she were a real buyer.

There had been just one truly sickening moment when Jamie had feared that, for sheer badness, she was about to blow it. Here was the problem with Lucinda: everything to her was such a hoot. 'I'm Arabella Sloane,' she had announced to Audrey Atkins on arrival, offering a hand for shaking as she swanned across the threshold.

'But I thought . . .' Audrey had murmured.

'Er, I think what Mrs de Lannoy-Hunt means . . .' Jamie had interjected, taking up a position behind Audrey, menacing his girlfriend, drawing one finger across his throat in dire warning. 'That is, I imagine Sloane is her, er . . .'

'Maiden name.' Lucinda had flashed him a grin. 'I am Lucinda de Lannoy-Hunt, née Sloane. One of *the* Sloanes. Of Chelsea.' And, 'You see,' she had added, the wicked, wicked girl, with her face all dangerous and dimpled, 'de Lannoy-Hunt is such a mouthful – aren't you Giles, darling?'

'Delighted, I'm sure,' a flustered Audrey had said. Then, plainly fancying she was in the presence of minor royalty, and uncertain of the protocol, she had taken the proffered hand and for one excruciating moment looked as if she might drop a curtsey.

After which, it had gone quite swimmingly.

The place, within as without, was every bit as big and beastly as Jamie had remembered it. It was a valuable pile, no question, though the ambience would not be to everyone's taste, and it was this morning redolent of cabbage.

Had Jamie been looking in earnest for a customer, there were a few tips he might have passed on to Audrey. Fresh cut flowers, he would have told her, were always beguiling. And the lavatory seat was better down than it was up, revealing a stained and crusty bowl for all the world to see. Then, while certain foody smells – coffee, fresh-baked bread – had proven buyer appeal, boiled greens were somehow more resistible.

'I believe they're seriously interested,' he hissed to the old dear now, catching her at the top of the stairs, as she trailed after Lucinda in a wake of Chanel. And he raised his two hands, with fingers crossed, to demonstrate that they were in this together, he and she.

'You think so?'

'I do. I honestly do. I'm slightly concerned that they're on a tight budget. Nevertheless . . .' He put a finger to his lips and shushed: a signal that this must be their secret. 'I have a hunch we may get somewhere near the asking price.'

'Uh . . .' essayed Mrs Atkins. And, as so often, failed to follow through. They had got her, Jamie decided at that moment, they had definitely got her, hook, line and proverbial sinker.

She had phoned, as he had somehow known she would, on Monday. (The merry toot, the jaunty wave, had surely done the trick.) 'Mr Rawlings?' she had said. 'Is that Mr Rawlings?' And although he had instantly recognised the agitated tremolo, although it had called to mind the querulous little woman, he had played it super-cool. 'Yes. Who is this?' he'd replied. And then, suavely, 'Ah, of course! I've placed you now! Forgive me, Mrs Atkins. For a moment, I couldn't put a face to the voice.'

'It's about the house.'

'You've come to a decision?'

'Yes, I have. Well, I think so.'

'You've decided to instruct us?'

'That's why I called. To, er . . . Yes, to instruct you.'

'Jolly, jolly good. And I explained to you, did I, the advantage to you if you give us sole agency? What say? You can't recall? Rightie-ho. No problem. I can pop round to you on . . . Let me see. We're in luck. I can drop in this afternoon and take you quickly through it.'

Then, round he had popped, armed with the all-important piece of paper, which he had read aloud to her with exaggerated slowness, sentence by sentence, clause by clause, pausing at intervals, ostensibly to allow the text to sink in, but actually to prolong her evident agony.

'"You will be liable to pay remuneration to us . . . if at any time unconditional contracts for the sale of the property are exchanged with a purchaser introduced by us" – this is standard stuff, of course; usual estate agency guff. We have to cover ourselves, as I'm sure you will appreciate. Now, where were we? "You will be liable to pay remuneration to us . . . if a ready, willing and able purchaser is introduced by us in accordance with your instruction . . . even if you subsequently withdraw and unconditional contracts for sale are not exchanged, irrespective of your reasons." Do you follow? Well, look, don't fret. Keep the contract, read it through. I always urge my clients: sign nothing till you're sure in your own mind.'

Well, she'd cut up a bit rough, she'd raised objections, but eventually she'd put pen to paper, she'd signed on the dotted. And he had taken the opportunity to reveal that, while he shouldn't want to raise her hopes, he did know of this delightful young couple, two simply charming people, who were looking for something out of the ordinary. A large place, they had specified, at an accessible price, which they could do up for their family. So – who knew? – Clovelly might be right up their street.

'Just the job,' declared Giles, bluffly cheerful, slipping in through the back door and stamping about on the mat. 'You know, you could get a half-size billiard table in that outhouse.'

'Oh, darling, *honestly*!' Lucinda went to stand beside him, laced her fingers through his, smiled indulgently up at him. 'My husband has no sense of priority,' she confided to Mrs Atkins. 'I imagine yours is just the same.'

Which was true, of course, insofar as Audrey's husband had scant sense of anything.

'They're all little boys at heart, aren't they? I say, might we just whizz round again? There are things I want Giles to see.'

'Er . . .' said Audrey Atkins.

'I'm sure that would be fine,' put in Jamie. 'Wouldn't it, Mrs Atkins? Audrey?'

'A quick shufti,' Giles insisted. 'Check out the lie of the land.'

'Such an unusual property. So much to think about. So much to take in at one go.'

'I'll put the kettle . . .'

'Ah, yes, please, Audrey!' Jamie beamed at her. 'I'm parched.' How much better if Giles were to do the grand tour, do his stock-taking, without the vendor always at his heels! He sat himself down, rested his hands, his fingertips, on the kitchen table, studied them for a few moments, then raised his eyes expectantly. He would drink a gallon of disgusting tea, he told himself, Audrey could fill and refill 'Dad' for him, if by so doing he could confine her here while Giles made his rounds.

'We-ell,' he said once they were alone. 'What do you think? What is your hunch? My instincts tell me we could be in business.'

'Yes?' She stood there holding fast to the kettle, till he got up to relieve her of it, set it on the hob, turned the old-fashioned gas tap and lit the ring. 'I should stick out, my dear, for almost the full whack. A hundred and twenty thousand pounds. That should set you up in style.'

'If you think . . .'

'Oh, I do. I have long experience. Now, we ought to talk, you and I, about precisely what sort of place you will be looking to buy.'

'We did it!' said Jamie, exultant. 'We bloody well did it!'

'We did it,' Lucinda contradicted him. 'Giles and I, didn't we darling? I mean, you had only to be yourself, Mr Estate Agent.'

'And Giles had to be *himself*.'

'OK, but *I* didn't, I had to be his lady wife.'

'And very good you were too, my dear,' Giles complimented her. 'I felt well and truly married to you.'

'It was a masterly performance,' Jamie agreed.

'Mistressly,' said Giles.

'Wifely,' said Lucinda smugly.

They were sitting on a bench on Streatham Common, drunk with self-congratulation, swigging Lanson from the bottle and laughing until they ached.

'What about the house, then?' Jamie wanted to know.

'What *about* the house?' responded Giles rhetorically.

'It's ginormous,' said Lucinda.

'Stupendous,' said Giles.

'And the stuff?' Jamie pressed him. 'What about the stuff? It's worth a few bob. Am I right, or am I right?'

'You're right,' Giles allowed with a nod.

'Your face, Jamie,' mocked Lucinda. 'The look on your face when I introduced myself to her as Arabella Sloane. It was priceless! I nearly wet myself.'

'So did I,' Jamie told her sternly. 'You realise, you could have blown us all out of the water?'

'Not a chance of it.'

'I can't think what possessed you.'

'Oh, it was just a bit of fun, you know. A bit of a lark. In fact, I was going to say that my name was Sloane-Ranger, or even Range-Rover, but it went clean out of my head.'

'Thank the Lord for that, then.'

'She would never have fallen in. She's addle-brained.'

'I shouldn't count on it.'

'Come *on*. She was a pushover.' Lucinda whipped off her Alice band and shook her blonde hair at him. She snatched the bottle from his hand and tipped champagne down her throat.

Jamie was, as always, both dazzled and faintly repelled by her. His guts felt squeezed. Her bewitching beauty, her amorality, were an awesome combination. She made no provision for shame and self-disgust. She did not suffer, as he did, for her sins. She moved through life without conscience the way the queen is said to move without money; the assumption was that someone else should pick up the tab.

He closed his eyes to exclude her from his consciousness, but she was there, on the inside, smirking at him. 'I'm telling you,' he said flatly, 'I wouldn't be so sure of anything.'

———— • ————

'I do not expect', said Ivy Burston, snapping on the Marigold gloves, 'to find children's potties all over my nice clean floor.' And she did a disappearing trick with her mouth, hiding it away inside her face, suturing the join.

Kayleigh raised her eyes to the beamed ceiling and sighed extravagantly. One baby, she thought. One potty. A lot of silly fuss about nothing. Still, she scraped back her chair, shoved aside her plate of toast and honey, snatched up the offending item, slopping its contents, and carried it long-sufferingly out to the downstairs bog. She emptied it into the pan, rinsed it under the tap, swilled it around, emptied it again. Then, since she was there, she had a pee.

A funny sort of room, it was. There were smelly old books on a shelf behind the cistern, and a spider plant hanging in some tatty string cradle fandangle, and a rude notice about not washing your balls.

When she returned she found Ivy sweeping toast crumbs off the table, scooping them with one hand into the other, then dusting her palms off, twiddling her fingers fastidiously over the swing bin. The kitchen reeked pointedly of pine disinfectant, and there were wide, wet Squeegee stripes on the tiles.

Ben looked on from his wooden high chair – on loan from some people called Horscroft – whimpering unexpectantly. 'What's up with you?' Kayleigh demanded, snatching a newly laundered teatowel to scrub at the jam smears round his mouth, then handing him a spoon to bang. 'Here, that should keep you quiet.'

She was not paid, Ivy would complain later to Angie, to go running around after some idle little slattern and her offspring. There'd been nothing said about that when Dee Rawlings had engaged her. Then, no, no, Angie would sympathise through a baffle of Battenburg cake. And, hoisting her legs so her mother could Hoover the Axminster under her, she would agree that Dee Rawlings was taking advantage. Yes, definitely trying it on.

'Have you made your bed, young lady?'

'Not yet,' said Kayleigh, yawning.

'Well, don't you think you should?'

'Maybe presently. What's the difference? No one's going to see it. No one's going to sleep in it but me.'

Such an attitude infuriated and confounded Ivy. She had no answer to it. Or, rather, she had an answer too complex to articulate. In the years that she'd kept house at Foxholes, the beds had always been made and the bedrooms tidied by ten of a Monday morning; the carpets had been vacuumed by eleven; the woodwork polished by twelve; the bathrooms and kitchen had been gleaming by one o'clock, when she would close the door with deep personal satisfaction upon a good job jobbed, and go home.

For only when these tasks had been accomplished, had she been able to rest. An untidy house was unfinished business, it preyed on her mind. She could close her eyes and see rumpled linen, unwashed cups forming rings on the tables, scurfy tidemarks in baths and basins, and she'd not be able to think straight for the mental clutter.

But try explaining this to a do-nothing little miss with her hair uncombed and teeth unbrushed and with the sleep still in her eyes. Try explaining the need for order, for symmetry, to someone who understood only chaos, who said 'What does it matter?' and 'It can wait', and who left her fag-ends standing up like soldiers on every available surface.

Ivy had, of course, until now, had the run of the place. She had had it to herself. It had been, from Monday to Friday, her domain. When she popped in each morning and found it pristine, empty, it had given her intense private pleasure. And against all reason she had always resented the weekend intrusions of the Rawlings mob, the uproar and mess which ensued.

So how much more bitterly did she now resent this greater intrusion. When she had learned from Dee on Sunday night that she was going to have to work around a new incumbent, she had been, to put it mildly, not best pleased.

'She'll hold me up,' she had protested vainly. 'She'll slow me down.'

'You'll manage, I'm sure,' Dee had told her, breezily, over the phone. 'I have complete faith in you, as you know.' Then, 'Kayleigh can give you a hand,' she had decided, with a wild misreading of character. 'You set her some daily chores, Mrs B. She can help to lighten your load.'

Ha! That was a good one! Lighten the load. It was now a quarter past eleven, and Dolly Daydream was not yet out of the T-shirt which she wore to sleep and flop about in. Her breakfast plate, her knife and mug, would have to be cleared.

As for the proposition that Kayleigh might be set to work, well, as Ivy would inform Joyce Pearcy from the village store when she came by in her new white Rascal van with a delivery of groceries, chance would be a fine thing.

The worst of it was that the house was never tidy now for so much as a minute. There had not been a day this week when Ivy could close the door upon it with the slightest satisfaction. It was like painting the fourth bridge, she told herself, wondering vaguely about bridges one, two and three.

She had been that close, *that* close to walking out, she would further confide to Angie, making a mingy little gesture with thumb and forefinger, pincering them in front of her face. And Angie would say that she wouldn't blame her; she wouldn't blame her one bit.

'There's nothing to do here,' Kayleigh grumbled. She began literally to kick her heels, to scuff one bare foot against the other, chafing skin against parchment-dry skin.

'If you're looking for ways to improve the shining hour,' Ivy chided acidly, 'you can start by cleaning your bathroom.'

'Don't feel like it.' Kayleigh draped herself over the dresser, cradling her head in one arm, resting her cheek against the planed surface, breathing the sharp smell of varnish, as with her free hand she picked at a splinter of wood.

'Which means it will be left for me to do.'

'That's what they pay you for, isn't it?'

'To skivvy for you? I should think not!'

'I didn't ask to come here, you know.' Kayleigh began to open and close the cutlery drawer, to slide it repeatedly in and out.

'Well, push off then, back to where you came from.'

'Can't, can I?'

'*Why* can't you?'

'Because.'

'That's no kind of answer.'

'And it's none of your business. I was invited to stay here, to make myself at home. No one said anything about making beds. No one mentioned cleaning baths.'

'So go out, can't you, and get a breath of fresh air? You'd be a lot less groggy if you took some exercise. It would do that boy of yours good, too, poor mite, to feel the sun on his face.' Ivy gestured impatiently towards Ben, who, truth to tell, touched nothing within her. Big, bonny babies with rosy cheeks and dimples were one thing; neglected, misbegotten scraps were quite another. 'And *I* could get on with my tasks in the meantime.'

'What sun? It's not sunny.'

'It's not a bad day, it's quite mild.'

'Oh, all right then. If you like.'

'It's not what *I* like. Since when did anybody bother about what I liked? I'm just trying to think what's best for you. I'm trying to think of ways for you to keep yourself amused.'

'Okay.' Kayleigh slid the drawer home decisively. She straightened up and stretched. 'I'll take him to see the horses,' she said, unlatching the hinged tray and springing him from his borrowed high chair. 'Want to come and see the gee-gees, Ben?'

But her baby merely flopped against her, as if in a state of advanced exhaustion, and made no reply.

———————— • ————————

They took up an awful lot of room, the television people. They made an awful lot of noise. They were dreadfully disruptive and behaved for all the world as if they owned the place.

What a shemozzle, Nancy thought, clamping her head with her hands, stopping her ears with her fingers. None of this would have bothered her, she told herself, if she hadn't had a pile of paperwork to get through. But it was difficult to attend to the job in hand when you had people constantly buzzing around you, unpacking equipment in front of your desk, setting up lights and cameras, boxing you in, calling to one another in ringing tones across the top of your head.

Add to this the comings and goings of colleagues from other departments, and you had, in the 'Dear Dee' office that day, a situation reminiscent of Piccadilly Circus in the rush hour.

In a rare gesture of caring and sharing, Chloë from Cookery had dropped by to see if Edie and Nancy would like to taste a truly delicious sweet vegetable torte which they'd just rustled up in the test kitchen. Then Kristina from beauty had brought samples of moisturiser which the girls might just like to try. Yasmin had come looking for a possible taker for a putative free health-farm weekend. Harriet, the chief sub, had popped in once to see if Edie had checked the proofs, and a second time because she'd left her typescale the first time. John, the chief designer, had paid them three informal visits to talk discursively about layout.

And it was marvellous, really, how cool and professional each of them had been. None of them had shown the slightest interest in the camera crew. Indeed, they hadn't even appeared to notice them. They were all very brisk and businesslike, sparing the lighting man, the make-up girl, the guy with the clipboard, not so much as a glance.

'Must dash,' Chloë had said with an eloquent shrug, 'I have a meat loaf in the oven.' 'Have to go,' Kristina had told them, smoothing her Arabella Pollen skirt against her slender thighs, 'I'm needed on a cover shoot.' And, 'I can't stop,' Yasmin had announced, pausing at the door to toss her luxuriant blue-black hair this way and that, 'I'm off to be Rolfed.' Harriet and John, for their part, had spoken earnestly and knowledgeably of running turns, of bastard measures, of pics, of trannies, of four-colour black, and of the use of white space which gives a page integrity.

'No peace for the wicked,' said Edie loudly, biting into a sardine sandwich and glaring through her specs at a young man in jeans, who was rolling a long sheet of paper, rustling it unnecessarily, flapping and snapping it about. 'Are you not going out for your lunch, young Nancy?'

'I haven't time,' Nancy confessed. 'I'm all behind.'

'Like Barney's bull.'

'I beg your pardon.'

'It's an old saying: all behind like Barney's bull. Although quite who Barney's bull was – or Barney himself, for that matter – I regret I cannot say.'

'Oh, I see. I'd never heard of either of them. What I meant was, I'm not making very good progress. I don't seem able to concentrate, somehow.'

'Who could wonder at it?'

'It's probably just, you know . . .' Nancy blushed hotly, anxious as ever not to cause offence, to make anyone feel snubbed or unwelcome. 'It's maybe just one of those days.'

'It's one of those days, all right. It's a blasted nuisance, this,' said Edie, gesturing with her hand towards the battery of lights. 'We can't hear ourselves think. Such a kerfuffle, just for a few minutes of telly. Where is Superwoman, anyway? Where's the star of the show?'

'Dee? She's nipped out to Nicky's to have her hair done. She won't be very long.'

'She won't have to be. They're almost ready to start filming, I believe. Aren't you?' she challenged the man with the roll of paper. 'Aren't you about to begin?'

'Not for a while yet,' he told her distantly, and walked out.

'Ye Gods! What a performance!'

'Edie,' ventured Nancy softly, now that they found themselves, briefly, alone.

'Yes, dear?'

Nancy peered at her computer screen. She scrolled slowly through the text of a letter, gnawing her thumbnail, reading as she went. 'Oh, nothing,' she said with a sigh. There was no point, she decided, in sharing her concerns. Edie would only wave them away, she'd say life was a glorious cycle of song, a medley of extemporanea. She'd say love was a thing that could never go wrong – and she was Marie of Romania.

Besides, it would be terribly indiscreet to raise doubts, with relays of strangers traipsing through the office.

Goodness, here was Jennie Gosling, wearing something long and silvery and knitted like a suit of chain-mail. 'Nancy, we were wondering, could you be an absolute darling and rustle up some coffee for the team?'

'Uhm, yes, of course. No bother.'

Probably she was wrong, Nancy told herself, as she filled the kettle and plugged it in. (She would have to make at least three jugfuls, she calculated wearily, if there was to be enough for everyone.) What did *she* know, for heaven's sake? She had led a sheltered life, she had not been anywhere or done anything.

Then, who was *she* to comment, she asked herself, when she finally returned to her keyboard, to her screen. Who was she to say that these latest responses, replies to the most recent batch of letters, seemed ever so slightly – well, certainly more than usually – off the wall? She had long ago realised that Dee's answers were informed by a higher logic than that to which she could aspire. She understood only how little she understood.

So she sighed and resumed typing, faithful to the last dot

and comma of Dee's original draft. And if, every so often her eyebrows shot up, if they disappeared completely under her fringe, no criticism, no lack of confidence in her superiors was implied.

———————— • ————————

'I just don't think she's suitable,' said Shirley Clarke, wife of Roy, mother of Colin, for whom suitability was a precise concept and a guiding principle. There was nothing in life that could not be judged by her either suitable or otherwise, such distinctions being modified to some degree, of course, by circumstance.

Sherry was a suitable drink to serve with soup, for example, and a riesling or German Moselle with fish, but it would be unthinkable to serve either with roast beef.

The *Daily Mail* was a suitable national newspaper. Acrylic was suitable for machine-washing; junket for someone with a delicate tum. 'Cloakroom' was a suitable word for the lav. Ten o'clock was a suitable time to go up the wooden hill to Bedfordshire; seventy-five a suitable age at which to turn up one's toes.

Junk jewellery was unsuitable, as were trendy vicars, tattoos, toplessness, thigh boots, bare feet, blue jokes, body piercing, black lingerie, uplift bras, ankle chains, identity bracelets, bubble-gum, basket meals, second helpings, four-letter words, hitch-hiking, hipsters, homosexualism, vegetarianism, rastafarianism and, come to think of it, most of the isms – not to mention a certain asm.

The Labour party was not suitable to run the country; adulterers were not suitable to hold office. Ponytails were unsuitable for men. Cheese was unsuitable last thing at night. Coley was suitable only for cats.

'What's wrong with the lass?' Roy wanted to know, sitting on the bed, unballing a pair of silk socks and shaking them out. 'She seemed very pleasant to me.'

'Ah, yes, well.' Shirley looked to the left and snapped on a gold knot earring. She looked to the right and snapped on its twin. She inclined towards the mirror to pinkwash her face with foundation, to damp down her natural colour.

She could not deny that Sandra Rawlings was very pleasant, she was a nice enough girl, and her food had been perfectly tasty.

But it had also been, to Shirley's mind, a tiny bit *outré*, it had been more than a little way out.

She had heard of Dinah's Dinners from a neighbour. Anne Marshall, it was, who had commended the service, and who had pressed upon Shirley a business card. 'You won't be disappointed,' she had promised. But then, Anne was from a theatrical background, she was slightly bohemian, she dressed in a kaftan, and smoked cheroots, and rescued donkeys. Lemon *aïoli* Anne would take in her stride. Mango and cilantro vinaigrette would be right up her alley.

Not that the Clarkes' dinner party last week had been an unmitigated disaster. There had, indeed, been clean plates and compliments all round. 'How unusual!' guests had said. 'How imaginative!' But then, they would, wouldn't they? They would say 'How nice!' And when one's only son announced that he was dating a caterer who dabbled in the exotic, one was forced to ask oneself if she was, well, suitable girlfriend material. To which the sun-dried tomatoes said no. The *rucola* said resoundingly no. They said she was deeply, deeply suspect.

'All right, she's no oil painting,' allowed Roy, fiddling with his bow-tie, yanking it about. 'But then, neither, let's face it, is young Colin.'

'That's a nice thing to say!' Shirley snatched up a phial of perfume – Femme, by Marcel Rochas, which was too heavy for day wear, yet suitable for evening – and sprayed herself sparingly on her pulse points.

'I'm simply facing facts.'

'What facts? It's only your opinion. Anyway, I'm not talking of looks. Looks are by the bye.'

'What then?'

'I simply feel . . .' Shirley sighed. She inspected her neat, polished nails. 'I don't feel she's right for him somehow.'

'Help me with this, will you dearest?' Roy came to stand behind her, he rested a hand on her shoulder and danced a cufflink in front of her eyes. 'I'm all fingers and thumbs this evening.'

'I'm busy just now, as you see,' she said, shrugging him off.

'Well, when you've finished titivating.'

'Please don't use that word, Roy.'

'Why not?' He admired his moustache in the mirror, a thin pencil line on his upper lip.

'I don't like it, that's why not.'

There was a knock and, after a moment's hesitation, Colin came shuffling, crabwise, in. He had never felt at ease in his parents' bedroom, where he had had first picked up the spoor of the unknown beast.

As a small boy he had learned from his mother that there were *some things we don't talk about*. Doubts about these things, too secret to bear discussion, too awful to name, had beset and disturbed him throughout his young life. Here was a riddle wrapped in an enigma. And he had somehow known that the answer lay behind the bedroom door.

It had been Marchmont, his best friend at St Joseph's primary, who had given him the gen on where babies came from. 'Pukey,' he had reacted, only half believing that which was anyway, as he would eventually discover, only half true. Then the pair of them had made vomiting noises, pretending to chuck up in the shrubbery, reeling among the rhododendrons, as a means of expressing their disgust.

And all these years later, to be honest, though he'd come round in a big way to sex, he had still to get his head sorted out in the matter of his own conception. The idea that here, in this very room, in this very bed – or one not unlike it – Roy and Shirley had done the business of which he had been either the product or the by-product, was frankly rather a facer.

Few people are completely sanguine about their parents' sexuality. And, with parents such as Roy and Shirley, the imagination positively boggled.

No wonder they had botched it. Colin was, in his own estimation, a typical first attempt. With practice, they might have done better.

His father was a pocket Adonis, a small man, but perfectly formed. His mother was pretty in an inconsequential sort of way. It was inexcusable that they had contrived to produce a son so lacking in their finer qualities.

Having said which, Colin was on reasonable terms with himself. He was content in his own sum and substance. Lack of ambition, lazy acceptance, were comfortable to live with. He seldom felt driven or despairing or down on his luck, and, though he affected a special brand of glumness, mild amusement lay ever just below the surface. Even his chronic hypochondria, a faint, unfounded suspicion that he might not be long for this earth, did nothing to dispel his enjoyment of it, and if anything sharpened his appetite for life.

He had gone without a fight into the family firm, where he was popular with the work force for his easygoing, unassuming nature, his lugubrious presentation, and his awful jokes which made everyone wince and suck on their teeth or shriek with hysterical laughter. The older women, the secretaries, the tea lady, in particular loved and mothered him – as though he had not mother enough.

Still, he took it all in good part. There was no indignity, so far as he could see, in purveying drawing-pins to the business community, in supplying the staplers and sticky labels, the wallet files and window envelopes which kept the wheels of commerce turning, or in wolfing down the cakes and biscuits which the kindly matrons pressed upon him.

It was not as if it had been given to him to be an artist or a writer, although at St Joseph's his poem about a robin had won critical acclaim, and his depiction of a fire engine had been up on the classroom wall for weeks.

'I have to go,' he announced to Roy and Shirley. And he rotated his chin above his starched collar, then inserted a finger at the neck and ran it back and forth. 'This thing is throttling me. I said I'd drive over and pick Sandra up.'

'Be careful, mind,' said Shirley, dipping into the jar of hair gel. She turned to him with a glob of the stuff glistening on her fingertip, then turned away and glued a kiss curl to her cheek.

'Of course.' He bent to give her a peck. Then, 'Do I look all right?' he asked, backing away from her.

'You look fine.'

'Don't be late,' warned Roy. 'Bad form to be late.'

'I shan't,' Colin promised. 'Trust me.'

'And go easy on the drink,' put in Shirley, who could imagine no greater disgrace (well, few greater disgraces) than a positive breath test. Such ignominy to be asked to blow in a bag, or to have to do a wee-wee in a bottle.

'Scout's honour.' Colin saluted her. 'See you.' And he was gone.

From the latticed window of their Tudor-style executive home, Roy Clarke watched as the boy folded himself up like a deckchair into his MG midget. A whisp of blue smoke from the exhaust pipe signalled that he had started her up. Once the engine was ticking over, Colin clambered out again to close the panelled up-and-over garage door.

Big girl's blouse, thought Roy affectionately. He was, himself, a nothing kind of person, a cipher, who adopted that relentlessly jokey approach to others which can pass for personality. But he was not without heart or soul or perspicacity. It was all very well, he told himself, for Shirley to quibble, to find fault with the girl. But Colin could do worse than this Sandra. She could at least cook.

———————— • ————————

Alison rang to say nothing. And nothing, of course, takes a great deal more saying than something, it takes an awful lot more time.

Sandra, twitching at the end of the phone, longed for her to come to the point. But there was, it seemed, no point to which she might come. The conversation was diffuse. It had no beginning, no middle, and, Sandra began to fear, no end.

'Uh-huh,' she said briskly, glancing at her watch. Six twenty. Colin would be here in less than half an hour.

And, 'Mm,' she said, distantly, discouragingly, as she strained at the flex, groping vainly for a mug of Earl Grey which stood cooling on the bookcase just beyond her grasp. She was literally and figuratively at the end of her tether.

'I have to go,' she said desperately. And, 'Did he really? What a sauce!'

Then, two minutes later, 'My bath will be getting cold,' she all but pleaded. And, 'No, I don't think you should ring him. Wait. Keep him guessing. Let *him* call *you*.'

Finally, after a further two minutes, she was reduced to fibbing. 'There's someone at the door,' she said urgently. 'It's probably Colin. I shall have to dash. I'll call you tomorrow. Byee.'

She was fond of Ali after a fashion, and grateful to her for the loan of a dress (a swishing blue satin, off-the-shoulder number which, though it made her look broad, did bring out the grey-blue of her eyes in an unexpected way). But she would have to go like stink, she told herself, to be ready by a quarter to seven, and for that she did not thank her friend.

In the event, it took her no more than fifteen minutes to prepare herself, mainly because she had reduced her routine, not so much to a fine art as to a bare minimum. Clean, combed and mascara'd, with a smidge of grey eyeshadow, and with a squirt of Diorella behind each ear, she was her version of dolled up. If she were to put more effort into her appearance, she knew it might repay her. (On the other hand, of course, it might not, then what a fool she would feel!)

Most attractive women are basically ordinary. They work with what they have, they make the best of it (how few, actually, can just wash and go). Sandra was aware of this, but she could never quite bring herself to strive harder. She had a basic disbelief in her own possibilities, a feeling that, at the end of it all, this indefinable quality, this *je ne sais quoi* would still elude her. She had resisted her mother's persistent urgings to seek professional advice, to turn herself over to Colour Me Beautiful, doubting in her heart of hearts that there was such a colour. Besides, she had a strong puritanical streak, an abhorrence of vanity, a reluctance to fill her day with anything so footling as Alexandra Marie Rawlings.

Occasionally, in some half-hearted attempt at self-improvement, she would buy new cosmetics, skin-care products, expensive shampoos and conditioners. But there were, for her, no minutes more dead than those spent waiting for nail varnish or for fake tan to dry. And the chipped, streaked, blotched results of her experiments with these bore testament to her frantic impatience with the beautifying process.

So, when her doorbell rang at precisely six forty-five, she had nothing to do but to drape a shawl about herself, and to reach for her bag, her purse, her keys.

'I'll be right down,' she said into the entry-phone.

'Can't I come up?' asked a muffled, disappointed voice.

'Well, of course, if you want to.'

'I do. I want to see where you live.'

'Okay. Push the door.'

She buzzed him in, then went out to wait for him, hung over the banisters, and was surprised by the joyous sense of recognition, a rush of elation fizzing like champagne, when he appeared around the last bend in the stairs.

'Flat top,' he said, as if to himself. 'Bell four. Flat bell. Top four. Ah, there you are!'

'Here I am.'

He seized her by the elbows, steered her round in a slow, unchoreographed dance out there on the small square of landing. 'You look lovely.'

She ruthlessly suppressed a desire to refute this, then could not resist a facetious response. She knew she must some day acquire the grace to accept a compliment, instead of parrying as was her way, but this was not that day. 'You're not so bad yourself,' she said, looking up, looking down, looking up again, grinning into his face, his funny, funny face, into the round, brown, teddy-bear eyes.

'You like the tux?' He fingered his lapel.

'Very smart.'

'It's hired.'

'Then we're both in borrowed plumes. This dress belongs to a pal.'

'It suits you. The blue.'

'Thank you.'

'And your hair is different.'

'I hope it's an improvement.' She jabbed at it with her fingers and shook her head vigorously so the curls flopped about. 'The perm's a lot looser, thank goodness.'

'You look terribly glamorous. Like someone out of *Dynasty*.'

'Oh, crikey! I hope not.'

'Well, only a touch. This is great,' he said, following her through her front door, and gazing around him at the simple studio flat.

'It's fine for my needs.'

'It's better than that.' The place exerted a powerful pull upon him, it drew him right in to the centre, where he knocked his head against the paper globe lampshade and set it wildly swinging, looping on its flex. 'It's so straightforward,' he told her appreciatively as the light sluiced first this wall then that one, illuminating by turns her bookshelves and prints, the trestle table, the calico sofa, the single armchair, throwing exaggerated shadows. 'It's so sparse.'

He was thinking of his own home, his parents' house, picturing the swags and bows and drapes, the frills and tassels, the cosies, covers and chintzes, valances and knicker-blinds, the metres and metres of surplus material with which it was festooned.

Colin's mother, who knew nothing of Mies van der Rohe, of his dictum that less is more, and who would anyway discount absolutely the views of a native German, was of the firm conviction that more was more, she liked things to look pretty, and went in for a fine excess.

For years he had dreamed of moving out, of finding an apartment of his own. He would furnish it with packing cases. He would pin a sheet up at the window. He would live very simply, he would sleep on a mat, eat his meals off the floor, straight out of a tin, he would be able to *breathe*.

But it was a tricky one, this leaving-home dilemma. It was delicate. It didn't bear discussion. The few times that he had broached the subject, Shirley had looked so pink and stricken, he had been quite unstrung, unable to pursue it.

He had heard tell of the empty-nest syndrome, the sense of loss and desolation and futility that can settle on mothers when their children move away. For some women, according to an article he had read by Dee Thingamy in one of Shirley's magazines, it could lead to insomnia, to depression, to a feeling of futility, a sense of staring at a blank wall. 'If only I had not given myself so completely to my child,' such women would cry, 'but had devoted more time to myself!'

Colin was not sure if Shirley had ever set eyes on a blank wall, or if she could envisage that phenomenon. But he could well imagine her crying out, 'If only . . .', he could imagine how she would suffer from insomnia and depression, and be under the doctor, on strong medication.

There was, it had come to him, an awful lot invested in him. His responsibility was immense. If he walked out of the door, he would take with him his mother's hopes and happiness. And he wasn't sure that he could live with himself after.

It might have been easier if he'd had a brother or sister, but of course he had neither.

Poor Shirley! She had put all her eggs in one basket. Poor Colin! He was that basket.

'What are you thinking?' asked Sandra at his side.

'Nothing.' He smiled at her. 'Are you an only child?'

'No, I have a brother.'

'That must be nice.'

She spread her hands in an ambiguous gesture. 'It has its advantages. Its disadvantages, also. Why? Whatever made you think of it?'

'Nothing, really. Does your mother have a job?'

'Yes.'

'A career?' he pressed.

'Very much a career.'

'What does she do.'

'Uhm . . . counselling,' she extemporised.

'That's good.'

'Yes, it is.'

'Can I kiss you?'

'What, now?'

'Or later. Should I make an appointment?'

'Now would be fine.'

His face was prickly. His small, sharp teeth grazed her lip. For once she felt no shyness, no shame, no need to apologise for herself. She felt only happiness.

'Pity we have to go to this do,' he said close to her ear.

'Must we, then?'

'Well . . . My parents would be very upset.'

'In that case, certainly we have to go.'

'It might even be fun.' He offered her his hand. 'And there'll be prawn cocktail to start.'

'There will?'

'Or melon.'

'Honeydew?'

'Yes. D'you?'

'Do I what?' She blinked at him.

'Honey, d'you think that you and I might be an item?'

•

7

'This is a funny little car,' said Sandra, hauling herself up and out of the MG. There was a chill in the air, and a smokiness, a faint foretaste of winter. A habitual mouth breather, she took great gulps of it, felt it curl on her tongue and catch at the back of her throat. Cones of mist drifted in the headlamp beams until, with the flick of a switch, Colin doused them.

'I'm a funny little *person*,' he rationalised, stretching across, peering up at her, addressing her through the passenger door in the instant before she closed it.

'Try again.' He reopened it, gave it a shove. 'It needs a good slam.' And, 'That's it,' he mouthed through the window glass, as she rammed it home and he locked it.

'You're not so little,' she laughed as he unpacked himself, all arms and legs, on to the tarmac and stamped about.

'But funny?' He regarded her over the hooded roof of the MG, fiddled with his key in the lock. 'You concede that I'm funny?'

'I suppose so. Funny ha-ha.'

'Not funny peculiar?'

'Well, maybe just a touch.'

She hugged the shawl protectively around herself, and gazed across the car-park to the whitewashed public house, which archly called itself an inn and promised traditional country fayre. It stood off from the road behind a half-circle of lawn out of which grew a tall, swinging sign and a scattering of those incommodious, plank bench-and-table climb-in-and-out affairs designed to snag stockings and to thwart anyone in a short, tight skirt.

'We've just time for a quick one,' said Colin, glancing at his watch. 'We don't have to get to this shindig on the dot.'

'We don't?'

'No. In fact it's better not to. The first half an hour is always pretty dire. Everyone just stands around clutching drinks, checking out everyone else, and feeling awkward and overdressed.'

'But you did say that we shouldn't be late.'

'Not late late. That would be inexcusable. But early late is permissible.'

'You have to think of your parents.'

'Yes.'

'I expect they look to you to be there mingling.'

'Oh, sure. And I shall do. I shall mingle with the best of 'em.' He dug her in the ribs with his finger. 'Come on.'

'What's the occasion, anyway?' she wanted to know, as she picked up her skirt and fell, rustling, in step with him. 'The reason for the bash?'

'It's our annual Christmas knees-up.'

'Christmas is weeks and weeks away.'

'It gets it over with.'

'Well, if you look at it like that . . .'

The lighted windows of the pub were deceptively welcoming. She felt suddenly, absurdly excited. 'How's your eye, by the way?' she asked as he ushered her into a large bar room which had been camped up to recall an Edwardian salon, with plastic potted palms, and with button-back armchairs, deep sofas and low quilted stools arranged in little huddles. Pub pop music trickled from invisible speakers like some minor indiscretion, best ignored.

'My eye?'

'I seem to remember you had a tic.'

'That's right,' he confirmed, as they arrived at the gleaming counter. 'A sort of pulsing. I thought it was a symptom of some terrible sickness. I thought I had yaws.'

She raised an eyebrow.

'Go on then,' he prompted.

'Go on, what?'

'You're supposed to say "What's yaws?"'

'But I know what yaws is.'

'Then *I* say, "That's jolly decent of you, I'll have a gin and tonic." '

'You want a gin and tonic?'

'Certainly not. I'm driving.'

'Because I'll buy you one with pleasure. Only I have heard of yaws, of course. It's a tropical disease. It affects the skin, though not, so far as I'm aware, the eyes.'

'Then I can't have had it, can I? Look, this is on me,' he fingered his stiff shirt collar. 'What would you like?'

'Uhm, I'd like a . . . er. What are you having?'

'Low-alcohol lager, but only because I'm at the wheel. I wouldn't recommend it to you. It's not the stuff to put hairs on your chest.'

'In that case, I'll have a glass of dry white wine, please, if you recommend that for hirsutism. Thanks.'

'You go and bag us a seat.' He dropped his keys on to the counter and dug around in his inside pocket for his wallet as the landlord bore down upon them, bidding them a gloomy good evening. 'Make yourself comfortable. Pull up a Chesterfield.'

'Okey-doke.' Sandra scanned the room in search of a quiet corner, and found herself spoilt for choice. On Saturday nights and Sunday lunchtimes there would be standing room only in this kind of place, but early on a Thursday evening it was all but deserted.

After a few moments' deliberation, she opted for a sofa by the window, where she sat and watched with amusement as Colin was served. What was it about him that so endeared? There was something immensely appealing in his very posture, his gestures, in the tilt of his head. The hired suit sat oddly upon him; it just sort of hung and did nothing to help him. He seemed very loosely strung together, and he dipped at the knees like a puppet. She shut her eyes, and they filled with tears, joyful tears.

What was going on? And what did it portend? She had, she realised with compunction, never before been out with anyone good and gentle and kind and undemanding. She had always been perversely attracted to ruthless, selfish, unreliable types. She had been stood up, let down, blown out, passed over by a succession of bastards, had allowed herself to be misused and exploited, and had even . . . well, 'revelled' would be the wrong word, but she had certainly wallowed in it. She had been hooked on emotional pain, and had found a sort of sick satisfaction in being proved right in her harsh self-assessment.

So, either she must be growing up, growing out of her stupidity, she told herself, as he came gingerly towards her with two brimming glasses, or there was something very special indeed about Colin Clarke.

When he set the glasses down, their contents lapped over. 'Enjoy your drink,' he droned in a fair imitation of mine host, as with his fingertips he tested the instability of the table, wobbling it so more liquid slopped out.

'Did he say that? The landlord?'

'He did. Budge up.' Colin sat down beside her and nudged her with his hip. 'Enjoy your drink,' he said again, as if for practice.

'But not "Have a nice day"?'

'No, he didn't say that.'

'Well, that's a blessing.' She picked up her wine, using her free hand as a saucer to catch the drips, and sipped demurely.

'How is it?' he asked.

'Not bad. Quite palatable. You know, it's getting worse. The Americanisation, I mean. I was in Ravel the other day, and, if you can believe it, when I went up to pay, the girl at the cash desk said "Enjoy your shoes." '

'Perhaps she thought you were kinky. Some people, after all, get a lot of enjoyment from shoes. They have a funny thing about them.'

'Some people have all sorts of funny things.'

'Yes, so I understand. Well, you know what they say . . . ' He ducked down as if he were bobbing for apples, and siphoned up some flat-looking lager without lifting the glass. 'There's nowt so queer as folk.'

'But you don't have any?' she asked.

'Any what?'

'Any, er, funny things? You're not into rubber? Or bondage? Or women's underwear?' Perhaps, after all, there was a flaw in him which she had failed to spot?

'None of the above.' This time, he lifted his drink to his lips. 'I'm boringly ordinary where all that is concerned. I used to think fetish was a Greek cheese.'

'And isn't it?'

'I used to think peccadillo was a yellow sauce you had with hamburgers. I thought cunni –'

'Enough already.' She held up her hands. 'Please spare me the old one about the Irish airline.'

'Oh, all right, spoilsport.'

'Anyway, ordinary's not boring.'

'It isn't?'

'I don't think so.'

'That's good.' He considered for a moment and smiled at a private recollection. 'I once got thrown out of a sex shop,' he confided.

'You did?' She took another sip of wine.

'Yes, truly. They said, "We don't want your sort in here." '

'Meaning . . . ?'

'Meaning that they could tell. They could see through me. They had me bang to rights. Something – the clean raincoat, perhaps – must have given me away. They took one look at me and thought, "We've got a right one here." '

'A browser?'

'Precisely. So they threw me out and said never to darken their dildoes again.'

'Maybe they took you for some kind of inspector.'

'A police inspector?'

'Or a trading standards officer.'

'Do I *look* like a trading standards officer?'

'A little bit. In certain lights.'

'Well, thank you.'

'Don't mention it.'

'So, anyway, what I am trying to tell you, in a roundabout fashion, is that I am not sexually adventurous. You do not see before you, the Don Juan *de nos jours*. You do not see a Magic Johnson.'

'Or a Masters and Johnson?'

'No. So, if you're looking for a great lover, a man of prowess, of experience, or of imagination, you have come to the wrong address.'

'I see.'

'You're barking up the wrong tree.'

'I understand.'

'Never ask me to make love to you five times in one night.'

'I shan't.'

'Or to discover some new erogenous zone.'

'Uh-uh.'

'Or to do it on top of the wardrobe.'

'All right. I have fitted cupboards, in any case.'

'That's a blessing.'

'It would be possible to do it *in* the wardrobe.'

'Yes?'

'But I don't think I'd like to.'

'No?'

'No. I'm a bit claustrophobic.'

'The thing is, I've led a quiet life.'

'I should imagine you have,' she nodded, thinking of Shirley, thinking of Roy – thinking, too, how much more erotic was this line of chat than the usual male braggadocio. It was almost irresistible to her. Here was someone who would laugh her into bed. However, 'It's early days yet,' she told him primly.

'Ah, yes, early days. But for future reference . . .' He drank another draught of lager. 'I felt you ought to know.'

'I appreciate it.'

'I thought I should put my cards on the table.'

'Thank you.'

'Because I don't get out much, I don't put myself about. I'm too busy at home, doing my chores.'

'What chores?'

'That's jolly decent of you,' he yelled in triumph, punching her on the arm. 'I'll have a gin and tonic.'

———— • ————

Dee withdrew the boeuf bourguignon from the oven and gave three hearty cheers for Marks & Spencer. She might differ with M&S in her definition of a portion, she might be at odds with them over serving sizes (they did not, let's face it, cater to the trencherman – or, indeed, to the trencherwoman), she had bought double helpings for her son, her husband, herself, but apart from that she had nothing but praise for their food, she found it simply first rate. Of course, given the leisure to do so, she would always prefer to prepare the family meals herself, to make them from scratch, from the finest raw ingredients, following the latest exciting recipe dreamed up by the *Mia* cookery team. But, as every superwoman knew, it was smart sometimes to cut corners, to make artful use of the contents of the refrigerated counters. For whom else, if not for working wives and mothers, had the cook–chill process been developed? One could surely compromise without, as it were, being compromised.

And wasn't it wonderful the way Marks had made available to the great British public cuisines from around the world? St Michael was, now she came to think of it, a great leveller. The rich man in his castle, the poor man at his gate, all could tuck in to a nice paëlla, or jambalaya, or tiramisù.

Admittedly, their stuff was not cheap. But it was value for money, this was the great thing, and there was absolutely no waste. You just popped a dish in at regulo five, sat down with a dry Martini until the timer went ping, dished up, added a garnish – a radish rose, a carrot curl, or a lemon butterfly, that little extra touch to give a meal plate appeal – and Bob was your uncle.

It had never been easier, either, to provide adequate nutrition, what with all the labelling on packets. There was no excuse for anyone to feed their kids an inferior diet, to fill them up with frozen chips and burgers and fizzy pop, or to bribe them with lollies, when there were so many healthy options. It ought to be brought home to people – and she would make it her mission to do so – that poor nutrition was the source of many social ills.

Low intellect, hyperactivity, vandalism and other criminal behaviour had all been traced back to vitamin deficiency and to orange food colourings, to the azo dyes. You had only to look at some children to know that they wanted for mother love and good home cooking. And you had only to glance in mum's supermarket trolley to confirm the lamentable truth.

Ben, for instance, Kayleigh's child, would do a great deal better on the free-range chicken, the farm-fresh eggs and vegetables which she had ordered in from Joyce Pearcy in the village, than he would on fish fingers and crisps. The girl herself, come to that, should be beefed up a bit; she was emotionally, as well as physically, starved. Dee could not think when she had met a more surly, silent, lacklustre, unresponsive little ingrate. Oh, yes, she was ungrateful! And, while one did not of course look for thanks, some small show of recognition, some tiny token, some expression of appreciation would nevertheless not go amiss.

'How are you?' Dee had asked on the telephone earlier this evening.

And, 'All right,' Kayleigh had replied after a moment, in gruff and grudging tones.

'You're managing, are you? You have everything you want?'

'I couldn't find the brown sauce.'

'Well, we don't usually . . . It's not a staple, you know, of the Rawlings store cupboard. But I can buy some at the weekend if you must have it.'

'Okay.'

'Or there's home-made chutney in the pantry.'

'Chutney?'

'Mrs Bastable's green tomato. She makes it for the village fête. You'll like it.'

'Okay.'

'And apart from that? You're coping?'

'Mm.'

'And Ben?'

'Uh-huh.'

'That's grand. Well, you know we'll be down tomorrow night.'

'All of you?'

'I don't think Sandra will be coming, no. I believe she has a booking, a twenty-first birthday party to cater for on Saturday night.'

'Oh.'

'I'm sorry. I'm sure she would have liked to see you.'

'And Jamie?'

'Jamie? Uhm . . .' Frowning, Dee had reached out and stripped a page off her calendar, a picture of Lake Superior, of which she had grown heartily sick. It was now, after all, October. 'I don't believe he's made any plans to join us.'

'I see.'

'So I expect it will be just me and the old man.'

149

'Right.'

'Until tomorrow, then. *Ciao ciao.*' She'd blown a kiss. But Kayleigh had, by then, hung up.

Ho hum, thought Dee, as she took the pretty, hand-painted Divertimenti dinner plates from the warmer. She would have to work with that difficult girl. She would have to give her lessons in home economics. She would point out, first of all, how delicious and how nourishing was such cheap and simple fare as jacket potatoes and baked beans on toast. She would teach her to make fresh vegetable soup, to knock up an omelette with salad. (It was not as if Kayleigh had anything better to do with her time.) She would also teach her, if she could, to mind her Ps and Qs.

All at once she felt furious. Indignation rushed up inside her like vomit. It was clear to her that others took advantage of her giving nature. 'Will someone please lay the table?' she called out sharply to her husband, her son. And, when answer came there none, 'Eric, do you hear me? Can you *please* lay for me?'

Jamie could do it, of course. But Jamie had been working, he had earned his rest.

'Oh, and open a bottle of wine, there's a darling, ' she cajoled, bringing her temper under control, when her husband came out to the kitchen, set down his crystal tumbler of whisky, and started raking around ineffectually in the cutlery drawer. 'A nice drop of red, what do you think?'

'Anything you say, my sweet,' he responded with, if she did not mistake it, the faintest suggestion, the merest hintette of sarcasm.

She had noticed of late a certain chippiness, a dissidence in her normally amiable spouse. At moments he could be downright cussed. Dee was not, however, unduly perturbed. She had a shrewd idea what ailed him. Here was a textbook case of the male menopause, on which subject she was something of an expert, having recently written a leaflet.

It was perfectly common for a man in mid life to suffer some kind of crisis. Not that Eric could strictly be said to be in mid life, unless he proposed to survive beyond a hundred, to have his telegram from the monarch, which was a very long shot, given that neither of his parents had clocked up their three score years and ten. Dee was more or less reconciled to the fact that she would outlive her husband. She would be devastated by the loss, but she would cope. Widowhood, grief, would be yet another great learning experience, it would give her a valuable insight.

Anyway, 'mid life' was a mere figure of speech (as, for that matter, was 'menopause'). The point was that Eric, poor lamb, was going through a period of imbalance. It happened to many, many men in their late forties and early fifties. They went decidedly peculiar, began wearing strong aftershave, playing their Grateful Dead records very loud, and combing their hair in thin, greasy strands across the bald patch. Often they became withdrawn, obsessed with their health. At worst they went ever so slightly insane.

They started to question life in all its aspects; they turned against their partners, they longed to break out, yet their souls seemed immured. They measured their achievements – or, as in Eric's case, lack of achievements – against their early aspirations, and they sank into despair.

Having said which, there was no need to worry, since the condition was purely episodic and, like all things, must pass. It was not, in that sense, serious, nor was it based in physiology, although there might be some small biochemical change, and a resulting diminution of the sex drive. Recent researches had suggested an age-related rise in sex-hormone-binding globulin, which adheres to testosterone and renders it inactive. But, pfooff, who really cared? What was a slight loss of libido between friends? (Because they *were* friends, she and Eric, she had said as much today, to camera: 'Eric, my life partner, is my best and dearest friend.')

Truth to tell, she would welcome a certain relaxation in their sex life, an easing up in the intercourse department. It was a source of pride to her that her man still found her desirable, but she fancied she detected, in his performance, an increasing desperation, as if he feared that he must use it or lose it, and she was tempted to explain to him that he need not make the effort.

That was not the way, though. He must come to terms himself with his declining virility, and must formulate a new set of plans more appropriate to his age. She would give him her support, and would forbear to argue with him for as long as he was in this delicate mental state.

He was fortunate, actually, to have so understanding a wife.

Many in his situation did not, and it was they who got up to all manner of sillinesses. Some made fools of themselves, chasing after young girls. Others, under a pernicious American influence, apparently took themselves off to the woods to 'find themselves', to beat drums, and to sniff each other's anuses, if you can conceive of such a thing.

It was a blessing, in some respects, that Eric had few opportunities, that he was not in a milieu where he might meet younger women, or be led astray by male colleagues, encouraged to weep, to engage in sword play, and to be generally primitive and hairy.

'How was your day, my darling?' she enquired of him sweetly.

'The same as every day.'

'Don't be like that.'

'Like what?'

'Don't be despondent.'

'I'm not. I'm merely saying . . . You asked me how it was, and I told you.'

He went through to the lounge. She heard him banging down the knives and forks on the table in the dining alcove. Poor Eric. Perhaps, after all, she should suggest testosterone replacement, which was the latest buzz, the coming thing. On the other hand, perhaps she should not.

'How's business?' she asked Jamie as she bore in the plates of steaming food.

'Slack,' he replied shortly, and he groaned as he dragged himself off the sofa.

It would be the recession, Dee supposed. The slump in the housing market. That must be terribly frustrating for a bright young man with get up and go.

'There's rumours of a new agency opening round the corner,' he disclosed.

'Another Richmond in the field?' said Dee with sympathy.

'Gascoigne-Pees,' said Jamie.

'We've all got to go some time,' put in Eric.

The pop of a cork was a cheering sound. And, as he poured the wine, everyone seemed momentarily to brighten.

'I spoke to young Kayleigh,' Dee reported, seating herself at the head, riding her chair in till her bosoms rested on the table.

'She's still there, then?' asked Jamie, picking up a fork and jabbing about with it, moving food around his plate.

'She is.'

'You're going to have to get rid of her, you know,' he told her sternly. 'You're going to have to move her on.' He shovelled in a cube of meat and worked it over. 'The longer you let her stay, the more difficult it will be,' he lectured her through the masticated beef, paining his mother, causing her to wonder where he had acquired these appalling manners.

'Ah, no, no. She's not in any doubt that it's a temporary thing.'

'Well, the sooner she shoves off, the happier I shall be.'

'Jamie! That's most uncharitable.'

'No, well, charity was never my thing.'

'It's not as if she's doing you any harm.'

'She's not doing me any good. Or you, either.'

'Now, now,' put in Eric to Dee's surprise (he'd changed his tune since last week!), 'have a bit of humanity, have a heart. Let the kid stay, I say, for as long as she needs a roof over her head. We ought to share our blessings, oughtn't we?'

———————— • ————————

'Where can they have got to?' Shirley, sucking on her slimline tonic water as if it were strong drink, felt her eyes drawn once more to the doorway, half expecting at that moment to see Colin there, half knowing he would never come. She had visions of mangled metal, of blue flashing lights, of scurrying figures black against the white-hot sheets of flame. Her head was full of sounds – a squeal of brakes, a sickening crash, a siren's plangent tone. Footsteps rang in the chill, clinical corridors of her imagination; voices echoed; a drawer was rumbled out to reveal the cadaver, poignantly naked, and ribby and skinny and pale. 'Yes, yes, that's him. That's my baby.'

This was an exquisite form of torture which she had devised for herself the day Colin was born, which she had been tweaking and fine tuning ever since. Over the years he had unknowingly suffered a thousand cuts, he had died a thousand deaths.

He had been abducted, lured away by bad men in shabby suits who sidled up to him with crumpled bags of sticky toffees.

He had been snatched by bank robbers, taken hostage ('Nobody moves, or we blow the boy away'). He had drowned in the school swimming-pool, in ornamental lake and open sea. He had been beaten up by bigger boys crazed on solvents; he had been torn limb from limb by marauding dogs. He had been knocked off his bike by a hit-and-run motorist, to lie undiscovered in a ditch. He had been brained by a cricket ball at silly mid on . . .

The world had never seemed more wicked or more fraught with peril, the newspapers more full of nameless horror, than they did in motherhood. If Colin was so much as fifteen minutes late, Shirley would be climbing the walls with anxiety. And he was seldom less than fifteen minutes late. As an infant, he had been the last in his year to learn to tie a shoelace. And how slow had been the process of packing a satchel, of buttoning a blazer, of setting cap on dreamy head, while Shirley waited, fretful, one of a dwindling band of mothers at the school gate.

The simplest errand, a trip to the shops for a bag of self-raising flour, or the quarter-mile walk to Cubs, had presented young Colin and his chums with endless diversions. There had been deep, black puddles to stir with sticks; squished slugs to probe; toads' spawn, and snail trails and stinkhorn to investigate ('Pooh, pongo, Marchmont, what a stench!'). There had been birds' nests and burrows; tree stumps frilled with bracket fungus; owl pellets, sad little parcels of bone and fur; sticky buds, catkins, ash keys, acorns holed by weevils. There had been conkers, great big sixers, winking at him amid the earthy-smelling amber drifts of leaves. And – horrors! – there had been hemlock, henbane, yew berries, belladonna, death caps, destroying angels, nux vomica, red and spotted fly agaric.

'What have you been up to?' she would demand of him, as he came trailing home at last, his pockets pulsing ominously, stuffed with offerings for the nature table of wriggling, wiggling wildlife.

And, 'Nowhere,' he would say bemusedly, blinking at her, unable to account for it, to recall time as lost and gone for ever as days lost to alcoholic oblivion.

'He'll be here any minute,' Roy told her blithely, swigging back the fizzy wine, beaming around him at the loyal band of workers and their partners, all in high spirits, in their party best, now filtering into the function room of the Crosskeys Hotel and Country Club. 'You worry too much, you know that, Shirl?'

'It seems to me', she scolded her husband sniffily, as she nodded and waved to Reg from purchasing and his hypertrophic wife Doreen, 'that you don't worry half enough, Roy Clarke. And please don't call me Shirl. Especially in front of people, don't do it.'

'Hey, hey, look, the gang's all here.' Roy jabbed her with his elbow and nodded in the direction of the door, as the band struck up 'New York, New York'. 'What did I tell you? So much fuss about nothing. I said he'd turn up like a bad penny.' And he began, tunelessly, to sing along. 'Start spreading the news. I'm leaving today. I want to be a part of it, New York, New York.'

'Oh, do be quiet, Roy. You're making a spectacle of yourself.' Abject terror was displaced by outrage. Shirley would have liked to smack her son for being so dilatory, she would have liked to shake him for turning up now, with the ungainly, big-boned, plain-faced Sandra at his side.

The young woman was carapaced in blue satin, in a style, a cut of dress, which did not become her, and she was showing an unsuitable amount of . . . *embonpoint*. More infuriating yet was her expression, her swanky smile, her air of self-assurance. 'Smug' was the word that came to Shirley. Sandra was smug in her son's affections.

Almost, almost, the flashing blue lights, the sheets of flame, the mangled metal would be more endurable than this.

Oh, Lord, thought Sandra, hanging on to Colin's arm, braking hard, as a liveried man announced Miss Sandra Rawlings, Mr Colin Clarke. Her gaze was drawn to Shirley who stood very stiff in viscose and acetate, in a shade somewhere short of damson, clutching a glass, exuding hostility and dismay. She's going to hate me, she realised. She's going to loathe and detest me for stealing her precious child. She is going to try to come between us. I can see it in her face.

'Sorry, sorry, sorry.' Colin towed her over to his parents, offering the breezy, meaningless apologies of one for whom the concept of punctuality is, at best, a bit abstruse.

'Where did you get to?' queried Shirley with a fine show of casual concern. 'Did you have a puncture, hm? Hm? Or lose the way?' Then, 'Hello, my dear,' she greeted Sandra, who stood off a little, unable to suppress a nervous, humourless, wholly inappropriate smirk, and who focused grimly on Shirley's manicure, ten perfectly shaped plum nails, rather than meet her glinting eye.

'We popped into the Peacock for a quick one,' Colin explained.

'Colin, I hope you haven't . . .'

There were the blue lights again, the sirens and the sheets of flame.

'Don't worry, Mother, not a drop has passed my lips. Or no more than a drop. One part of alcohol to a hundred parts of deeply disgusting lager.'

'Then you'll have a glass of something now,' coaxed Roy, very jovial, flagging down a waitress, 'you'll have some of the hard stuff.'

'Roy,' Shirley frowned at him, 'you shouldn't encourage . . .'

'Safe limits, my darling. Safe limits.'

'I think,' said Sandra, who felt suddenly strangled by her own tension, 'if you would excuse me . . . I must just pop to the loo.'

'Have a nice time,' Colin called heartily after her, in his best yankee accent. 'Missing you already.'

Fire doors snapped at her heels as she hurried out into the long, lowlit corridor. Thick red carpet stole her footfalls: as if to deny her existence, the springy nylon pile returned no sound to her.

In the stuffy box that was the ladies' powder room, she dipped into a dispenser of violet tissues, damped one under the tap, and dabbed at her forehead as she sank into a complaining boudoir chair. She would have to keep herself together, to see the funny side, if tonight were not to be an intolerable strain. She remembered a wonderful piece of advice, a trick for reducing your worst experiences to farce. The idea was mentally to set the situation to loud circus music; and this she did, at full volume, with whistles and cymbals and fire crackers and plenty of oom-pah-pah.

Cheered, she stood up, smiled at her reflection in the mirror, a proper smile without a hint of a smirk. The fear that she might commit some dreadful social gaffe was quite misplaced. And Shirley Clarke was not important. Colin liked her. Colin *fancied* her, of this she felt quite confident. And they were in this thing together. That was, after all, what mattered.

She took several deep breaths to clear her head, succeeded only in making herself feel woozy, sat down again heavily, stood up, said 'Stuff it', and set off to rejoin the party.

'Promise me,' Shirley Clarke seized the moment to implore her son, and she lowered the glass with which she had been shielding her face, to fix him with a penetrating stare. 'Please, Colin, promise me, you won't get too involved.'

For as long as he could remember, she'd been doing this to him, exacting solemn undertakings, declarations, pledges, demanding that he mortgage his freedom to her, denying him independence, volition, choice.

With unerring acuity, she had always known those things which he most fervently desired, and would move in to pre-empt him, to bind him up with honour bright.

Well, okay. He had gone along with it, he had promised, albeit reluctantly, not to swap his Scalextric for Carlisle's crossbow and the arrows with the rubber suckers; not to play kiss chase with the girls from Selbourne Manor; or to drink aspirin in Coca-Cola; or to climb on the shed roof; or to take his hands off the handlebars; or to spend his dinner money on sweets. He had promised not to have a puff of Marchmont's dad's pipe, or to copy Broomfield's algebra homework, or to brazen his way into adult movies, or, latterly, to have his ear pierced, or his hair streaked.

But he was grown up now, and he would not be so shackled. Besides which, he thought, as he watched eagerly for Sandra to return, he was really keen, really taken with this lovely, sweet-natured, honest, open person. Everything in him was attracted to her. She made his heart bulge in his chest. So, 'No,' he responded, 'I won't, I *can't* promise, Mum.' Then, because she looked smitten, 'In any case, you're jumping the gun a bit, aren't you? This *is* only our first date, you know.'

'I know,' she conceded with a sniff. And she thought, first of many.

'I can't see what you've got against her.'

'Nothing, Colin. I have nothing against her. I'm sure she's perfectly charming. I'm only saying . . .'

'Then, for heaven's sake . . .'

'Now, don't for-heaven's-sake me, don't talk back to me, I'm your mother. You're very young, that's the thing, and impressionable. You always *were* easily led. If Daniel Marchmont had told you to jump under a bus, I do believe you would have done so.'

'No I wasn't. And I wouldn't have. That's absurd.'

'Yes, you were, dear, you were his patsy. I'm sorry, but it's true. And now, as then, I am only thinking of you.'

'You are?'

'Of course I am,' she snapped. And, moving seamlessly into hostess mode, 'Hello, Pauline, how nice to see you! Hello Jack. I'm so glad you could make it with that hip of yours.'

'You're a dark horse, young Colin,' teased Pauline from bought ledger, one of his office aunties, approaching, puckering, with a kiss for Shirley. 'You never let on that you were courting.'

'He isn't,' said Shirley crossly.

'Not exactly,' said Colin, and for the hundredth time his hand flew to his stiff collar, to fiddle with it irritably.

'She cooks for me,' claimed Shirley without a flicker of embarrassment. 'She caters my dinner parties. And she's very innovative, I must say. Only last week we were entertaining clients – because, of course, we do a lot of entertaining – and they were most impressed.'

'Ah, they say that the way to a man's heart . . .'

'They do.' Shirley's upper lip went back like a roll-top desk to reveal an orderly file of teeth beneath.

'So, will it be wedding bells?' Pauline persisted.

'I was just asking the same question. But "It's early days yet," Colin said to me. "Aren't you jumping the gun a bit, Mum?" ' Shirley made a silly-me gesture, and uttered a self-deprecating little laugh.

'It's the first time we've been out together,' explained Colin to Pauline, suddenly weary.

'He's not courting as such,' insisted Shirley.

'Still foot loose and fancy free, eh?'

'Oh, yes.' Shirley placed her hand in the small of her son's back, rather as if he were a ventriloquist's dummy; and, like a ventriloquist's dummy, he rolled his eyes in his head. Then, 'He's still very much a bachelor gay,' Shirley pronounced, betraying a poor command of the vernacular. 'Ooh, they're bringing in the melon gondolas. Isn't that grand? And, you see, Roy is making frantic signals. We must go to our tables. Have you found your place card, Pauline, dear? Good, good. We'll see you later.'

'How are you doing?' asked Colin, as Sandra returned to his side. Then very deliberately – almost, she felt, as if to make a point – he took her hand, tucked it under his arm, clamped it firmly there, and led her to the top table where he shovelled her up with a chair.

'This looks nice,' she said politely, hopelessly to Shirley, opposite, and she waved a hand vaguely, indicating silver, napery, crystal.

'Doesn't it? Well, they always do us proud.' Shirley smoothed the skirt of her dress, which she had bought especially for the occasion, at Raggety Anne's in the high street, in the little local shopping centre which called itself a village. They knew her there – her style, her size – and had never let her down. 'We've been coming here for years, you see. We're valued customers.'

A waitress was doing the rounds with a basket of bread rolls, distributing them with tongs. One dropped from a great height on to Sandra's side plate, and bounced on to the floor. 'Oops. Sorry,' said the girl, delivering another.

And, 'Sorry,' echoed Sandra, because she always took these things upon herself.

'Not your fault.' Colin, beside her, ducked under the table and retrieved the roll.

'Leave it, Colin, do,' his mother chided, picking up a spoon and digging into her melon. 'Tell me, Sandra, where did you learn to cook so beautifully?'

'Well, in the first place, from my mother. And then, after school, I trained . . .'

But Shirley, having tabled the question, had turned away from her and was talking to her neighbour, a bald man with white side-whiskers. Sandra felt the blood rush up, like cherryade up a straw; her face was awash with it.

Only, then a hand closed upon her knee and gave a gentle, reassuring squeeze. 'Miss Rawlings,' said Colin softly, sweetly, 'will you promise me a dance?'

'I'd like to.' She shot him a smile of gratitude. 'I'd like that very much.'

'What do you call a judge with no thumbs?'

159

'I beg your pardon?'

They were one of perhaps a dozen couples, dancing very close, while the band played 'Cabaret', and while everyone else sat talking and drinking, amid the debris of dinner and half-filled coffee-cups. She felt incredibly safe and cosseted in Colin's embrace. He was no better and no worse a dancer than she; they were in perfect time with each other, if not always with the music.

He propped his chin on her shoulder, rested his heavy head. 'I said, what do you call a judge with no thumbs?'

'I don't know. Pray tell me: what *do* you call a judge with no thumbs?'

'Justice Fingers.'

'For Pete's sake!' She thumped his shoulder with a clenched fist, and started laughing absolutely silently; he felt the spasms of mirth.

'You're wobbling like a jelly.'

'You say the nicest things.'

'Are you happy?' he mumbled in her hair.

'Mm. Yes. Surprisingly, yes I am. You?'

'Ditto.'

'Except, I'll just die if we win a spot prize.'

'Have no fear. We don't stand an earthly.'

'How can you be so positive?'

'Well, A, because we've got to be the worst movers on the floor tonight. And, B, because it's rigged. It has to be. It would never do for the boss's son to walk off with the magnum of Krug or the picnic hamper, would it?'

'What a break!'

'I know. Isn't it?'

'We're in the clear, then?'

'Completely.'

'Colin . . .'

'What?'

'I don't think your mother likes me very much.'

'She probably thinks you're after my body.'

'How dare she?'

'You mean, you're not?' He feigned disappointment.

'We-ell . . .'

'Oh, go on, eh,' he wheedled.

'Well, maybe just a little bit.'

'A tad?'

'I hate the word tad.'

'What about tad*pole*?'

'That's all right. Tadpole's fine.'

'Then, what abou-out . . . ?'

'You can't think of any other tad words.'

'I can.'

'Name one.'

'I could if I wanted to. I could name hundreds. Thousands, probably. Tadcaster. There!'

'Proper nouns don't count.'

'How about improper ones?'

'They're fine.'

'And improper suggestions?'

'If you must.'

'Okay . . .' he inhaled sharply. 'What about if I take you home and roger you senseless?'

Her knees threatened to give under her. 'I also hate the word roger,' she said in a small voice.

'How about bonk?'

'That's even worse.'

'Ravish, then?' He clamped her bottom with his fingers and pulled her to him. 'Do you like ravish?'

'Mm.' She pressed her face against him and grinned like an idiot into the cloth of his jacket. 'Ravish will do nicely.'

———————— • ————————

It was very dark beyond the bedroom window; it was a kind of darkness Kayleigh did not know. It was noisy here, too; it was noisy in a way she did not understand.

In London the night sky was grey and watery, with a thick, sulphurous sediment, it was flushed with squandered sodium street light; it was never this uncompromising, all-enveloping black.

In London, also, the sounds made perfect sense: the screech of tyres, the wail of a siren, the clang of dustbin lids, the shrill wheee-wheee of a car alarm, the frenzied barking of a neighbour's dog. Often, voices raucous with drink would intrude upon your sleep. Or there would be some terrific argie-bargie, thuds and yells and the smash of china, the din of a 'domestic' spilling out of the flat opposite and spiralling down the stairway. Then the wind would rock you gently in your tower-block bedroom. And you would be lulled by the mindless chatter of trains far below you, or by the soporific murmur of next door's TV, of the adult channel, beyond the thin dividing wall.

How different was the countryside at dead of night, when there was no traffic, and there were no voices, no trains or televisions, only weird yelps and yaps and hoots, a persistent scritch-scratching in the roof cavity, and the leaden chimes of the church clock by which to measure your insomnia.

She sat cross-legged with the duvet drawn up to her chin, and gazed ahead of her till she began to hallucinate, as drowsy shadows passed behind her eyes. She listened hard, and her ears filled up with nothing.

She would have liked to go down to the kitchen to make herself a cup of tea, a slice of the sawdusty wholemeal bread which Dee favoured, spread thick with peanut butter. She had ventured once on to the landing, to the banisters, and had peered into the inky well. She had even dipped a toe before her courage failed her and she scurried back to the safety of her bed, there to take comfort in the presence of her sleeping baby, another living creature in this lonely, alien place.

She, who had always lived in flats, on a single floor, in a small, square, densely peopled space, found something very, very disquieting about upstairs and down, about so many corridors and alcoves and empty rooms and vast dimensions. And she was constantly spooking herself.

When she was down in the kitchen, or in the sitting-room, she would fancy she heard the soft pad of footsteps, the click of a latch above. When she was up in the bedroom, it would be the creak of a floorboard, the rattle of a window in its frame, or a curious scraping, or a knock-knocking, or the sound of something weighty, inert, being dragged across stone flags below.

None of this was actual, of course. These were not real sounds as were the yaps and hoots and yelps without, or the grumbling of timbers or the groaning of pipes within. They seemed to happen inside not outside her head, and, straining after them in hope of a reprise, she would hear only the singing of her own blood, rushed around by her wildly beating heart.

This was the worst part, the teeming hours before pale sunlight stole in to drive back the shadows. So often she would lie there, wakeful, scheming, planning her escape. Even a women's refuge, it would seem to her at such times, or a hostel, or some poxy B&B, would be preferable to this. And it would be five, six, seven in the morning before she fell into a fitful sleep, to be woken by Ben's fussing, or by the welcome sound of Ivy Burston roaring in behind the vacuum cleaner, railing at her for her idle, good-for-nothing ways.

It was now, after midnight, that she felt most homesick, missing London, missing her family, missing Greg. But she had learned that the night terrors would abate, that the day would bring with it an uneventful normality, a reassuringly dreary routine.

In the daytime, too, she would count her blessings. As soon as Ivy had done her disapproving stuff and departed, Kayleigh would run delicious hot baths laced with scented oils, in which she would steep herself till her skin was crepey. She would make herself huge doorstep sandwiches, she would pig out in front of the telly. She would swig whisky straight from the bottle, then stand, starkers, by the radiator, warming her hands, watching – actually seeing – the ripples of heat, and marvelling at so much undreamed-of luxury.

Or she would tour the house, touching things, playing with things, snooping, prying, rooting through cupboards and drawers. She had tried every one of Dee's perfumes and cosmetics. She had examined every scrap of paper, from the sheet music in the piano stool to private documents in the bureau, most of which meant sweet Fanny Adams to her.

She could no more follow notation, decode crotchets and quavers and demisemiquavers – could no more sight-read and hum to herself the tune of 'I Love a Lassie' or 'Green Grow the Rushes, Oh' – than she could decipher Dee's Will, with its wax seal, its green ribbon, and its impenetrable legalese ('Sections 31 and 32 of the Trustees Act 1925 shall be applicable hereto modified as appears in the first Schedule hereto . . .')

She had read all Sandra's, all Jamie's school reports, from which she had learned with no surprise that Sandra had been

conscientious, attentive, hard working; that Jamie had been indolent, arrogant, unco-operative, roguish, a boy after her own heart.

The only family member of whom she found no trace was Eric,
the husband, the father. He might not have existed, so slight was
the evidence of his being. She had sifted through the photograph
albums, of course, and through wallets of snapshots, through the
entire Rawlings archive. She had pored over pictures of a plump,
complacent Dee Rawlings, an awkward and embarrassed Sandra, a
relaxed, a super-confident Jamie. But nowhere was Eric captured
on film. She supposed he had been always behind the camera, in
which case his eye was in there somewhere, his presence was at
least implied. All the same, it was creepy, the way he contrived
by his absence to be so conspicuous.

The words of a nonsense poem, a silly rhyme she had heard
from her Nan, came to her now and teased her.

> Late last night upon the stair,
> I saw a man who wasn't there.
> He wasn't there again today.
> I wish that man would go away.

Christ, it was enough to give you the heebie-jeebies, to give
you the screaming abdabs! Oh, Jamie, Jamie! From under her
pillow she extracted a photo, a recent image of her beloved,
lounging against his Porsche, with his arms folded, and with one
leg slung negligently across the other. For a moment she studied
it, then she pressed it to her lips and, closing her eyes, breathed
the intoxicating scent of fixers.

It pleased her to pretend that Jamie might protect her: his
picture was a treasure and a talisman to ward off evil. Still, when
there issued from the gardens, at that moment, a cry so unearthly,
so *satanic* that she felt her scalp crawl, she began to doubt if even
he could save her.

Leaping from the bed, she hauled a small, handpainted chest
of drawers, fussed up with a stencilled flower-and-leaf motif, in
front of the door. She was busting to go to the toilet, but dared
not make a bid for the bathroom. She would hold on till morning
if it killed her.

To occupy her frenzied brain, she took up a paperback, an

old and musty-smelling Penguin from the downstairs carzey, a book called *When The Green Woods Laugh*. The woods were not laughing tonight, she thought. The woods were howling. And here was a peculiar thing: the story turned out to be about the Larkin family, whom she always thought of vaguely as the Buds, the darling Buds. They were all there – Ma and Pop and Mariette. So the television people must have ripped it off. How disgusting!

Kayleigh had never been much of a reader. Now and then she would plough through a Mills & Boon, for the unique satisfaction of reaching an end which fulfilled her every expectation, like pudding at the end of a meal. But literature was not her thing; she'd never listened to a word in English lessons, to classmates standing up and droning on, reading aloud, without tone or emphasis or interest, murdering *Huckleberry Finn*.

So here was a second surprise: that the book was so engrossing. She read slowly, with difficulty, mouthing as she went, working abstractedly at her loose front tooth with her tongue until, with a nauseating rasp, a crunchy, grating feeling, it finally broke away and fell out.

And, well, you can imagine: there was blood everywhere.

———————— • ————————

'You look', said Colin, 'like an ice-cream. All pink and white and yummy.' And he ran his tongue up from her navel, across her abdomen, between her breasts, with an exaggerated slurping sound.

'Eek!' Sandra protested, wriggling, kicking her heels, drawing her knees up defensively. 'Get off. You're a nutcase.'

Then he gazed into her eyes and, like an ice-cream indeed, she melted.

'You're gorgeous,' he told her gruffly.

'So are you,' she responded with sincerity. Because, in his awkward, skinny, way, with his bony knees, his jabbing elbows, his pigeon chest, his freezing cold feet, and his prickly face, he was, oh, just divine.

His love-making was delightful, it was exuberant and energetic. He approached it in the spirit of some schoolboy escapade, a piece of harmless mischief, madcap and hilarious, in which he involved her completely.

There were none of the usual worries about cellulite or sagging breasts or jodhpur thighs or wobbly bottom which can be so dreadfully distracting for a woman. He was so patently thrilled by her body, so overtly admiring, for once in her life she felt luscious.

'Well . . . ?' He rolled on top of her, snorted like a horse, executed a slightly precarious box press-up, levering himself off her, and smiled down at her, one of those huge, curly smiles that brought his every feature into play.

'Well . . . ?' she countered, grinning lazily.

Then, as he lowered himself back on to her, 'Again?' she asked, impressed.

'Again,' Colin insisted.

Her head was swimming slightly. Lack of sleep, or hyper-ventilation – all that panting, all that gasping – made her dizzy. She was sore, too, and burning with her own body fluids, and his. She felt bruised on the inside by his long, thin, thrusting prick. But in no part of herself could she resist him.

She had waited apprehensively for familiar responses of doubt, disappointment and dismay. She had waited for post-coital *tristesse*, or for a visitation of disgust. But her dominant emotion was still bliss.

There was none of the iffiness she had come to associate with sex. In the past she had found that it could turn you on, and then turn on *you*, it could leave you suddenly cold. You could want it most desperately, you could be aching for it one minute, and regret it utterly the next.

A wrong word spoken, a crass remark or a coy one, an indelicate action or a loveless look, and she would all at once perceive herself as ugly, pitiable, wretched, a dupe, and her gorge would rise, she would be physically nauseated. (She had a similar reaction, now and then, to mashed potato.)

But nothing about Colin displeased her. If he had, for one moment, forgotten her name; if he had, in an access of passion, cried out for someone called Vanessa; if he'd entered her with indecent haste, without so much as a kiss, and had ejaculated with equal dispatch before turning on his back and snoring; if he'd scratched her with his toenails; if he'd referred to his penis in the third person, if he'd christened it, affectionately, Dick, or George, or John Thomas; if he'd committed any one of the atrocities of which past lovers had been guilty, it would all have been over in an instant. But he hadn't, he'd done nothing wrong, except to say 'bonk', which was redeemed by the inverted commas implicit in his tone.

'I love you madly,' he told her urgently as she writhed beneath him.

'I love you, too,' she said, and meant it.

He paused mid-thrust and rolled his eyes as he checked a climax. 'Quick,' he said, 'say something funny.'

'I can't think of anything.'

'Well, you're a lot of help!'

She giggled. He giggled. And he lost the erection which he had so heroically sustained.

'Sorry,' he said.

'*Don't* be. Why should you? You were wonderful.'

'I *was?*'

'Sensational.'

He kissed her shoulder. 'You're a pal.'

'Thanks.' She closed her eyes. 'Do you do this a lot?'

'Do what?'

'Well . . . You know. Make love.'

'No, not often. Not on a first date. Not all night. How about you?'

'Occasionally,' she confessed. 'But never like this. It was never so good before.'

'Aw, shucks.' He affected bashfulness. 'You're just saying that.'

'No, no, I'm not. I mean it. Cross my heart.'

He rolled away from her and stretched out luxuriantly. 'If a Martian came down to earth,' he said, 'how would you explain about sex to him?'

'What?'

'I mean, the urgency. The irresistibility. The way it turns your head and takes you over. It would be incomprehensible to an outsider. How would you make him understand? He'd think we were cuckoo.'

'Well, for a start, "he" implies gender, it implies sex. Which means he would already know about it.'

'No he wouldn't. All Martians are male.'

'The same as mules?'

'The same as surgeons. And eskimos.'

'Really?'

'Yeah. You know the brainteaser? A young man is knocked over by a car and rushed to hospital. The surgeon looks down at him and says "This is my son". And yet the surgeon is not the young man's father, so who is he?'

'I haven't a clue.'

'His mother.'

'Then why did you say "he". You said "he" again.'

'I didn't.'

'You did. You said "Who is he?"'

'Okay, then, that just goes to prove my point.' He held his hands up to the lamp, palm to palm, hinging them at the heel, making a snapping motion, throwing a giant shadow on to the ceiling. 'Look,' he said, 'an alligator.'

'Frighteningly realistic.'

'And now look.' He hooked his thumbs and fluttered his fingers.

'An eagle?'

'No, a bustard.'

'Well, it doesn't look like one.'

'It's a silly bustard.'

'They have these long, sticky-out feathers under the mandible.'

'How come you know so much? Are you up on whats-i-thology?'

'Orni . . .'

'Yes, 'orny as 'ell. You?'

'Not now. Not any more. The thing is, I just seem to collect information, you know. Some people collect beer mats. Or Mickey Mouses.'

'Mickey Mice.'

'Uh-huh. Or stamps or coins or whatever. But I just collect useless facts.'

'Oh, I'm sure you will find a use for them one day.'

'Do you reckon?'

'You could make something with them.'

'Such as?'

'You could sew them together and make a factotum.'

'I'll think about it. Let me sleep on it.'

'Already? But it's only . . .'. he groped for his watch and squinted at it. 'Five to five.'

'Won't your parents wonder where you've got to?' She voiced, at last, the anxiety she'd been feeling for him.

'I should imagine they'll have guessed. My mother will put two and two together and make trouble.'

'Are you worried?'

'Just a bit.'

'I'm sorry.'

'You're not to blame.'

'I somehow feel I am.'

'It takes two to tango.'

'So they say.'

She snuggled up to his back and wrapped an arm around him. 'I'm shattered.'

'Me too.'

'When I wake in the morning –'

'This *is* the morning,' he reminded her.

'When I wake up, will you still be here? Or is this all a dream?'

'It's all a dream.'

'I was afraid so.'

'I'm a figment of your imagination.'

'You don't *feel* like a figment. You're all warm and solid and vivid . . .'

'Maybe I am real, then, after all.'

'I hope so.'

'So do I.'

'Good night, then.'

'Night, night.'

'Sweet dreams.'

She closed her eyes and was drifting contentedly into un-consciousness when he asked suddenly, brightly, 'What do you call a prehistoric monster with poor eyesight?'

'I don't know.' She groaned and clamped her hand to her forehead. 'I don't care.'

'I-don't-think-e-saurus.'

'Shut up,' she said, smiling into her pillow. 'Shut up. Be quiet. Go to sleep.'

'All right.' He reached behind him and patted her thigh. 'I love you,' he said, 'honest injun.'

8

The worst had happened. Colin was dead. Shirley Clarke lay, rigid with shock, beside her supine, insensible husband, staring raw-eyed at the ceiling, mentally making the funeral arrangements, and struggling to come to terms with her tragic loss.

Denial – always a first reaction to bereavement – was strong within her still. She couldn't believe it. Yet she knew it to be true.

This was the day she had awaited with both cold dread and obscure longing – the day when she could confront her sorrow, and deal with it, and go beyond it, and pick up the pieces of her shattered life. She would never smile, never laugh again, but at least, at last, the torturous wait was over.

'See you,' her son had said to her last night, so blithe, so gay, so *vital*, as the strains of the last waltz died away, and the lights went up to reveal red wine spills on the starched white cloths, a mess of pastry crumbs, of cocktail sticks, and cigarette butts, and cellophane wrappers, and slugs of ash all over the patterned carpet.

In that instant, also, had become apparent the many little imperfections of dress and hair and make-up, the crooked seams and snagged tights, the tangles and wrinkles, the smudged lips, the panstick and powder, the dark roots and stained teeth, the blocked pores, the thread veins that kinder lights had conspired all evening to conceal. And some instinct of self-preservation had sent people scurrying – like Cinderella on the stroke of midnight – to the cloakroom for hats, coats, scarves.

So . . . 'See you,' Colin had said. 'I'm off now to run Sandra home. Great evening Dad, Mum. Thanks. Cheerio.' Then he had kissed her lightly just . . . She located with the tip of her finger the precise spot where her cheek burned with the memory . . . Just here.

And 'Goodbye,' she had said, little knowing that this would be their final farewell. 'Drive carefully, mind.'

They would sing 'Abide With Me', 'Jerusalem', 'Soldiers of Christ Arise'. There would be a sweet rendition, by a boy soprano, of 'The Lord Is My Shepherd'. They would have vases of tall, pale Madonna lilies, mute trumpets to fill the church with white noise. Finger food would be most suitable. Tea. Sherry. The best china. Wedges of quiche. Bridge rolls with fish pâté and cress. She would wear a mantilla and –

Oh, please, God, no! No! Not my baby boy!

Tears slid from the corners of her eyes and trickled into her ears. Nice, neat, shell-like ears she had, with pretty, rosy lobes. The gold cluster earrings had looked well on her, as had the purple gown from Raggety Anne. The bright lights had found *her*, at any rate, innocent of flaws. She must not, now, let herself go. Appearances still counted for a lot.

But what was she thinking? How the mind wandered when one was in such dire distress!

They had arrived home, she and Roy, at a quarter to one, and she had sat cleansing her face, talking nineteen-to-the-dozen, quite carefree, quite *up*, until she saw in the mirror that her husband's jaw had dropped, his eyes had closed, and he had nodded off.

She was a sensitive person, of course, she was highly strung and lived on her nerves. But she had her lighter moments, and she had enjoyed the dance, it had all gone off without a hitch. 'You know,' she had confided, tissuing off her lipstick as if staunching a wound, then examining the blooded Kleenex before balling it up and dropping it into the bin, 'I don't believe Colin is the slightest bit serious about that girl.' And, as she dabbed on her cold cream, 'I suspect it is a mere flirtation. Boys can be so fickle at his age. I asked him about it, actually, and he seemed to laugh the whole thing off. "You're jumping the gun, a bit, Mum," he said. "This is just the first date." Now, I have a feeling there'll not be a second. What do you say, my dear? I mean, seeing them together. What did you make of it? Darling? Are you listening? Oh, Roy, for heaven's sake!'

She had eased in beside him, and very soon, too, her own eyelids had fluttered and closed, as she was beguiled by a dream in which Her Majesty the Queen featured, albeit in a supporting rôle, running the cake and provisions stall at the harvest bring-and-buy.

But three, four hours later, she had woken with a crushing sense of dread, with the absolute certainty that something was horribly wrong. Because a mother always knows, doesn't she? Even in the deepest sleep she hears things. Or, as it might be, *doesn't* hear them.

What Shirley had not heard, though her subconscious had harked after the familiar sounds, was the crunch of tyres on the drive, the grumble and squeal of the garage door, a key in the latch, a stealthy tread upon the stairs, the blundering of somebody trying his clumsy best to be quiet, or the flushing of the you-know-what, the lubi-loo.

'Roy, Roy, wake up.' She had prodded and shaken him back to awareness of sorts. 'Call the police this minute. Colin's not come home.'

'What's the matter? What's all this fuss? Don't be daft, woman, he'll be here. He probably popped in to Sandra's for coffee.'

'Popped in? Popped in! But it's four o'clock in the morning.'

'He's a big boy, now, Shirley. You have to accept it.'

'He's had an accident. I'm as sure as I can be. A mother's intuition. It's all your fault, Roy, for pressing drink on him, tipping wine down his throat as if it were going out of fashion.'

'You're being ridiculous. He had one glass, maybe two.'

'Ring the police, please, Roy, and don't argue with me.'

'If he had had an accident, Shirley – though, perish the thought – the police would be calling *us*. They'd identify him from the vehicle documents and come knocking on our door with faces like fiddles, never fear.'

'Not if . . .'

Not if – she had been about to say – his little car had been engulfed in a ball of fire. She had framed the sentence in her head, but had found herself unable to give it utterance.

'Call the girl, then. At the very least do that for me. Ask her if he's with her. The number's written under C for catering.'

'I'll do no such thing. Give it a rest, Shirl, and go to sleep. Take one of your pills if it helps.'

'I don't want to take a pill. I don't want to sleep. Not until I know Colin is safe.'

She had sat there for an hour, maybe more, staring into space, as the floral wallpaper blurred and her vision jinked like old ciné-film.

And yet, amazingly, she had dozed, and, teasingly, in her sleep, Colin had come to her, he had stood over her in his old football kit and said, 'There, now, Mum, see, feel, I am alive and kicking.'

When she woke a second time, before first light, it was with feelings of confusion not of comfort, and she had hastened with beating heart along the landing to his room, to find that his bed had not been slept in.

So the hopeless dawn found her, lying thus, with her hands crossed on her breast, with her mind flitting from her choice of outfit, to the order of service, to the filling of sandwiches (because a funeral, like everything else in life, must be approached wardrobe first), until the alarm clock beeped gratuitously and the day officially began.

She was in the kitchen making tea when he came home. She heard the sound of an engine, the slam of a car door, heard him stomping about on the doormat, making a huge production of wiping his feet.

'Colin?' She gave a strangled cry, clasped her hands in an attitude of prayer. But her overwhelming sense of sweet relief was swiftly displaced by a somewhat inappropriate sense of anti-climax.

'Yes.'

He came in looking sheepish, as well he might.

'I've been out of my mind with worry. Where have you been?'

'I . . .' He took a step towards her, staring fixedly at the teaspoon which she wagged at him. Then he raised his eyes to her, and shrugged his shoulders, spread his hands, palm upwards, much as he used to do as a child when he'd been dabbling around in ditches while she went practically insane with fear for him. And all he said was 'Sorry.'

'You were with *her*. Don't try to deny it.'

'I wasn't about to.'

'And never a thought for me.'

'Mum, I –'

'You promised me, Colin. You gave me your word.'

'I did no such thing.' He swelled up with sheer indignation before her startled gaze; he turned quite red, and looked as if he might burst. 'I gave you no promise. I care very much for Sandra.'

'You scarcely know her.'

'She's a lovely person.'

'She's loose, if you ask me?'

'I don't ask you, actually.'

'To allow you to stay with her. To share her bed.'

'She *said* you didn't like her.'

'So you discussed me, did you?' Shirley turned away and nipped her lip, as she dropped teabags, uncounted, into the pot. 'You had a good laugh at my expense. I am the subject of your pillow talk.'

She began to cry softly; her voice was choked with tears.

'Please don't,' implored Colin, unmanned. He took a step towards her, but dared not touch her. 'I love you,' he offered meekly. 'That will never change.'

'If you loved me, you would listen to me. You would be guided by me. I'm only thinking of you.' Shirley Clarke never told a lie: at worst, you could say, she made up the truth as she went along.

'You have to let me live my life.'

'Even if I see you making a mistake.'

'Even then, yes. Even *if*.' Colin leant against the work top, propped his weary head on one bunched fist, while with the other hand he played with the breadbin, opening, closing, opening the lid, which had a sort of up-and-over mechanism, like the garage door.

'Your generation is so different from ours,' his mother admonished him. 'We would never have gone against our parents' wishes.'

'No?' This ran counter to everything Colin had heard or read about the children of the sixties, who, according to mythology, had been rebels to a man. But then, Shirley Clarke was untypical. By

175

no stretch of the imagination could he picture her in mini skirt, or kinky boots, or with a transfer of a daisy on her cheek. The very idea made him smile, and he felt cheered. He had been sick at the prospect of this confrontation, but it came to him that he could handle it, he could handle mother.

'It's not the end of the world, you know,' he told her fondly. 'I've got a girlfriend, that's all. Now, let's have some tea and toast, shall we? Then I'll get ready for work.'

———————— • ————————

'What's up with you?' demanded Ivy Burston, who was shining the brasses at the kitchen table, looking, as ever, as if she were sucking on blotting-paper (her mouth had a peculiar, wry, dry, disagreeable, downward skew). She had lined up the ornaments, in descending order of size, on sheets of newspaper, and was going at a tall umbrella stand with Duraglit and vigour, setting up a powerful vibration, an agitated metallic clamour.

There was something increasingly exaggerated, a touch of burlesque about her busy-ness: she seemed almost to be acting out the tasks of mopping, sweeping, dusting, polishing, to be miming housework, performing for Kayleigh's benefit, with the aid of props, an elaborate charade of the kind that occasions ever more wild guesses ('Little Women', 'Good Wives', 'A Broom of One's Own', 'It's a kitchen sink drama!' 'Abelard and Elbow Grease').

'Nothing,' mumbled Kayleigh, behind her hand. 'Leave me alone.' And her eyes wandered excursively over the dresser, taking in the plates, the cups, the cow jug, the Oxo tin, the cracked Victorian cheese dish. . .

'Well, pardon me for asking. Now, since you say there's nothing wrong, you can stop mooching around like a lovesick chicken, and put the kettle on, you can make us a nice cup of tea. Always supposing, of course . . . ' Ivy laid aside her polishing rag for a moment, and she shared with her stretched reflection in the burnished brass a look of commiseration, she sympathised with her heavily burdened self. 'I mean, assuming it isn't too much trouble.'

'No trouble.'

Kayleigh slouched to the sink. She turned the tap with unnecessary force, so the water washed over, spattering the tiled floor. 'Oh, balls!' she said feelingly.

'Now, now, watch your language,' Ivy reproved her with uncharacteristic mildness. 'And have a care, will you? What are you trying to do, flood us out?'

The woman seemed, notwithstanding her scolding, if Kayleigh did not imagine it, to be *slightly* more kindly disposed towards her this Friday morning. Perhaps, in spite of herself, she was warming to the Rawlingses' house-guest. Then again, thought Kayleigh, furtively checking out Ivy Burston's sour expression, perhaps she was not. 'It was an accident,' she protested, dropping her head and muttering into her chest, the usual justification. Curtains of hair closed about her like the curtains of a confessional upon a miserable sinner.

'Well, think what you're about, that's all.'

Kayleigh filled the kettle and plugged it in. She drifted across to the dresser, dragged open the drawer, dipped in for the teastrainer, drifted back to the sink. 'Don't strain yourself,' said Ivy with heavy sarcasm, intending no pun.

For answer, Kayleigh merely sighed a deep and put-upon sigh, then, without a word of explanation, and with her hand still muffling her mouth, she wandered out of the kitchen. After a minute or two, Ivy heard the ting of the telephone in the sitting-room and supposed that the sly little madam was making calls.

The kettle worked itself up to a belligerent boil; steam jiggled the lid. The good-for-nothing child must have filled it to the brim. Huffing, Ivy went to see to it. 'If you want something doing,' she said painedly, addressing her words to the ceiling, to the heavens, 'then do it yourself.'

She made tea for two and was bearing it to the table when the frontdoor slammed. 'Of all the . . . !' And where would she be off to, the cheeky bitch? To the post? To the pub? To the village shop for more fags? Well, good riddance to bad rubbish, let her go!

Kayleigh had been more than usually disagreeable today, more than usually uncivil. 'Hangdog' was the word that came to mind. She was so obviously bored here, and restless, and peevish, she would probably take herself off back to London any time.

It occurred to Ivy Burston, then, that the girl might have walked out, she might have slung her hook, absconded. She went so far as to rehearse in her head the conversation she must have with Dee Rawlings about it ('Yes, yes, that's right, just upped and offed without the courtesy of a goodbye'). But it seemed too much to hope. And, yes, in fact it *was* too much. Kayleigh had gone no farther than the bus stop.

She had always feared the dentist, she had not been near or by one for donkey's years. The shrill whistle of the drill beyond the waiting-room wall and the antiseptic smell were enough to turn your stomach. But she couldn't go about like some toothless hag, with a gap at the front, and her speech all mangled, she couldn't let Jamie see her this way, she would have to get herself fixed up. To this end, she had leafed through the Yellow Pages, and had made herself an emergency appointment; she had written time and place in blue felt-tip on the back of her hand.

There was a bus that would take her to Tunbridge Wells, a single-decker job, she knew because she'd seen it. But the service was diabolical, it was worse than London Transport. Thirty, forty, fifty minutes later, she was still hanging about there, shuffling her feet, checking her watch in exasperation, and jigging the pushchair, making soothing, sing-song noises to quiet the grizzling Ben.

'Oh, bloody hell,' she said to him, squinting at the sky, at clouds bloated to bursting, 'it's only going to rain. That's all I need.' There was no seat here, or any shelter, except that afforded by a high stone wall, furred with sandy lichen, which nibbled at her cardigan when she leant against it. She was, as she put it to herself, pissed off rotten; she was almost tempted to go back to Foxholes and to bed.

But comes the hour, comes the van.

'Hey!'

A tatty Hiace with rust-scabbed paint and with a ladder on the roof puttered past her and pulled up at the kerb. 'Hi, there,' the driver called to her, leaping out and strolling towards her. She recognised at once the saucy beggar she had met on her walk with Sandra last weekend – the one with the long hair, who was probably some kind of didicoi, some kind of so-called traveller, and whose eyes had been all over her, licking around her like flame.

They were all over her again now, it seemed to her. They had a curious, intrusive quality which made her fidgety with ill ease. She suspected him of mentally undressing her, of visualising her without her clothes. She did not guess that he was looking even deeper, that he was seeing clear through to the core of her.

'Have you had your fucking three penn'orth?' she asked with studied hauteur, and her mouth ran away at the corners with displeasure.

'What are you waiting here for?' he asked unabashed, as if he had not heard the jibe. And now he was laughing at her, although not unkindly; those eyes were crinkled with mirth.

'For Christmas. What d'you think?' she told him coldly, trying once more to cut him down to size. 'Not that it's any business of yours.'

'That's all right, then. So long as you're not waiting for a bus.'

'And what if I am? What is it to you?'

'Nothing to me, ducks. But it'll do you no good to stand here.'

'Why not? It's a bus stop isn't it? It says so, see, on the sign up there, in sodding great big letters. B - us, St - op,' she read it aloud to him.

'Well, you've missed it, you know. The B - us. It went at nine o'clock from this St - op.'

'Then I'll wait for the next one,' she informed him, and, sniffing, dismissing him, she averted her gaze.

'Next one's not until tomorrow morning.'

'What?'

'There's only the one into town, you see. And the one out again at three o'clock.'

'Well, what kind of a service is that?'

'Not a great one, to be sure.'

She dropped her head, feeling suddenly, overwhelmingly ugly and battered and beaten. She saw herself, in that fleeting instant, as a pathetic victim and a hopeless case. This trip to the dentist, this one modest attempt at self-determination, had been doomed before it started. Yet again, those faceless pen-pushers, the men in suits had been working against her. Once again the bloody system had shafted her. She had been thwarted by a timetable. She might as well lie down right here on the cold pavement and let life roll over her. She might as well give up. 'Why does nobody complain?' she asked peevishly.

'Ah, but they *do*.' She appeared to him like a broken doll. She was so wan, with shadows under her eyes. The missing tooth lent her a sweet, childish aspect. Intuitively he sensed her despair, and he endeavoured to cajole her out of it. 'In fact, it's what they do best around here. They lead the world in indignation. They could complain for England, some of our local ladies. They could bore on for Britain. They'd carry the day.'

'Uh?' she asked, uncomprehending, wrinkling her nose at him, fluting her lip to reveal the unsightly space in her teeth.

'Oh, nothing, nothing. I was only kidding.'

'The thing is,' she confessed, not because she was any more drawn to him, just because he was *there*, because there was nobody else, 'I have to get into town to see the dentist.'

'And the good news is that I can take you. I can give you a lift all the way. I have to go in myself to buy some paint. White with a touch of peach for Mrs Venables. Hop in and I'll hand the little fellow up to you.'

Without further consultation, he bent to unstrap Ben from his buggy, and, in a practised, unabashed manner, lifted him out. 'What's your name, young man?' he said to him. 'Speak up now. Tell old Charlie. Don't be shy.' Such a strange and unresponsive mite he'd never seen. Ben would not trade smiles with him as other children do, but regarded him dubiously, his wispy brows knitting. He was heavy, literally, and lumpen, weighed down with his own sadness.

'He doesn't talk,' said Kayleigh, dithering, uncertain. This guy was a bit too familiar for her liking, he came on too strong. He could be a sex maniac, for all she knew of him. He could be a rapist. He was a virtual stranger, and, as Margaret had always cautioned her, 'Don't never take lifts from strangers.'

On the other hand . . . On the other hand, she needed to see the dentist, to fill the bloody great hole in her face. And she had no other means of getting there, of getting patched up. And – wouldn't you bleeding know it? – it was starting to piss down; she was pelted with fat, wet drops of rain.

'I'm Charlie Horscroft, by the way,' he said, as she hauled herself up into the cab beside his silly, floppy, friendly dog, who budged up obligingly, turned a skittery circle on the torn plastic bench seat, and flopped down again.

The interior of the van smelt powerfully of paint, of varnish and thinners. 'Phew-ee!' said Kayleigh rudely, and fanned her face with her hand.

'Alli-oop.' Charlie bundled her boy-child up to her and she received him unceremoniously on to her lap as if he were no more than a bag of washing. He went around to the back of the van, opened the door and slid the buggy in. 'I'm not sure if this is altogether legal,' he said, his voice resonating in the tinny space. 'I've got a feeling kids are meant to travel in the back seat. To be strapped in or something.'

'There *is* no back seat.' Kayleigh stated the obvious.

'No, but you could maybe sit on the floor and hold him.'

'*I'm* not sitting on no floor. It's all greasy. And, for your information, these jeans were clean on this morning.'

'As you wish, ma'am.' The rear door slammed. The van walls hummed. In a moment, Charlie appeared at the driver's side and hopped up behind the wheel. 'Get outa here, Pol, and give us some room.' He nudged his dog, who shot obediently over the back of the seat and ran up and down yipping. When he turned the key, the engine wheezed, it coughed productively, came to life.

'I didn't catch your name,' he said, revving hard, raising his voice to be heard above the roar.

'I didn't drop it.'

'And of which particular charm school are you a graduate?'

'Huh?' She pulled that face again, crinkling her nose, pleating her top lip, disclosing a dental catastrophe.

'Listen, I'll tell you what, let's start again. I say, "I'm Charlie Horscroft". And you say, "I'm delighted to meet you, Charlie Horscroft. I am the Duchess of Dagenham and this is my son Augustus." '

'Horscroft? I've heard that name.'

'I dare say you have. So you are . . . ?'

'I'm Kayleigh, okay?' She gave the information out like pocket money to a grabby child. 'And Ben is Ben.' She seemed about to offer a hand, which was scuffy and red, and had blue hieroglyphs inked upon it, but then thought better of it and withheld it.

'Kayleigh? That's an unusual name,' he remarked disingenuously, because he knew, of course, who she was, he had heard all about her from his mum, who had heard it from Ivy Burston.

'Not really.' She snuffled juicily. 'There were three at my school.'

'And where was that?'

'You ask a lot of questions.'

'I know. It's a fault of mine. I'm incurably nosy. I'm sorry. Take no notice of me.' He dabbed at the misted windscreen with the back of his hand, jiggled the column change, engaged first gear, and they moved off.

For the first few miles they travelled in noisy silence, exchanging no words, as the wipers went squelch, thud, squelch, thud, and the rain rattled ceaselessly on the tin roof.

Charlie Horscroft, eh? He was, Kayleigh told herself, as she stole a sideways glance, not bad looking. Yeah, she had to admit he had *something*. He was sort of well made, slight of build and yet strong. His eyes were the same charcoal grey as his sweatshirt, they were dark, yet they flickered with their own peculiar light beneath the strong arch of his brow. His features were rather fine; the skin stretched taut over prominent cheekbones. His mouth was mobile and expressive, it was very suggestive: it brought thoughts of hot, wet, deep, sexual kisses, unbidden, unlooked-for, to mind.

But he was not at all her type, her ideal man. He was no Jamie Rawlings. He lacked that special style, lacked class. She could not picture him at the wheel of a Porsche, with a portable phone to his ear. She could not picture him scented and suited, with his shirt nicely pressed and his shoes nicely shone. She could not picture him showing her the high life, the way Jamie did in her wild, wild imaginings.

The windows were very steamed up now, she could see almost nothing out of her side but the occasional black shape of a tree. Oh, dear! She wrapped her arms around Ben, rested her cheek on his warm, sweet, noddy head, and gave herself over to contemplation of her secret pain.

The aching and yearning was doing her head in. It was almost more than she could bear. For how long would she have to endure it? The five days since she first saw him felt more like five months. How many more day-months must she wait?

She had had an idea the other night, a wheeze which, by some mysterious alchemy, had firmed up rapidly to diamond-hard conviction. Fate, she believed, had brought her here to Kent. Their meeting – hers and Jamie's – had been written in the stars. And she, who had depended all her life on other people, was counting now, with no more or less presumption, upon Destiny.

Charlie, who saw everything, saw mother hug child, he saw one small, solitary human being clinging to another, seeking solace, he saw a sort of inverted dependency, mother love gone arse upwards, and he felt a surge of pure and unexpected tenderness.

She was a strange person, this Kayleigh, so frail and fierce and furious. Years ago he had found a kitten tied up in a cloth shoe bag in a ditch. He had taken it home and fed it with a dropper until it was strong enough to stand and could feed itself. It had been smaller than his hand, yet as brave as a tiger; it would take on all comers with tooth and claw. Spitting neatly, spitefully, it would terrify the boxer dog next door. Sparky, Charlie had christened the kitten. And, at his mother's insistence, he had let him go to a good home. There was a hint of old Sparky about Kayleigh, Charlie told himself now. And he grinned at the notion, with genuine, generous affection.

'So how are you liking it at the Rawlings place?' he enquired conversationally.

She brought her head up and regarded him sharply. 'It's all right,' she told him stiffly, wondering what he had heard about her (did he know all her bleeding business?).

'Nice house, Foxholes.'

'Uh-huh.'

'I have to do some work there next week.'

'You do?'

'Or the week after. Some tarting up, some tiling, in one of the bathrooms. It'll take me a few days.'

'I may not be there then. Not the week after next,' she said distantly.

'You won't?'

'Well, I shall have to see. They want me to stay, but I've not decided. It's dead boring here in the country. There's nothing to do. Not like London.'

'What do you do, then? in London?'

'We-ell . . . ' She made a shrugging movement with one shoulder, a motion of rejection, of closing out. 'Maybe go bowling, or down the boozer, that kind of thing.'

'You must get a bit lonely in that big place on your own. Especially at night.'

Uh-oh, thought Kayleigh wearily. Uh-*oh*, here it comes! Next he'll be offering to share my bed.

But no such offer was forthcoming. Instead, he said, 'Still, it's a safe old house. It's very secure.'

'I suppose so.' She covered her mouth, spoke into her cupped hand. 'There was this horrible noise last night – this, like, screaming.'

'That'll be your fox,' he said knowingly. 'Just a silly old fox, though he sounds like the devil himself.'

'That's all it is?'

'I reckon so.'

'I nearly wet myself, I was so scared.'

'But you have your baby with you for a cuddle. And you have the cat.'

'Oedipuss.'

He slowed and drew up at a junction and, as the traffic-lights changed from amber to red, he reached over and took her left hand in his, drawing it towards him. 'Come on, give,' he said firmly, when she made a tight ball of it and snatched it away. 'Show me a minute, will you? It's the address of your dentist I'm after, time and place, not your body, Okay?'

So she offered the back of her hand and he read it. 'Right you are. I know just where that is. And you're dead on time. I'll drop you outside. Then I'll pick you up in . . . what do you think? Half an hour? Or three-quarters? I'll pick you up, drive you back.'

'You don't have to.'

'It's no trouble.'

'Well . . . Okay,' she grudgingly assented.

'Oedipuss,' he mused, as the traffic began to move away. 'Ridiculous name that is, if you ask me.' Flipping his indicator, he moved to the crown of the road. 'He was Sparky', he revealed, 'when I had him. Good old Sparks! Do give him my regards when you next see him.'

———————— • ————————

'Mrs Atkins. Audrey. *Good* morning to you.' Jamie Rawlings

sounded very chirpy, very spry today. You could search far and wide, his tone implied, you could go to the ends of the earth and not find a sandboy, or a Larry, as happy as he.

Francine, who was standing over him fluttering papers at him, saw him rock back in his chair, she saw him make expansive, twirly motions with his free hand, she saw the very embodiment of *joie de vivre*, even as his insides seemed to liquefy and to run down into his boots. And she did not for one moment guess how strong was the urge in him to thrust her away, to knock her flying.

'That's right, yes, it's James here. Mabey Estates.' Up went his hand, then down flat on the top of his head, to smooth his sleek, pomandered hair.

'These need to be signed,' said Francine, shoving the papers under his nose.

'Me? Ah, tremendously well. And yourself?' He picked up a paperclip; rotated it between finger and thumb.

'Then I can catch the midday post,' said Francine.

'A nasty head cold? I'm sorry to hear it, my dear.' Tap went the paperclip on the desktop.

'You did say they were urgent,' Francine pressed him. 'You said to get them typed before lunch.'

'The time of year? I'm sure you're right. They do say the change in the weath– Audrey, my dear, could you just hang on one sec . . .' He put the call on 'hold' and snarled at his secretary, 'Will you bugger off?'

'Charming!' Francine went flouncing back to her own desk, she flung herself into her chair, tossed the letters into the bin, poked her tongue out at him, made antlers of her hands. What was his problem, anyway? She could see no reason why he could not read and sign his letters while he spoke on the phone. *She* could complete the coffee-break crossword in *Mia* magazine, she could read a short story, read the *Express* from cover to cover, *and* do her nails, while she was on to her mum, or to her best friend Elaine who had boyfriend troubles. Was it *her* fault if the great Jamie Rawlings, the Big I Am, could not walk and chew gum at the same time?

'Have I any news for you?' Jamie was saying. 'Audrey, have *I* got news for you!' Now he drew himself in, he huddled over the phone, he cuddled up to the receiver. 'I am the bearer of glad tidings. Those nice de Lannoy people have made us a rather handsome offer. One hundred and fifteen thou.'

Francine rolled her eyes, she opened her mouth and poked a finger down her throat to show how sick he made her.

Chitter-chatter went the Atkins woman on the other end of the line, chitter-chitter-chatter, as Jamie bunched a fist, as his knuckles blenched.

'I'm sorry you feel that way,' he said with the merest tremor. He unfurled his fingers and studied his nails. 'You know, it's quite a thing, in these troubled times, to get within a sniff of the asking price . . . No, well, I do see what you're saying. But Audrey . . . Yes, but . . . Audrey, Audrey, Audrey.' He patted the air placatingly. 'People are settling for twenty, thirty, even forty thousand less than they asked. They're taking half what they might have done five years ago. We are in the depths of recession, in financial crisis. And the Lannoys are cash buyers, remember, who are not even proposing to commission a full survey of the property – which can of worms, quite frankly, is far better left unopened. Still, if you feel so strongly, I shall see if I can edge them up. What say we ask them to split the difference; to offer one-seventeen-five?'

Chitter-chitter-chat.

Jamie took a deep breath, he filled out like an inflatable doll, became open, expansive once more. 'Right you are then. I'll get on to them this minute. Keep everything crossed till you hear back from me. Cheerio, now. Oh! Whoa! One more thing. I was forgetting. They would like to talk to you about some of the contents. It's a matter for you, and for them, not for me, but it should bring you in a nice bit on top.'

Then, 'Silly old bag,' he muttered as he slammed the phone down. 'Stupid, avaricious old trout.'

'Who was that?' Francine wanted to know.

'M.Y.O.B.'

'What?'

'Mind your own bloody business, Francine, and get on with that photostatting I gave you.'

'*Ooh*, we are in a crab this morning, aren't we?'

'I am *not* in a crab, Miss. You would try the patience of a saint.'

'I shan't get your lunch for you unless you're nice to me. *Or* make you coffee.'

'You'll do whatever I tell you. In fact, you can make some coffee now. And in future kindly do not interrupt me when I'm on to a client.'

'It's not part of my job, you realise? It's not in my contract that I have to make coffee.'

'You won't *have* a contract if you don't shape up.'

'Says who?'

'Says I.'

'*You* can't sack me. I'm employed by Mr Mabey, and *he's* got the hots for me, in case you haven't noticed.'

'That's ridiculous.'

'He has. He calls me poppet. He says I remind him of his niece.'

'He has the hots for his niece as well, does he?'

'Don't be filthy.'

'I'm not.'

'You're mental.' She retrieved the letters from the bin and dusted them with a tissue. 'Are you going to sign these or aren't you?'

'Very well. Bring them here.'

'Because it's no skin off my nose.'

'I dare say not.' He beckoned her over, took the letters from her, made a visor of one hand, and perused them.

If only she would not stand so close, smelling of Diorella, peering over him, always prying! Had no one ever told her that perfume should be subtle? Had no one told her not to poke her nose into others' affairs? 'She didn't accept the offer, then?' she asked.

'Who didn't? What offer?'

'Whoever you were speaking to. Mrs Aubrey.'

'Atkins.'

'That's it. Atkins.'

'She's being a bit bloody minded, that's all,' he confided, for fear of appearing secretive. 'She's digging her little heels in, the way they all do. But if I can edge the buyer up a bit, I'm sure she'll budge. We all have to be realistic.'

'It'll be the first thing we've sold in ages.'

'Don't talk daft. We moved a very nice place in Brancaster

Road only this Monday.' He signed the letters with a flourish. 'And I think I have something to suit the Atkins couple, I'm going to drop round there with the details.'

'Why drop in? Why not post them? I'll do it if you want.'

'You'll do what I tell you. Now make us that coffee. Then look me out the bumf about Forlorns.'

'Eh?'

'The wrinklies' retreat. The twilight zone.'

'Oh, *Fairlawns*, you mean. The retirement places.'

'The retirement places. Make me a folder. We'll present it nicely. It could be right up their street.'

'Anything else while I'm at it, Sir? Polish your shoes? Massage your ego?'

'No, just button your lip.'

'Well, thank Crunchie it's Friday, that's all I can say.'

'I wish it were.'

'Eh?'

'I wish it *were* all you could say.'

'What you doing this weekend?'

'The usual, I imagine.' He began aimlessly to tidy up, to rearrange documents at random into piles, as if by ordering his desk he might also order his emotions. 'Humping my girlfriend silly,' he added with forced jocularity.

'Fancy yourself, don't you?'

'Not half as much as she does. She can't keep her hands off me.'

'You're staying in town, then?' Francine mocked. 'Not going to the country seat for a spot of shootin' and fishin'?'

'Not this time, no. My people have some ghastly little oik staying with them, a lame duck my mother has rescued. I shan't go down again for as long as she's billeted on us.'

Suddenly Jamie felt weary. Sick to his stomach and exhausted. He screwed up his eyes, ground his knuckles into them. Everything was going precisely according to plan. Was it, perhaps, going *too* well? He would not sleep easy until it was all over; his nights would be troubled by terrible dreams; stress would play merry hell with his digestion.

There were moments such as this when he wondered if the game was worth the candle. There was still time to back out of the whole deal. Or was there?

'Look sharp,' he said tetchily, 'and sort out those details. Fairlawns, remember? Then coffee.'

'I thought you wanted coffee first.'

'Er, yup, yup, I do. Coffee now.'

He slid open his desk drawer and dipped in for the Rennies. And he told himself pettishly, reaching to the phone as it began to ring, I have to see the quack.

---------- • ----------

She knew he would be in touch with her. That was what made it so very different: the confidence, the certainty, this time. There was none of the old queasiness, none of the paralysing suppressed panic, as in the past, when only days of endless, accursed waiting would tell if she was embarked upon a grand affair, or had merely, foolishly, as usual, invested heart and soul in some futile enterprise, in just another loveless one-night stand.

Even so, when the phone rang, she felt the blood surge, felt her face burn, her nerve-endings bristle. Her hand shook perceptibly as she reached for the receiver. And the bright, impersonal 'hello' she summoned, was delivered as a breathless, abbreviated 'lo'.

'It's me,' said a familiar voice. 'How are you doing?'

'Oh, hello, Ali,' responded Sandra tonelessly, as her heart slowed, as the fizzling stopped.

'You sound really pissed-off. What's the matter? Got a hangover? Been crossed in love again? Ha ha!'

Sandra took a deep breath to steady herself, as a rush of unreasoning temper swept over her. How dare the silly cow ring now! Had she no insight, no imagination? She squeezed her eyes shut, squeezed her face like a wet rag. This was the trouble with Alison: she was utterly insensitive, and her timing was rotten. She was also one of those tedious people who are constantly metering their achievements against the failures of others. So long as Sandra weighed more, so long as she earned less, so long as she had smaller tits, a bigger waist, a heavier mortgage, heavier periods, heavier thighs, so long as she was manifestly, measurably inferior, their friendship was sustainable.

It would have given Ali no small satisfaction, now, to learn that her best pal had been stood up. Well, for once she would be disappointed. 'I'm fine,' Sandra assured her. 'I had a perfectly lovely night. I'll tell you all about it – but not now. As a matter of fact, I'm standing by for a call from someone else.'

'Anyone I ought to know about?'

'Just a client.' Sandra crossed her fingers, lest she be struck dumb for telling such outrageous lies. 'Look, Ali, we can talk later. In half an hour, maybe. Only this person, Mrs Gamlin, is supposed to be getting right back to me to discuss the menu for her daughter's birthday party tomorrow. It turns out one of her guests is food combining. And another is a vegan.' Then, overdoing it somewhat, she added, 'And another is watching her cholesterol.'

'That must be boring.'

'What must be?'

'Watching cholesterol. Still, I suppose it can't be any worse than watching *Neighbours*.'

'Oh, very amusing. You are a one! Look, I simply must get off the line, but I'll ring you soon, I promise. We'll have a nice long chat, a good old gossip, okay? Thanks a million for the loan of the dress, by the way.'

'Was it all right? Did it fit you?'

'Like a glove. It was perfect. Just the thing. I shall get it cleaned, of course, before I give it back.'

'Don't bother on my account. Keep it if you like. It's much too big for me, you see. That's why I thought it would do you. Listen, San, I have to dash. Cheerio. Be seeing you.'

Sandra had barely replaced the receiver when the telephone shrilled again, causing her to jump back as if the current had run through her.

'. . . lo.'

'Hello, sweetheart. How are you?'

'Oh. Hi, Mum. I'm great. Fine.' She beat her brow with the heel of her hand in sheer frustration. She half-believed her own story – the one about the vegan. About the food combiner, and the cholesterol-watcher. She half-believed she had been waiting for an urgent business call. Besides, she had to make a marinade.

'I'm so glad I caught you. I know you're frightfully busy these days, but I'd like you to come for Sunday lunch.'

'I'm not sure if I ca–'

'We'll eat at one o'clock, but I shall want you there for eleven to give me a hand. I thought we'd have something a little bit special. Better still, spend the weekend. Wouldn't that be nice? Drive down with us again on Friday night. I know Kayleigh would be glad of your company. She made a point of asking, when I spoke with her yesterday; she said . . . And, you know, I was rather touched by this. She said, "Will I see Sandie on Friday night?"'

'But I *can't*. Not for the whole weekend. I'm sure I told you, I'm doing a dinner party tomorrow in Fulham.'

'Sunday it will have to be, then. You're not working on Sunday, too, I take it? You don't have another booking?'

'Not an actual booking, no. But I do have other plans.'

'Cancel them, hm? Reschedule. Take a rain check. Be at Foxholes instead, that's my girl.'

'But I honestly . . .'

The urge to weep was almost irresistible. Tears prickled her eyes, she had to sniff them away. It's lack of sleep, she told herself, wiping her nose in the crook of her elbow. It has nothing to do with me and my mother, with the way she doesn't ever seem to hear me. Of course she doesn't mean to trivialise me; it's just her manner. I'm dead on my feet, that's what this is about.

'They're filming, you see. For the *Superwoman* series. You remember, I told you all about it? Scenes from family life. The four of us – or, rather, the five, as we now are.' Dee laughed delightedly. 'The Famous Five foregathered around the dining table. Won't that be fun?'

'Six,' Sandra corrected.

'Mm?'

'I said "six". We will be six, with Ben.' Will, not would. Thus, by her choice of tense, did she signal her capitulation.

'Ah, of course, if you count . . . Yes, six it is.'

'I'm not sure if I want . . . ' Sandra blurted. But how to say it? How to tell her mother, 'I don't want to be in the rotten telly programme'? How to explain, 'I love you, but I want no part of it'? How to say 'I am dying inside at the very prospect'? Well, there was no way, of course, without causing a row, so instead she asked, 'Then Jamie's going to be there?'

'Naturally.'

Oh, yes, naturally! Naturally! Jamie had already been asked.

'Get him to bring you,' Dee suggested. 'That would be jolly. Give him a buzz at the office and suggest it. He's there. I've just this minute spoken to him. He has a touch of indigestion. They work him too hard in that place. Anyway, I'm sure he'll pick you up if you ask nicely.'

'No, there's no need. I can drive myself. I'd rather.'

'Well, if you prefer your old jalopy to his souped-up sports car . . .'

'It will be easier, that's all. In case he wants to leave before me – or I before him.'

'It's up to you, of course. Yes, I do see your point. Always the practical one, Sandie. As you wish, then. *Ciao, ciao.*'

And for a second time, the phone went cold in her hand.

So that was the weekend written off. Oh, rats! Oh, come on Colin, *call me.*

He rang an hour later, when she was in the loo.

'I'd just gone for a pee,' she grumbled happily, and this time, when she screwed up her face, it was in secret exultation. Oh, joy, to hear his voice!

'I'm sorry I inconvenienced you.'

'That's quite all right.'

'I just wanted to ask . . .'

'Yes?' she prompted.

'How was it for you?' A joke – and not a joke.

'Not half bad,' she assured him, sensing his insecurity. 'And for you?'

'The same.'

'I'm glad of that.'

'Do you love me?' he dared to enquire.

'Mm-hm.'

'How much?'

'A bit. More than a bit.'

'That much, eh?'

There followed a few moments of not uncomfortable silence. Then he confessed, 'I've been walking around in a daze all morning.'

'Me too. I don't know if I'm coming or going.'

'I rolled back at the traffic lights, into a Peugeot. Didn't do any damage, but the guy took a dim view of it.'

'Can you blame him?'

"He called me names.'

'He didn't!'

'He did. He called me a big daisy and a great long drink of water.'

'How rude!'

'Yes, wasn't it? That's not how you regard me, is it?'

'Absolutely not, Colin.'

'You promise?'

'Hand on heart. I've never thought of you as . . . ' She began to giggle. 'As a great, long drink of water. Hey, how was it when you got home? How was your mum? Did she know you spent the night here?'

'She knew. She was distraught.'

'I'm sorry.'

'It's not your problem.'

'I suppose she thinks I led you astray?'

'You did.'

'I did not!'

'Yes you did. You seduced me.'

'What did she say?'

'Ah, well, you know . . .'

'I *don't* know. Talk me through it.'

'She said, "Cassio, I love thee; but never more be officer of mine." '

'Honestly?'

'Or words to that effect.'

'You mean she . . . ?'

'Banished me? Threw me out on my ear? No, not exactly. But she threatened to.'

'She wouldn't, would she? Ever? I just can't imagine it.'

'Not a chance. She did suggest that I treat the place like a hotel. She shoved some tea and toast at me, and said if I wanted any more I should ring for service.'

'That old routine!'

'She said I might like to sign the visitors' book.'

'Sarky, huh?'

'Ooh, dead sarky. And she said, after all she'd done for me . . .'

'Such a cliché.'

'The thing was . . .'

'Yes?'

'She kept crying. And I felt like shit.'

'Poor you!' Sandie sympathised. And then, with genuine if unexpected sympathy, 'Poor her!'

'This is the thing, you see. This is why I'm stuffed. Because she may be possessive and uptight and daft as a brush, but she is also my mum, and I love her.'

'Of course you do.'

'Then you see my predicament?'

'Very clearly.' And she thought: Already that woman is working against me. She will make it impossible for us if she can.

'However . . .'

'However?'

'However, I'll take care of this end.'

'Fine.'

'And you take care of that end.'

'There's nothing to take care of here, only me.'

'Then take care of yourself.'

'I intend to.'

'Can I see you tomorrow?'

'Yes. No. I mean, I'd love that, but I have to do a dinner. I told you.'

'You did. I forgot.' He made no attempt to conceal his disappointment.

'I could manage tonight,' she offered tentatively. 'I have a bit of prep to do. Marinating and so forth. But it won't take me long.'

'Er, tonight could be difficult. Fridays, I take Mum to Sainsbury's while Dad goes to snooker. We have our supper together.'

'Dinner à deux?' The weariness was on her again; the tears were too close to the surface. 'How cosy!'

'Sandie, Sandie, don't be like that, it's unworthy of you.'

'No. Sorry. That was uncalled for. Sorry, sorry, sorry.'

'I just felt, after last night, you know . . . '

'I understand.'

'Do you?'

'Sure.'

'I don't want to seem to . . .'

He sounded thoroughly miserable, now, thoroughly wretched. Sandie was mollified. She wanted to reach down the miles and hug him. 'Listen, don't worry,' she soothed him. 'There's no need to explain. You ought to help with the shopping, you ought to eat with your mum. There'll be plenty of other times for us.'

'Sunday, to name but one.'

'Ah, yes. Sunday. The thing is, I have to go to Kent, to lunch with my family. My mum is insisting. You see, you're not the only one who must do the dutiful bit.'

'Sunday evening, then. Would that be poss?'

'Sunday evening would be lovely. Could you ring me, do you think? In the afternoon. At my parents' place.'

'Give me the number. I shall write it on my heart.'

'Don't do that. You might lose it.'

'In my address book, then.'

'Ready? Have you got a pen?'

'It's poised and waiting.'

'Okay.' She rattled it off. 'Call me after midday. By then I should have some idea what time I'll be back in town.'

'You can depend upon it.'

'I shall.'

'Any other business?'

'I don't think so.'

'Until Sunday then. Byeee. I love you lots.'

For a few moments after he'd hung up, she stood there, motionless, with her head spinning, holding the phone to her, as if loath to break the connection.

This would be one in the eye for Alison. This was the real thing, it was love.

Then she went to make herself strong, black coffee, drank two big mugs of it, and took herself off to bed, to sleep the clock round.

———————— ✿ ————————

He never asked about the dentist, about her missing tooth or anything. 'All right?' he enquired neutrally, helping her up with Ben and buggy. And, 'Yeah,' she said neutrally in reply.

Then, perversely, Kayleigh felt piqued by his apparent loss of interest in her, and was moved to volunteer in crotchety tones.

'He's fixing me a bridge. A new tooth on a wire. It'll be ready next week. It will look just like the real thing, he says.'

'That's good.' Charlie narrowed his eyes as he made fine adjustments to the rear-view mirror, which she had knocked out of line with her head in the scramble with Ben.

'I can't wait to get it.'

'I'm sure.' He frowned in concentration as he indicated and moved out into the traffic. His mind was obviously on his driving, not on her.

'I feel a complete tit to be honest, with an effing great gap at the front – if you'll pardon my French.'

'It doesn't look so bad,' he assured her offhandedly, overtaking a cyclist in yellow PVC cape, giving him a wide berth. 'Don't worry about it.'

'I can come here on the bus,' she said after a moment's silence, which he declined to fill with conversation. 'Now that I know what time it goes.'

She had half expected him to offer to drive her, to make a special trip, but he merely nodded in reply.

Sod you, then, she thought huffily. If you don't fancy me, that's your look-out, mate, because there's plenty of others do.

She was ambivalent towards this young man, as she was towards the male sex in general, towards the beloved enemy. She resented, now, his seeming indifference, quite as much as she had earlier resented his questioning.

Kayleigh had a robust, a dauntless attitude to men in the street. She gave them as good as she got. She could better cope with their unwanted attentions than she could with their teasing inattention. (If there was one thing more unnerving than walking past a building site of jeering, whistling workers, it was walking past in eerie silence.) She liked to know where she stood.

In the same way, she would have liked, at this moment, to know where she stood with Charlie Horscroft, who had mysteriously gone cold on her. Was he playing a funny game with her? Did he want to give her one, or didn't he?

Probing the space in her teeth with the tip of her tongue, she stared dumbly, glumly out of the window, as the road raced past a garden centre, as it swooped under a railway bridge, and swerved up a hill. Very suddenly town gave way to countryside. It had stopped raining, thank goodness. A pale sun shone, chill as the fridge light, through a chink in the white clouds. The curtains of mist had lifted upon a scene of sodden grass and weeping woodland.

There was something oddly lovely about this dismal vista. And there was a sense of superiority, of exalted status, in sitting up high, peering down. She could see over walls and fences, into fields and orchards, into paddocks where the horses stood, dejected, hanging their heads, breathing steam. She could see on to gardens, and in through their lamplit windows, see people moving around behind the glass, like characters in a soap opera, acting out their lives, with the sound turned off.

Little by little, the anger, the sourness, left her. She felt almost tranquillised, lulled into a dream state, fuddled by fumes from paint-soaked rags, soothed by the sound of the engine, the hiss of the wheels on wet tarmac.

The journey took them off the main road and on to a narrow lane. They crested a hill and ran down through a water-splash with a satisfying whoosh. They made stately progress along the straight, and Charlie, who had been holding off until he sensed this softening in her, chose this moment to throw her a smile. Caught off her guard, she smiled back.

But next minute she was up in arms, as an oncoming truck forced them over, so they ran right alongside the squeaking hedgerow and came to a skidding halt.

'Wanker!' she mouthed in fury, twisting in the seat to make graphic masturbating gestures at the offending driver.

'Kayleigh, Kayleigh.' Charlie covered her lewdly motioning fist with his hand, forced it down on to the seat and subdued it there. 'Don't do your nut,' he said easily.

'But he almost shoved us into the ditch,' she protested in such dudgeon that he laughed out loud. He was constantly amazed by other people's capacity for outrage. His own, by comparison, was very limited. Certain things, it was true, made his hackles rise. Robin redbreast in a cage and all that stuff. But the piggishness of other motorists was par for the course, it was all in a day's work. Let these idiots try to prove their manhood if they must; he was secure in his own. 'My Greg would have had him,' she boasted, as if to taunt him. 'He wouldn't of let him get away with that.'

'Your Greg?'

'My boyfriend. Well, he *was* my boyfriend till I left him and came here.'

'Bit of a hard man, is he?'

She wasn't sure she liked his tone. He didn't sound duly impressed. 'He's useful, you know?'

' "Useful", eh?' He puckered his forehead. Would this explain the missing tooth? The faint umber of a bruise on her cheek? 'Was that why you had to get out?' he quizzed her. 'Was he a bit too "useful" around the house? Did he knock you about?'

'It wasn't always like that,' she said defensively. 'We had some great times.'

'Still, he roughed you up?'

'He was very jealous, you know how it is. Not that it's any concern of yours.'

'No. I'm sorry.' He made a small, conciliatory, conjuring movement, a smoothing of the air with his palm. 'It's no concern of mine.'

Yet it *did* concern him. It appalled him. He could not bear to think that anyone should do violence to this ferocious, fragile, stroppy, soppy little person. There was something about her that touched him profoundly. It tore at him to imagine what she had been through, and to what she might return. Not just for her own sake, but for the sake of her strange, solemn baby, she must never, ever go back. He banged his head down on the steering-wheel, then brought it up and grinned at her appealingly. 'I'm sorry. I didn't mean to . . . I promise I won't press you. Can we say no more about it?'

'Fairy nuff,' she agreed magnanimously.

'We'll talk about something else, shall we?' he proposed, and he edged the van forward, out of the thorny clutches of the hedge. 'Change the subject, eh?'

'All right.' She chewed on her lip, considering, then said, 'What do you think about abortion?'

'I don't . . .' He had been going to say, he didn't care to generalise.

'I could of had one when I fell for him,' she nodded vaguely at Ben, indicating with her chin the top of his downy head. 'My

Mum said I should, only I couldn't do it. I don't believe in it – still, that's me.'

'I expect you're glad. I mean, now that you've got him.'

'Oh, yes, I suppose so. I wouldn't be without him,' she said mechanically, without emotion.

No one has ever loved her properly, he told himself. No one has ever looked after her. And unless she is properly loved and looked after, she won't love and look after her baby. Not properly.

And it was there and then, without a word, and with circumspection, that he appointed himself Kayleigh Roth's guardian angel.

———————— • ————————

Nancy Wilkins gathered up the papers on her desk, she tap-tap-tapped them into a neat sheaf and slipped them, with self-conscious efficiency, with an air of finality, into the cardboard folder.

She had done all she could for today. She had dealt with the routine letters, the requests for leaflets or for information. She had referred people on to appropriate agencies – to the doctor or debt counsellor, to social services, to marriage guidance – she had passed the proverbial buck.

She had typed out Edie's terse, no-nonsense responses, which were, as ever, perfectly sound, if shot through with fatalism. (So life is no rose garden, she seemed to say. Whoever promised you a rose garden?)

Now, what was the time? Five past four. Dee and Edie were out of the office at the weekly editorial meeting (or 'conference' as it had come to be known since Clare Constantine arrived). Dee had yet to address herself to the trickier correspondence which had been mounting up all week. This was understandable: she had had a lot on her mind, what with the television programme; she hadn't had a moment to herself. None the less, it was a source of concern for Nancy, to whom those letters represented so much more than a mere pile of papers. People had poured out their woes to Dee Rawlings. Some of them were in parlous straits, they could be suicidal, they needed urgent prescriptions, words of wisdom, words of kindness and consolation.

Perhaps, Nancy thought, she could help in some way to lighten Dee's load at this difficult time. She would go through everything again, to see if there were any problems to which she might, after all, be equal. She would rough out possible replies and hand them to Dee for her approval. Or, failing that, she could send holding letters, she could write and say hang on, don't give up, help is on its way.

She took the file for signatures through and laid it in Dee's 'pending' tray. She removed the unanswered mail from the 'in' tray and bore it back to her work station. And there she sat with her head in her hands, wading into the Slough of Despond.

Oh, it was terrible what some folk must endure! It was all in here, in black and white: incest, infidelity, loneliness, guilt, obsessive jealousy, abject fear, financial hardship, homelessness, racial persecution, rejection, illness, addiction, death. . . And, in the short time that she had worked at *Mia*, she had seen it grow worse, seen recession reap a terrible harvest.

The truth dawned finally, belatedly on Nancy – and wasn't this what Edie, the realist, was always telling her? – that there was only so much you could hope to do for your fellow human beings; that some people were beyond help, some problems intractable; that no one could play God.

Dee must be aware of this, of course, though she made very light of the matter. She must know the limits of her influence and expertise. She must know that a single side of A4 bond would not serve to paper over all the cracks in someone's life. Her breezy matter-of-factness must, therefore, be a kind of front, a cover. It was her . . . Nancy, pondering it, came up with the phrase 'bedside manner'.

This was, when you came to think of it, the secret of Dee's huge success. She never dealt in despair, or in the deferment of hope that maketh the heart sick, but held out a promise for happiness ever after. She had an admirable can-do approach, an ebullience, an optimism which inspired. She had answers for the unanswerable, help for the helpless, she had opinions, she had those certainties for which the human race was hot. She said 'Do this, do that', when lesser mortals, fainter hearts, might simply shrug and say 'Well, *I* don't know, don't ask me.'

Dee would not sit agonising, hour after hour, over the case of Rachel K, for instance, whose little girl just might not be her husband's. Should she, Rachel asked here, tell him the truth? To which Dee would reply yes, or no, as the mood took her. She would pause for no more than a moment, with her eyes raised to the ceiling, considering, before saying that confession was good for the soul – or that all truths were not to be told.

Then, given that there was no absolute right or absolute wrong, and given that Rachel would probably, as Edie always said, do whatever she wished in the end, it maybe didn't matter what one said – so long as one said something.

The thing was, Nancy decided, to give every problem your best shot, to bring to bear upon it a cool head, common sense, compassion. You had to ask yourself where lay the most happiness for the most people.

With this in mind, and with a certain diffidence, she considered the dilemma of Rachel. 'You have a beautiful daughter,' she wrote in Dee's style, stern but kind, 'you have a loving and devoted husband. If your guilt drives you to destroy all this, how much more guilty will you feel? Now, dearie, this is what you're going to have to do. . .'

CHAPTER

—————— • ——————

9

The wind was up before anyone that Sunday morning. Charlie Horscroft woke to hear it skirling in the chimney cavity, in the black and silted lung of his living, breathing bachelor house. The side gate had been creaking and banging monotonously for the past hour, as though unseen hands were working it, trying to wrench it off its hinges, and he could no longer exclude these sounds from his consciousness.

He brought with him, out of sleep, some useless, incoherent scraps of memory, the remnants of a gratifying dream. He had been with a girl, with a woman, but could not recall her face, only a kind of teasing after-image, a subliminal impression recorded in the blinking of an eye. The sensations were somehow all still in him – the melting warmth, the oneness, the fierce devotion which can attend upon the sex act and beatify it – but the subject of his ardour had flown. There she was, gone.

His mood of euphoria was rapidly displaced by something far less soothing, by sexual frustration, an unsettling condition. He felt a sense of real desolation, felt the absence of his dream partner, he missed this figment as if she were flesh. Strange to think that nothing had actually happened, while he still felt the glow of it, felt its imprint on his skin. If only this wonderful nothing would happen again!

He lay for a while with his eyes closed, hoping that sleep

would reclaim him, then, impatient with himself, he threw back the quilt, cast a disparaging glance at his tumescent state, and went at once to look out of the window, to see what havoc the gale had wreaked. But the sky was still a deep and dusky lavender, streaked with cloud. It would not be truly light till long past seven, for these were the final, fugitive days of so-called British Summer Time, and he could barely discern across the choppy meadows the black and huddled form of the woodland.

His old army greatcoat was slung across a chair. He shrugged it on over his nakedness, relishing the cold as a kind of counter-irritant, and went downstairs to make tea.

Polly exhibited her usual unalloyed joy at seeing him, grovelling at his bare feet, bouncing up at him, pitter-pattering around him, smiling as only a dog can smile, hugely and unstintingly.

'You want your breakfast, do you?' he said, tugging her floppy, velvety ear. 'Right you are, then. Wait a sec.'

When he opened a tin of her favourite dog food (a particularly noisome brand), he was mugged by the musty, meaty smell of it. 'Christ, it's revolting! How can you face this stuff so early in the morning, Pol?'

Then, 'Just watch me,' she seemed to reply.

He spooned the slurry into her bowl, set it on the floor for her, and stood over her a moment as she snaffled it up, loving her for her enthusiasm.

She had her own dreams, of course, her own night-time adventures, in which she nosed down gamey rabbit holes, ran the neighbourhood cats ragged, and, for all he knew, was covered by a disreputable retriever or a foppish Afghan hound with breath like a charnel house. Sometimes, too, in dreams, the rabbit grew fangs and bit back at her, and marmalade cats the size of elephants came pounding after her howling for her blood, so she scrabbled with her paws and whimpered pitifully.

But she always woke with pleasure and with optimism; each new day brought new doggy delights. Her simple happiness was very cheering. She was such fun to have around.

'What shall we do today, Polly Perkins?' he asked as he filled the kettle. 'Shall we go for a walk? To the pub for a pint? You decide.'

He opened the back door to let in the agitating wind; to let Polly out for her run. She would forage in the garden while he had his tea, looking anxiously in on him every few seconds, making sudden sallies to the threshold to chivvy him. He dragged a chair into the doorway and sat there, shivering, to stare with dark and hankering eyes, as the daylight crept up like the tide, washing over the fields, to lap at the house. His usual contentment, his equanimity, his sense of wholeness, which had been subtly undermined by his dream, were slowly restored to him. After all, his life was full, he needed no one.

Meanwhile, at Foxholes, Kayleigh Roth lay, spiny as a caterpillar, cocooned in a sheet, and dreamt that the silken skeins that bound her floated free, and she emerged, a silver-winged fritillary, to flutter in the open rides of ancient woodlands, darting in the silver shafts of sunlight, feasting on violets. Or something of the sort.

She dreamt that Jamie Rawlings kissed her, and the kiss wrought a magical transformation. And she was released.

At the other end of the landing, in the big master bedroom, Eric, too, dreamed of kissing. He dreamed he was kissing Kayleigh.

His wife, at his side, was also deep in love with someone – she was deep in love with Dee.

Thirty-five miles away, in the Clarkes' neo-Tudor Surrey home, Colin dreamt he had been given a box of liquorice allsorts, and when he opened it he found they were not in fact all sorts, but one sort, the pink coconut kind which get in your teeth and for which he didn't much care. The dream was more disturbing than it should have been.

At the same time, in her attic flat in Camberwell, Sandra Rawlings dreamt she shopped in marble halls, she pushed her metal trolley down endless echoing aisles, between tall shelves of outlandish foods, and somehow it was never filled. Indeed, the more she shopped, the less she had to show for it.

And in Clapham, Jamie lay motionless, with parched mouth, with a sick headache, and listened as the wind tore into everything, snapping branches, snatching tiles from rooftops, rocking the parked cars till they shrilled with electronic hysteria.

The noise was enough to wake the dead, it sounded to him like the end of the world, all that weeping and gnashing. Yet he could sense Lucinda lying there, oblivious, on her back; he could picture her smiling that familiar, infuriating, pleased-with-herself smile.

There was no way she was suffering, as he was, from the excesses of the night before. She had a truly prodigious capacity for booze. They *all* had – Luce, and Giles, and even Hennie. They would slug back champagne with abandon, talk louder and louder, declare themselves thoroughly sloshed, but in truth they would be scarcely affected, and would not pay a penalty as he must on the following day.

They were different even in their constitution, he decided despairingly. Their materials, their very stuff was of a better quality. They did not shrink, or run, or lose their shape, or fall apart after a soaking.

He eased himself gingerly to the edge of the bed (any sudden movement could, he feared, prove fatal), rolled off it and went down on hands and knees. When he opened and closed his eyes, it was as though he were a camera; an image of the carpet, of the pattern, was retained inside his head.

You have no one to blame but yourself, Jamie Rawlings, he told himself. But there was a small part of him that did not buy this; a small part of him blamed Lucinda and her crowd.

He had not even tried to keep pace with them, as they quaffed the bubbly, but had drunk at his own steady pace, as his spirits had dulled, and as a sense of his own separateness had stolen over him.

The others had been like a train, a racketing, streamlined express, from which he'd somehow become uncoupled. They had simply left him behind.

He began to crawl towards his bathroom, relying on radar to guide him, since he dared not open his eyes a second time.

The thick pile of the carpet beneath him gave way to creaky, lavender-polished wood. He negotiated the door and progressed on all fours across the bruising tiles to the pedestal basin, where he knelt a moment in an attitude of prayer, composing himself, before hauling himself to his feet.

He blinked, and thus took another snap, this time of his own face in the mirror, a candid shot, an image of red-veined eyes, of raddled cheeks and puffy flesh.

'Never again,' he said aloud. 'Never, ever, ever again.' He

would have to spend the day in bed, sleep off this crashing hangover, the nausea, the emotional frailty, the hot flushes, the aches and pains, the depression, the bone weariness that follows drugged and dreamless slumber. If he could just lie completely still, in the darkened room, he would by six or seven o'clock tonight be sitting up and taking nourishment.

But, of course, that was impossible, it was out of the question. He had been summoned to Kent, to his mother's home; his presence was required at the family table. The prospect of lunch, of greasy food, of roast potatoes and gravy was ghastly enough; the prospect of the television crew, and the eventual screening of the programme, curdled his blood. But how could he have refused? He had never been a match for Dee at her most determined. He had never been able to resist her. The favoured child is, after all, a burdened child.

Black coffee. That was the answer! Or was it? Had he not read that it made matters worse? Sweet tea, then? Or Bovril? He craved both salt and sugar.

He filled the basin with cold water, ducked over it and rinsed his face before blotting it with a towel. The bathroom seemed to rotate, first clockwise, then anti-clockwise, through three hundred and sixty degrees.

The girl would be there at Foxholes, of course, with her repellent, snivelling offspring. The whole thing was perfectly bloody.

He opened the bathroom cabinet and found paracetamol in a child-proof bottle. God, how he wished he were child proof! Rashly he choked two tablets down; they seemed to stick in his gullet.

> *O Death, where is thy sting-a-ling-a-ling,*
> *O Grave, thy victoree?*

'Jamie,' Lucinda was calling to him imperiously from the bedroom. She sounded to be, as he had predicted, thoroughly eupeptic, she sounded to be in the pink. 'Stop arsing around and come back to bed this instant. I'm screaming for a fuck.'

And the bells of Hell go ting-a-ling-a-ling
Not for you, but me.

———————— • ————————

Sandra drew the sirloin of beef out of the oven and basted it liberally with spluttering juices, as Eric, behind her, performed some rather dashing swordplay, clashing steel against steel till the sparks flew. To carve the joint, his manner implied, was man's work. And, indeed, the Rawlings family conspired to make it so. It was a job for the head of the household; masculinity, seniority were essential to its successful execution; no lowly female would essay it.

Charged with this most crucial role, he seemed actually to grow in stature, to rise, quite literally, to the occasion. He looked, Dee remarked with satisfaction, very much the part, truly a domestic gladiator.

It was a shame about Sandra, however. The girl was as usual letting the side down. She was wearing an air of abstraction with her inevitable greys and blacks, she had her hair drawn back from her round, plain, unpainted face, she appeared a tiny bit fey and decidedly dowdy, like . . . well, like lamb got up as mutton.

Still . . . 'That smells good!' Dee said heartily, setting her vexation aside, and she grabbed a fork and moved into shot, to jab purposelessly at the carrots in their pan. 'The roast beef of old England!'

The film would show a rumbustious, slightly chaotic scene, recalling her old 'I, Me, Mine' column, her hilarious despatches from the home front. It would show her beautiful farmhouse kitchen, the warm, pulsating heart of the house, with everyone lending a hand to rustle up a veritable banquet. Her husband, her kids were all absolute stalwarts, Dee would proclaim, in the commentary to be dubbed on later: without their love and support she would not be where she was today.

There would be glimpses of them sitting around the table, exchanging news, opinions, anecdotes, overlaid with her voice, as she reflected upon the breakdown of the family, laying the blame squarely where it belonged, at the door of the junk-food industry, the manufacturers of TV dinners.

All right, signalled Jennie Gosling to the camera crew. Enough.

And, 'Mega,' she said approvingly, picking up the glass of sherry which Dee had kindly pressed upon her. Jennie was very much in the vanguard today, very *à la mode*. She was one of the first to embrace the latest French Resistance look – a black leather cap, a leather jacket over a black satin *bustier*. In the age of the fashion victim, Sandra noted with private satisfaction, it was nice to see fashion come off worst for once.

She herself was positively embalmed in happiness, wrapped from head to toe in it, blissed out, besotted. Every few minutes, thoughts of sex exploded in her head like fireworks, sending out cascades of white-hot sparks. The 'fey' look which Dee had discerned was the look of a woman in a daze of love and lust; the 'dowdy' grey and black were a disguise. And through Sandra's head ran the words of a song:

> *To-night, to-night,*
> *Tra, la, la, la, la la-a. . . .*

Even the acute embarrassment of being filmed *en famille*, and the knowledge that she might be seen on network television, were not enough to dampen her spirits. What did she care? It was, after all, a piece of harmless nonsense.

In the sitting-room across the hall, the telephone began to ring. Sandra made as if to tear off her apron (of course she could not talk to her lover while she was so attired).

'Sandie,' said Jennie, 'can we see you at the stove again? Just you on your own this time.'

The ringing stopped.

'Jamie's got it,' said Dee tranquilly. 'He'll tell them we're filming. He'll take a message for me.'

'Yes,' Jamie spoke curtly into the receiver, 'this is seven eight four eight. What? Sandra? Er . . .' He cast around the empty room with a wild surmise, as though she might be hiding thereabouts – perhaps trying to pass herself off as a pot plant. He knew perfectly well, in fact, that she was in the kitchen helping to prepare a sumptuous lunch, but he could not summon the will or the energy to gather himself up, to heave himself out of the chair, to go to the door and call her. Even the merest swivel of his eyes, which bulged with blood in their raw, red sockets, was, in his estimation, beyond the call of duty.

He still felt decidedly dicky; he was in no mood just now to get busy, to rush around after other people. 'No. I mean, yes,' he said, making a cool compress of his hand, applying it to his fevered brow. 'Yes, she's here, but she's a bit tied up at this minute. Can I . . . ? Uh-huh. Mm. Very well, I'll tell her. Yeah, yeah. Okay. She'll call you right back.'

He hung up and yawned cavernously. His system craved oxygen, but he feared to breathe deeply while the aroma of fatted calf was seeping under the door.

I am fed up, he thought, with feeling this way. I've been living on my nerves for too long. All this worry is driving me to drink. It's wrecking me, doing my head in.

The solution was suddenly obvious. He must pull out of the Atkins deal, he must pull the plug on it. He would urge Audrey Atkins to take the house off the market, he'd advise her to wait for an upturn, to hang on for a year, maybe two, for the promised recovery.

He would lose face, of course, with Giles, with Lucinda, although maybe not with soppy Henrietta. He would forfeit something of their respect, along with the spondulicks. But, if that was the price of peace of mind, it was surely a price worth paying.

He hesitated for a moment while he checked himself out. He had been known in the past, in a similarly fragile emotional state, to say things that he'd lived to regret. He had even once, on a reckless impulse, gone so far as to propose marriage to an earnest girl named Clemency, who had seemed to him, in his vulnerable condition, to embody all the feminine virtues, but who, on subsequent, more rigorous assessment, had turned out to be a prize-winning dog, Cruft's champion of champions.

The problem was, of course, how to know. Could he trust himself, in his present humour, to act to his own advantage? He felt weepy, sentimental, harking back to the age of innocence before he ever heard of a house called Clovelly. The not-so-distant past, in retrospect, seemed bathed in a kind of golden aura, as in a plank of sunlight filtered through the high rose-window of a church.

He longed to return there, to put the clock back. But was he in his right mind? Was he sound?

Ach, to hell with it! He picked up the phone and, before he could have a change of heart, dialled Giles's number. If he lived to repent the impulse, then so be it.

'Giles? Hi-ya. James here . . . Jamie . . . Jamie *Rawlings*. Remember me? We had supper together last night. For Christ sake, stop farting about.' There were times when he found intolerable the relentless jokiness of his upper-crust friends, their refusal to engage with the serious issues.

'Jamie, you old reprobate!' Giles chaffed him. 'Yes, *I've* got you. Of course, of course. How are you? You were looking a bit green around the gills when last I saw you. You were drunk as an owl, in fact. Have you not heard the term "moderation"?'

'I'm fine,' Jamie told him brusquely. 'And I wasn't drunk.'

'Admit it, you were squiffy. Pissed as a parrot.'

'Oh, all right. If you say so.' Jamie pillowed his head with his free hand. Owls? Parrots? What did it matter? His tone was one of resignation.

Giles, by contrast, sounded to be in rude health. His voice was strong, and shook with stifled mirth. 'Anyway, what can I do you for, dear boy? Why are you phoning at this ungodly hour? What is the burden of your song? Be brief, if you can. I'm a bit tied up.' Snorts of laughter, male and female; great guffaws of merriment. 'I've got somebody with me, you see. Yes, I'm up to my eyes in it. Ha!'

'Some rather bad news. A bit of a body blow.' Jamie paused a second to inspect his perfect pink fingernails. This would teach Giles to take the piss out of people; this would wipe the smile off that sneering de Lannoy-Hunt face. 'Re the Atkins place.' He pronounced it not ree, but ray, as he had heard Giles himself do. 'Audrey Atkins has pulled out of the deal.'

'What?'

'She's dropped out. Changed her mind. Can't bear to leave the ancestral home. Sorry, and all that. Still, *c'est la vie*. Nothing to be done about it. Some you win, some you lose, huh?'

'I don't believe in losing, Jamie. Not if I can help it. Anyway, when did all this happen, eh? How long have you known about it? Why did you not mention it last night?'

'Ah, well, you know what they say.'

'No. What *do* they say?'

'Never mix business with pleasure.'

'But business *is* pleasure. At least, lucrative business is pleasure.'

'Indeed,' Jamie agreed. He spread his fingers, considering. He had big, smooth, plump, pale hands, which, but for their size, would have appeared girlish. He was thankful not to have the rough and horny hands of a labourer.

'She can't do it,' Giles informed him.

'She's done it.'

'I say she can't.'

'And *I* say she has.'

'You misunderstand me, my friend.' Giles spoke coldly, adamantly. 'I will not allow it.'

'Not a lot you can do about it, is there?'

'Oh, but there *is*, me old cock sparrow.' Giles assumed his cheeky-chappy persona, the highly comical, cor blimey, cockney barrow-boy parody that always had Lucinda in stitches. 'Or, at least, there is something *you* can do about it.'

'What d'you mean?' Jamie clawed at the knot of his tie, which seemed to be throttling him. 'How so?'

'Did you not tell me . . . ?' Giles's delivery was syrupy with sarcasm. 'You said she had signed on the dotted. You said . . . Now, let's see if I can recall your precise words. Ah-hah! Yes, I have it! You said she was caught like a rat in a trap.'

'I don't remember –'

'You had only to find a ready, willing and able purchaser – as it might be, *moi* – and she would be liable to pay your remuneration, *irrespective of reasons, and even if contracts were not exchanged.*'

'Yes, yes, I know all that, but . . . ' Jamie felt as if he were being irradiated, microwaved, cooked from within. He could not order his thoughts. Then, to make matters worse, the door opened abruptly and, without a knock or an excuse me, Kayleigh came doggedly through it.

She was dressed in jeans and a big, white shirt, which he recognised with incredulity as one of his own. She wore no shoes, and the chipped red varnish on her toenails somehow gave the impression of unwashed feet.

She padded over to the sofa, sat down and began to twiddle with her hair, to pick at the split ends, while regarding him sneakily from under lowered lashes.

With a superhuman effort he brought his emotions under control, marshalled his thoughts, modulated his voice. 'I take your point, of course,' he said urbanely into the telephone. 'However, I don't think we would wish to invoke that clause.'

'Don't be an absolute pill, Jamie. Just remind the silly old bat about the contract. Point out that it will cost her an arm and a leg to pull out.'

'At Mabey Estates, we like to think –'

'She's panicking, that's all. She's in a funk. She's lived in that hideous great pile for the past hundred and twenty-nine years, and she can't imagine living anywhere else. But she'll be much better off in a nice retirement flat, among people of her own age, with a community centre, and a warden on call, and ramps, and a handrail round the bath. You'd be doing her a great disservice if you didn't persuade her of that.'

'All right. I hear you. I'll give it a go.' Jamie heartily wished he had never rung. What on earth had possessed him to do so? When would he ever learn? He had suffered this humiliation for nothing.

On the plus side, he would still be in for his cut when the house was sold on, he would make a killing as planned. He would thank Giles, in the end, for holding him to it. In the meantime, his most fervent hope was that Lucinda would not be too punishing when she got to hear – as she was bound to do – of his weakness and indecision. She might be the most heavenly fuck on God's earth, but there was no denying, she could be a first-class bitch.

'Right-ho. Tell you what, old man, leave it with me. I'll have a word with the client and come back to you.'

'Bye, then, you scoundrel. Keep your powder dry till we're ready for action. Got to go now. I've an erection a yard long and there's someone here trying to climb up it.' More mirth, more snorts of laughter, and then silence.

Jamie replaced the receiver, cleared his throat self-consciously, straightened his tie. He'd been jangled by the conversation, but he fancied he had not by so much as a flicker betrayed it.

The accursed girl was still sitting there, fiddling with her hair, apparently absorbed in this mindless occupation, although he had sensed her both watching and listening.

For some reason he felt he had to say something, to explain away his end of the dialogue. He wanted something from her. What? Her simple, unquestioning support? Her understanding? She had a crush on him, hadn't she? She wouldn't sneer at him or patronise him. She wouldn't snort like a horse with suppressed laughter. She would be on his side, right or wrong. 'Client,' he offered with a rueful smile. And, as she raised her eyes and regarded him opaquely, 'No rest for the wicked, hm?'

She cupped her hand over her mouth before replying, and 'No' was all she said.

'An agent's work is never done.'

She dropped her head again, and mumbled, 'I s'pose not.' Of course, she must be overawed by him. She would not have met, not mixed with his like before. But did she have to be quite so taciturn?

'Where's the brat?' he enquired jovially, to put her at her ease.

'Ben? With Sandie.' She addressed the words to her lap.

Sandie? Ah, yes! He had a message for his sister. Colin somebody had called. He had asked if she'd call back. He must relay this information to her – if he could be bothered.

Oh, bloody Sandra! Bloody Sunday! Bloody hell!

'That shirt . . .' Without warning, he went on the attack. (What was he doing, for heaven's sake, talking to the little scrubber?)

'What shirt?'

'The one you're wearing. Where did you get it?'

'Found it.' She brought her knees up and hugged them self-protectively.

'Found it where?'

She shrugged.

'It belongs to me, as a matter of fact.'

'Sorry.'

'And I should like it back.'

'Okay.' She frowned as she made a minute examination of a hangnail. 'Now?'

'No, of course not now. Not this minute.'

213

She rested her face on her knees. Her hair flowed about her shoulders like a waterfall. It looked freshly shampooed, more healthy, less ratty than it had done just one short week ago. 'It was in the jumble bag,' she said.

'What jumble bag?'

'Some stuff your mum sorted out. For the church sale. For Somalia.'

'But that's a Paul Smith. It's far too good for . . . ' He shook his head in disbelief. 'What can she have been thinking of? I tell you, nothing is safe from her do-gooding. Lock up your valuables when Lady Bountiful is in town.'

'See, I thought if you didn't want it −'

'I know, I know, you thought you'd help yourself.'

'It was being thrown out.'

'It was being given to charity, which is not the same thing. It was to go to a good cause.'

'They say charity begins at home,' she replied with sudden verve and spirit, tossing her head, baring her teeth at him, to disclose an unsightly gap. The effect was faintly shocking: Jamie averted his gaze.

'It's like taking the bread out of the mouths of the starving,' he lectured sanctimoniously.

'Listen, mate, don't you start on at me about Africa. People like you, you don't know you're born. Besides . . .' In a revealing gesture, she stroked the shirt front with a small, scarred hand. Christ! She really did have a thing for him. It was not, after all, the shirt itself she coveted, not the cloth or its cut, but its owner. She wanted something of Jamie next to her skin; perhaps to work some sympathetic magic, or simply to feel close to him, as if the essence of the man himself were caught up in the warp and woof of the cotton.

Well, dream on, baby, he thought callously. And, in a conscious endeavour to wound, to offload some of his own misery, 'What happened to your tooth?' he demanded.

If he had expected her to blush, however, he had sorely underestimated her, for she was made of sterner stuff. 'I left it for the tooth fairy,' she told him defiantly. 'What do you *think* happened to it? I put it under my pillow, and in the morning I found a silver ten-pence piece.'

At which moment they were interrupted by a call from Dee, summoning them to the table.

'What's eating you, Jimmy James?' Sandra ambushed him in the hallway. She had Ben in her arms, she was encumbered, otherwise she would have made a grab for him. Instead, she bumped him with her hip in a matey, faintly conspiratorial manner, and tipped him a wink. 'You look a bit the worse for wear.'

'There's nothing "eating me", as you put it,' he hissed, glaring at Ben, who was gazing at him meditatively, thumb in mouth. 'Though I could do without this telly fandango, I can tell you. I could do with being elsewhere. And *don't* call me Jimmy James.'

'Isn't it frightful?' she cheerfully agreed. 'Excruciating. I don't think I could bear to watch myself on the box. It must be even worse than hearing oneself on tape.' Her face was lit up like Selfridge's window, with everything on show. He supposed she must be in love again, poor cow, and probably deluded. She really put herself up for it, didn't she? She really went for it. She had no wiles, no guile, no subtlety or mystique. Small wonder she frightened the fellows away.

Ben uncorked his mouth and studied his thumb which was sequinned with spit. 'Isn't he a poppet?' queried Sandra. 'Who's a little poppet, then? Benjie is.'

'Do you have to?'

'What?'

'Do you have to go all gooey and cooey over the little devil?'

'Ooh, isn't Jimmy James a crosspatch, Benjie. We'll take no notice of him, shall we? Uhm, who phoned, by the way?' This in an offhand, a casual voice.

'What?' James thrust his hands into his pockets and scowled at her. He was not disposed to pass on messages while she was deliberately goading him. What was he, anyway? Her social secretary? Her personal assistant? Her answering service?

'Someone called. About ten or fifteen minutes ago. Was it . . . ?'

'Oh, that.' He passed his hand over his eyes. 'Wrong number.'

'Not for me, then?'

'No, Sandra, not for you.'

'Ah, well. I just wondered.'

'You're expecting a call?'

"Yes. A bit later, maybe.'

'Maybe,' said Jamie and, stifling a malicious smirk, he went ahead of her into the dining-room, to take his place at his mother's side.

After lunch, while Ben slept, Kayleigh sat at the bedroom window, staring out over the garden, as the wind chased stripes of light and shadow across the lawn, as it flurried the leaves and got under the skirts of the conifer bushes.

She folded her arms on the sill and rested her cheek in the crook of her elbow. In her head she saw Jamie, and she closed her eyes tight against his escape, she imprisoned him in her imagination.

He had spoken to her at last. He had made conversation of sorts. And yet. . . Reviewing their intercourse, she could not decide quite what had been its character. 'A client', he'd said, amiably enough. And 'No rest for the wicked'. And 'An agent's work is never done'.

But then he'd started on at her about the shirt, which she had after all taken in good faith. And he'd very rudely drawn attention to her tooth. She had stuck up for herself – well, you have to, don't you? – but inside she had felt like dying.

Dinner had been a truly weird experience, with people talking in high, forced voices, laughing inordinately, trying too hard to be natural, to ignore the camera zooming in on every mouthful.

She had kept her head down and eaten stealthily, feeling more than ever like an outsider. And she had resisted all attempts to draw her in.

Now, the TV crew had packed up and gone, and a Sunday torpor had settled on the place. Dee had retreated to her study, Eric to his armchair, Jamie to his bed. Sandra was down in the kitchen, presumably clearing up, for she seemed not to have heard of women's lib. Kayleigh had half a mind to go and help – but, then again, she had half a mind not to.

Her thoughts turned towards home, to her own family, who must by now be missing her. Greg would have been round asking for her, he would have caused a ruck, he'd have gone apeshit. She should ring her mum, but last time she'd tried, she'd got the 'number unobtainable' signal, so the bill had most likely not been paid.

She could drop them a line, she supposed, just to say that she was safe and well and living at a secret address. She wasn't a great one for letters, however. Last time she'd tried it, she'd written to 'Dear Dee', and look where that had landed her. You never quite knew, when you put pen to paper, what you might be letting yourself in for. It was probably better never to commit yourself in such a way.

At the far end of the garden, Oedipuss appeared on the wall. He stood for a moment as the wind did its best to blow him inside-out, then he tricked down into the flowerbed and ran across the lawn.

This glimpse of him brought Charlie Horscroft briefly, inconsequentially, to mind, even as the man himself arrived at the Rawlingses' door.

'You asked me to drop by,' Charlie reminded Eric. He stood there on the step, with the changeful light behind him, with his shirt billowing, his hair streaming loose about his shoulders. In a past life he must have been a swallow. Or a curlew. Or a condor. In a past life he would have had wings.

'That's right.' Eric knocked on his forehead with his fist, as on a block of wood. 'I'm sorry. What with one thing and another, I clean forgot. Come on in.'

He led the way through to the big, homey kitchen, where his daughter, Sandra, was swabbing down the worktops, while the dishwasher made juicy, sluicy noises in the corner.

'Hello.' Sandra gave Charlie a proper smile, with eyes and teeth and dimples, but there was a hint of abstraction about her as she waved a sponge cloth at him in greeting.

'Take the weight off your feet,' Eric urged, pulling a wheelback chair out from the table. 'We must have a chat about our bathroom. Madam wants a recessed basin with an eau-de-nil tiled frame and a wooden shelf under. She wants a tiled surround for the bath.' This last he addressed to Sandra, who nodded comprehendingly. There was evidently, between father and daughter, a tacit understanding.

'So long as I know exactly what she has in mind.'

'Well, we have a photograph. She saw it in her magazine, the style of thing she's after, so she tore it out.'

'You show me, then, and I shall see what can be done.'

'Will you have a cup of coffee?' enquired Sandra, drying her hands on her striped apron, with the air of someone who is ever anxious to appease. Charlie liked her unguarded expression, her manifest honesty, her lack of side. No one could call her pretty, he reflected, but she had *something*. If it weren't for her off-putting self-effacement – if only she were more robust – he might almost have been attracted to her.

'No, thanks very much. Not for me.'

'You're sure?' she dutifully pressed him. Then she glanced wildly at her watch, and at the clock, and once more at her watch, and, in an eloquent gesture, she pleated the hem of her apron with her two hands.

'Yes, I'm quite sure.' Charlie, too, was prompted to check the time. It was twenty past four, and the day had all but blown itself out.

'Hello, hello.' Dee Rawlings was, it seemed to Charlie, more an event than a person. She did not so much arrive upon the scene as she happened to it. She happened to her husband, and to her daughter, who seemed diminished by her presence. 'I thought I heard the door,' she said heartily. 'Well, Charlie Horscroft, so it's you! Is your mother well? I don't know how she copes, I'm sure. Such a handful those children must be! My leaflet on vasectomy might be of interest to her. Now, has Eric told you what I'm after? Good, good. We'll go upstairs and take a look. But first, a cup of coffee. Wouldn't that be nice? Sandra, make some coffee, there's a love.'

'But he doesn't want any. I did ask.'

'No, really, not for me.'

'Well, I shouldn't mind a cup myself. Do be a dear and put the kettle on.'

As Sandra, with the merest sigh, did her mother's bidding, Dee took up her position opposite Charlie, she rested her elbows on the table, propped her chin on her clasped hands, smiled at him a practised, polished smile, while regarding him shrewdly through sandbagged eyes.

He had heard all about her, of course. He had had the goods on her these past few days from his mother, who had had them from Ivy Burston. He had been thoroughly primed.

He had heard how Dee Rawlings swanned around; how she put on airs and graces; how she fancied she was the bee's knees; how she imposed upon her cleaning lady, while never herself lifting a finger. Still, he had come to this house, as he went everywhere, with an open mind, and if he did not warm to the woman, it was instinctive, for his opinions were not informed by village gossip.

A spacious human being, he could accommodate most people, and yet, unusually, unreasoningly, he had no room for this one. His gut reacted rather violently against her. And, in consequence, he felt no enthusiasm for recessed basins, for wooden shelves and eau-de-nil tiled surrounds. He would undertake the work for her; he would do an expert, an excellent job. But – though the keenest observer would never know it – he would withhold something vital of himself.

'I thought I could smell coffee.' The son James was next to materialise. He was a tall young man, and in theory, on paper, good looking. He was almost preternaturally clean, as though he had just come back from the laundry, his hair was neatly combed, and yet there was about him an unwholesome, crapulent, bloated quality, which suggested he had recently had a skinful. His shoulders sagged, his eyelids were pursy, his mouth was a miserable circumflex which qualified his stubborn chin.

He glanced with lizard eyes around the kitchen, taking rapid stock. His face registered indifference to his father, to his sister, and to Charlie himself, though he worked up a smile of sorts, a faint twitch of the lips for the visitor, before going to sit by his mother, to whom he seemed to have some kind of powerful attachment, as if by an invisible umbilicus.

'You know Charlie Horscroft, do you?' enquired Dee, favouring her son with a look of love and pride. 'The family live next door but one to Ivy. I was just saying – wasn't I, Charlie? – that his poor mother really has her hands full. She's like the original old woman who lived in a shoe.' This in a deep, stentorian voice, to make the bone-china cups on the cup-hooks sing.

'You want coffee, do you, Jimmy James?' put in Sandra, blushing, mortified, endeavouring to cover for her mother's indelicacy. 'I imagine you need it. You look absolutely whacked. Did you get legless last night, or what?'

It was Jamie's turn to blush, this time with anger. He positively fluoresced with it. 'I have a touch of flu, if you must know,' he responded, glaring in pure hatred. 'I ought really to be in bed.'

'Well, you poor old thing,' Dee sympathised. 'Why don't you pop upstairs and lie down again? Sandie will bring you a hot drink.'

'No, no. I must be getting back to the metrop. I have to see a man about a house.'

Dee clucked with disapproval. 'You're working too hard. You need your rest.'

'I'm all right. It's nothing. Besides, I need to earn the extra if I'm to have my car fixed up. I expect you noticed, it's been scraped. I left it outside the house and whammo! A hit and run, so no hope of claiming on the beggar's insurance. And I'm not about to forfeit my no claims. Look, are we having this coffee, or aren't we?'

'Coming up,' said Sandie, plonking a cafetière down in front of him. 'I'll go and see if Kayleigh wants a cup.'.

Ah, yes, thought Dee, Kayleigh.

Ah, yes, thought Charlie, Kayleigh.

Ah, yes, thought Jamie, Kayleigh.

Ah, yes, thought Eric, *Kayleigh*.

'Can I come in?' said Sandra softly, pressing her ear to the door of the spare bedroom, grasping the handle, depressing it gently.

'Sure,' said Kayleigh, and she yanked the door open from the inside.

Sandra uttered a gasp of shock, as if she had been caught eavesdropping. Then, 'Do you want some coffee?' she tendered.

'Not particularly.'

'Or tea?'

'No.'

'What have you been doing?'

'Thinking.' Kayleigh padded over to the bed and sat down, wrapping her arms around herself. There was a crease on her cheek, corresponding to a crease in the shirtsleeve. The sight of her was strangely poignant. She looked small and rumpled and miserable.

'Are you homesick?'

Kayleigh shrugged.

'Well, you must be, of course. You're bound to miss your own place. Be it ever so humble – Oh, I don't mean . . . What I meant was . . .'

'Humble?' Kayleigh seemed to chew on the word for a moment. 'I suppose you *could* call it that. Myself, I call it a tip.'

'All the same . . .'

'Yeah.' She hugged herself tighter and rocked back and forth. 'The thing is,' she blurted out, 'I don't know what to do.'

'We'll sort something out for you, I promise,' soothed Sandra, misapprehending. 'Find you somewhere nice where you can be with Benjie, safe and sound.'

'I have to stay here for the time being.' Kayleigh's tone was urgent, insistent. 'I don't want to go just yet.'

'No, well . . . That's understood. You can stop for as long as it takes to get you fixed up.'

'That's not what I'm on about.'

'What, then?'

'You see, the thing is . . .' Kayleigh lay back, clasped her hands behind her head, stared at the ceiling. Her chest rose and fell. The shirt parted to reveal her midriff, the perfect, pert, pink poke of her navel.

Sandra plonked down beside her. Kayleigh felt the mattress dip. There was a waiting silence, as the urge to confide came and went. 'Oh, nothing,' she said at last.

Downstairs, the telephone began to ring. Sandra jumped. She stiffened. She caught her breath and held it till her face contorted with the strain.

'Expecting a call?' queried Kayleigh nonchalantly.

'Er . . . yes. Maybe.'

'Some chap or other?'

'That's right. Some chap. Or other.'

'Boyfriend?'

'Well, you know . . . It's early days.'

Sandra got up and went to the door. She opened it a crack and stood there, tense, with her head cocked, listening. There was no shout, no summons, no sound but the murmur of voices from the bathroom at the end of the landing, where Dee was in earnest negotiation with the Horscroft guy.

'They're all the same, aren't they?' Kayleigh commiserated. 'They only want one thing. And then, when they've had it, they don't want to know.'

'Oh, dear, that does sound bleak!' Sandra, frowning, turned to stare at her.

'It's true.'

'Of some guys, maybe. Not of every guy.'

'Pretty well every guy.' Kayleigh sniffed. 'Greg at least stood by me,' she conceded, in a spirit of fairness, 'once he'd got me in the family way.'

'Do you love him?'

'Not now. I don't think so.'

'But you did?'

'Dunno. I guess I must of done.'

'He must be wondering what's become of you.'

'You bet. He'll be doing his nut.'

'And your mum. She must be worried. She must be out of her mind.'

'Not really. It's not the first time I've done a runner. But I'll write her tomorrow. I'll let her know I'm okay.'

Wearily, disconsolately, Sandra closed the door. 'What's it like', she asked, 'having a baby? Is it agony?'

'No worse than shitting a football.'

'That bad, hm?'

'That bad.'

'But then, I imagine it's a natural sort of pain. Not like, you know, having a leg off.'

'P'raps,' allowed a doubtful Kayleigh, for whom a pain was a pain was a pain.

Sandra did a bit of pacing, back and forth, back and forth.

'Sit down,' commanded Kayleigh, 'you make the place untidy.'

'Sorry.' Obediently, Sandra sat.

'Good-looking, is he, this mystery man?'

'Uhm . . . ?' Sandra laughed and felt cheered. Whatever was she fussing and fretting about? Colin would call her in his own sweet time, she could rely upon it. 'Not exactly,' she admitted.

'Mind you, they tend to be the worst, the good-looking ones. They tend to be the most big-headed.'

'That's right, they do,' Sandra agreed, with feeling.

'Think they're the effing cat's pyjamas.'

'Colin's not that way. He's a bit self-deprecating.'

'Uh?' Kayleigh wrinkled her nose.

'You know, modest. Apologetic.'

'Oh.'

'Sends himself up the whole time.'

Kayleigh made no reply.

'Always kidding around.'

Again no reply. Sandra sighed. 'It's nice to be able to talk to you about him. There's no one else I can share it with.'

'What about your mum?'

'Good gracious, no! I've never been able to unbosom myself to her.'

'Un*bosom*?'

'That is, to bare my soul. To share my secrets.'

'I don't see why not. It's her job, isn't it?'

'Yes, and yet . . .'

'Yes?'

'Perhaps it's just more difficult when you're close to someone,' Sandra reflected. And she thought, No, that's not it, it *isn't*. The truth was that Dee was not there for her. She did not make herself available. To run to her for answers was like running into a duvet.

'Your dad, then?'

'He has his own troubles, in case you haven't noticed?'

'I noticed.' Kayleigh paused, considering. 'He's stuffed, basically, isn't he?'

'That's it exactly.' Sandra could not help but laugh. 'He's truly stuffed.'

'And how about . . . Jamie?' The hesitation was brief but telling, and there was a tiny bit too much treble when she said his name.

'Jamie?' Sandra raised her eyebrows. 'We don't talk much any more, he and I.'

'So he wouldn't, erm, tell you what he felt or nothing? He wouldn't . . . unbosom himself to you?'

'I'm afraid I should be the last person.'

'Oh.'

'Why do you ask?'

'No reason.'

Dear God, thought Sandra, in alarm, the poor thing's really smitten! She was panicked by the thought that Kayleigh might solicit her opinion (for what, in all honesty, could she reply?). Because there was no chance, let's face it, that snobby Jamie Rawlings would be attracted to an unmarried mother, to a scruffy little kid who dropped her aitches. And even if he were . . . Well, could she, his sister, with her hand on her heart, give Jamie a character reference? Could she declare him a good bet?

The fact was, though she could scarcely bear to face it, that Jamie was a shit. He was a weak, impressionable, ruthless, avaricious social climber. It hurt her even to think these things, it made her heart ache. He was her brother, and she loved him more than life, but she could not commend him to anyone. Still less could she badmouth him.

She stood up abruptly. Her anxiety propelled her to the door. 'I have to . . .' she offered vaguely. 'Er, I must go and . . .'

At the head of the stairs she met Jamie himself. 'Hi, Jimmy James,' she said guiltily.

'Hi,' he responded coolly.

'The telephone . . . ?'

'What about it?' He grinned, inexplicably, from ear to ear.

'It wasn't for me?'

'Were you expecting a call?'

'Yes. No. Well, I just thought . . . And you made sure to put it back on the hook?'

'What do you take me for, an imbecile?'

'No. Sorry, sorry,' she placated him. And, to the newel post at the foot of the stairs, as she blundered into it, 'I'm so sorry.'

To be Sandie meant forever having to say you were sorry.

So that was it. She didn't want to know. Colin sprawled on the sofa, flipping, unseeing, through the *Mail on Sunday* and cursing the name of Sandra Rawlings.

He had called her twice, as arranged, and each time he'd been given the bird. Some guy with long, drawly vowels had come on the line to fob him off with lame excuses, to say she was too busy to talk – a likely story, hah! – and that she would call him back.

He had waited and waited for her to ring. He had sat there staring at the inert and silent ivory telephone, willing it to come alive, until it swam before his eyes.

Who had he been, the guy with the drawl? A boyfriend? A lover? Almost certainly, yes.

She had taken him for a fool, that was clear. She had toyed with his affections.

Memories of a night of passion, which he had cherished until now, had been debased. Colin had once seen a stage hypnotist convince a guy from the audience that he was in love with a mop. The guy, in an altered state of consciousness, had danced with that mop. He had clung to it. He had cuddled it and stroked its stringy hair, and would almost certainly have given it one, only it hadn't been that kind of girl.

Now, Colin felt about Sandra Rawlings pretty much how the poor guy, once woken from his trance, had felt about the mop.

Because that mop had trifled with him. It had teased him. It had smooched with him and led him on. It had made a priceless ass of him, then it had gone all wooden on him.

And the worst part about it – the real bugger of it – was that he had believed in her. In Sandie, Colin had fancied he had found a soul-mate, he had thought her a beautiful, a very special and singular human being.

Well, rats to her! See if he cared! She could go fry her face.

'Where are you off to?' called Shirley from the stairs, half-way up, or half-way down, as Colin banged out of the sitting-room.

'Nowhere.' He glowered at her.

'Where's nowhere?'

'Nowhere.'

'You're going to see that Sandra,' she challenged him, and she reached for the banister to steady herself.

'What Sandra?'

'What do you mean, "what Sandra"?'

'I mean', he shouted – yes, *shouted* – at her, 'that there *is* no Sandra. So far as I am concerned, Sandra Rawlings is dead. Have you got that?'

The door slammed on his heels, and moments later she heard his car start up, heard him revving the engine like a madman then go roaring off up the road.

With a tut and a shake of her head Shirley descended to the kitchen. He'll kill himself, racing around in that old rattle-trap, she thought as she reached, for comfort, for a cherry Bakewell. And she waited for the familiar, sick sensation, the fear and trembling to assail her. But it never came. Only a sense of private triumph, of exultation.

'There *is* no Sandra Rawlings. So far as I'm concerned, she's dead.'

CHAPTER

———— ● ————

IO

Clare Constantine sat at the vast walnut-veneer desk, in the editor's office at *Mia*, the following Thursday morning, brooding darkly on her difficulty. And she said to herself – for such was the tenor of her inner dialogue – 'Oh, who will free me from this turbulent priestess?'

The room had been reorganised, at her commissioning, at company expense, by a practitioner of Feng Shui; it had been rebalanced, the furniture realigned to dispel negative energy and to promote a constant flow of positive chi. In her newly harmonised work environment, with the chi positively surging around her, she was able to think more clearly, more creatively, more ingeniously, her intellect was honed to a razor edge, sharp enough to let blood, yet *still* she could not cut through the big question.

Dee Rawlings was going to have to go, of this there was no doubt. By some means she must be ousted. But, wondered Ms Constantine as she dipped into her drawer for her Evian spray and veiled herself in a refreshing mist, how was this end to be achieved?

The whole bloody business was beginning to obsess her. She lay upon the pillow each night, a head so full of argument, she could not sleep for the din.

It wasn't fair, it really wasn't. *Cosmopolitan* had smart, shrewd, estimable Irma Kurtz. *Company* had the bright, attractive Donna

Dawson. And meanwhile she was lumbered with ludicrous, vulgar, overblown, ebullient, mumsy, homesy Dee Rawlings.

It was the sight of the woman, above all else, not just in the flesh around the place, but in the magazine, that so affronted her. Clare Constantine had seized the opportunity of a redesign to shuffle Dee's pages from the front to the back of the mag, to the 'graveyard', among the small ads and the fag-ends of features, where her picture by-line could cause less serious offence. But its very existence in *Mia* pained her sorely. The presence of a plump, middle-aged columnist spoiled the whole line of the publication, it was an abomination, like a visible panty line, knicker elastic showing through a sleek Chanel skirt.

She had implored management, from the day she was appointed, to pension off this superannuated auntie figure, to make Dee redundant, or to redeploy her. This would liberate the space, it would allow her to set up on those pages an expert counsel, a panel of advisers qualified to deal with a better class of problem.

But, no, Dee Rawlings was apparently fire-proof. And why? For no better reason than that the public liked her. She had a following. Readership surveys had consistently shown that hers was among the best-read elements of the magazine, it was the main reason people gave for parting with the one-pound-fifty cover price. Which only went to prove what Clare Constantine had long suspected – that *Mia* was attracting the wrong sort of reader altogether.

She was not happy that the product should fall into the hands of the hoi polloi. If she'd had her way she would have barred them. No one over the age of, say, thirty-five, no one over nine stone, no one north of St Albans, no one in a shellsuit or velour tracksuit should be permitted to buy it.

She wanted to appeal to the As and Bs in society, to the professional and managerial classes, to the metropolitan smart set, the types she met at supper parties, at book launches, at first nights, at the opera. High-quality gloss paper, perfect binding, were wasted on the Cs and Ds; they should go elsewhere for their entertainment, they should make do with newsprint and staples.

She had argued forcefully for a relaunch, an opportunity to reposition *Mia* in the market. But, sadly, her arguments had not convinced the 'suits' upstairs, the pusillanimous, pussy-footing, profit-conscious, penny-pinching directors. Well, if she could not prevail in the boardroom, she must rely upon her own low cunning.

With a sigh, she rose from her desk and went – rufous as a fox and twice as foxy – over to the fish tank which bubbled by the door. She had chosen black mollies, not only because their slinky, velvety look reflected her taste, but because, according to her Feng Shui guru, black fish would rid the place of evil forces.

There were supposed to be six of them, that was the magic number, but now she counted only five gliding silently around behind the wall of glass. Damn! What a bore! She must send out at once for a replacement. Maybe she could have one biked over? The greedy little beggars had presumably eaten their fellow. Fish did that sort of thing, didn't they? God, how gross! She despised an appetite out of control.

She was on a cleansing diet at the moment, herself, she was on a detox programme, a forty-eight-hour fruit fast, and something about the process – about the elimination of poisons from the system – made her more than usually unforgiving. All the same, disgust gave way to grudging admiration. She could not but be awed by this extraordinarily effective method of reducing the head count. It gave her the germ of an idea.

'Good morning.' Dee burst in upon her, fluffy as a bunny in white angora, knocking gratuitously, if not indeed facetiously, at the door, even as she passed through it. 'Only me.'

Only!

'Oh,' said Clare, straightening, glaring at her, 'you. What is it you want? I'm very busy.'

'I've had a wheeze.'

'You have?' Clare responded with infinite cool, raising one quizzical eyebrow, and she returned to sit at her desk, to regard Dee across it with eyes as green and glacial as arctic ice, in a vain attempt to subordinate her.

'I do indeedee.' Dee plonked herself down in a leather armchair, severely winding it. 'The royals!' she pronounced in triumph.

'The . . . ?' Clare sighed. 'What *about* the royals?'

'The ultimate dysfunctional family. An in-depth discussion feature for the February issue. I advise the Queen on how to deal with her wayward children. I urge Charles and Di to kiss and make up. We put Diana on the cover and it's a sell-out.'

Clare shuddered. She actually shuddered. She was racked by

emotion. She closed her eyes, pincered the bridge of her nose between thumb and forefinger, as if to ease a headache. And she said, simply, weakly, 'Please!'

'You don't go for it?'

'I *hate* it. It's unthinkable. Unspeakably naff. It's the stuff of tabloids. Besides which, we have no idea, have we, what might happen between now and next year? The Waleses may very well split up. That Diana book has done irreparable damage.'

'Oh, no.' With airy complacency, Dee waved away the proposition, as the Weight Watcher Success of the Year might wave away the dessert trolley. Plainly, she was having none of it. 'Those two won't part. Take my word for it. For the sake of her boys, Di will want to keep her family together.'

'You can't be sure of that.'

'But I can. I have an instinct for these things. I am, after all, a mother.'

'It's too much of a risk. Besides, it stinks.' Clare's nostrils twitched as though she could actually smell it. 'It reeks to high heaven of prurience.'

'I'm sorry you feel that way.' Dee tugged her skirt over her ample knees. She had a face like a doughnut, Clare privately noted, she had a mouth like a squish of jam.

'I do.'

'Bob thought it was a real corker when I put it up to him.'

'You spoke about it to . . . ? You've already talked about it with Bob Tanner?'

'Well, just *en passant*. You know how it is. He dropped by my office. We were chewing the fat.'

The image was altogether too graphic for Clare. She grimaced, covered her mouth with her hand. Her headache was no longer a metaphor; it was a thumping reality. 'I should remind you', she said, with iron self-control, 'that I am the editor. You should discuss your ideas with me before talking to anyone else.'

'Of course, of course,' said Dee soothingly. 'I do apologise.'

'Well, kindly bear it in mind for the future.'

'Just as you wish. You're the boss.' (Was there, then, in her tone, a hint of derision? Or was it merely Clare's fancy?)

'It's simply that we've long been in the habit, Bob and I, of having these little chinwags.'

This was it! Here was the rub, the very nub of the problem. Because Dee Rawlings and Bob Tanner went way back. They had a shared history. He it was who had appointed Dee to *Mia*. She was, in a sense, his creature. And it was this that Clare was up against.

'I should prefer you to save your ideas for conference. They should be discussed by the team, around the table, not in some hole-and-corner manner with the director.'

'Right-ho.' Dee hauled herself out of the chair, she made as if to go.

'By the way,' Clare told her snappily, 'we've a meeting with those incompetent fools from promotions on Monday at twelve-thirty. I expect all senior staff to attend.'

'Monday?'

'Yes, Monday.'

'But I can't. *We* can't. Have you forgotten? It's the Women of the Year Lunch. I mean, surely you been invit – No? I see you haven't. I'm so sorry, I just assumed . . . *I've* been asked every year since I-don't-know-when. It's terrific fun. All the most fascinating, influential women are there. Everyone who's anyone. Never mind. Maybe next time. But, hark at me, chattering on! I must leave you to your work. *Ciao, ciao.*'

At the door she paused to glance at the aquarium, then turned back to beam at Clare, who was sitting very stiffly at her desk, as if she had been starched, and looking, even by her own standards, pale. 'Cichlids,' Dee pronounced.

'Mollies,' Clare contradicted, barely moving her lips.

'Molly's. I had supposed they were yours. You know about cichlids, of course. The males are repelled by tough, go-getting females. If a lady cichlid is too aggressive, too dominant, she will never find a mate. She is doomed to a life of dried-up spinsterhood. Oh, yes, left on the shelf, absolutely. Always the bridesmaid, never the bride. I dare say there's a lesson in that for us all, don't you? Now, I do have to dash. Toodle-oo.'

—————————— ❀ ——————————

Dear Mum, Dad and Lisa,
Just a note to let you know I'm alright. I had to get

away as I'm sure you'll understand. I have written to Greg also, and told him it's for the best. I have told him to forget me and find someone else. Ben is okay. I hope you are all okay. I am with friends. They are very good people. They say I can stay till I get fixed up. I lost a tooth but I got a new one yesterday. Well, I think that's all my news. I'll ring you sometime, when the phone is back on. Look after yourselves.

Love always,

K

xxxxxxx

Kayleigh frowned and sucked on her lower lip as she read the letter over to herself. It would do, she decided. It would have to do. It wasn't poetry, exactly, it didn't sing, it would not win any prizes, but it served its purpose, it said what she wanted it to say, no more, no less.

Better go at once and post it. She'd take Ben in the buggy. It was a dismal old day – the sky was a liverish yellow, freckled with dull brown birds; the black earth oozed moisture; skittish breezes stirred the branches of the oak trees, shivering the leaves – but it was probably better outdoors than in.

She was feeling horribly cooped up this morning, horribly confined. She had never in her life had so much space around her; and it was this space, it seemed, that pressed in on her.

'Want to come down the shop with mummy?' she asked Ben, who sat on the floor chewing on the ears of Sandra's old teddy, Horace, with his legs curled round like a rubber ring. She squatted beside him and peered into his china-blue eyes, as she tried to unscramble what she felt about him.

There were times when she thought it had ruined her life, falling for a baby when she was not yet seventeen. True, she'd had nothing much planned for the next sixty years, she'd had nothing much on for the rest of her days. But a child could really cramp your style.

What chance had she with Jamie, for instance, when she was so encumbered? Would he be willing, even if she won him over (which, itself, was a pretty iffy if), to take on another man's son? What if it came down in the end to a choice between Jamie and Ben? How would she ever decide?

Her response to Jamie Rawlings was clear and straightforward. She defined it as love, and would stand by that definition. If you cannot love someone whom you scarcely even know (and people will argue that you cannot), how to explain the aching heart, the emptiness, the fevers and flushes? Then, if it was not the man himself, but the *image* of the man that so allured her, would someone please say where the image ended and the man began? And what is the distinction, actually, between being in love and merely believing yourself in love? Doesn't it hurt just the same? Others might call it infatuation, but Kayleigh called it loving. And it was *her* heart, after all, that was doing the aching.

The fact that she had been through this before, with Greg, did not bear upon her reason. The past is more easily discounted than the present or the future. It may be endlessly rewritten, recast, or reduced. If her feelings for Greg had been half so intense or so pure as they were now for Jamie, she could not remember it.

Her baby, on the other hand, aroused in her such incompatible emotions. At moments, she truly, truly hated him – and yet, in spite, she would have died for him.

She smiled at him, and he smiled back after a fashion, mirroring her expression earnestly. Up and down went his sketchy eyebrows, up and down. He raised one short arm, waved it jerkily about, unbalancing himself.

With a tentative hand she smoothed his hair, felt the heat of his scalp with her fingertips. Wouldn't it be funny, she thought, if people weren't warm? If they were cold to the touch, like fish? She imagined lying with Jamie, in a cool and slippery eel embrace. Then she imagined his body, warmed by heart's blood, wrapped around and around her own. Mm-mmm.

When she got to her feet, her knee joints made cracking sounds, as if she were a very old lady, but her reflection in the mirror told a different story, as she practised seduction, snarling to admire her new incisor *in situ*. It was at least as nice as the real thing, perhaps nicer. She thrust her tongue into her cheek to make it bulge, swept her long, fair hair up with her two hands, swooshed it around, let it flow loose about her shoulders. She looked, she thought, dead sexy. She looked gorgeous. She had filled out ever so slightly in her short time here; her skin fitted more closely, somehow. And, like a spindly tulip watered by soft spring rain, she was standing straighter, she was holding her head up, she was beginning to bloom.

She tilted her chin, regarded herself through half-closed eyes, pouted at her reflection. She cupped her hand at her chin and blew a kiss. No man on earth – Jamie Rawlings included – could be immune for ever to her charms.

'What's all this, then?' Poison Ivy came in at that second, surprising Kayleigh in this small display of vanity. In her hands she carried a duster and an aerosol can; the expression on her face said she meant business.

'D'you mind?' Kayleigh rounded on her, blushing hotly, making hard, defensive fists. 'This room is private. You can't just barge through that door whenever you feel like it. No wonder they call you Mrs Burst-in. Why don't you leave me alone?' Because, it was true, there was no hiding-place for her here at Foxholes, from the avenging cleaning lady. Wherever she went, there Ivy would be, upstairs and down, with mop and bucket, with scrubbing brush or broom, drawn to the scene of domestic chaos by the same grim fascination, perhaps, as draws spectators to the scene of an accident. (Or was it the mother in her, answering to the child in Kayleigh? Was she, improbably, against her nature, starting to adopt the girl, much as one sometimes reads in the tabloids that a Rottweiller is parenting baby chicks?)

'Private or not,' she rebuked Kayleigh now, 'it's a bloody tip. You pick up those things so I can vac.' She raised the can, took aim and squirted: puff, puff, puff, the liquid vapourised in choking clouds of rose-scented reproach.

All houses have their own particular smells, their own bio-chemistry, their own ineradicable, individual secretions to which their owners are inured (returning after weeks of absence, breathing again the scent of home, they will think, for a fleeting instant, Ah, yes!). But the natural odours of this house were so heavily overlaid by a chemical pot-pourri, by the smells of bleach and pine and factory flowers, as to be almost undetectable.

'Oh, leave it, will you? Give it a miss for once. It doesn't need doing.' Kayleigh flung out her arms to embrace the unmade bed, the strewn clothes, the open drawers spewing bras and tights.

'I'll do no such thing. The very idea! I'm paid to clean, and clean I shall. Come along, chop chop, pick that stuff up off the floor, put it away nice and neat and tidy.'

'All right, all right, all right.' Kayleigh snatched up a pair of jeans, a T-shirt, knickers and crammed them in the wardrobe. 'There. That do you? Okay.' She wrested the teddy from an affronted Ben and sent it spinning on to the bed, dragged him off the floor, made for the door and slammed out with him.

Someone was whistling loudly, melodiously, down the landing in the far bathroom. It was a rare and emotive sound in this inhospitable place; Kayleigh drifted, unresisting as a piece of flotsam, towards it, and, as she recognised the tune, she began to sing along, in that husky voice which would now and then move perfect strangers to offer her a throat lozenge.

> Those were the days of our lives.
> The bad things in life were so few . . .

'Hello, there,' said Charlie Horscroft, throwing her a smile when she materialised in the doorway, before returning to the job in hand. 'How's it going?' He was down on his knees, unscrewing the hardboard panel from the side of the bath. It came away with a squeak of protest, to expose two clawed, cast-iron feet, a dark and secret place of filth and fluff and rubble beneath the tub, a pink plastic nailbrush, a little mouse of pumice, a small, amber oblong of Pears soap.

He was wearing a begrimed white T-shirt with his torn and faded jeans. His dark hair was floured with dust. But his grey eyes were lustrous, they shone in that disconcerting way which might or might not be sensual (she was no longer certain of it).

'Not so bad.' Kayleigh shrugged.

'And you, my friend?' Charlie spared another glance, a grin for Ben, who waved a pointing finger in response, and mouthed like a goldfish. 'How are you keeping?'

'He's fine,' Kayleigh reported, setting him down.

'That's good.'

'Also, you see, I've got my tooth.' She peeled her top lip, the loose flap of flesh, back with thumb and forefinger.

'I see. Yes. Lovely. So you caught the bus okay?'

'I'm not completely helpless, you know.'

'Of course not."

'I don't need a wet nurse.'

'I'm sure.'

'I'm not a baby.'

'No, you're not.' He whistled another few bars of the song. Then, 'Did you say something about a cup of tea?' he prompted.

'Nah.'

'Oh, go on, there's a pal.'

'What did your last slave die of?' But she was arguing for argument's sake. Or out of habit, because such had been her relationship with Greg.

'It's just that I'm busy here,' he said reasonably, wiping his brow with his forearm. 'And I'm parched.'

'Well . . . all right, I guess.' But still she hesitated. 'Bit of a mess under there.'

'So it is.'

'Better not let Ivy anywhere near it.'

He laughed shortly, amusedly. 'No, better not.'

'Five minutes, then. Okay?'

'Okay.'

'Where's your dog?' Kayleigh wanted to know. She was sitting, now, at the kitchen table with her arms folded in front of her, propping herself, watching over the teapot, which nestled under a quilted cosy. Ben stood fastened, unnoticed, unrewarded, to her knee, swinging himself back and forth in a slightly fractious manner. Charlie had never met anyone so inert as this young woman; such energy as she possessed seemed to exert a downward pull upon her.

Turning from the sink, where he had been soaping his hands with washing-up liquid, he reached for a package of paper towels which, he noted, made much of being one hundred per cent recycled and of being so *long*, as if there were virtue in profligacy. 'Polly?' he said. 'Outside.'

'Outside where?'

He balled up the sodden towel and deposited it in the swing-bin. 'Outside here.' He nodded towards the back garden.

With a flex of her legs, Kayleigh shoved the chair back on the squealing tiles, she brushed Ben off her, and went to the window to gaze out. 'I used to want a dog, but I was never allowed. Where? Where is she? I can't see nothing.'

'Here, look.' Charlie hooked her around the waist, drew her over to a better vantage. Then, having positioned her, he stood there behind her, with his hands resting lightly on her hips, watching over her shoulder, as Polly made the rounds of the borders.

'That's pretty,' said Kayleigh, nodding to indicate a pale pink musk rose, its blossoms clustered on dipping, bobbing branches. She was talking mindlessly, just talking, to cover her sudden confusion. She could not stand so close to a man, she could not feel his touch, however matey, without being put forcefully in mind of sex. This was not to say she was attracted to him. (No, Charlie definitely wasn't her type.) But it was a bit like standing by a fire, *any* fire – she could not but feel the heat.

'Which? The rose? That variety's called "Ballerina".' His words whiffled in her ear.

'Is it?'

'Yes.'

Kayleigh sniffed. 'A bit late in the year, isn't it, for roses?'

'Not for this one. You're right, it's a beauty. My mum would love it. I must take a cutting and plant it in her front garden.'

'Huh?'

'A cutting. For my mum's garden.'

'What's that, then?' She twisted around to look at him with genuine, unguarded curiosity.

'Well . . .' It took him a few seconds to comprehend her incomprehension. (When you know a thing so thoroughly, it is hard to understand another's ignorance of it.) 'You can snip off a bit and plant it,' he mimed the process, oversimplifying slightly, 'and it grows. You get a whole new plant.'

'You can? You do?' She registered utter disbelief. His story did not seem plausible. It sounded like sleight of hand. Like pulling something out of a top hat. So she studied him minutely, to see if he was joking. But he was not, after all, so easily read: his face had a sealed look, and the filmy sunlight conspired with his eyes to exclude her. 'You *can't*,' she decided, finally.

'Sure you can. It's easy. I mean, you have to know what you're doing – whether to cut hard wood or soft wood, and what time of year – and they don't always take, but . . .'

'You're telling me that you can lop a bit off that rose bush, stick it in the ground, and it'll grow into another rose bush?'

'That's about the size of it.'

'Well, stone the bleeding crows,' she said, impressed. 'It's a shame it won't work with other things. Like, with beer bottles. Or with fags. Or money. With fifty-pound notes.'

'No, that would never do.' Charlie went and took two mugs from the dresser, making a conscious choice, selecting a pale blue one for Kayleigh, dark blue for himself. Oxford and Cambridge, he thought fatuously, meaninglessly. 'If money grew on trees, so to speak, it wouldn't be worth a fig. Hey, what about Ivy? Will she want some tea?'

'But it isn't anyway, is it? Not without health and happiness. Hey, hark at me, getting all philosophical. Nah, she won't have any, she'll of had some already. She'll be wanting to finish upstairs and piss off.' Kayleigh fetched milk from the fridge. She disappeared into the pantry, to emerge with a packet of shortbread biscuits under one arm, with one biscuit already clamped between her teeth. 'She doesn't like me being here,' she added with difficulty, through clenched jaw, plonking herself down on her chair. The biscuit wagged about.

'Ah, well, I'm sure . . .' Charlie was about to refute it, but innate honesty prevailed. Of *course* Ivy Burston didn't want Kayleigh there. How could she keep the house the way she liked to keep it, with someone actually in residence? At Foxholes, all traces of human habitation were folded away, or were sluiced down the drain, or sucked up the Hoover pipe, or incinerated, or dumped outside for the dustmen. The place simply didn't seem lived-in.

But then, reflected Charlie, in a way, it *wasn't*. Not properly. The Rawlings family, like so many weekenders, were playing at country living. They existed in quite a different manner from the long-time residents to whose lifestyle they fancied they aspired.

In the big old country houses, handed down through generations, the rain seeped through ill-fitting windows and stained the ancient velvet curtains; sunlight faded the drapes and upholstery; huge pieces of furniture stood propped on Tunbridge Wells phone books from 1972 and '73; the sills and light shades were black with heaps of desiccated flies; smelly dogs slept on the sofas, they whelped in the master bedroom; the grounds came in, year by year, through the back door where the wellington boots were stacked. And no one had time to hand-stencil the wallpaper, or to sew a patchwork, or to distress a wardrobe. Nor would they have dreamed of doing so, life being altogether too short for such whimsical nonsense.

He thought, then, with dislike, of Dee Rawlings. And he said to himself, It's a game to her.

'She's always going on at me. She gets on my tits, to be honest.'

'Who's that? Ivy, you mean? Well, I guess it makes a lot of extra work for her, your being here.'

'That's right, go on, you take *her* side.'

'I'm not taking sides, Kayleigh, but . . . Look, let's have that tea.'

She picked up the pot and, with wavering hand, began to pour, drizzling the golden liquid now in the mugs, now on to the tray. If she would only stand up to do the job, he remarked to himself, she would be able to exercise more control. This was not, however, a critical thought, it was merely an observation. And he sat tight, forbearing to get up, to go round and take over from her. Too many people, already, in his opinion, were doing that to Kayleigh Roth.

'You're all right here, are you, otherwise?' he asked conversationally. 'I mean, apart from this thing with Ivy.'

'S'pose so.'

'Not too lonely?'

She shrugged. 'What do *you* think?'

'I don't know. I quite like my own company. But this is a large house. And you're a long way from friends and family. I guess there must be times . . .'

'It gets a bit boring, that's the worst of it. Still, there's always the telly. And I'm reading this book.'

'What book?'

'About . . .' But she could not, then, muster an answer. Even idle talk, at times, demanded more of her than she could readily supply. She rested her head on her spread fingers, drove them into her hair.

'What will you do?'

'Huh?'

'You must have some plan.'

'I'm staying put for now.'

'Yes, right. But . . .'

'But what?'

'It's none of my business, of course –'

'No, it isn't.'

He took a biscuit and snapped it in half. 'If ever you need anyone, in the evening, in the middle of the night, you only have to ring me.'

She shot him a look of dark suspicion. Her mood was combative again. She had been right all along: he was like all the rest, he was only after one thing. 'You should be so lucky,' she told him nastily. And, 'I don't know what you take me for?'

Her approach to members of the opposite sex was at most times confrontational. Her manner was the same when she was flirting with them as when she was seeing them off. And on occasion she was barely less confused than they were by her contradictory stance.

If Charlie was confused, however, he gave no sign of it. He smiled, not with his eyes, nor with his mouth, nor with anything visible, but on the other side, the inside of his face, where she could sense rather than see it. 'If you thought you heard burglars,' he told her easily, 'or if a pipe burst, or a fuse needed mending, *then* you might give me a call.'

'Oh,' she said shortly. 'Yes.'

'And don't be so bloody chippy.'

'All right.'

'I'm not trying to take advantage of you.'

She brought the cup up to her mouth, breathed in the steam which moistened her lip, lowered her eyelids demurely. When she took a sip and swallowed, he saw the movement of her throat, and felt renewed tenderness for her.

'Sorry,' she said gruffly, clanking the cup down after a pause.

'Don't be,' he reassured her. And he gave her a proper, open, outside smile, which brought into play his eyes, his mouth, even his nose.

She smiled back. How could she not? He was probably the closest ally she had in an alien world (for even Sandra, she sensed, needed something from her).

'D'you know,' she said softly, confidingly, 'I –'

'Look at this, if you please. Look at this!' With a tedious

inevitability, Ivy was back, flurrying a pillowcase at Kayleigh.

'What?'

'A cigarette burn, that's what. In this nice, lacy pillowslip. You've been smoking in bed again, haven't you? Or are you going to tell me it's the moth?'

'No.' Kayleigh doubled at the waist, she reached for Ben, hauled him on to her lap and ducked down behind him, using him as a shield. 'Sorry,' she offered meekly, having used up her reserves of fight.

'You'll have to pay for it. It's only fair. The best guest linen.'

Charlie looked into his cup, swirled the last of the tea around and drank it down in one mouthful. He got up purposefully and went to the sink, to wash up after him. And he studiously ignored this contretemps.

He wanted to go to Kayleigh's aid, to put his arm about her, to fend off her accuser. He wanted to shout that *he'd* buy new sheets, new pillowcases, new anything, only, for Christ's sake, leave the poor kid *alone*. And he had to remind himself, very, very firmly, that this was not the means by which she would be helped. It would be wrong and cruel and stupid to encourage her dependency.

So he dried the mug, hung it on its hook, and made for the door, whistling nonchalantly ('These are the days of our lives . . .'). Only, then he couldn't help it. He absolutely couldn't. As he made his exit, he tipped Kayleigh a furtive, supportive, we're-in-this-together type of wink.

That was the day Sandie wasted two hundred quid. Not that she saw it as waste at the time: she regarded it, rather, as a sound investment in herself, in her spiritual and physical well-being. Only later was she forced to the dispiriting conclusion that she had simply chucked good money after bad.

She had woken very early, stiff with new resolve. An urgent sense of purpose had propelled her from her bed to her table, where she had sketched out her agenda. No more mooching around, no more moping, no more harking after what might have been, no more self-doubt or disillusion. She was going to take matters firmly in hand.

She had had an unspeakable week so far. Everything that could go wrong had gone wrong. Shocks, hurts and misfortunes had homed in on her like smart bombs until she felt positively devastated.

On Monday, when she was shopping for fish, she had taken a chance in the residential parking in Notting Hill, even though she had known this to be folly. Too fretful to think straight, she had bought brill instead of the bass she had intended, and had forgotten the shrimps altogether. Then she'd gone haring back to where she had left her little car, just in time to see it borne away on the back of a tow truck, calling plaintively to her and flashing its hazard lights. This had meant, of course, a trip to the pound, where she'd parted with an extortionate sum to reclaim it from an unsympathetic, sanctimonious jobsworth in a peaked hat, who had taken obvious delight in delaying her.

The next morning there had been a bit of argie-bargie at Marble Arch with a fat man in a Mercedes who, mauve with rage, had lowered his electric window to bawl at her that she wasn't fit to push a pram, let alone be loosed upon a public road. And, in her demoralised state, with wrong at least partly on her side, she had been scarcely able to disagree.

Finally, last night, she had cooked for a party of truly hateful people, spoilt young Chelsea types, who had all got disgustingly drunk and tipped plates of *linguine* over one another and used the *crostatine di frutta fresce*, perfect little fruit tarts, for ashtrays.

She had wanted very much to tick them off. She'd had a strong urge to inform them that they were over-privileged brats, delinquents, parasites. She'd had a good mind to evoke the starving millions in the developing world, but had checked herself, not so much for fear of forfeiting her payment (though she could ill afford to do so), or because they would only jeer at her, but because she had realised, appalled, that this was her mother speaking through her, the way mothers do (you just open your mouth, and out come their words, their sentiments, unmediated, unedited, like radio interference).

Well, enough was enough, she had concluded on waking today. She was having no more of it. She was tired of being a soft target. She was going to get hard, to shape up, to fight back.

She was not especially overweight, but was deeply at odds with her body, uncomfortable with its slopes and planes, its ins and its outs. She would have killed for a smaller waist, for leaner thighs, for a well-defined muscle here, a powerful sinew there, for a bum that might fairly be called 'pert'. And, since these things were all achievable, she swore to herself that she would have them.

Every now and then she would make these private pledges, she would promise herself the earth – subject to some pretty stringent terms and conditions. She would resolve to give up tea, coffee, alcohol for the benefits that abstinence would confer. She would swear off red meat, or chocolates, or Coca-Cola. She would vow to rise early, to run five miles a day, to enrol for evening classes, to learn French, or Spanish, or Cantonese, or car maintenance, to take an open university degree. She had, in other words, a history of making solemn resolutions – and of breaking them.

Her diary was littered with purposive statements, affirmations, admonishments, imperatives, as over and over she set herself up for failure. Had she sat down to read it through, she might have seen it was a testament to self-deception. But she never referred back, and each new entry was written with the same conviction, with much recourse to cliché and to platitude.

No pain, no gain, she had reminded herself abrasively on the twenty-fourth of April. Failure and unhappiness were self-inflicted, she had noted high-mindedly on the twenty-third of May, while success and happiness were self-bestowed. The eighteenth of July had found her in reflective mood, musing on long-term aims and short-term sacrifice. The thirteenth of September had been the first day of the rest of her life – as in their turn had been the thirtieth of January and twentieth of June.

If this book were to fall into the hands of a stranger, he or she would probably visualise its owner as a big Girl Guide called Pollyanna. About her love-life, however, the stranger would learn nothing. It was far too sensitive to be committed to paper, except in a kind of cryptic, coded form. ('Met C. Asked out.' 'Dance. C stayed. Great!' 'C rang.' 'No word from C.' How could anyone guess what a tale this told? A brief and tragic love story with beginning, middle and end.)

Her uncertain humour was all down to Colin, of course. He was responsible. It was his fault she had felt such a victim. But she was going to turn this thing around, she was going to harness the energy of her anguish to beget change.

So here she was, at a very swish gym, signing on for a year, confident that she was embarked upon a whole new chapter of her life. She would come here four, five, maybe six times a week, to pound a kind of rolling road, or to pedal an immobile bicycle, to go nowhere very, very fast. She would attend aerobics classes, stretch classes, step classes, she would lift weights. In a few short weeks, you would not know her. The two-hundred-pound joining fee would thus be money well spent, twelve pounds a week membership a mere bagatelle.

All right, she did not warm to the lithe blonde with the sunbed tan who greeted her at reception, who flicked and clicked her fingernails as she spoke, and who offered laconically – one might even say 'grudgingly' -- to show her around. Then, yes, she was a mite intimidated by the beefed-up blokes she saw flexing their tempered bodies before the full-length mirrors, so narcissistic, so single-minded. She also, to be honest, felt a tiny bit disadvantaged by the beautiful young women who were swanning around wearing funny Lycra knickers, Batman fashion, over their leggings (now, what could be the point of *that*?) The atmosphere in this bright-lit, subterranean world was curiously torpid, as if Time itself were working out with weights.

The old Sandra Rawlings would have turned and fled. But it was a very different Sandra Rawlings who filled in a membership application form, and who dashed off a cheque without flinching. She had, after all, been reborn.

'This entitles you to free access to all the club facilities,' the receptionist intoned. Flick, flick went her fingernails. 'That is, the gym, the studios, the steam room and jacuzzi, showers, changing-room and vanity area, the salad and juice bar. Also, use of hair-drier plus one small and one large towel per visit. But physio and beauty therapies are extra.'

'Oh, quite.'

'As are the sunbeds.'

'Right-ho.'

'No black-soled shoes to be worn in the gym or studio.'

'No, of course not,' said Sandra virtuously. (Perish the thought, her tone implied.)

'And no vest tops, please.'

'Fine.'

'Because we can't have members perspiring all over the machines.'

'Yes, I do see,' she concurred, breaking out in a sweat.

'We will write to you as soon as your application has been processed, probably early next week. Then you must come along for a fitness assessment with one of our personal trainers.'

'That will be great.'

'Payments are pro-rated, which means, if you start half-way through the month, you will be charged accordingly.'

'That seems very fair. Well . . . until next week, then.'

She was positively boiling with enthusiasm as she bounded up the stairs (if steam had poured out of her ears, she would scarcely have been surprised). She could not wait to get cracking, could not wait for the day when she too was a vision of loveliness in snappy Lycra.

She wrestled with the street door, endeavouring to push it when it ought to be pulled. And she stood well back, flattening herself against the wall, as a clean-cut young man with wavy brown hair came shoving in through it.

'Jamie!'

'Sandra!' The surprised expression gave way to one of puzzlement, then, rapidly, almost comically, to one of petulance. 'What are *you* doing here?'

'I . . . er. I just joined.'

'You joined *my* gym?' he queried, incredulous.

'I didn't know it was yours,' she told him hotly. Her face prickled as if it had been scoured. 'I didn't know you belonged – let alone that you *owned* the place.'

'Don't be funny. Of course you knew. You must have known. That's why you've come here, isn't it? You never could allow me my own space. You've always been jealous of me, that's your problem. Well, look, I can't stop you, can I? It's a free country, after all. But at least do me one small favour, will you? If you see me here, don't hang round me, don't talk to me. Especially if I'm with the other guys, keep *stumm*. We don't know each other, right? We've never met.'

'Jamie,' she replied, choking, as her eyes filled with astringent tears, 'I *don't* know you. We *are* strangers. Who are you, actually? I mean, who the hell do you think you are?' Then, without waiting for an answer, she bundled out through the door and headed for home, vowing never, ever, ever to set foot in that hateful place again.

———————— ● ————————

Colin Clarke sat at his desk, playing cat's cradle with a long, inelastic rubber band, and brooding on his bitter disenchantment. He was simply not himself at the moment, as Vi Wheeler in despatch had remarked to Pauline from bought ledger only this morning. (And, yes, there was something not quite right there, Pauline had agreed. Girl trouble, perhaps? That would be it.)

He had a pile of paperwork to process, but he could not bestir himself. His tray filled up with orders, invoices, enquiries, like a steady drip of rainwater into a bucket, until the lot ran over under his distracted gaze.

He had a good mind, he told himself, to ring that Sandra Rawlings, to give it to her straight from the shoulder. He had a good mind to denounce her, to cry shame.

He looped the rubber band over two fingers to make a catapult, pulled it taut and pinged it at the calendar, which showed a nice west view of Exeter Cathedral and did not deserve to bear the brunt of his ill will.

What kind of moral coward was she, who would not even come to the phone to speak up for herself, to say 'I'm truly sorry, I think this has been a mistake', or, 'It was nice, but . . .', or, as might be the case, 'No thank you very much, I don't want to see you, you're a long streak of piss and a laughable lover, you're absolutely hopeless in bed'?

She had taken him for a fool, that was evident. He had been thoroughly impressed by her, and thoroughly bamboozled. She had seemed so sweet, so sincere, so straight-up-and-down. She had been all lovey-dovey – then she'd given him the bird.

Colin was, when all things were considered, pretty well adjusted. He had got his head together. If he did not love like a brother the young man who greeted him in his shaving mirror each morning, if his looking-glass self was not David to his Jonathan, or Castor to his Pollux, the two had at least reached some kind of accord.

In his teenage years he had been ruthlessly self-critical, he had hated his face, blitzed as it had been with spots and so very far from perfect. He had prayed to God for outrageous good looks, he had put in as a matter of urgency for powerful sex appeal. Then, although the former had quite plainly been denied him, the latter had, he'd fancied, been bestowed upon him in some small measure.

Well, so much for that! He had plainly been deluded. Now, all his hard-won confidence was gone. He was ridiculous once more in his own eyes; he was back at the adolescent acne stage, returned to youthful fearfulness, reduced to the critical contemplation of his willy.

He could not escape the feeling that he had been the victim of an elaborate tease. He was sure that he had been used. He felt, indeed, the way any woman would feel who had been taken to bed on a promise, then dropped like a hot brick the next morning.

I have to talk to her, he determined, reaching for the phone.

I *can't*, he demurred, chickening out. His stomach was in knots. He could not even bring himself to eat the currant bun which Vi had brought him for his tea. It sat there on a saucer, staring at him through its many beady eyes.

Sod it, he decided, I *will* phone her. I don't care what she says. I shall feel so much better for telling her she's a first-class bitch.

But as he grabbed up the receiver, an internal call came straight through. 'That was quick,' said Pauline, down the line. 'I didn't even hear it ring.'

'No. I was about to dial out.'

'Oh, I'm sorry, my ducks.'

'That's all right,' Colin told her, picking up a plastic ruler and waving it about. 'It was nothing important. Nothing at all.'

———————— ❀ ————————

Nancy Wilkins sat back in her chair and closed her eyes, the better to imagine what it was to be twenty-eight-year-old Anita P, who felt ugly and frumpy and lonely and thwarted, who had never had a boyfriend, never been kissed, and who despaired of ever finding true friendship, let alone love.

This was how she went about her work now. She tried to *be* each person, to know what it was to live a particular life, to experience someone else's particular reality. She endeavoured to solve problems, as it were, from the inside, which seemed like the best way to approach them. And at long last she was beginning to apprehend what was meant by 'reading between the lines'.

She had worked hard and long, over the past four days, to clear the backlog of Dee's correspondence. Now, at 6.30 on Thursday night, she had all but brought it up to date.

Through the week, she had envisaged herself variously bankrupt, battered, obese, anorexic, agoraphobic, unhappily married, widowed, divorced, sexually compromised, harassed, coerced. . . . She had put herself in a great many pairs of other people's shoes. And she was developing a style of response – an engaging mix of her own genuine empathy and Dee's long experience, her own native wisdom, Dee's greater worldliness – which would bring genuine solace and inspiration.

Nancy was not twenty years old. She was a virgin. She lived, as she had always done, with her parents. This job at *Mia* was her first. And, in an almost childlike manner, she could state certain shining truths to illuminate a situation. People at their wits' end, receiving word from her, would feel a little less alone, a little less afraid. They would see that, yes, they still had possibilities.

Her letters were softer in tone, less assertive, less scolding than Dee's. They were also intellectually honest, they were forthright, they had the clarity and practicality of an uncluttered mind. She said, not 'Do this', but 'Consider this'. She said, 'Look at it this way'. She understood instinctively that one could only work with what one had. She took into the final reckoning all the fears and frailties that bedevil human nature. And when her message was one that the recipient would not wish to hear, she delivered it with a palliative charm.

Sometimes she would go home and sleep on an issue, and when she awoke her subconscious mind would offer up to consciousness a happy resolution. Or she would talk a problem through with her family as they sat over their meal at night, and between them they were sure to think of something.

Not that there was invariably consensus. (The jury was still out, for example, in the case of Maureen from Peterborough, whose husband, having scarpered with a younger woman, had seen the error of his ways and was begging to return. Should Maureen have him back? Could she trust him? What of her new-found independence? 'Give the guy another chance,' Nancy's dad had urged, forking shepherd's pie into his mouth. While, 'Not on your life!' her mum had argued, wagging her knife like a reproving finger.) But it did mean that they covered all the angles.

At four o'clock each day, Nancy passed the fat file of correspondence through for Dee to sign – and sign Dee duly did, making no comment on her labours, beyond a complacent, jokey, 'Well, now, my sweet, I can see I'll have to watch it, or you'll be doing me out of a job.'

So, there was Nancy, on her own in the office, empathising for all she was worth, inhabiting the world of the unloved, unlovely Anita, who had never learned to cherish herself, who had a great big hole at the centre of her being which must somehow be filled; there was Nancy, experiencing Anita's pain and isolation, when the cool, pale scent of L'Eau D'Issey wafted up her nose and made her eyelids flutter.

'Oh!' she said, startled, glancing up. And then, 'Oh, crikey!' For Clare Constantine, was standing by her desk, reading the thoughts she had jotted down in her ring-bound notebook, words of comfort and encouragement rehearsed in longhand. (Nancy could think so much better, somehow, on paper than on a computer screen: notions seemed to flow like ink from her brain, down her arm into her writing hand, and to spill on to the page.)

She had scarcely any contact with the editor from day to day. Clare Constantine was not a regular visitor to the 'Dear Dee' office. It was, indeed, something of a backwater. And Nancy Wilkins was, after all, just a minion, a very junior member of staff. She was terribly in awe of this beautiful, aloof, chic, self-contained creature with a mouth like a poppy, with hair so red it seared the back of the eye, and with a gaze cold enough to give you frostbite.

'Where's Dee?' asked Clare in her deceptively soft voice.

'Uhm, she's left.'

Clare made no reply, merely raising one eyebrow a bare millimetre.

'She's not been gone five minutes,' Nancy offered loyally, protectively. 'She had to, er . . . er . . . go.'

'And Edith?'

'Edie. No, she leaves at six on the dot. Always. Because of having to catch her train.'

'I see.' Clare reached over her to pick up the letters file, and proceeded to leaf through it. She read without a word, her lips tight shut so that no thought should slip out, as Nancy sat frozen, hardly daring to breathe, too nervous to utter a sound.

'Who wrote these?' asked Clare at length, tersely, riffling the pages.

'Er . . .'

'Not Dee, surely?'

'Well, you see . . .' Nancy had heard it said that human beings blushed only on exposed parts of the body. If a woman was wearing a low-cut dress, apparently, her blushes would spread to her chest, whereas if she was wearing a high-necked sweater, the blush would stop at the chin. Now she wondered how anyone could possibly know this. It was much like the fridge light conundrum. How could they tell what went on beneath one's clothes? In fact, she was absolutely sure she was blushing, at this very minute; under her ribbed polo-neck jumper, she was sure she was pink right to her navel.

Clare replaced the file on the desktop, she pinned it down with her fingertips. 'These are your replies,' she said firmly.

'Well, yes and no.'

'Meaning . . . ?'

'Uhm . . .'

'Either they are yours, or they aren't.'

She was about to be given the sack, Nancy realised in dismay. She was going to get the push for so far exceeding her authority. What right had she, a secretary, to meddle in the affairs of *Mia* readers? What right had she, a mere nobody, to tell anyone what they should do? 'The thing is', she said in a rush, 'we were a bit behind, so I thought I could help. I've typed hundreds and hundreds of Dee's letters since I've been here, and I've sort of got the feel of it, I know how she answers people. And, of course, Dee goes through them all before she signs them, she reads every one. And, in any case –'

'Shush,' said Clare, and made a cut-off gesture with her hand. 'Remind me, what is your name?'

'Nancy Wilkins.'

'Ah, yes.' Then, as Nancy squirmed in the glare of her speculation, Hmmm, Clare thought. And, Maybe. . .

This moppet, this poppet, with flittery eyelashes and a jittery smile, with her hair bunched up in a scrunchie, was not the most likely protégée, and yet. . . There was something of My Little Pony about the girl, and My Little Pony could be groomed.

She would infinitely prefer to see, at the head of the problems page, a photograph of sweet, sympathetic Nancy Wilkins, than that of Dee Rawlings simpering at the camera, wise in her own conceit ('Love me, love my dogma,' Clare would react with distaste, whenever she looked upon it).

There was an innocence, an artlessness about the girl which was all to the good. She could work with those qualities. Miss Wilkins was going to help her to unseat La Rawlings – and she wouldn't even know it was happening.

DECEMBER

CHAPTER

•

II

'How are we doing in here?' asked Dee, advancing her bright, importuning face around the door, her small eyes darting. Then, when no one responded, 'All right, everybody?' she entreated. 'Mummy? Daddy? I say, why are you sitting in this Stygian gloom?'

She snapped on the light and something happened to perspective: the room, the people in it, seemed to zoom towards her; the garden beyond the window stepped smartly back into the shadows: indoors was suddenly very in; out was very out.

'Are you warm enough?' she fussed, though the central heating was going full blast, and she glanced distractedly over at the fire. It wasn't burning up at all, she noticed. Flames licked playfully around the apple logs but would not bite. The damp, sappy wood hissed and spat contemptuously. The reflection in the round-bellied brass coal scuttle was thin and milky. Eric ought to do something. Why would he never trouble himself? He showed no initiative whatsoever.

Uttering little snorts and clucks of consternation, little farmyard noises, Dee went to close the curtains on the cobalt afternoon. 'Isn't this nice?' she said tonelessly, because, frankly, it wasn't, it wasn't nice at all.

The normally comfortable sitting-room at Foxholes had taken on the aspect of a special clinic; the atmosphere was at once tense and tedious, with everyone apparently huddled over his or her own private misery, waiting for the worst.

The dozens of greetings cards looped on ribbon above the fireplace, the beady holly boughs, the winged mistletoe with its waxy berries strung from the beams, did nothing to lend cheer, but rather pointed up the lack of it. In the corner stood the Christmas tree, moribund and moulting, silently shedding its needles and, like a child hugging to itself a secret, declining to give off so much as a whiff of pine.

Weird, thought Kayleigh, watching this seasonal pantomime in disbelief. *Well* weird. She would never have credited it. Here was a very different, a far less exuberant Dee Rawlings from the one she had so far encountered. Since her parents' arrival yesterday, Dee had, indeed, become positively cringing.

Mind you, it wasn't any wonder. The couple were enough to give anyone the screaming ab-dabs. What a pair of creeps! Innes, Dee's dad, was a tall, thin, grey-faced man with thick, wavy, sulphur-tinged white hair, which he wore greased down and comb-harrowed. His eyebrows met in such a tangle at the bridge of his bulbous nose, they somehow gave the impression that his face had burst open and was spilling its stuffing. He said almost nothing, showed no inclination to talk, and was absorbed in his pipe, which appeared to need continual servicing (he would plug it with tarry tobacco, tamping it down with a stained and spatulate thumb, then puff it alight, suck his way through it, knock it out, clean it assiduously, blow down it like a wet fart, refill it, and light up once more, fugging the place with throat-catching fumes).

His wife, Jean, however, could elicit from him the occasional grunt, by positing that today's young people had no grace or manners or respect for their betters, that television turned their foolish heads, that Christmas just wasn't Christmas any more, and that the *Sun* newspaper had committed a crime tantamount to high treason, by publishing this morning, two days before transmission, the text of the Queen's Christmas message. (The junior royals, she averred, had no one but themselves to blame for their misfortunes, but Her Majesty had done nothing to bring down upon herself such ill luck.)

Jean Crabtree was a tiny, wizened woman, with cross-stitch at the corners of her cavilling mouth. She seemed so dried, she might have been sucked out, shucked off, sloughed, shed like snakeskin; there might have been nothing of her but husk. She wore a moth-holed lilac jersey with a lacy crochet collar, and with a balled hankie bulging up the sleeve. Her hair was dyed a curious shade of tangerine, and grew in sparse clumps, as if it had been pricked out; her scalp showed luminously through. She dipped from time to time into a crumpled bag of barley sugars, twisting off a cellophane wrapper and rattling a sweet, like a pebble, against her dentures.

The Crabtrees, Mr and Mrs, held for Kayleigh a gruesome fascination: she could scarcely take her eyes off them. When she did allow her attention to slip, her gaze to slide, she would be brought up short by the sight of Eric, who sat in his usual chair, juggling Oedipuss on his lap, awkward as a TV dinner, and who stared at her with unconcealed lust.

'You can say what you like,' Jean addressed her daughter, defying her, with a look, to say anything at all, 'but no good has ever come, or ever will, of so-called women's liberation.'

'No, Mummy.' Dee stood at the window, fussing a curtain, shaking down the folds, and seemed, by her silence, to concur.

'Is it any wonder', Jean demanded, 'that modern marriages end in divorce, when these uppity wives are forever off gallivanting? Paul tells us', she continued, calling upon a higher authority, 'to submit ourselves unto our own husbands. For the husband is the head of the wife, even as Christ is head of the church. As the church is subject unto Christ, so let the wives be to their own husbands in everything.'

'Christ!' muttered Kayleigh irreverently. And who, she wondered, was this Paul? She waited for Dee to sound off, to respond with anger to her mother, to reply with her customary force that the idea stank. But Dee merely sighed and subsided on to the sofa, where she hunched herself forward, trapping her hands, palm to palm, between her ample knees and squeezing hard. Who was she to argue with this apostle, with whom her mother was on such cosy first-name terms? Who was she to argue with her mother? And with what, precisely, anyway, would she be taking issue?

Jean might have been making reference to the Duchess of York, whose antics had exercised her over supper last night. (It was her habit to return to a topic, one day, two days, even three days later, as you might return to a cryptic crossword, with your mind refreshed, your pen poised, having summoned the answer to Five Down. 'As I was saying,' she would remark, quite out of the blue. Or, 'And another thing'. 'As I was saying, I've no time for the Pope.' 'And another thing, this Nintendo.') Equally, she could have been speaking of marriage in general. Or she could be impugning the Rawlings partnership in particular, all arsey-versy as it was, all back-to-front and upside-down and against nature. She could be getting at her daughter, or at her son-in-law, or both. Her trick was to be that bit vague, to dissemble, to play the game of Now You See Me; Now You Don't.

Let it pass, let it pass, Dee soothed herself, rocking just perceptibly back and forth. Jean didn't mean any harm. No, certainly not. She had old-fashioned values which one must respect. She was just of that generation.

But Eric, *dear* Eric, would not let it go. 'You're quite right there,' he bantered, stroking Oedipuss, who purred ecstatically, jacked up his tail-end, stapled his front end to a Terylene trouser leg. 'You hear that, Dee? Submit unto your husband. Head of the household, *et cetera?*'

'I must away to the kitchen, my liege,' said Dee with a sickly smile, 'and warm some mince pies. We'll have tea, and then afterwards we can play the Parson's Cat.'

'Play the parson's cat at what?' Eric joshed her.

'Oh . . . *you.*' Dee snatched up a tapestry cushion and made as if to lob it at him. She was laughing, Kayleigh noticed, but with a kind of desperation. She appeared ever so slightly off her head.

Weird, she thought again. Wee-urd. The place was a madhouse. She rummaged down the back of the chair for her fags, hung one on her sullen lower lip, cupped her hand, flick-flicked her Zippo alight. The flare showed red for an instant through the thin flesh of her fingers as she drew on the flame. Then something about the presence of these visitors – Jean's sniff of condemnation, Innes's own dogged, disgusting, almost aggressive smoking habit – discouraged her. With a sigh, she ground the unsmoked cigarette out in the ashtray, squashing it till it frayed and split. Jamie might, she told herself, find the taste, the smell of tobacco a turn-off. Come the New Year, she would kick the habit.

Jamie. Oh, yippee! The day after tomorrow he would be here to spend Christmas. It was such ages since she'd seen him. Weeks and weeks. Now she counted the hours till he would come, till the moment when she might offer him his Christmas present.

Deirdre Rawlings, née Crabtree, stood in the kitchen at Foxholes, wringing a teatowel in her hands and staring into space. She felt about eleven years old, she was returned to the plain, plump child she used to be, in a drab frock, with her hair cut short above her ears, and with her heart simply breaking.

She had had (although she could not, even now, fully confess it) a rotten childhood. She had been born in 1940, into a world at war. She had been a baby in the days of clothing coupons, in the era of the utility scheme when, under the Making Up of Civilian Clothing (Restriction) Orders, materials were skimped, when the use of pleats and frills, wide hems, long sleeves and buttons was curtailed, when all embroidery, all trimmings except knicker elastic were banned.

Thrift, austerity, the make-do-and-mend ethic, had found in Jean and Innes Crabtree its most enthusiastic exponents, for parsimony was their middle name. When the government introduced comprehensive rationing, it had been playing their tune. And when all rationing was finally abolished, it seemed no one had bothered to advise the Crabtrees. They had continued with their cheese-paring, penny-pinching, sides-to-middling regime, much as a few lone Japanese soldiers continued to fight World War Two in the jungle, refusing to surrender, to believe it was all over, years after hostilities had ceased.

The young Deirdre had dreamed of silk tulle and taffeta, of tiered skirts that spun out like soup-plates when you whirled around, of velveteen-trimmed hems, of sky-blue and pink, of ankle straps, or smocking, of pearly buttons, and rick-rack binding, and long pigtails with butterfly bows. But these had been no more available to her than was a nipped-in waist. Instead, she had been issued with standard school uniform, thick grey socks, sensible shoes, a grey gaberdine, and a 'new' Sunday frock, a spare-parts job, customised from two outgrown ones.

She was hungry in those days. And lonely. But most of all she remembered being always cold. Well, of course, so was everybody else. But in her schoolfriends' homes there had at least been little islands of heat, there had been hand-pulled hearth rugs before glowing coke fires, there had been sputtery blue gas fires to roast bony shins; there had been great, big, rumbling boilers, and hot water enough for an occasional decent bath. Her friends' parents had not gone around, as Jean had done, switching off this, damping down that, unplugging the other, always in the name of economy.

'Put another woolly on,' Jean would admonish her miserable lump of a daughter. Or 'Run around and get warm, why don't you?' Deirdre, however, had not much cared for sports, for playing out. She had always studied hard, cramming her head with facts and figures, to pass exams, to be a wanted child, to make her parents proud.

They had hoped for a son, you see, to raise to manhood, at that intense moment in history when all Britain was in love with its 'boys'. In the happy event of future conflict, they would kiss him off with indecent pride to almost certain death. A girl, on the other hand, had been somehow not the thing.

Deirdre had always understood this, deep, deep down, the way children do, without it ever once being spoken of. She had known she was a bitter disappointment, a lamentable mistake. She had known she had come to the wrong address. And she had embodied this knowledge; it had been as much a part of her as blood and bone, and had grown with her into adulthood.

Still, she had won through in the end, had she not? She had earned their love and regard. She had been vindicated. No boy could have achieved more in life than she had done (she was on telly, for Pete's sake, she was famous).

She had also, incidentally, sides-to-middled her past, she had made do and mended, she had salvaged something useful, a colourful remnant from her childhood. 'I have suffered hardship,' she could boast to her readers, 'I have gone without. I had humble beginnings. We were poor, yes, but we were happy. It was character-forming. It has made me what I am. So don't talk to *me* about underprivilege. That is not an excuse.'

Jamie would tease her endlessly about this. Such a wag, was

Jamie. 'Tell us', he'd beg, 'about when you were a girl. When you lived in a shoe box. When supper was a single baked bean between the three of you.' Then, always the sport, Dee would laugh and laugh at her own funniosity. She'd say, 'No, it was *two* baked beans on a Sunday.' And strangely, somehow, it seemed even more true, for the fact that they joked about it.

Returned now from her reverie to the present, to her reinvented self, Dee Rawlings shook out the teatowel and hung it on the rail. If only, she thought, Mummy and Daddy would show, by the merest of gestures, something of the appreciation they must surely feel, if only they would unbend a bit, say, 'This is nice!', or 'Oh, how lovely!' or 'Well done!', if only they would learn to express emotion, her happiness would be complete.

Year on year they came to her for Christmas. Year on year she put up a magnificent spread. They slept in a warm room, under a duckdown duvet, and were woken in the morning with tea and toast on a tray. 'I never could get on with these continental quilt affairs,' Jean would grumble. And, censoriously, 'I dread to think what your electric bill must be.' 'Rich food', she would say over dinner, 'never did agree with me.' While Innes harrumphed in agreement.

Never mind. It was just their way, the quaint old dears, Dee told herself forgivingly. The habits of a lifetime die hard, they really do. At Foxholes the Crabtrees found themselves in the very lap of luxury. Understandably they were overwhelmed and perhaps somewhat defensive.

Thank goodness she had been able to do so much better by her own two children! Thank goodness she had learned from experience! She had been open and loving with the kids. She had never disparaged or belittled them, never pushed them too hard or retarded them, never put them down or denied them, but had loved them and nurtured them, and had encouraged them to be themselves, to believe in who they were. She had stinted them neither materially nor emotionally: she had been lavish in her generosity to them.

'Oh, it's you,' she said shortly, as a draught from the back door sliced through the kitchen, and Sandie blew in, marbled with cold, bearing gifts. 'I was hoping Jamie would be here today, too, that we'd have a full house,' Dee added, offering a cheek for a kiss, 'but needless to say he is working.'

'I can't honestly imagine', Sandie replied, dutifully touching her cold lips diffidently to her mother's pillowy face, before stooping over the table, spreading her arms, depositing the gaily wrapped parcels in a jumble, 'that anyone much will want to buy or sell a house just a couple of days before Christmas.'

'But he'll have paperwork to do, and book-keeping, I don't doubt. On top of which there's the property management side.'

'Yes, there is that.'

'I'm sure he's hard at it.'

'Mm.' Sandie unwound her scarf, which was sparkly with moisture, she peeled off her gloves, tossed them on to the dresser, helped herself to a sheet of paper towel and sneezed into it, a whooping and – to Dee's mind – intemperate sneeze. 'I've been pretty busy myself, as you can imagine,' she said, screwing up her eyes and nose against a second explosion. 'Dots of pardies. Dots of shopping. And dots of lubbly bomb scares.' She twitched her nostrils like a hamster, then relaxed her face. Privately she hoped this was not the beginnings of a cold. It was all too easy, when you were depressed as she was, to let the buggers in. 'Police cordons everywhere,' she continued in her normal voice, 'just to add to the fun and festivities. I left my car in Piccadilly in the hope they'd think it was suspect and blow it up. I've got to take it for its MOT and it hasn't a hope of passing.'

'No?' Dee turned away to stoop over the Aga. When she opened the creaking cast-iron door, a smell of mincemeat, of cloves and cinnamon and burnt sugar, wafted up her nostrils. She would have liked to help Sandie out with the car, she reflected. She would have been pleased to give her something towards the expense. But Jamie had touched her only recently for money towards the repair to his Porsche, which some despicable person had scraped while it stood parked, and frankly, one could not be forever bailing out one's children, could one? It wouldn't, in the long run, do them any good. It wouldn't encourage enterprise. 'Granny and Gramps are here, by the way.'

'Three cheers! That's made my day.'

'Now, Sandra, darling, *please.*' Dee transferred the singing mince pies on to a cooling tray, picking them up very quickly, one by one, going ouch, ouch, then dusting her fingertips and puffing on them.

'I know, I know. Don't worry, I'll be on my best behaviour. But it's not as if they could care less, they haven't the slightest interest in me. Jamie's their blue-eyed boy.'

'That's nonsense. They're extremely fond of you.'

'Ha!'

'They *are*. They're not demonstrative, that's all. They're very repressed.'

'You can say that again.'

'But they mean well.'

'Hmm.'

'You're not leaving those gloves there. Or that dirty old scarf.'

'It isn't dirty.' Sandie picked up the offending items and crammed them, anyhow, into her pockets. 'How's Kayleigh? Still with us?'

'Still here.' Dee passed a hand over her brow. 'She's quite impossible, I find. A stubborn little madam. I can't think what we're going to do with her.'

'Would you like me to have a chat with her while I'm here? A girlie heart to heart? To ask her what plans she's making?'

'Oh, no, no, no, don't dream of it. It's a delicate matter. Best that I handle it.'

'As you wish.'

'Well, I do wish. I *do*. Now, these packages . . .' Dee circled her hand to indicate the parcels on the table, each one so beautifully, carefully wrapped and labelled, marked to so-and-so from Sandra, with love, kiss, kiss, kiss. 'They can go under the tree.'

'Okey-doke.'

'Take them through. Say hello to the folks. Then you can come and help me with the tea things.'

'All right,' Sandie assented, shrugging off her coat as she went into the hall. At the sitting-room door she hesitated, took a deep breath, steeled herself for this encounter. Here we go, she told herself resignedly, for the prospect of seeing her grandparents filled her with a peculiar despair. Here we go, here we go, here we go. . .

———————— • ————————

Charlie Horscroft sat at his kitchen table, with Polly's heavy head in his lap, and contemplated his handiwork in a mood of utter satisfaction.

Every night for more than a month he had laboured at it, inclining over it till his neck muscles creaked, his dark brow furrowed with concentration, his mouth set in a grimace. He had sawed and planed and carved, he had screwed and glued and sandpapered, taking meticulous care over the fiddly bits, paying close attention to detail, pausing only to dash aside the lock of hair that fell repeatedly over his eyes. There must be no rough edges, no nasty splinters to spear little fingers. All paints must be non-toxic, and no piece small enough to swallow.

A sturdy little ark, he had built, complete with the rosy-cheeked Noahs, Mr and Mrs, plus a veritable menagerie of pigs and horses, stripey tigers, sheep, tortoises, geese, giraffes. . . The figures were actually rather crude and representational. They could not have been called true to life. Approximation only had been possible in the time; verisimilitude would have taken longer. The main thing was, he told himself, that you could tell your aardvark from your elephant.

He threw a booted foot over his knee, tugged at the lace, as, mightily pleased with himself, he began to whistle, 'The animals went in two by two', and to shout, 'Hurrah! Hurrah!' This sudden outburst set Polly skittering on the lino, up and down, up and down, up and down. 'It's all right, honey,' he soothed her, when she came to a halt and started barking, bouncing, her front paws lifting off the ground. 'I've not lost my head. Look, though, what a lovely thing I've made.'

He had conceived the toy for Ben, as a surprise, as a present for Christmas, because that funny little fellow had such worried blue eyes, and a nose like a button; because Charlie had taken him to his heart; because the kiddie had next to nothing, while most had so very much.

These, at any rate, were the reasons he had enumerated to himself. Kayleigh, and the feelings she aroused in him, had not been in his accounting.

In the front hall, the telephone began to ring. He went at once to answer it, trailing a bootlace, hauling his sweater over his head, dropping it on to the stairs. It was his habit to undress this way, to shrug off clothes willy-nilly. By the time he got up to the bathroom for his shower, he might be wearing one sock and a singlet, or just his jeans, or nothing.

It occurred to him, fleetingly, that this might be the call he'd waited for – the call from *her*. 'Ring any time,' he'd said nonchalantly. 'If there's something you need. Or just for a chat. Whatever.' But she hadn't. Not yet. Since he finished work at Foxholes in early November, there had been no word from Kayleigh.

'Hello,' he said, with no great hope or expectation. (What would be, he had determined, would be. The choice was hers. It was unthinkable to him that he should force his affections upon another human being.)

'Charlie,' said his mother, 'is that you?'

'Yes. What d'you think? Who else?' He hung on to the newel post with his free hand. He felt tired in his bones, yet alert; he felt the way an old man feels, whose mind is still young and green and keen, whose imagination is errant and indomitable in a decrepit body.

'I don't know, do I? Listen, do me a favour and look at my tap. It's the washer or something. The water just keeps gushing out, it's driving me mad. I'd get your dad to see to it, but he's working nights. Have you eaten yet? Only there's plenty. Stay for your tea. Come now and we'll have it before *Coronation Street*. What with that and my Achilles tendon. Did I tell you I pulled it? Yes, isn't that daft? Not badly, I don't mean – nothing to worry about – but it hurt like hell at first, it was crippling. I'm getting too long in the tooth for this aerobics malarkey. Still, you have to try, don't you? Can't let yourself run to fat. And it's much better than it was. Everything's fine otherwise. *You're* all right, are you? Been keeping busy? Ivy was saying, Angie's Geoff saw you over Eridge way. Yesterday, that would have been. No, the day before, because he had to go to Crowborough with his verruca. Oops, I have to hang up, the rice is boiling over. It's all scummy.'

'Better run, then,' Charlie told her fondly, amused. It was perhaps an effect of having so many children, so many calls upon her attention: at any time of the day or night, Ann Horscroft had a dozen or more things on her mind. Mostly, they were contained, confined, but at moments of high excitement they spilled out just any old how. The effect, at the receiving end, was like opening

263

an overstuffed broom cupboard, to be engulfed in an avalanche of polish tins and sponges and scrubbing brushes, to have mop and bucket come clonk you on the head.

'It will be good to see you. We can catch up on the news,' she said finally, bewilderingly. (There was *more*?)

'All right. Ta-ta,' he responded, and hung up.

He would take the ark round and show it to her, he decided. He would set it out for her to admire while he got to work on her plumbing. 'Ah, Charlie,' she'd say, 'that's smashing.' And, 'Clever old cock, aren't you?' Not that he hungered for praise; that wasn't the point. Nor was he lonely, or insufficient to himself. It was just that, every so often, it was nice to look at something *with* someone. It was like when you stood gazing at a beautiful view, and you turned to the person next to you and said, 'What about that, then?', and it made it more real in a strange way, it sort of validated it for you, and it deepened your appreciation.

Now, how long had he got? It would be, he reckoned, about twenty to seven. Like most people who do not wear a watch, Charlie had his own quite accurate internal clock. His subconscious was attuned to nature, to the changing seasons, to sound and light, to lengthening shadows, to people and routine. It heard traffic rumble and birdsong and the chimes from St Aubyn's. It registered the rhythmic to-ings and fro-ings of his neighbours, a car starting up in the damp early morning, a clump on the stair; the clack of the letterbox, the chuckle of water in the wastepipe; the *News At Ten* music through the party wall at night. And, without ever having to think about it, or to make calculations, he knew, he just *knew*, within a minute or two, what the time was.

He would take a shower, *rapido*, and pull on some clean clothes, and be round at his mum's as she was setting the table. He would join in the bunfight which at Jubilee Terrace was called 'tea'. Then the little ones would be shushed or packed off upstairs, and his mum could sit down in comfort for her thrice-weekly fix of 'The Street'. (So happy-go-lucky was the Horscroft family, so free and easy and untrammelled their existence, that Ann was seldom at full emotional stretch, and she looked to the soaps to take up the slack, to tug at her heartstrings, to provide her, vicariously, with problems.)

He cast his jeans on the landing, his socks at the bathroom door.

On his return journey to the kitchen he would scoop them all up and ram them in the washing-machine for laundering. Then he would hang them out to dance on the line; and he would bring them back in starched and scratchy with cold.

In the uncurtained bathroom window, he saw his own ghost, saw himself afloat, adrift out there in the darkness. A thousand years from now, he mused, it would be as if he never was. He would leave nothing behind him, would he, not even a memory?

It was not, after all, such a desolating thought. It was even, in a way, a comfort. It was a kind and forgiving system.

It would have been nice, of course, to be an artist or author, a Leonardo, or a Lawrence, even a Limerick, and to enrich the culture. But it didn't matter that one wasn't, for that was granted only to an exceptional few. Besides, posthumous fame was all very well, but you would still be as dead as dead.

The gratifying part would be to give humanity, in one's lifetime, something like the Macintosh or Tarmacadam, the Biro or Belisha beacon, or Braille, to know that you had made a practical contribution, that it would ever after bear your name. But what was there still to give?

Sometimes he had fancied he might dream up some great invention. This was, however, easier said than done. Innovations were all too obvious once those other guys had thought of them. (You went, 'Oh, well, of course.' And 'Why didn't *I* think of that?') But to conjure something from the ether, the abstract, *this* was the real challenge.

What could the world want, that it did not already possess? What single item, what idea was missing? What would a Horscroft be. What would it *do*? ('I just don't know how I managed before I had a Horscroft.' 'An absolute godsend.' 'It's certainly changed *my* life.')

Then how about a medical breakthrough? Horscroft's disease? Horscroft's syndrome? Horscroft's complex? Horscroftiasis? ('It's bad news, Madam: you have Horscroft's disease.' 'Just wait till I get my hands on that bastard Horscroft!')

No, no, no. The fact was that he was one of the vast majority who do not make a mark. Was this why people were so anxious to reproduce? If you couldn't come up with a photocopier or a food processor or facsimile machine (and, let's face it, Charlie could not even have *re*invented those things; he hadn't a notion of their workings), you could still leave a small part of yourself, a drip, drip, drip, becoming ever more dilute, down the ages.

Well, it wasn't a good enough reason to father a child. You should have them, not to be linked into posterity by some tenuous silver thread, but for pure, unselfish love.

If he ever had children, it would be to cherish them in the here and now. And that was a not inconsiderable if. It depended on finding the right woman, who, to this day, had eluded him. Unless, unless. . .

———————— • ————————

She had written him a letter, hadn't she? A Dear John style of thing, giving him the heave-ho. It was all for the best, she had said, as she hoped he would understand. He was to try to forget her, and not to come looking for her, because she was at a secret address, she was staying with a friend. Which meant, of course – and it didn't take Sherlock bleeding Holmes to work it out – that she'd got herself fixed up, she'd got a bloke. Some toerag must be getting his leg over. Nice, eh?

Greg spread Kayleigh's letter out on the floor, smoothing the creases with his fingertip. For the hundredth time he read it over, scowling at the unruly script, scrutinising it for any hint as to her whereabouts. He even held it up to the light and squinted at the watermark. But the more he looked, the less, it seemed, was revealed to him.

When he had first opened it, weeks ago now, he had fancied he would find the answer in there somewhere: the communication had seemed to him stiff with clues, with whats and whens and wheres. But it was like when you thought you could smell burning, or when you caught a niff of gas, and the more you sniffed, the less information went up your nose.

He snorted, thinking about it, and swept the page aside in disgust. Hopeless. He felt hopeless. And cheated. And wronged. He rammed the heels of his hands into his eyes and sobbed out loud.

He was not, after all, an evil man, or an insensitive one. Rather the reverse, indeed, for he was too easily wounded, he was driven by righteous indignation, by grudge and grievance, and he believed in fighting his corner. His actions were always sparked by his vocabulary. Words such as 'atrocious', 'diabolical', 'pathetic', would come into his head and trigger an outraged, often violent reaction.

He comported himself with his own style of dignity, according to a rigid personal code. If someone had a pop at you, you were honour bound to hit him back. If your woman was lippy, if she cut up rough, if you suspected her of playing away from home, you had to give her a smack. (Well, what d'you expect? She had it coming to her.)

Insofar as he was capable of love, he loved Kayleigh. Loved his little boy, too, his Ben. He had never meant to hurt the silly tart, never stopped hoping that she would come back to him, never stopped listening for her key in the latch, or watching for her boot face to come round the door. If she only knew how she was crucifying him, if she knew the tears he'd shed since she walked out, it'd break her bleeding heart.

He sobbed again, experimentally, an unproductive sob which dredged nothing from his soul. He felt dried up inside, and wasted.

When he dropped his hands and opened his eyes, his gaze fell on the Tanto. The Ninja Tanto. The legendary blade of the masters of Ninjutsu, the so-called Shadow Warriors, the Silent Ones, that small élite band who came under the cloak of night, and whose secrets remained untold to this day.

He had ordered it from the *Sunday Whatsit*, the colour supplement. He'd put in for his advance reservation, he'd sent the first instalment, and in due time the knife had fetched up, along with its Certificate of Authenticity.

It wasn't the real thing, of course, but it was a true collector's piece for the connoisseur, a magnificent recreation of the sixteenth-century Ninja knife, an extraordinarily faithful replica, crafted with consummate skill. It had a glinting, tempered stainless steel blade and twenty-four-carat gold electro-plate embellishments, and, like the original, it would reflect the status of its owner. Anyone with a taste for the legends of the past, for this thrilling period in Japanese history, would want to own it, and to pass it down to future generations. This, at least, according to the blurb.

Well, nuts to that! So much for future generations! He would have liked to show Ben the Tanto, to lift him up, to let him have a closer look at it, and to watch his face light up with awe. He'd have liked to tell him tales at bedtime, of the Shadow Warriors, the Silent Ones, to fill his infant head with fantasy. And with what pride, when the lad was old enough, would he have handed down to him the useless sodding object.

This had been somewhere in his mind when he had ordered it. He had pictured himself placing it with great solemnity in his grown son's hands, inviting him to admire the exquisite craftsmanship, to marvel at the workmanship which wrought the golden dragons on the tsuba (whatever the fuck a tsuba was).

Now he thought he might just take advantage of the hundred per cent buy-back guarantee, which, according to the advert, would permit him to enjoy the knife for up to thirty days, then return it without affecting his statutory rights.

There seemed no point any longer in his investing in this rare and beautiful object to display in the home. There seemed no point in living. For, finally, miserably, he had accepted the fact that Kayleigh wasn't coming home.

———————— • ————————

Jamie had indeed, as his mother had speculated, been hard at it that afternoon. Even as Dee was warming the mince pies in the Aga, he had been in Clapham, warming himself on Lucinda, getting in amongst her, lapping up her lusciousness, delighting in her accessibility, which was by no means a given.

At best, in bed, she had a kind of wilting loveliness, a fragility, she would open to him like a flower. Her body was so beautifully made, her waist so small, her breasts so full, her flesh so firm, she was the perfect female confection, whom it was his privilege to enjoy. So if he now and then wished that she would be more . . . well, demonstrative, that she would play a less passive role, he would banish the churlish desire.

All right, he would have liked her, maybe, sometimes, to get on top, to go down on him, to go crazy with lust. But he supposed she was just not that sort. She was by disposition indolent, and had been accustomed all her life to servants; in bed, as elsewhere, she expected to be served.

In fact – though who would have guessed it? – Lucinda's enthusiasm for sex was in the nature of a fad: she would go off it in later years as completely as she was presently on it. She would come, in time, to regard it as a chore. It would be just another tedious wifely duty, like walking the dog, or doing the school run, or inviting those frightful people from number twenty-nine for martinis. She would produce a couple of beastly children and lose interest, devoting her energies instead to the running of the house, to harrying the domestic help, to issuing instructions. She would wear a box-pleated skirt with a Fair Isle jersey, and would shout up the ladder at the window cleaner, or down from the upper storeys at workmen on the street; she would follow the gardener around with a stick, pointing out the weeds he had missed. She would make frequent trips to Harrods, where she'd have an account, and where she would brass her way up to the front of any queue. Then at bedtime she would slap on the night cream, retire with a good book, plead exhaustion, and would be done, if she could, with 'all that'.

Her likeness to her mother, on the day she had posed as Mrs de Lannoy-Hunt, had been more than mere chimera: it had been prefigurement. They were a long time adolescent, the members of Lucinda's set, then suddenly, dauntingly, they were all grown up, they took upon themselves respectability.

Jamie, however, had no inkling of this. In his imagination she was endlessly youthful and sexy, endlessly lascivious; they were for ever at it, he and she, like knives. (*He*, at any rate, would be at it like a knife; there was, even now, perhaps more of the spoon about Lucinda, she being somewhat of a lapper-up.)

He had made up his mind that he must marry her. He had set his heart upon it. Their affair, fun though it might be, was altogether too precarious, it made him rattle with insecurity. He needed to claim her, to formalise their relationship, not merely because their association could lend him greater credibility than his fast car or his Gold Card ever could, but because he was mad about her. She might be hard to love, but would be harder still to leave. She was in his system like a drug, she was his habit.

He had entertained, momentarily, the possibility that she would reject him, but had reasoned it away. He counted above all on her inertia. He must catch her in her sleepy, acquiescent mood – late tonight perhaps, or early in the morning – when an outright no, a refusal, would demand too much of her, when a yes and a yawn would seem altogether the easier option.

It was a matter, in other words, of time and place. And if this was a somewhat cold-blooded scenario, so much the better, since Lucinda's sort were overtly despising of romanticism. Express too much raw feeling around them, and you'd have them honking with derision and ya-hooing at you, clasping their hands to their bosoms, or serenading you with imaginary violins. Emotion, to them, was pitiable weakness. All that hearts and flowers stuff, they implied, was for the plebs.

The manner of the proposal, the form of words would thus be of the essence. No good to drop down on one knee, to declare undying love. 'What say we tie the knot?' might just hit the spot. Or, 'How about we get spliced, you and me?' Then, before she had time for second thoughts, slip the ring on her finger and shake hands on the deal.

He had gone secretly, yesterday, not to Regent Street or to Bond Street, not to Garrard or to Asprey, but to a cramped little shop in Clerkenwell, a specialist in antique jewellery, where, breathless with his own initiative, he had selected a sapphire-and-diamond engagement ring, a fine gold band worn thin with age and attractively priced.

It had been his great-grandmother's, he would explain to Lucinda, not to claim for it the sort of sentimental value which she scorned, but to convey a lack of choice (like it or not, he was stuck with the thing). Family honour, obligation, heirlooms, inheritance, manipulative forebears, wills, conditions, codicils, these were things she understood. The wishes of some cantankerous old ancestor must of course be observed. One did the square thing by great-granny.

Now, at seven in the evening, they sat in the champagne bar, waiting for Giles and Hennie, with whom they had planned to celebrate the sale of Clovelly, which had finally gone through. Giles was the legal owner. Audrey Atkins had been installed in a retirement home, a manageable flat, with poor, bewildered Cyril. The agency had done very nicely, thank you, out of both transactions. And the best, for Giles and Jamie, was yet to be.

Jamie dipped into his pocket, stroked with his fingertips the miniature casket in which the ring nestled, and felt a rush of pure elation. Suddenly everything was coming up roses. He wanted to shout aloud, but he didn't, of course, in case people turned to stare.

At this early hour, the place was not crowded. A few couples inclined over marble-top tables, their heads almost touching. The barman, an Italian with heavy-lidded eyes and a sensuous, slightly feminine mouth, lounged against a back-lit display, probing his teeth with a cocktail stick and staring in a concentrated manner at Lucinda, who every so often screwed round on her bar stool to pucker up enticingly over one raised shoulder at him, or at her own reflection in the mirror behind him. 'Don't do that,' Jamie longed to scold. 'Don't flirt with the lecherous bastard. Behave.' Instead, 'Too bad', he said lightly, pitching for her attention, 'that we must each spend Christmas with our people, Luce. I should have far preferred us to spend it together, you and I.'

'Yes,' she responded in a discouragingly neutral tone, 'too bad. Still, never mind. Needs must and all that. Cheerio.' At which, she tipped back her head, poured champagne down her throat, half a glass at one glug, gave an alcoholic belch, dashed her hand across her mouth and blew the barman a peach of a kiss.

She had on rather more perfume than she had clothing: she was wearing about a gallon and a half of Ysatis with a dazzlingly plain, tight-fitting black dress, which had ridden up almost to her crotch. Her long, strong, slender legs, in satiny sheer black tights, were spread in a teasing, unladylike fashion. She raked back her platinum hair with her hand, shook her head about and pouted. Despite the fact that she'd spent the best part of an hour in the bathroom, douching him off her and out of her, she looked, Jamie remarked, somehow terribly post-coital, as if she'd just dragged herself from his bed.

'Maybe next year, eh?' he suggested casually. And he frowned into his glass as if he saw a speck of cork, a fly, a foreign body floating there.

'Oh, good God, Rawlings, that's an eternity away. We may all be dead and in our graves by then. Hey, hey . . . ' She jabbed him brutally in the ribs with her elbow, and bounced up and down in childish glee on the bar stool. 'Here comes the de Lannoy-Hunt contingent. Giles, Hennie, how are you? What will you drink? No, no, put that away Giles. Jamie is buying, aren't you darling? We'll have another bottle of Bollie, yah?'

'Why not?' Jamie rubbed his hands together. 'It's been one hell of a week, after all. Giles, hi. Hennie, hi-ya.' He inclined to kiss Henrietta gallantly on either cheek, and she giggled mindlessly.

'Let's all get pie-eyed,' proposed Lucinda, helping herself to a large green olive, stripping the flesh with her pearly teeth, then tossing the stone over her shoulder. 'Let's all get completely ratted.'

'Don't we always?' said Giles, the smoothie, stepping between her encircling legs, cupping her right breast, and snogging wolfishly with her, until Hennie punched him hard in the small of his back and said to pack it in this minute.

'Enough, enough,' Jamie turned from the bar, where he'd been vainly brandishing banknotes at his Italian friend, to join Henrietta, albeit jokily, in her protest. It was not for him – at least, not yet – to be possessive. Lucinda would only call him a complete prat, she'd say not to be so bourgeois, or accuse him of being on a jealousy trip. His best course was to grin and bear it, but that was to tax too far his limited self-control.

'Come on, Jamie,' Lucinda chivvied him, 'stop faffing around. Where are the drinks?'

'I'm just getting them, aren't I?'

'Well, get on and get. Oy, over here.' With a beckoning finger, a flex of the wrist, she summoned the barman. 'A nice bottle of Bollinger and four straws for us. Oh, and whatever you're drinking. It is Christmas, after all.'

'What are you doing for Christmas, Jamie?' asked Hennie with an amiable smile.

'Oh . . .' He made a bung of his fist, covered his mouth, cleared his throat. 'Er, spending it with my folks, as usual. Over Tunbridge Wells way.'

'You know, I have yet to meet his mother,' Lucinda confided, swinging her legs, first one, then the other, out in front of her, pointing her dainty toes, admiring her shapely calves. 'He's not introduced us. Do you think he's ashamed of me, Hennie? Giles?'

'Don't be absurd,' said Jamie miserably. His hand flew to his throat, to pluck at his collar. 'I'm not in the least. Why should I be?'

'I did meet Daddy, though, didn't I, once?'

'Yes, you did. Briefly.'

'He liked me.'

'Yes, yes, he liked you.'

'I had an idea that he did. Call it feminine intuition.'

'Well, doesn't *everybody* like you?'

'*Men* do.' She held her champagne flute aloft for the barman to fill, then waved it around extravagantly. 'Some *women* aren't so enamoured.'

'My mother would, I have no doubt, be very taken with you. Look, why don't we drink up and move on somewhere else?' Jamie shot his cuff and checked his watch unseeingly.

'Let's eat,' said Hennie.

'Too early,' scoffed Lucinda.

'But I'm hungry.'

'You're *always* hungry, Henrietta. You'll be as fat as a pig when you're forty.'

'I expect so,' agreed Henrietta serenely. 'I fancy Chinese. Does anyone else?' She tugged at the hem of Giles's jacket. 'What about you, Cuddlebum? I could kill for some crispy duck and pancakes.'

'*I* wouldn't mind,' offered Jamie thankfully. It was a relief to be off the subject of his parents. But, of course, there would have to be a meeting soon with Dee, if Lucinda were to be his wife. ('Mum. Mummy. Er, Mother, this is Lucinda Blackstock . . .') He dipped into his pocket, closed his hand on the ring box, but this time drew such cold, cold comfort from it.

———————— • ————————

When Kayleigh opened the window, banging the swollen wood with the flat of her hand to unstick it from the frame, a smell of wet soil came up in a rush, as if the earth were yawning. She leaned on the sill and hung herself out, breathing in the black air, her face aching with the cold.

There was a perfect square of light, like a carpet, unrolled on the terrace outside the sitting-room window. Elsewhere, though, there was only darkness. She listened and heard the squeak-creak of creeper branches rocked by the breeze, wearing away at the brick fabric of the house. Then there were all the usual scritching, scratching, scurrying, animal sounds which had scared her witless when she first came to this place. She wondered, now, what it was that she had feared, so accustomed was she to the snapping of twigs and the rustling of leaves, the comings and goings of the night shift.

How bright the stars were in the countryside! The city lay under a pall of exhaust gases, lit from beneath. But here it was so clear and shimmery, you could see all the way to heaven.

It was spooky when you came to think of it, that each of those little points of light was a planet of some sort. They looked as if you could hold them in the palm of your hand and watch them melt, or string them together for earrings. Yet they were at least as big as the world, some of them. They must be hundreds and hundreds – no, probably thousands and thousands – of miles away.

The idea made her feel extremely small and obscurely insulted; it seemed to diminish her. It was difficult for her, for a moment, to hold on to the conviction that she was the very centre of the universe; her perceptions wobbled precariously, then righted themselves.

Kayleigh was not content to think, as Charlie Horscroft did, that she was the merest of mere mortals, that she had but one life to live, that this was all there was. She preferred the other theory, the one about God. And she liked to believe she was indelible; she might never be rubbed out.

As her eyes adapted to the dark, things began to emerge from the background. Rose bushes with preposterously late white wadded blooms, pink clusters of viburnum, the skeletal branches of whitewashed bramble, the roof of the shed, the pale stone birdbath, the garden roller, one by one presented themselves to her.

A tawny owl loomed silvery against the night sky, then parachuted silently down upon its prey. (A vole, perhaps? A woodmouse? A shrew?) Owls had wing feathers like velvet, with which they sort of stroked the air. They laid eggs the size of ping-pong balls. And here was a funny thing: when the food supply was low, when there weren't a lot of little mice and things for their babies to eat, they laid fewer of them.

All this she had learned from Charlie Horscroft, who apparently knew everything there was to know about nature and that.

She had grown to like Charlie when he worked at Foxholes. She had grown to trust him. He still had that predatory look, as though he might pounce upon you, he still stared right into you with darkling eyes to make you fidget and shuffle your feet. But he was really kind. Whenever Mrs Burston started bending her ear, nagging and moaning and name-calling as she did, Charlie used to say firmly, 'Now, Ivy'. Just that. 'Now, Ivy.' And she would say, 'But . . .', and 'Well . . .', and 'I don't know', but always in a better humour, with a suggestion of a smile in her voice.

'Ring any time,' he had told her. 'If there's anything you want, you call me.'

Well, there was something she wanted, but she hadn't called, since it was not in Charlie Horscroft's gift.

The day after tomorrow he comes here, she told herself, tugging at the window, slamming it shut, then writing his name on the misted pane.

J-A-M-I-E.

• ————

12

Jamie Rawlings was not what you would call a thoroughly bad lot – at least, he was pleased to think not. The words 'lovable rogue' seemed to him to meet the case: he had tried them on himself and they had fitted.

True, he pulled the odd stroke, he got into the odd scrape, the occasional piece of white mischief – the Atkins scam, the Clovelly wheeze, being but one example. Yet no one, in that instance, had been unhappy with the outcome. No one felt bad. Audrey, in her new home, was surely like a pig in muck. So what harm could be said to have been done?

No, Jamie was not wicked, nor was he stupid. He had a fine head on his shoulders, a brilliant business brain (see above). All in all, he was one hell of a guy.

So why did this Christmas morning find him so low in his own esteem, so demoralised, so full of self-disgust?

Because in bed yesterday morning, Lucinda had turned him down. He had popped the question, and she had said no, not nicely, not with delicacy, or with any hint of equivocation, but with an ear-splitting yelp and a resounding slap on his naked thigh, which had left her hand imprinted there, a red splat which had melted only slowly away. He should not be such a dickhead, she had said. He should not be so witless.

'Listen, I'm quite serious,' he had rashly insisted, allowing the mask of insouciance to slip, his flippant tone to firm up into something far more purposeful, and he had opened the box to hold up as proof the sapphire ring, had offered it in his palm. But she'd thrust his hand away with impatience, sending ring and box flying, and had told him, for goodness' sake, to stop behaving like a character in some ghastly B movie.

'I mean to say,' she had expostulated, 'it's not as if . . .' And this was supposed to be answer enough.

'It's not as if *what*?' he had enquired bitterly.

'Well, you know.'

'No, I don't know. You tell me.'

Which she would not. She had simply refused to fill in the blanks, to elucidate. Instead, she had walked around him on her knees, had attached herself to his rounded back, nuzzled his neck, breathed in his ears, and rubbed herself lewdly against him.

'Come on, don't sulk, it's Christmas Eve. We're all right as we are. We have fun.'

'Ah, yes, of course. Ain't we got fun!'

'You *are* sulking. You really are, you great big girlie,' she had whooped triumphantly, imposing her weight upon him till he doubled at the waist, then rolling off him to lie in a convulsive heap beside him.

'Get off me, can't you?'

'I am off.' She had gnawed on her fist to suppress a laugh. Then, reaching in between his legs she had played with his flaccid penis, coaxing it out. 'Ah, diddums, is he in a huff?'

'Look, lay off me, will you? What say we simply forget it?'

'Suits me, sweetie, Oh, Jesus, God, I feel like shit this morning.' This with her usual indecent high spirits, in her usual strong voice. He doubted if she even knew what a hangover was, though she would sometimes affect one, presumably for the hell of it, or because he might not have anything she did not. She would screw up her eyes against the unforgiving daylight, she would groan and pass a hand across her fevered brow, and the next minute she'd be cavorting around, demanding a sausage sandwich, or scrambled eggs and bacon.

'You deserve to,' he had told her censoriously. 'You behaved abominably in the Chinese restaurant.'

'Did I? Did I *really*?' The idea plainly tickled her. She sprang up from the bed and went to the mirror, where she stood tilting her head first this way then that, studying her reflection as one might a work of art.

Well, she *was* a work of art, of course, Lucinda Blackstock, cunningest pattern of excelling nature, for we by no means invariably get the looks we deserve.

'You and Giles, fencing with chopsticks. Making infantile cracks about prawn balls. Calling out for special fly lie. Telling the poor waiter to watch your rips.'

'Ah, well, it's Christmas, after all.' She had granted herself absolution as if it were mere formality, something to be stamped and nodded through. 'Anyway, it was Giles's fault. He dared me to tell that chicken joke.' Then, purely for her own amusement, she had told it again. '"Waiter, waiter, this chicken is rubbery." "Aww, thank you, Sir!"'

'It wasn't funny then, and it isn't now.' Good grief, he had sounded like his mother! That was how upset he had been.

Now, as he waited in Deptford for the traffic lights to change, as he hammered at the steering-wheel with his palm and whistled like a kettle with nervous tension, he tried to tell himself it had been his own fault, that he'd come on too strong or screwed up on timing. Fools rush in, he told himself, moving away on red-amber, burning off the Citroën that had ludicrously tried to pass him on the near side.

When he crested the hill at Blackheath, he saw a huge silver sky full of kites. There were graceful bird models with beating wings; elaborate boxes with streaming tails; swooping, slapping, snapping, showy-off stunt kites describing arcs and loops and figures of eight.

Couples were walking dreamily, hand in hand, or throwing sticks for their dogs. Over on the greasy pond, fathers would be sailing their sons' new toy boats. Middle-class London was at play in earnest, it was showing off what Santa had brought in the night.

'Cretins,' he muttered, jabbing the button to switch on the stereo. 'Peasants. I hate the lot of you.'

He drove very fast past rows of pedimented houses behind high garden walls, then round the roundabout, down the slip road, on to the main highway, to thread like a needle through the fast-moving traffic into the offside lane. The speed relaxed him. He felt momentarily more sanguine. He and Lucinda were still together, after all, they were still a couple. She had bought him a silk Versace tie, which she had knotted round his neck. Then she had seized it and pulled him to her, to kiss him smack on the lips. So all was not actually lost.

This break from each other would do them both good. It would give him time to get over his pique. And she might even, in the next day or two, repent.

Would she hell! He was kidding himself. 'It's not as if . . . ' she had objected, and though she had declined to be drawn, to say one word more, he had intuited the rest. It was not as if he had real money. Or status. It was not as if he were truly of her social class. *This* was what she had been telling him, and there had been no need for her to spell it out.

Lucinda Blackstock was properly posh. She came, as Jamie put it to himself, from an old Wiltshire family (as though all families were not similarly 'old'; as though a Rawlings might not reach back into the distant past and find forebears).

But then, what he meant, of course, was that the Blackstocks had property. They had an estate. Lucinda's grandparents owned an historic house with a headless ghost, and with ancestral portraits glowering down from the walls, whereas he and his sort were much more of the here-and-now.

'She is no better than I,' he said aloud, but without conviction. And, 'Who does she think she is, anyway?'

God, this Christmas ritual was a drag! He could picture the scene that would greet him at Foxholes, with the family sitting around in the pristine new sweaters Dee would have pressed upon them, talking inconsequences, with the unspeakable Jean Crabtree pick-pick-picking, with Innes uttering the occasionally affirmative grunt, and with that wretched, impertinent girl and her mewling, puking offspring. He hated being among these people, for they seemed to tarnish him: exposure to them left him, somehow, dimmed; for a day or more after, he would shine less brightly.

Then there was the cost, the sheer needless expense. In a carrier bag on the seat beside him he had a bottle of Chivas Regal for his father, wrapped in blue tissue paper with a twist at the top; he had perfume for his mother, pink bath salts and lilac talc for the beastly Jean, two ounces of shag for Innes.

He had despatched Francine to the chemist for the smelly stuff, to the stationer for gift wrap, and had looked into the off licence himself for the tobacco and booze. He had not, it must be said, worn himself to a shadow walking the streets in search of the perfect present for each person. Still, he had shopped, he had put himself out, which, for a busy young man such as he, was quite beyond the call of duty.

He could not wait for January now, for the return of sanity, when the Barclaycard, the Access and the Visa bills came in, and the populace went, subdued, about its work once more.

Next year was going to be a biggie for him. Giles would sell Clovelly on, then he, Jamie, would trouser his share of the profit, and would look to the next project. What might that be? He had yet to decide, but his brain teemed with brilliant ideas. Soon he would have a very nice wedge, he would have a whack of capital. He must invest it wisely.

He roared up behind a Ford Orion in the overtaking lane and flashed his lights. When the driver refused to move over, he nipped by on the inside. No one – and this could be his New Year's resolution – *no one* would get in the way of James Rawlings.

———————— • ————————

The parson's cat was an angry cat. He was an astute, an artistic, an amenable, if an awkward cat. He was a belligerent, a cantankerous, a demonic, and an eccentric cat.

'The parson's cat', said Dee beaming with counterfeit merriment, playing the life and soul as usual, striving to whip up a mood of frivolity, 'is a flamboyant cat.'

'The parson's cat', said Eric, subversively, 'is a flatulent cat.'

'The parson's cat', said Sandra, 'is a fluffy cat.' Then she rested her hands flat on her knees, leaned forward in her seat and smiled around her, as if inviting everyone to picture, if they would, this endearing ball of fur.

'The parson's cat', said Kayleigh, in some bafflement, 'is a physical cat.'

'That's not an F!' Jean Crabtree pounced upon her, demonic as a parson's cat. 'It's a P Haitch. You ought to know that, a great big girl like you. I can't think what they taught you at school. Those teachers always shouting about money, they're always on about pay, and they can't even teach the three Rs.'

'I do know it's not F,' said Kayleigh, sullenly. 'I just forgot.' And she folded her arms defensively across her chest. This was a stupid game, anyway, which they would insist on playing. It was a waste of time. She couldn't see the point of it. Round and round and round it went, and finally up its own bum.

'You could have "fidgety",' tendered Sandra kindly, hoping that this didn't sound too condescending. 'Or "finicky".'

'Or we could let you have "physical", this once, as it's Christmas,' Dee offered with an air of magnanimity, a wink of complicity, which raised condescension to new heights.

'If you must know,' Kayleigh snapped, 'I don't much care about the effing cat. I don't much care about him one way or the other to be frank.' She dropped her head and picked at the ribbing of the sweater which Dee had given her, a jazzy handknit with a daffodil motif. It was really gross, not her style at all, or her colour, for it made her look sickly. She had been coerced into trying it on, and then had felt constrained to keep it on, as everyone kept insisting how nice it looked, how well it suited her, how perfectly it fitted.

'The effing cat?' Eric wondered aloud. 'Should we accept it? The F word? I don't see why not.'

'Enough of that, thank you,' his wife reproved him. 'Expletives most definitely don't count.'

'Look, you lot play without me,' Kayleigh suggested. 'Go ahead. Don't mind me. You'll get through much faster that way.' They would be hours at this rate, it seemed to her, coming up with words for every letter of the sodding alphabet, from soup to nuts. Z (zestful, zealous, zany, zetetic, zonked) seemed a lifetime away.

'Don't let's take this thing too seriously,' pleaded Eric. 'It's supposed to be *fun*.' He glanced a shade desperately up at the clock. Was it time for a drink? It was after eleven. No, he dared not suggest it for at least another hour. To do so would be to invite from Jean some censorious remark about intemperance; from his wife, a joking reference to his weakness.

'Actually,' said Sandra, 'I could do with a bit of exercise. I might stroll up to the farm. Stretch my legs.' She hauled herself out of her armchair and went through a little flexing and stretching routine, as if to demonstrate. 'Would you like to come, Kayleigh, to keep me company? And bring Ben?'

'If you want,' Kayleigh assented. Anything, *anything* to get out of the house for half an hour. Then, by the time they returned, Jamie might have arrived, for he was pledged to be there by midday. She pictured herself coming in through the door, with her hair blown about, with roses in her cheeks, with the radiance of daylight in her eyes. 'Phew, I'm hot,' she would gasp, tugging off the new Christmas sweater, pulling it over her head, so her breasts rose and fell beneath her thin cotton blouse.

She went upstairs, then, to fetch from her bedroom the tan leather shoulder-bag which had been Sandie's gift to her, a really, really smart one which had so pleased and confounded her, she had been able to utter no more than a gruff, 'Ta, thanks.'

She had been more confused than touched to receive from these people a variety of presents. Particularly when Ivy Burston had thrust at her a parcel so well Sellotaped as to be almost impenetrable, Kayleigh had been totally discountenanced. 'Here,' Ivy had said before she left yesterday morning, shoving the thing into her hand. And, 'Don't say I never give you nothing,' she'd added with a hint of humour, as she buttoned her coat right to the neck.

'I'm afraid I haven't got . . .' Kayleigh had responded. 'I mean, not for anyone.' And, 'No, well . . .' Ivy had said with faint disparagement. (Like, 'No, well, *you* wouldn't.' Like, 'No, well, who would expect it of you?') Nevertheless, when Kayleigh had extricated from the shredded paper a gift set of Body Shop cosmetics (avocado this, coconut that, peppermint the other), and had been moved by an impulse to kiss Ivy's cheek, the woman had momentarily softened and looked flustered. 'My Angie got 'em.' She had hastily distanced herself from her own kindness. 'Just a little token. Nothing much.' And, finally, because she never could resist a dig, 'Now you'll be spending even longer in the bathroom, I dare say.'

Sandra's present, the bag, was on the chest of drawers beside the mirror. Kayleigh picked it up, opened it, buried her nose in it and breathed the pungent, calfskin smell. Then she came up for air, made a brief inspection of her face and turned to go.

She found Sandie in the hall, down on her knees in front of Ben, their heads bent together, crown to crown, as she buttoned him into his new duffle coat. He was inspecting it critically, as a man might at a fitting of a new bespoke suit. He smoothed it with one small hand, looked up at Sandra, at Kayleigh, and a rare smile lit up his face like a starburst.

'Aren't we smart, eh?' Sandie asked him, pulling a woolly bobble hat down almost to his eyes, then sitting back on her heels to consider him. Still smiling, he reached up for the bobble, but it was beyond his tiny, grasping fingers.

'It looks great,' said Kayleigh. 'It looks smashing. But you shouldn't of.'

'It was nothing.' Sandie shook her head vigorously. 'I mean, it was ever so cheap. And it gave me pleasure. I just love children's clothes, I can't resist them.'

'I haven't bought . . . Because I didn't think that . . .'

'Oh, please! Please don't worry about that. No one expects . . . I mean, why should you?'

'I feel a bit . . .' Kayleigh squeezed her eyes shut and went inside her head for a moment, in search of the right word, coming up at last with 'inadequate'.

'I wish you wouldn't. You're very much not. In fact, I think you're amazingly adequate.' Because Kayleigh was holding her own here; she was standing up for herself, she was standing her ground. Families are such strange hermetic units, and this one was surely stranger, more exclusive, than most. In Kayleigh's position, Sandie felt, she would simply have died.

I do like her, Kayleigh thought. She's lovely.

I do like her, Sandie thought. She's sweet.

And in this mood of mutual admiration, they set off up the lane.

'I've called to see Kayleigh,' said Charlie, standing there staring straight into her face in that dark and dauntless way of his which Dee misread as insolence.

'What a shame! You've missed her.' Her tone was almost triumphant; no hint of regret there. 'She's gone for a stroll with Alexandra.'

'I have something for the kiddie.' Charlie held out the box, as if to show proof, and rattled it. The wooden pieces made a satisfactory clunking sound inside their cardboard casing.

'Ah, yes, well . . .' Dee was tempted, in that instant, to wrest it from him, to thank him on Kayleigh's behalf, and to close the door upon him.

He was an artisan, a tradesman, albeit a fine and a conscientious one. He came from the other side of the village, from another milieu altogether. And while, heaven knows, she was not a snob, she somehow felt he oughtn't to be encouraged. This was not just her taboo, it was a fact of life in Ashcombe: there were certain social barriers which people might not breach. Quite what harm would come upon them if they did, she did not trouble to reason to herself, beyond some vague notion that it might be confusing for such simple folk, that they might not be comfortable with such social ambiguity.

'Very kind,' she murmured distantly, and she held out her hands, palm upwards, indicating, with a nod of her head, that he might entrust his offering to her.

At once he withdrew it, tucking it under his arm. 'Will she be long, d'you think?' he enquired, lounging against the door, fixing her with that unwavering stare, looking dangerously feral.

Even setting social class aside, there might be no question of inviting him over the threshold. There was quite enough chemistry under one roof today, thank you very much, without adding his hormones to the mix. 'I'm afraid I can't say. But when she gets back we'll be having our lunch. If you like, I can –'

'Charlie Horscroft, it's you, as I live and breathe!' Eric, who had drifted from the sitting-room into the hall in his wife's substantial wake, now appeared at her shoulder. He insinuated his face into the doorway and showed his teeth. At last, an excuse to make merry! He did not especially thrill to see young Charlie boy, who stirred in him such profound discontent, such acute envy. But he would have ushered Attila the Hun into his home at this hour, he would have greeted Vlad the Impaler like a long-lost brother. Christ, at a pinch, he would even welcome Jamie Rawlings, for the excuse of opening a bottle. 'Compliments of the season,' he cried. 'Glad tidings to you and your kin. How is the beautiful Ann? I've not seen her in a while, out and about on her bike.'

'No. She's strained a tendon.'

'Too bad. Do give her my regards. Have you time for a drink? Step inside, lad. We'll sip a schooner of pale dry amontillado and sing some rollicking Yuletide carols.'

'But it's only . . .' Dee protested, hitching up her sleeve, exposing her wrist, a blue vein, a bracelet of fat, but no watch, since she had left it on the dresser when she went to do the sprouts.

'I came to call on Kayleigh,' Charlie stated, as if to set the record straight.

'The sun's well over the yard-arm,' insisted Eric. 'Besides, it's Christmas. Come through, come through, and have a small glass of dandelion and burdock.'

Charlie, whose ambitions towards friendship were no higher than Dee's, who had no more wish than she to be matey, and who knew instinctively when he was being used, none the less heard himself accepting, saying 'Just a quick one, then. Just a drop. Thanks.'

Dee took a step back and glanced down at his feet, thinking with chagrin of her cream-and-gold washed Chinese carpets. She could not however fault him, for he was respectably shod in soft black leather, and no grime attached to the hems of his jeans.

'This is Charlie Horscroft who did our bathroom.' Stiffly, she made the introductions. 'Charlie, these are my parents, Mr and Mrs Crabtree.'

'How d'you do,' said Charlie, nodding to Jean and Innes, accepting with equanimity the glares which winged their way to him, like hate mail, by return.

He drank his sherry standing up, with his pelvis tilted rakishly, resting his left foot on the toe, apparently completely at ease.

Dee consented to a half a glass, and said 'When, when, whoa, when', as her husband filled it to the brim.

Jean and Innes would have none of it. Their faces were set against the enterprise.

When Oedipuss barged through the door, made straight for him and wound himself around his legs, purring ecstatically, Charlie set his glass down on the bookcase and squatted to fondle him. 'Hiya Sparks,' he said. 'Hello, Sparkie. How're you doing?'

'Oedipuss,' Dee corrected him in a tone that brooked no argument.

Oedipuss, shmoedipuss, thought Charlie scornfully, what does it matter so long as he loves his mother?

'Atishoo,' said Jean loudly.

And, 'Bless you,' said Charlie, who had never heard a less convincing sneeze.

'I have an allergy,' she informed him peevishly, sounding, somehow, as if she held him to blame.

'Can't abide cats,' Innes grumbled 'Beastly animals. Very sly.' He knocked the dottle from his pipe, an evil nest of shag cemented with saliva, and shrilled down it. He pitched to the left, drew his tobacco pouch from his jacket pocket, then returned with some difficulty to the perpendicular. 'I'd drown the lot of 'em in a bucket if I had my way.'

Charlie did not for one moment doubt it. Without comment, he scooped the black-and-white tom up into his arms, gazed a moment into his yellow eyes, then bore him out of the room and set him down at the foot of the stairs. 'You'd best keep well away from that lot,' he warned him, *sotto voce*. The animal's back arched with pleasure when he ran his hand along it. 'So should I, for that matter,' he added, 'but there's Kayleigh to consider.'

'Drink up,' urged Eric, when he rejoined the happy throng, and he cocked the sherry bottle like a pistol, aiming at his head. 'Have a top-up.'

'No, no, I'm fine.' Charlie capped his glass with his hand.

'Well, *I'm* ready for another, I must say. What's got into you all? You're no fun any more.' Eric, having made up his mind to get drunk as a lord and disgrace himself, saw no reason to wait for the alcohol to take effect. 'Why not let your hair down for a change? Have a knees-up?'

'With *my* knees,' said Jean, with a martyred air, 'I don't think so.'

Through the window, Charlie saw a red Porsche glide by. The window panes throbbed with engine noise.

'Jamie!' said Dee with sudden animation.

'Jamie,' confirmed Eric, toasting them all with his glass.

Jamie, Charlie told himself grimly. And he made his excuses and left.

It was a nothing sort of day, a climatic non-event, as if the weather were taking time out. The sun was off somewhere behind the clouds. A little breeze loitered among the branches. The cold had a residual feel, it was yesterday's left-over chill. It was yesterday's rain, too, which leached out of the embankment, yesterday's rain which lay in shallow puddles on the road, drying out at the margins (splish, splash, hiss went the wheels of the buggy, riding through them).

'At least it's not snowing, that's a blessing,' remarked Kayleigh. And she stopped abruptly while she cleared her throat, hawking raucously.

'Do you think so?' said Sandie, imagining evergreen and glistening white; electric lights burning in cottage windows; bird tracks and church bells and mulled wine and mistletoe; and everywhere an enigmatic silence. 'But I *love* a white Christmas. Especially in the countryside. It's magical.'

'Well, if you look at it that way. It's pretty, I grant you,' Kayleigh was prepared to concede, though her own imagination offered up treacherous glazed pavements and piled slush, it offered a freezing, powdery wind, and hissing car tyres throwing up soaking black spray. It offered the singular darkness of the downstairs lobby at E block, chill as a fridge, echoey and awash. It offered the world in monotone.

'So long as you can keep warm,' Sandie continued, forging ahead, plodding heavily on splayed feet, deportment never having been her thing.

'That's it, isn't it?' Kayleigh agreed. 'It's no fun if you're frozen half to death.'

'It's the old people one feels so desperately sorry for.'

'Yeah.' Kayleigh, sparing a thought for poor old buggers everywhere, felt warm in her own virtue. 'Shame, innit?'

'Mm.'

'Like the other week. About a fortnight ago. Cold enough to freeze the bollocks off a brass monkey.'

'Balls.'

'Huh?'

'The expression is "to freeze the balls off a brass monkey".'

'Same difference.' Now, when Kayleigh sniffed, it signalled dismissal or reproof. She was less snuffly than she had been when she first arrived, less adenoidal.

'It isn't, in this case, no. It's a different sort of monkey from the one you have in mind.'

'It is?' said Kayleigh, who had, indeed, vaguely envisaged a well-endowed simian, an ape with brass knobs on.

'Yes. A "monkey" was the thing they stored the cannon balls on.'

'How come?'

'I've no idea. It just was.'

'Oh. Right. Well, anyway, it was bleeding taters, that I *do* know. And I thought then, What about the poor old folk?'

'It's a scandal, if you ask me. A national disgrace. They work all their lives, and for what? For a pitiful pension, barely enough to keep body and soul together.' Sandra had salvaged a stick from the hedgerows. She beat it absent-mindedly against her flank until it snapped, then tossed it into the bushes. She looked, Kayleigh noticed with surprise, quite het up, she had high colour in her cheeks. 'Bloody Thatcher,' she declaimed. 'Bloody John Major.'

'And the other lot are just the same. There's nothing to choose between them, my dad always says.'

'Well, I don't know about . . .'

'They're all as bad as each other, with their jaw, jaw, jaw.'

'I suppose so, but . . .' Sandra sighed. It was too vast an issue to bear discussion, and the contemplation of it made her miserable.

'We don't vote,' Kayleigh boasted. (Thus, her tone seemed to imply, was the politicians' hash settled.)

'Yes, I do often wonder if there's any point in doing so. Here, for instance, needless to say, the Tories always win. And where I live in South London, it goes to Labour.'

'I tell a lie. My dad did vote last time.'

'Who for?'

Kayleigh shrugged. 'Can't remember. I'm not even sure if *he* can.'

'And why did he bother? I mean, if they're as bad as each other.'

'He'd been down the pub, you know. And he gets that way when he's had a few: he gets to thinking he can set the world to rights.'

'Tall oaks from little acorns grow,' said Sandra fatuously, and she winced at the sound of her own voice. 'Every little helps,' she added, which sounded more excruciating yet.

'Would you look at this!' Kayleigh stood wrinkling her nose. 'It's disgusting.' The lane up ahead was black with mud, where the cows were driven daily up to the farm to be milked, bringing large chunks of their field on their hooves. She aimed a kick at a clod, which was spiked with straw like a hedgehog. 'Ouch!'

'Perhaps we should carry the pushchair,' Sandie said anxiously. 'It will be a bit yucky, I'm afraid. But I thought Ben would like to see the farmyard. Then we can come back via the horses if you want.'

'Don't mind.'

'Right, then.' Sandie stooped and picked up the front of the buggy, Kayleigh hung on to the handles, and they stretchered the child between them.

Ben, tipped back in his seat, seemed to like this new vantage; he gazed around him and waved one arm imperiously, as to an invisible crowd of cheering onlookers. 'Mummum,' he said. And, unexpectedly, 'Horsy.'

'Listen!' said Sandie, delighted.

'Oh, yes,' Kayleigh confirmed, in a matter-of-fact sort of way, as though she had always known he would come good, 'he does that now. He says cat and dog and loads of other words. He's coming along fine.'

'You must be thrilled.'

'I guess.' This time, when she sniffed, it had a different import. 'His granny must be missing him.'

'Oh, dear! Yes, she must. And *you*. She must be missing you. And you, her.'

'A bit.'

'Are you dreadfully homesick?'

Kayleigh did not answer, but seemed intent upon negotiating a path through the slurry.

'This can't go on, can it? We've done nothing to help you. We shall have to get you fixed up for the New Year.'

But, 'I'm fine where I am for now,' Kayleigh told her, thrusting out her jaw in defiance. Sandie had a sense then of extraordinary obduracy, and of a powerful, compacted ego. Inside that small exterior something huge had been crammed.

Then, 'Fwaw! What a pen and ink!' Kayleigh exclaimed. 'I mean, hums a bit, doesn't it?'

They dumped Ben, somewhat unceremoniously, on the verge, and leaned side by side against the high stone wall, breathing through their mouths to exclude the smell of ordure.

The farm was a disappointment. Kayleigh had visualised something cosier, rosier, more idyllic. A thatched farmhouse, perhaps. And a cobbled area, with stabling, with horses peering over their doors. Chickens pecking on the grass; a rooster crowing on a whitewashed gate. She had even sketched in a dovecot, and an old grey donkey, for she owed her notions of rural life almost entirely to the charming fictions of children's television.

The collection of ramshackle buildings which now confronted her, their rotting doors hanging off their hinges, was not the least what she'd expected. There were no cobbles, just some fractured concrete, carpeted with shit and soil and poultry feathers. The shell of an ancient Citroën 2CV sat on its axles in one corner, and apparently served as a henhouse. Nothing grew there but nettles and dock. Seeing it through Kayleigh's eyes, Sandra had to admit it was not a pretty sight.

'Shall we go into the barn?' she asked doubtfully. 'There are chickens in there. And there might be calves.'

'I don't think so, on the whole. I'd rather not.'

'You're probably right. It does look a bit sludgy. Besides,' Sandra checked her watch unseeingly, 'we should be getting back. Will we go by way of the fields? Say hello to the horses?'

'No,' said Kayleigh bluntly, impatient now to return to the house, and – please God – to Jamie. 'We can see them any day. Besides, I want to do a wee.'

'You could pop through that gap in the hedge. No one would see. I'd keep guard.'

'No, I'll wait. I'd rather.'

'As you prefer.'

Their mood of amity dissolved. They were, after all, strangers, and from different worlds.

They walked back to Foxholes in silence.

———————— • ————————

There was somewhat more congenial company to be had in the public bar of the Hare and Hounds that lunchtime, than ever there was *chez* Rawlings. Charlie straddled a bar stool and sunk a pint of draught bitter very fast. Then, feeling marginally more human, more sanguine, more settled, he consented to play darts with Brian Truefitt, a mate of his since school-days.

He had a wide circle of friends and acquaintances, on whom he made no emotional demands, needing little from them beyond their conversation, the odd game of pool, the occasional jump-lead on a winter's morning when, complaining bitterly of the cold, the clapped-out van refused to start.

'I saw that blonde tart up by Scott's farm this morning,' revealed Brian. He swigged his Guinness, shaved off a foam moustache with his index finger and flicked it on to the carpet. 'The cockney sort. The one that's moved into the Rawlings place. Her and the kid. She was with the daughter. Sandra with the thighs. Arrows, please, Joyce, when you've got a moment.'

'Don't call her that name,' Charlie admonished him, picking up a packet of cheese and onion crisps, tearing it open with his teeth.

'What, "Joyce"? What's wrong with "Joyce"? Ta, my lovely.' Brian took the rusty old panatella tin which the barmaid slid across the counter. It contained a motley assortment of darts, all different lengths, some with plastic flights, some feathered, bedraggled.

'No, "tart". Don't call Kayleigh a tart. Don't call anyone a tart. Especially when you don't even know her.'

'Whoops,' Brian mocked him, 'did I put my size-nine boot in it or what?'

'Or nothing. I just don't like name-calling. It's unnecessary.' He managed somehow not to sound pious when he said this: his tone conveyed genuine affront.

'Now I come to think of it . . .' Brian took the frayed and filthy square of towel and smeared the blackboard with it. 'I'll do chalks,' he volunteered distractedly. Then, remembering, 'Now I come to think of it, you were there for a couple of weeks, weren't you? Month or so ago?'

'I was doing a bit of tarting up, that was all. A spot of carpentry. Some plumbing.'

'Don't say "tarting". It's unnecessary.'

'Oh, very comical.'

'So what I'm asking myself here is . . .' Brian's hand hovered for a few seconds over the tin of darts as over a box of the finest handmade Belgian chocolates, while he agonised over the choice. Finally, arbitrarily, he singled one out, examined it doubtfully, weighed it in his hand, scratched his chin with the bent plastic flight and continued. 'Maybe she went for a handyman like you. So what were you up to in there, eh? A bit of the old tongue and groove, was it? A bit of pipework?'

'Knock it off,' Charlie told him tersely.

'Listen, chum, if I had your advantages . . .'

'Do give it a rest.'

'No, I'm serious. If I had your looks, if I had half your opportunities . . .'

'What opportunities? Stop talking such crap, Truefitt, and chuck a dart. Double three. Hang on. My throw. Treble eighteen. Me to start.'

'Beginner's luck,' Brian sought to dismiss Charlie's minor victory, as he chalked up a squeaky C, an ear-splitting, tooth-grating B. 'No, I kid you not, if I had your advantages, I'd be all over that blonde one like butter over hot crumpet.' Then, with a masterly mix of metaphors, 'I'd be up her like a rat up a drainpipe.'

'Double twenty,' Charlie told him. 'I'm away. Pay attention if you're going to score. Twenty plus twenty. That's forty off.'

'And you're telling me *you* didn't? Hand on heart?'

'Didn't what?'

'Well, *score*, of course, what else? With what's-her-name. Kayleigh, is it?'

'I'm telling you just that. I'm sorry if this disappoints you, but the only female in my life right now is Pol.'

'Ah, roly-poly Polly. How is she?'

'Who are *you* calling roly-poly?'

'What are you incinerating?'

'You're not exactly a sylph, yourself.'

'I'm a fine figure of a man. Where *is* Pol today?'

'At my mum's, where I shall be going shortly for my Christmas dinner.'

'We're having pheasant,' Brian boasted, cleaning his fingernails with the point of a dart.

'Been out in the moonlight, have we, with our gun?'

'Nah, these are oven-ready jobs, a brace from the butchers in

Edenbridge. Completely kosher. Well, when I say kosher, I don't mean, you know, *kosher*.'

'Brian, you're doing my head in this morning with all your nonsense. Will you give it a rest?'

'There you go again, casting nasturtiums.'

'Take that uncle of yours, Jim Bayliss. You're telling me he's not a poacher? That overcoat of his has more pockets than a billiard table. When you've finished your manicure, it's you to go.'

'Rabbits,' Brian insisted. 'He might bring back a rabbit. Never pheasant, never partridge, nothing of the kind. That's my story, and I'm sticking to it.'

'And flying pigs? Did he ever bring back one of those?'

'You can take a flying fuck,' Brian told him equably, peering through slitty eyes at the board before loosing a dart.

'Praise be to God! Double seven. We're off. Watch out, Horscroft, there'll be no stopping me now. Loser to buy the next round.'

'I'm not staying for another, but I'll buy you a pint, win or lose.'

'Very magnanimous of you, I'm sure.'

'Well, that's me all over. Generous to a fault.'

'And modest,' Brian prompted.

'And modest.'

'So you didn't – Oh, sh – ugar.' This as a dart hit the wire and rebounded, to embed itself in the floor at Brian's feet. 'Did you see that? That was the bull's-eye for sure.'

'It missed by a mile.'

'I'm telling you.'

'Well, tough, it doesn't count.'

'No, I do realise.' When Brian bent to retrieve the dart, to tug it out of the hard wood, a gymnastic feat for a man of his proportions, his zip-up jacket inverted over his head, the blood ran down into his face like sand in an egg-timer till it filled right up. 'So you didn't, like, hit it off with this Kayleigh tart?' he asked. He straightened up, and the blood ran back out again.

'You know what you are, Truefitt?'

'Yes,' said Brian proudly, 'I'm incorrigible.'

———————— ● ————————

What do fairies have for breakfast?

This question exercised members of the Rawlings family as they sat down to their meal amid the debris of coloured crepe paper and foil. Jean Crabtree sported a plastic ring like a daisy on her third finger. Eric blew a miniature whistle until people put their fingers in their ears and begged him to desist. Dee toyed with a geometric puzzle. Ben drove a tiny model jeep recklessly around the tray of the high chair.

It's like a bleeding madhouse, Kayleigh told herself, it's like a loony bin. She dropped a magic cellophane fish into her palm and watched with quiet satisfaction as it coiled. This was supposed to show that she was passionate. Only, then the stupid thing thrashed its tail, turned over in her hand and slowly uncurled, a sign that she was not. Ach, what did a rotten fish know, anyway? What did *anyone* know of her private torment, of the desire that consumed her? She brushed the fish on to the cloth with her fingertips, discarding it angrily.

Raising her eyes she saw Jamie opposite, sitting back, sort of skewed in his seat, with his head propped on his fist, with one leg hung over the other, disdaining the proceedings. Crackers, paper hats, idiotic riddles, all these were beneath him, his manner implied. His distaste was not, today, particularly for her, yet she felt encompassed by it.

He had brought gifts for his grandparents, for his parents, but nothing for Sandie, and nothing for her. Had she ever seriously entertained the notion that he might? No, she thought she had not, for why should he?

She had told herself stories in which he regaled her with flowers and perfumes and precious jewels, all beautifully parcelled and tied up with ribbons, but she had always known, of course, that they *were* only stories, that this was an exercise in make-believe.

And this morning, in the sitting-room, when she had stood with hands clasped in a fine display of innocence beneath the mistletoe – when she had imagined that he might stride across to take her manfully in his arms, when she had rehearsed in her mind her response to his impetuous kiss – that, too, had been sheer fantasy.

Now, seeing how he withheld himself, how he subtracted

himself so completely from the sum of the group, she felt, for the first time, close to despair. She said to herself, I give up.

'Give up?' demanded Eric with unseemly, slightly inebriate glee. He was enjoying himself mightily. Something about the occasion – the sheer ghastliness of it – appealed to the destructor in him. The atmosphere was highly charged. There would be one hell of a row before the day was out. There would be tears before bedtime.

'Yes, we give in,' Dee humoured him.

'Elf food,' he crowed, and he gave a long, shrill blast on his whistle. At which, as if it had a life of its own, a yellow paper crown rose up off his head with a sort of puff and went floating off on a current of warm air.

'Ooh, terrible pun,' Dee grimaced.

Sandra studied her own face, piecemeal, in a doll-size pink hand mirror – eye, nose, mouth, a pimple starting on her chin – building up a depressing jigsaw picture of herself. Dreadful cracker jokes, excruciating puns, brought Colin very pressingly to her mind. Elf food? He would have enjoyed that one. She felt tense and unaccountably fearful. Her heart seemed to slam about inside her chest, as if, imprisoned there behind her ribs, it had gone quite insane.

'No more riddles, now, please,' Dee implored, opening her arms in an unconscious mime of loving and giving. 'Stop titivating, Sandie, and put that away. Come on, all of you. Eat, eat.'

She had laid before them, with Sandra's help, an enormous spread. Turkey, ham, roast potatoes, boiled potatoes, sweet potatoes, carrots cooked with pancetta, brussels sprouts cooked with ginger, broccoli with red pepper sauce, a stuffing of wild rice and apricot, pork chipolata sausages . . . All this as an offering to her mother and father. The table groaned under the weight of her supplication.

'Of course, your father won't eat sprouts,' said Jean, 'they give him wind.' She helped herself, pointedly, to a morsel of this a morsel of that, a sliver of turkey, a single potato. Then she picked up her cutlery and smiled a smile of self-congratulation. Enough, said her look for all to read, was as good as a feast.

'Can't touch them,' Innes agreed. 'Pass the ham, James.'

'Sure.' Jamie picked up the platter, heaved it over, delivering it into his grandfather's clutches, and, as he did so, catching Kayleigh's eye, shot her a look of mischievous complicity which made her blood shout.

Insofar as they were both outsiders – because this was how he saw himself; as something other, not truly, inescapably family – he felt a slight affinity with the girl today.

Her appearance had improved since last he saw her. She had a full complement of teeth, for one thing. And her skin was brighter. And her hands were less raw. The insipid light of afternoon, slanting through the window behind her, became snarled in her long, fair hair, lending her a kind of aura. She had a nice little body, too; youthful and compact. She was still irredeemably common. She held her fork in a clenched fist and jabbed at the food on her plate. She had nothing to say for herself, no conversation, no small talk. But, in terms of pure aesthetics, she was the best that the room had to show him.

He had no lingering doubt that she fancied him. See how she glanced at him from under lowered lashes. See how her hand flew to her breast. See the telltale movement of her lips, the little twitch and pucker, when his eyes engaged with hers; then see how she moistened them with the tip of her tongue.

He could bed her if he wanted, just like that. She would be weak with gratitude for his attentions. Nor would she ever laugh at him, or slap his thigh, or say 'It's not as if . . . ' Her very presumption, the preposterous idea that she aspired to make love with him, was more pleasing to him than it had been. It was salve to his ego, it sweetened his temper and renewed his hope. He would have to be firmer with Lucinda. He would lay it on the line for her: this was what was going to be.

'Happy Christmas,' he said, to no one in particular, raising a glass of Fleurie in salutation, then drinking deep a toast to his own future.

'Happy Christmas, Jimmy James,' Sandie, alone, responded, getting up distractedly from the table, going to Ben, to cut up his food and to fuss over him, coaxing him to be a good boy and to eat it all up ('Here's a train, going into the tunnel, chuff, chuff, chuff,' she went, advancing some potato pap or a piece of sausage on a spoon as he opened his mouth and went 'O'.)

'You can say what you like,' said Jean, 'but these factory turkeys don't have the same flavour.'

'But it's a free-range bird,' Dee protested, wounded. 'Black Norfolk turkey.' And she added, as an afterthought, 'The best.'

'Too much wind in Norfolk,' Innes commented.

'Ah, that'll be the brussels sprouts,' said Eric.

'Eric!' snapped Dee.

'It's too flat, that's the thing, East Anglia. Give me hills, any day.'

'Yes,' Jean concurred, 'hills.'

'We're fortunate', tendered Dee, 'that it's quite hilly round these parts.'

'It is. Very hilly,' Sandie supported her.

'Tonbridge is terribly hilly,' Jean complained.

'You mean Tunbridge Wells, Mummy.'

'Very steep for walking.'

'I suppose it is a bit.'

'Too steep for my old legs.'

'Uh, huh. I say, Mummy, Daddy, we haven't told you our news,' said Dee, who had been almost bursting to do so, and she clapped her hands together as a child might. 'We're going to be on television. All of us. In the early summer. May, June time. In a programme about superwomen. You know, those of us who have successful careers, and lovely homes and families, who give of themselves a hundred and one per cent.'

'Here, what's this?' Jean poked with the point of her knife at the stuffing.

'It's wild rice, Mummy. And apricot. Now, as I was telling you –'

'It is?' Jean sniffed. 'You can say what you like, but you can't beat the old-fashioned parsley and thyme.'

'Can't beat it,' echoed Innes. 'Pass the salt.'

'Well, I simply thought it would make a change. Do try it, at least. And do try some sweet potato. It's cooked in honey.'

'That sounds like a funny idea.'

'But it's nice. If you'd just *try*.'

Any minute, Jamie told himself, exasperated, Dee would get up and go to her mother, she would bend over her with great solicitude, as Sandie bent over Ben, and spoon the sweet potato into her querulous mouth. 'Here's a train going into a tunnel. Chuff, chuff, chuff.'

'Thank you, no.' Jean paired her knife and fork, emphatically, and laid them side by side. 'I've had sufficient. I shan't make a pig of myself.'

'But you've had hardly anything,' Dee all but wailed.

'Enough', said Jean piously, giving voice to it at last, 'is as good as a feast.'

She'd done some ridiculous things in her time, but this surely took the bleeding biscuit. For downright absurdity, it knocked the parson's cat into a cocked hat.

The suggestion had been Sandie's, and what had possessed her Kayleigh could not imagine. They had been sitting around, the lot of them, full of food, lethargic, as night came down and enclosed the house, when she had sprung up, shouting 'Murder! Let's play murder! Oh, do let's!'

'Good idea,' Dee had responded. 'What fun!'

Fun? *Fun*! The idea was – if you could get to grips with it – that someone had to be the detective. Then you all drew bits of paper out of a hat, and the one with the cross on got to be the murderer. You shot off upstairs. The lights were turned out. And the murderer did one of you in. Then the detective had to give everyone the third degree, to find out who done it. Incredible.

What that meant was that you found yourself hanging around in the pitch blackness, waiting for someone to top you, which was not her idea of a laugh, oh, no.

Kayleigh lurked just inside her bedroom, pressing herself against the wall in irrational fright, hugging herself, straining to see in the darkness, straining after sound, lest anyone come to get her. She knew that it was all pretend, that nobody would really harm her, but the mere thought that one of them might even now be stealing up on her, that they might be preparing to bump her off, induced in her an abject terror.

What was that? She did not so much hear a movement as feel the stirring of the air. There was someone coming, there *was*. She stiffened, made defensive fists, curled her fingers into her palms, squeezing hard. If anyone so much as touched her, she'd just *die*.

Her thoughts raced out of control. Who was it? How close was he? She? Did they sense her presence as she sensed theirs? Was her rasping breath audible to them? Then, what evil designs had they upon her?

When a male hand brushed hers she leapt with alarm. But the next instant a great tidal wave of relief swept over and engulfed her.

It was Jamie. She *knew* it was him. He had come in here to find her, not to stab or shoot or strangle her, but for the illicit pleasure of a stolen hug and kiss. She remembered the way he had looked at her, the way he had caught her eye at dinner. At her moment of deepest despair he had reached out to her, he had come across, he had communicated. After all, as she had hoped and dreamed, he wanted her.

The hand sought hers again and pressed it reassuringly. 'Trust me,' the pressure told her. 'I'm not going to hurt you.' Their fingers laced together. With a sob, she turned to him, slumped against him, buried her head in his heaving chest.

When he stroked her thigh, she did not resist. When he forced his knee between her legs she was happy to accommodate him. She clung to the sleeve of his sweater, which smelled of soap powder and of man-made fibres. And she was visited by an image of Jamie, sitting there, so handsome, so artfully casual, so stylish, in a cotton shirt and lightweight, linen Armani suit.

A mouth covered her mouth fiercely. The tongue which was thrust into her mouth tasted powerfully of wine.

At the moment that Jamie's hands closed with unseemly relish around his sister's throat to throttle her, a scream slashed through the darkness like a knife through a shower curtain.

'Who was that?' asked Sandie in surprise.

JANUARY

'It's chucking it down out there,' said Nancy Wilkins, shouldering her way into the office, her hands full of sodden paper bags and polystyrene cups from the café.

Edie, glancing up from her work, shared the perception that it never rained but it poured.

'Still, I dare say we need it,' Nancy ventured, peeking into bags to check their contents, sorting them, setting them out on the top of a small filing-cabinet in a one-for-you, one-for-me fashion. 'That's Dee's cream cheese and pineapple. Her smoked turkey with avocado on granary. My chicken tikka pitta pocket.'

'Chicken tikka pitta pocket,' Edie chanted. 'Is that the tikka pitta pocket Peter Piper picked?'

Nancy giggled. 'You're so funny, sometimes, Eed. Now, let's see. Dee's cappuccino. My soup. Your tea, two sugars.' She carried it over and set it down before her colleague. 'I mean, it ought to please the water company. The rain, that is.'

'Well, so long as it pleases *someone*. Thanks, sweetie.' Edie prised the lid off the hot drink and raised it to her lips. Her spectacle lenses misted. 'Mm, I needed this. Though it's never quite like mother makes, I find, the tea from across the road.'

'It would taste a lot better out of fine bone china,' Nancy suggested, trying, as usual, and ultimately failing, to make the best of it. The café, for all its pretensions to frothy coffee and avocado, was a dismal concern, where industrial teabags sat steeping, bloating, in a huge aluminium pot; where crusty rolls pressed against the glass of the display cabinet, poking out despising tomato tongues at the customers; where runny butter was slathered on to pre-sliced bread, and sloppy bought-in fillings were spooned from the polythene containers, and the man always pinched her fingers and folded them into her hand around the change.

So much did the place dispirit her, so great was her antipathy to it, she would never have gone there were it not for Dee. 'Darling,' she would say, whenever she was lunching in, 'would you mind running over to get us a snack?' Thus, somehow, subtly, she managed to implicate Nancy, to suggest vested interest ('You will want to go there anyway,' she seemed to imply. 'There is something in this for you also.') And, increasingly, against her nature, in a small part of herself, Nancy resented it.

'Why should I?' a rogue voice would ask in Nancy's head. And, indeed, why should she?

It had been different when she first arrived, when she was so very junior, so wide-eyed and willing, when everything was touched with novelty. But now that she had taken so much more – and more *important* – work upon herself, the long minutes spent in that shuffling queue, waiting for complex orders to be filled, for baked potatoes and chilli to be microwaved, felt like time stolen from her.

'I say, where's Dee gone?' she wanted to know. For the door to the inner sanctum stood open and Dee's desk was unattended.

'She's just buzzed off down the corridor to bait the editor. They've asked her to do another telly thing, so she's gone to swank about it to Ms Constantine.'

'Oh, dear! What is it this time?' asked Nancy, remembering the shemozzle there had been last time a TV crew was in.

'It's all this Marje Proops business. Our foremost agony aunt confesses to a loveless marriage and a years-long affair, so some bright spark gets a notion to ask a group . . . Do I mean a group? Or a gaggle? A school? Come on, Nancy, help me out here. What is the noun of assemblage for agony aunts? You know, like a kindle of kittens, or a murder of crows, or an exultation of larks.'

'I can't think.' Nancy laughed again. 'A . . . consultation,' she suggested, beginning to dry her hair with her fingers.

'I like it! Right. So, some bright spark gets a notion to invite a consultation of agony aunts in for a studio debate along the lines of: do you have to be of stainless character, with your own life perfectly ordered, to do the job successfully? Or, does it help if you've suffered a bit? Should you, yourself, have experienced the darker side of life? I mean, I ask you! And they're calling it, believe it or not, *My Sainted Aunt*.'

'Gracious!'

'That was my reaction – more or less. Well, you can imagine how that will irk the ed. The more exposure Dee gets, the more Clare Constantine seethes.'

'I don't see why.' Nancy, frowning, sipped her soup. 'It's all good publicity for *Mia*. And it's bound to boost our sales.'

'You think she cares about sales? Don't kid yourself. Image is all that concerns Clare Constantine.'

'You know, I think you're being too hard on her.' Nancy regarded her half-slice of filled pitta bread, the chunks of bright red chicken, the ribbons of old lettuce, consideringly. 'Actually,' she continued, 'if you ask me, she's quite nice.'

'Really?'

'When you get to know her.'

'And when *do* you get to know her? Or, should I ask, when do *you* get to know her? I fancy your paths seldom cross (for which, much thanks, in my opinion).'

'Oh, she drops in sometimes at the end of the day.' Nancy dipped into the pitta, stirred the contents with her finger, extracted a piece of chicken, popped it in her mouth and pulled a wry face. 'Yuck. It tastes sort of sour.'

'What would you expect? You will buy that stuff. Yet you could make your own at home for a quarter of the price.'

'It's too much bother, I find. Besides, money's not a problem. I have enough for my needs, even after I've paid my mum. And, d'you know what? I'm getting a rise.'

'You're . . . ?' Edie registered astonishment. 'What do you mean, you're getting a rise? Not that I begfudge it, I hasten to say. You deserve it more than most. But I thought we had a wage freeze. No increases until the new financial year.'

'Well, I know. This is what I'm saying. This is why I'm telling you that Clare's really quite sweet.'

'Sweet?' Edie almost choked on a swig of tea.

'Yes, truthfully. She comes by now and then when I'm working late, and she's perfectly friendly, she stays for a chat. And the other day she said to me, "I've been looking at your salary. It's a bit on the low side. There may be room for manoeuvre on grounds of merit. Let me have a word with the suits upstairs."'

'You're sure about this? You didn't dream it? You haven't been taking those Ecstasy tablets about which I read so much?'

'Certainly not! No, I'm serious, Eed. It started a while ago. She put her head round the door and saw me there, so she came in to see what I was doing. And since then it's been a regular thing. And we chat about all sorts.'

'Well, I never! And is Dee aware by any chance, that you and she –'

'Hello, hello, we're back,' announced Dee at that minute, bouncing into the room, and it wasn't clear if by 'we' she meant herself, or Nancy, or both. 'D'you know, it's simply pelting down outside?'

'I know,' said Nancy.

'She knows,' said Edie. 'She was out in it.'

'That's young people for you. They don't seem to mind. It's water off a duck's back to them.'

'This is your lunch, Dee,' Nancy told her, gathering it up and bearing it through.

'Splendid! I'm famished. Now, do I get any change from my fiver?'

As if to see her visitor out, Dee waited on the threshold to her office, holding fast to the door, which she closed immediately on Nancy's heels.

She wanted to be alone a while with her exultation, for she was feeling tremendously bucked. She saw her appearance on this programme, with three of her most worthy counterparts, as a golden opportunity to shine.

Which of them could claim to have achieved so much in both personal and professional spheres? One had been more than once, and messily, divorced. Another was single, with a teenage child. The third was married to a notorious philanderer, from whom she had separated more than once. Alone among them, Dee could own to a perfect life.

She could claim, with only slight exaggeration, to be married to her childhood sweetheart; she could chalk up three decades of monogamy. She could point to her healthy, happy and successful son and daughter. She could uphold her beautifully functional family.

No, she would argue, it was not necessary to have made a catastrophic match, to have had an unplanned child, in order to be equal to one's job. No, one's life did not have to read like a catalogue of human error. Piffle, she would say. Piffle, poffle.

Grasping a sandwich in her two hands, she took a bite. Then she sat there chewing meditatively, musing on her ideal circumstances.

There had been a tiny problem with Eric at Christmas. A bit of horseplay, mere high spirits, a childish prank, and nothing to raise hell about. She had been cross with him at the time, it was true, for his crass stupidity, his lack of judgement. She had rolled away from him in bed, and had bitten on her lip and refused to talk. But very soon she had forgiven him, since it was just not in her to bear grudges.

This was what had happened. He had sneaked up in the dark on the girl, Kayleigh, and given her a playful peck. She, poor child, quite understandably, had jumped out of her skin. She had then tried to blow the thing way out of proportion, and, to be honest, in so doing, had entirely spoiled their Christmas for them.

It was much to be regretted, with fault on both sides. But it was a teeny-weeny incident in a long and blissful union. It was also a private matter: there was no reason whatever to broadcast the facts, to place them in the public domain.

So, yes, Dee had told the producer, she would be glad to appear. She would speak up robustly for the idea that an agony aunt should be above reproach: she would balance the debate.

Clare Constantine was not thrilled, of course. She had looked, when Dee told her, more than ever as if she were sucking on a lemon. But what could she say? Her hands were tied? 'I can't discuss it now,' she had said acidly, fixing Dee with those wintergreen eyes. 'I have a meeting with the printers.'

The truth was, however, that there was nothing to discuss. Ms Constantine held no sway with Dee Rawlings. She was completely and utterly powerless.

Kayleigh stood resting her forearms on the knotty wooden rail, her hands clasped in front of her, gazing down at the skipping, swirling stream. The water would be freezing, she told herself. She could imagine the numbing sensation if she were to plunge a hand in, the ache that would travel up her arm right to the shoulder and across her back, the deadening of her fingers. 'None of them believed me,' she complained. 'Not even Sandra.' Then, after a moment's thought, '*Especially* not Sandra.'

'We-ell . . .' Charlie Horscroft placed a restraining hand on Ben, drawing the child gently back from the brink by the hood of his duffel coat, as he gave the matter his earnest consideration. 'I suppose it must be very hard', he said, 'to admit that your own dad is an old goat.'

'*I* wouldn't find it hard.' Kayleigh skidded her foot moodily back and forth, squeaking the sole of her trainer on the slimy moss with which the plank bridge was clad. 'I'd believe anything of my old man.' A brief hesitation. 'Almost anything.'

'But Sandie's daddy's girl, isn't she? I sense between them a sort of . . . What would you call it? A solidarity. It's as if they were on the same team.'

'Even so . . .'

'Yes, as you say. Even so . . .' He went down on one knee to look, with Ben, over the lower rail, wrapping an arm around him to secure him.

'Fish in there,' said Ben conversationally, turning his face to him, smiling, pointing a wavering finger.

Charlie screwed up one eye and cocked his head to make the child laugh. 'I see no fish. And you're sure, Kayleigh, of what happened? Of his intentions? There's no possibility that you misunderstood?'

'Look, don't *you* start.'

'No. Of course.'

'I had hoped that you, at least . . .'

'Yes, I understand. I'm sorry.' She had come to him for support and he must provide it. She had told him a tale, and he must believe it. Without equivocation or condition he must do these things for her.

He appeared so genuine, kneeling there gazing up at her with that strange soft radiance in his eyes, she could not but forgive him. 'It's okay,' she said. 'I sort of knew it would be all right to confide in you. I knew that you, of all people, would listen.'

She had woken that morning to a beguiling false spring. She had looked out over the garden to see the sun flaunting itself. The trees had been rocking with birds. Already, though it was not yet February, yellow crocuses were busting through the lawn.

What ever time was this? She had glanced at the clock, and had seen it was barely eight. Why so early? What had roused her? Habitually she slept until nine or ten, she slept for as long as Ivy indulged her, and rose, then, only with the utmost reluctance from her bed.

Today had felt different, somehow. The air had seemed charged. A deep breath of it had galvanised her, and she had made up her mind to do something – though what was to be done, she had not been sure. She had thought she must talk to someone – but to whom?

'You just caught me,' Charlie had told her, ten minutes later, picking up the phone on the first ring. 'I was literally on my way out.' And, 'Sure,' he had responded. 'Sure I can. No trouble. I'll be with you soon.' As good as his word, he had dialled Mrs Richardson's number, to tell her that her tallboy would have to wait (there were worse problems in life, after all, he had put it to her, than loose knobs and sticking drawers). Then he had piled into the van with Polly, and had driven straight round to Foxholes.

'You did say to phone, if ever I needed . . .'

'I did. I meant it. I'm here, aren't I?'

Already the frivolous weather had begun to break. The sun had disappeared in a heaving scrum of cloud. Then the rain had come suddenly, theatrically, aslant, washing over them and moving on. Now the ground sucked with it; everything dripped with it, and the sun was back, it seemed, on sufferance.

'We'll go somewhere,' Charlie had said. 'We'll drive.' And he had brought her to the boisterous stream at the heart of the oozing wood, where he and his friends used to set up camp as boys, where they used to pan for gold.

There was a cool, green aquarium atmosphere under the canopy of leaves. The watery light shimmered. There was a persistent pitter-patter among the branches.

'It was his word against mine,' she said miserably, her vision swimming, 'that was the worst part. And he wasn't half convincing. I began to think it must be me. I thought, Hold up, what's going on here? I thought, How come it seems like I'm in the wrong. The dirty old git sneaks up in the pitch dark and gropes me, and it turns out that I'm the troublemaker.'

'They probably couldn't deal with it. None of them. They preferred to sweep it all under the carpet.'

'And me with it. Because that's how they made me feel: like a bit of dirt to be swep' aside.' She swung her leg up, rested her heel on the handrail, as on a barre, described a tulip shape with her arms above her head. 'I used to want to be a bally dancer.'

He did not say, slavishly, as some men might have done, 'I'm sure you would have been a lovely one.' He did not deal in flattery. He seldom said anything merely for the sake of it, preferring to represent his true perceptions. How would he know, actually, if she had the makings of a dancer? What did he know of ballet? He could visualise her in a tutu, but not actually performing, not up on her points turning circles like the ballerina on a musical box, for this was beyond the reach of his imagination.

'I'm not a liar,' she continued, with the kind of conviction that no one with an absolute regard for truth could hope to summon. Because of course she told fibs, not least to herself, of which this was but one. Now and then she told absolute whoppers. And in her selective retelling of events on Christmas night – her omission, for instance, of Jamie's name, her failure to confess how she'd hungered for his kiss – she was knowingly dissembling. But the fact remained that Eric had made a pass at her, and no one had properly believed her, no one had taken her side, so she was entitled to her righteous indignation.

'Why do you stay there?' Charlie asked her. 'It feels all wrong to me. As if someone were taking advantage of you.' And he was not thinking particularly of Eric.

'I have nowhere else to go,' Kayleigh replied. Another partial truth.

He knew better than to say, then, in reply, 'You can stay with me. I'll look after you.' He bit on that one and was silent.

In that silence her thoughts turned to Jamie as a sunflower to the sun, yet no warmth, no light was shed on her predicament.

When all hell had broken loose on Christmas night, he had offered no comment and no comfort, but had withdrawn further than ever from the proceedings, creating a distance that no one could breach. 'This has nothing to do with me,' he had seemed to be saying. 'I want no part of it, for it is all so very far beneath me.' Thus, once again, she had sensed his contempt, and she had known she was within its compass. And once again she had despaired.

'You should have your own place. Perhaps the council . . . ?'

'I've *got* my own place. My own council place, in London. Much good it does me.'

'Yes, but . . .'

'Greg is there, that's the thing. And the rent's not been paid. And there's money owing everywhere. And I've left him for ever. That's how I come to be here.'

'But it's not a solution. You must see that. You are nowhere, now. You have nothing. Only a new and completely unsuitable dependency.'

'It's only temporary, until something is decided.'

'And how long will that take?'

'Dunno.' She went into a sulk. He saw the shutters go up. And he thought, There are things she's not telling me. He was scandalised by all he had heard, dismayed by the whole rotten business. There was something deeply suspect about the set-up. He sensed perverse self-interest, sensed manipulation, exploitation, gross misconduct. He longed to spring her from this bizarre trap. But she did not apparently wish to be sprung.

'Do you think he'll try it on again?' he asked, his gorge rising, his throat constricting at the very notion of it.

'He won't get a chance to,' she said stoutly.

'You would always call me, wouldn't you, day or night, if things got really nasty?'

'I expect so.'

'No, never mind "expect so". You must promise.'

She stood there vacantly, idiotically, trying to touch the tip of her nose with her tongue, thinking that she could kill for a fag. She had not yet felt any benefit to her health from giving up; if anything, she felt worse. She couldn't remember, offhand, why she had wanted to kick the habit.

'Kayleigh,' he pressed her.

She sighed. She turned away. And she ran through, in her mind, all the good things he had done, his little kindnesses to her. He had never pushed his luck with her, never come on to her, never spoken out of turn. He had made a Noah's ark for her baby, her Ben, a gesture of sweetness so great it lay outside her comprehension, outside the range of her response, somewhere between love and despising, so she had simply not known what to say. ('Thanks,' she had offered gruffly, folding her arms protectively across her chest, when she had met him one day in the street. And with this he had seemed satisfied.)

'All right,' she said at last, when he had waited enough. 'If anything else happens –'

'Or just if it *might* happen.'

'All right,' she said again, in a tone which mocked both him and her. 'All right, all right. Don't keep on, will you. I swear I will. God's honour. I'll come crying to you.'

———————— • ————————

Jamie Rawlings had had an idea. And when Jamie Rawlings had an idea, he acted upon it *prontissimo*. He went from nought to sixty in under five seconds. Vrrrrroom. Watch his smoke!

He was feeling very pleased with himself this afternoon. Cock-a-hoop would about describe his humour. In the space of a single morning he had received three nice, big, fat instructions. He had sized up a mansion flat he felt confident of selling. He had shown a cash buyer around a house with a serious structural fault, talking it up such a storm that a spot of subsidence had come to seem, even to him, a minor inconvenience. And, to cap it all, he had at long last wrung out of old Richard May Be, the promise of a pay rise in April. Dynamic, or what?

But all work and no play would make Jamie a dull boy, so he had decided to give himself time out, to take the afternoon off as a reward for his endeavours. This was the idea, this was the action.

'I'll be out for the rest of the day,' he had told Francine, sliding papers into his briefcase, closing it decisively, snap, snap. 'If anything comes up, I'll deal with it tomorrow.'

'I'll call you on your mobile,' she had volunteered, looking up from the sheet of headed paper on which she had been laboriously writing her name four times over, with a clutch of coloured pens. 'Only make sure it's switched on.'

'No, don't do that. Give me a break. I shall be incommunicado. I have no wish to be disturbed, have you got that?'

'I'm not stupid, you know. I do understand plain English.'

'Yes?'

'Yes, so don't speak to me in that tone.'

'I'm sorry, my love, my poppet, my sweet. Now, please, be a good girl and do as I say.'

'So what am I supposed to tell his lordship?'

'He won't ask.'

Francine Scott, she had written again with her fistful of felt-tips, in a loopy script – red, green, black, blue characters overlapping, interlocking. 'We used to do this at school when we were given a hundred lines. Tried to write three at one go. Did you do that?'

'I was never given lines.'

'Oh, likely.' She had sat back and regarded him with scepticism. 'It didn't work, in any case,' she'd admitted as if this were remotely surprising. 'Perhaps if I'd had bigger hands . . .'

'Right, I'm off.'

'And if he *does* ask?'

'I shall leave that to you. Use your own ingenuity. After all, my little chick-a-biddy, you are, as you're so fond of telling me, no dumb broad.'

'You're expecting me to lie for you. I don't have to do that, you realise?' She had lowered her eyelids, made a prim little purse of her mouth, folded her too-small hands, one over the other in her lap. 'I was reading an article about this very subject. It said that no secretary should have to compromise herself for her boss.'

'Look, you don't have to lie. You can tell him the truth: that I told you I was going to see a client.'

'But you're not.'

'Who said I'm not?'

'You did. Or as good as. So I'm to be your partner in crime?'

'Don't over-dramatise. You make us sound like Bonnie and Clyde. Please, just do as you're told, and stop arguing.'

'Oh, *you*,' she had scolded him then, but her face had been shining. She loved it. The banter which for him was merely an amusing *divertissement*, plainly had a sexual dimension for the soppy little trollop.

Ah, well, she could be his guest. Whatever turned her on. He, however, was making other plans.

The first of these was to drop in on Lucinda, but when he cruised to a halt in front of her shop, Cado, he saw that the 'closed' sign was up. God, she was useless. How did she stay in business? Daddy must pay out hand over fist to keep her afloat.

Well, all that must change once they were married. He would not tolerate such a drain on their resources. Because they *were* going to be married, he was set upon it, and never mind 'No', never mind 'It's not as if . . .'.

Since Christmas Eve, when she had refused him, he had let the matter drop between them. Neither of them had mentioned it directly, and, whenever she had made the odd teasing allusion, he had put her firmly down. His approach to her was subtly altered: he was tougher with her now, he was more masterful, and he fancied that she was responding, becoming more susceptible, more compliant. Before long he would dominate her utterly: she would eat out of his hand.

His first reaction, on finding she was not at work, was one of extreme exasperation. He got out of the car and went to kick the shop door, to scowl in at the useless arty *objets*, bits of blown glass and ceramic, spindly candlesticks, for which there was apparently, incredibly, still a market in a Britain hobbled by recession. Shielding his eyes with his hand he pressed his face against the window pane, to reassure himself that she was not lurking somewhere within. But the place had that deserted air, that stillness which is somehow cumulative, a gathering emptiness (if she'd simply popped out for an hour, he'd have known it).

Then he saw that, as usual, there was an up side. It occurred to him that he might find her at home. He would drive around to her pad unannounced. He would sweep her off her feet. He would have her on the floor, on the stairs, on the kitchen table. He'd give her a good seeing-to. He'd give her 'It's not as if'! It would be a new and powerful Jamie Rawlings whom she'd answer to today.

As he motored towards Kensington, he ran through his performance, the words he would utter, his every action. 'By Christ, you're feckless,' he imagined himself scolding her. And, 'Well, feck me, then,' she would gasp, as she fell helpless, imploring at his feet.

So transported was he by his erotic fantasies, as he mounted the steps to her front door, that he could not erase the smile from his face, though he rubbed with his thumb at the corner of his mouth.

Lucinda lived in a first-floor flat, in a house like a wedding cake with a handsome portico supported on icing-sugar columns. Once, such a place had been beyond his wildest dreams – but no longer.

He punched the brass doorbell with his index finger, and in a moment a bored female voice issued from the entryphone. 'Yah?'

'It's Jamie,' he said, smoothing his hair with the flat of one hand and worrying his tie.

'Jamie?' The voice belonged not to Lucinda, but to her flat-mate, Sarajane.

'Yes, me. Ah, that's you, is it, Sar? Is Luce there?'

'Errr . . .' said the voice noncommittally. A few seconds elapsed in which he somehow knew she was yawning gustily, filling and then emptying her lungs. He thought he caught the sound of it, a faint susurration coming over the intercom; he half expected to feel the soft outbreath in his ear.

Sarajane was, if possible, more indolent than Lucinda. She had the slanting yellow eyes of a cat, and like a cat she slept most of the day, curling up wherever she found herself – on the sofa, on the hearth-rug, on the window seat in the sunshine, with her hands pawed beside her face. Whenever he called around to the flat, there she would be, in the act of waking, or of drifting off. She spent the daylight hours, it seemed to him, buoyed up on a lazy, ebbing, flowing tide of slumber.

At night she was different, Lucinda said. At night Sarajane went wild. But this was a phenomenon which he had yet to witness. 'May I please come in?' he implored, and he pushed impatiently, with splayed fingers, at the heavy panelled door, as if it might give under the gentle pressure.

Another few seconds, another yawn. 'Hold on,' she commanded. There was an electronic buzz. Then, 'Come up.'

He arrived on the first-floor landing, to find her slumped against the door jamb, dressed in close-fitting leggings and a sloppy mohair sweater which did more to accentuate than to disguise her slim figure. (How curious that these women were so effortlessly, undeservedly thin!) 'Hi,' she said, pushing her long dark hair out of her eyes, as she must do every few seconds, since she wore it parted on the side, tossed over the crown, unrestrained by clips or bows or bands.

'Hi.'

She stood aside for him and he went before her, through to the front room, but found no Lucinda there. 'Is she here or not?'

'In her bedroom.'

'Does she know I've come?'

'Uh-uh.' Sarajane shook her head. Her hair flopped once more over her eye.

'I didn't phone first, just called round on the off-chance.'

Sarajane pushed her hair back, right back, and held it there, revealing her smooth white brow, while she fixed him with a peculiar, teasing smile.

Was she after his body? Was that her game? There was mischief of some sort on her mind. Fleetingly, treacherously, he resolved he would one day make love to her (although not before he and Luce were man and wife).

'You can go in,' she prompted, lolling her head, unclasping her hair, which slid forward yet again.

'I shall surprise her.'

'Oh, yes.' Limp-wristed, Sarajane pillowed her cheek on the back of her hand. She smiled a dozy, angelic smile. 'It will certainly be a surprise.'

He went quickly down the carpeted passage to Lucinda's bedroom door, grasped the handle in his two hands, turned it noiselessly, rocked back and forth on the ball of his foot as he rehearsed his entrance, and burst in.

Lucinda was lying with her arms thrown back, with her head upon the pillow, with a beatific look on her lovely face. His first response was to the beauty of her expression; his second to the bulge in the bed. She seemed to have grown monstrously. The silk sheet strained over a large and moving hummock.

'Oooh!' said Lucinda. She slapped her hand over her laughing mouth like a plaster over a gash, but her eyes were stretched with mirth.

Jamie crossed the room in three long strides and stared down, his eyes riveted by the sight of two crepey male feet, one either side of his girlfriend, ten toes tucked almost into her armpits, a pair of male ankles, protruding whitely from beneath the sheet. Into his head popped an absurd question. And, 'What's afoot?' he heard himself demand.

He seized hold of the sheet, fought Lucinda for it as she hung on for grim death, and finally dragged it back, to find Giles de Lannoy-Hunt on all fours, burrowing like a truffling pig between her legs.

'I say, old man!' protested Giles, sitting back on his haunches.

'We weren't doing anything,' Lucinda insisted, and a scream of hilarity escaped her.

'Absolutely not. I'm her financial adviser.'

'No, no. We were playing estate agents.'

'Yes, that's what we were doing. I was taking vacant possession.'

'Oh, Jamie, darling, don't look so cross. I'm not your property. You don't have sole ownership.'

'Or sole agency.'

'Our sole agency.'

'Yes, arsehole agency.'

And the pair of them dissolved in fits of giggles, rolling on their backs, kicking their legs, groaning and clutching themselves with the joy of it all.

'You complete . . . bastards.' Jamie clawed at his eyes as if to pluck them out. He staggered backwards into a wardrobe, ricocheted into an armchair. He made fists and waved them blindly around. His face resembled a swede, with brown fading to mauve fading to yellow.

And the worst of it was, he saw it all. He seemed to stand back from himself, to watch himself, as if he were on film. He was witness to his own unspeakable humiliation.

He saw, then, too, what a dupe he had been, the plaything

of a rich bitch, the butt of her friends' jokes, an oik, an eejit, a self-deluding, willing victim of their buffoonery.

They had taken him for all they could – for drinks, for meals, for their amusement. If all the bottles of Bollie he had bought them were laid end to end, he thought acrimoniously now, they would stretch from Battersea to Bromley-by-Bow.

He dropped his face into his hands and stood there fighting back the tears, as he struggled for mastery of his emotions. 'I'm going now,' he told them through his fingers. Then, dropping his hands, lifting his chin, regarding them as levelly as he could, 'You deserve each other, d'you know that? You deserve to rot in hell. Goodbye for ever.'

With all the dignity he could muster, he made for the door, yanked it open, and exited.

'Does this mean', Lucinda's voice pursued him into the hallway, 'you won't be taking me to the Ivy tonight?'

———— • ————

Sandie whisked up a dressing for the torn leaf salad and tasted it with a teaspoon. Had she perhaps overdone the garlic? Should she start all over again? No, it was surely fine. It was, after all, a matter of taste. Some liked it piquant, some less so.

Her challenge tonight had been to produce for sixteen people a vegetarian fork supper, a hot buffet so 'scrummy' that the carnivores would not even notice the omission of meat. 'It's my husband's sixtieth birthday,' Mrs Hooper, the hostess had told her on the telephone. 'We've been veggies all our married life, and never a day's illness, not so much as a head cold. Oh, yes, we thrive on it. Now, I know you can do this for us. You come highly recommended by my dear friend Anne Marshall, who speaks very warmly of your *crespelline*, not to mention your mango and cilantro vinaigrette.'

Anne Marshall? Ah, yes, Sandie had placed her after a moment. 'The lady with the donkey sanctuary? How kind of her!' she'd murmured. 'How very nice!'

She was preparing *fettunta al pomodoro*, a *risotto ai quattro formaggi*, vegetable compôte with dry *zabaione*, stuffed, fried courgette flowers, a wild mushroom tart, plus various salads, with candied oranges or coffee water ice to follow.

She loved working with vegetables, she enjoyed their shapes, their textures, the crisp, fresh smell of them, their colours, and had been happily absorbed for the past three hours in her numerous tasks. It had all come together like a dream, and she had only to put the finishing touches to the spread. Then somehow she must bear it all through to the dining-room table as the guests converged around it.

'Let me help you,' insisted Maud Hooper, swishing into the kitchen in an emerald gown. And, clapping her hands to her bosom, 'You have done us proud! What a clever girl you are!'

'If we handed the *fettunta* around first . . . ' said Sandie. 'They're the tomatoes-on-toasty things. The white plate. That's right. Maybe you'd like to pass them among your guests, then I can bring the rest in a mo.'

'It's an awful lot to carry. I know, I have just the thing for you.' Maud Hooper bore away the plate of savoury toasts, and returned in a couple of minutes behind a squealing serving trolley. 'You can simply load up and wheel the lot through in one go,' she proposed with satisfaction. 'It steers to the left, so be careful, won't you? But it will make your job a lot easier, I fancy.'

Yes, Sandie said, it certainly would. And, wonderful. Thanks most awfully.

In practice, however, it proved less than ideal. Unloaded, the vehicle was more-or-less manoeuvrable, but once burdened with dishes it became shrill and crotchety, veering off unpredictably this way and that. It was bad enough in the kitchen, on a vinyl floor, where the wheels at least ran freely, but in the long, carpeted passageway it dug in and refused to shift.

She dared not push it too hard, lest it suddenly bound forward, shedding its load in the process. But a tentative nudge had no effect at all, it seemed well and truly stuck.

Oh, dear! And it had all gone so well until this moment. Maybe she should try to drag it back, then carry the stuff through on trays. But it was no more manageable in reverse than it had been in forward gear.

Perspiration started on her forehead. She began to feel menaced by the babble from the dining-room, to imagine them all waiting with mounting impatience. When she chanced a good shove, the trolley lunged forward, dishes skidding about on its polished tiers and clanking together.

She knew there was really nothing to panic about. Far worse things happened at sea. But her emotions had never been subject to her reason, and her nerves would not be subdued.

What would be so terrible about asking for help? She could look in with a rueful smile and prevail upon the nearest person. Some gentleman was sure to give her a hand. There could really be nothing simpler?

Yet she couldn't. She just couldn't. She seemed, like the trolley, to be embedded in the carpet, to be rooted to the spot.

At the end of the passageway the lavatory flushed. Then, a few moments later, the door opened and a lanky young man with round, brown, distracted eyes emerged, drying his hands on the flanks of his trousers.

'I say,' he offered, recognising her predicament a split second before he recognised her, 'can I give you a ha –'

'Colin!'

'Sandie!'

He advanced on her angrily, curling his fingers into his palms. She gripped the trolley as though she might ram him with it should he try anything. They confronted one another across the infernal chariot, across the dishes of glistening food, glaring, glaring, too furious to speak, like a couple of quarrelling children.

'You,' he mouthed at last, at the same instant as she did.

'What are *you* doing here?' each then demanded.

'I'm catering. What does it look like?' she sneered.

'Well, we're friends of the Hoopers.'

Friends, too, of course, she realised, of Anne Marshall. 'What a small world.' She gave a bitter little laugh.

'Yes, isn't it? Such a coincidence.'

'You didn't phone me,' she then accused in an undertone.

'You didn't phone me back,' he hissed at her.

'What? What are you saying?'

'It was *you* who didn't call.'

'You're off your head. You must be, Colin. You don't know what you're talking about.'

'And you're off your trolley. You think I don't know when I phone a person? When I phone her *twice*, in point of fact, and each time I get fobbed off by some bloke.'

'You're a liar.'

'I'm not. I'll thank you not to . . . I rang you, Sandie, twice, and each time I got some geezer saying you were a bit tied up. Like, you're in your parents' home, it's an ordinary Sunday afternoon, but you're too busy to take the call.'

'I *was* busy, as it happens. There were people there. We had something going. Not that it's any business of yours.'

'Something more important than talking to me, eh? More important than returning my calls?'

'I didn't *know* about your calls. I wasn't told.'

'Kept it from you, did he? This mysterious person, who, I'm thinking, might just be your boyfriend.'

'I don't have a boyfriend. There's nobody. I –'

Their voices had been rising steadily. She feared they would be overheard. 'I don't have a boyfriend,' she repeated more calmly, more quietly. 'It must have been my brother Jamie. He didn't tell me you'd been on. In fact, now I remember, he said it wasn't anyone for me. Oh, why would he do such a hateful, rotten thing? Because I was *longing* to see you, to talk to you, and I thought it was all . . . I thought we had . . . I thought it was special. And then, when I didn't hear, I supposed it was just . . .'

At which she began to cry.

'Sandie!' said Colin, stricken, and he edged around the trolley, to take her in his arms, and to kiss the tears from her crumpled, blotchy face.

In which unsuitable attitude Shirley Clarke found them, when she popped out to the little girls' room to powder her nose.

MAY

CHAPTER

———— • ————

14

Jamie Rawlings had been expected, his arrival anticipated. Any day, Giles had thought, the bad penny would turn up. It was tedious, but it would have to be faced. All the same, when he glanced through the window of his King's Road emporium and saw the sleek red bonnet of the Porsche Carrera nosing alongside the kerb, its flamboyant paintwork repelling the bright, darting needles of sunlight, he experienced a minor shock, a pricking in his veins, an adrenalin fix which he found not entirely disagreeable. Ah-hah, he said to himself, here comes nothing. Oh, we shall have some sport this morning!

With his hands buried in his trouser pockets, he sauntered to the door, which stood open to let in the dry London air, redolent of exhaust and of baked dust – familiar, summer, city smells, which pervaded his subconscious and stirred it like the embers of a bonfire, inflaming it, releasing ashes of memory, scraps of time lost, winking, glowing, disintegrating.

If he was nervous (and it was something of an *if*; 'on his mettle' was how he himself would have put it), he was in no way in as bad a state as poor old James. For, see what a rotten show he made of parking the car. Back and forward he went, back and forward, grinding the gears with each change of direction, twisting his body, hanging on to the passenger seat, craning his neck to peer over his shoulder, and finally letting the clutch up sharply, stalling the engine.

For a full two minutes Giles lounged in the shadow studying Jamie's profile as he waited for him to make a move. He noted the barely perceptible nodding of the head, a hint that Jamie was talking to himself, that he was psyching himself up for this confrontation.

It seemed at one point that his courage might fail him, and that he might simply drive away, leaving Giles with an indigestible mix of relief and chagrin, for he was a bully with a bully's relish and distaste for his own excesses. What had been done to him as a child at public school, he these days did to others, revenging himself, inevitably, on the wrong people, while his real enemies prospered in parliament, industry, the law. . .

Eventually, however, Jamie unlatched the door, rammed it open, and shot out on to the wide Chelsea pavement. Then he turned, reached in for his peppermint green jacket, hooked it over his finger and threw it across his shoulder.

With studied nonchalance he locked the car. And he was jingling his keys, he was whistling as he approached the shop, a whistle that died on his lips at the sight of his old adversary.

'Giles,' he said coldly.

'Rawlings, J.,' Giles greeted him enthusiastically. 'Long time no see. How're you doing?'

Jamie played a solitary game of ick, ack, ock, advancing and withdrawing, advancing and withdrawing his hand, offering it for shaking, thinking better of it, offering it again, having second, third, even fourth thoughts, while Giles, clinking the small change in his pocket, smiled urbanely, as if awaiting the end of the performance, when he might politely applaud.

'What brings you to these parts?' he enquired at last.

'I believe we have some business to discuss,' Jamie told him through tight lips.

'Better come inside if that's the case.' Giles indicated, with a nod, the cool, dark, deserted interior. 'You look a bit steamed up, old man. This weather not suit you? Too bad. I love it, myself. Come on through and have a refreshing drink.'

He went ahead to his office at the back of the shop, a glass-partitioned area with a phone, a desk, a couple of old wooden swivel chairs. 'Take a seat, do. Oh, whoops! Be careful. Sorry.

I ought to have warned you. That one does have a tendency to buck you off.'

'It's all right.' Jamie dusted the seat of his stone-coloured trousers. 'I'll stand.'

'As you wish. And how about a livener? A glass of Chablis? I have some chilling nicely in the kitchenette. I say, don't you just love ette words? Serviette, usherette, laundrette? Do have, at least, a drinkette.'

'I won't thank you. I'm not staying. I trust this won't take long.'

'Whatever, whatever, whatever,' Giles held up his hands placatingly. He sat down in his own, more secure swivel chair, at his mahogany desk, and raised his eyes expectantly. 'Usherette, majorette. . .'

'Cigarette?' suggested Jamie grimly, unhelpfully.

'Come now, tell me. I'm intrigued. What is all this about? Fire away.'

'But you *know* what it's about,' insisted Jamie. He propped one foot up on the desk, propped his elbow on his raised knee, propped his chin in his hand, a precarious construction of limbs and trunk, an uneven distribution of weight, which failed to convey the attitude of casual contempt after which he was striving.

Giles spread his hands, put his head on one side, smiled. Tell me about it, he seemed to invite.

'All right, all right, if you want to play silly buggers.' Jamie took his foot off the desk, he stabilised himself, he folded his arms across his chest. 'I know you've sold Clovelly.'

Up went the de Lannoy-Hunt eyebrows, one, then the other.

'I saw it advertised in the local press. I saw it in the agents' window. I saw the "sold" sign, so don't try to deny it.'

'And?'

'And when am I going to see my share?' Jamie's agitation moved him out of the glass box of an office, over to a display stand, where he loitered uncomfortably, snatching up at random, oddments of Clarice Cliff hand-painted Poole vases, lustre jars, *pâte de verre* figures, iridescent glass dishes, dressing-table sets and thingamies. 'When do I see my cut?' He inverted a jar, squinted at it, wondered where he had seen its like before, then set it down on its base once more.

'I bought a bit of property,' Giles's voice, his even, measured tone, followed him out there. 'I sold a bit of property. I made a bit of money, not a lot.'

'What? What's "not a lot"? One-fifty, two hundred thousand?'

'My dear chap, the housing market is in steep decline. There are no fast bucks to be made any more. But, of course, I don't need to tell *you* that. I dare say it's the bane of your life.'

'I'm quite aware, Giles, that you'll have to do some number crunching, what with solicitor's fees, stamp duty, the agent's cut, capital gains . . . I don't expect a straight fifty-fifty off the front. My whack was always to come off the back end, that was understood. Fair's fair, after all. But what I want to know now, at least approximately, is when and how much.'

'Well, to answer your questions in reverse order: nothing, and never.'

'I knew you would do this.' Jamie's voice cracked. His face crumpled with self-pity like a toddler's. As if a tap had been suddenly turned on, tears splashed from his eyes. 'You stole my girlfriend,' he sobbed, weeping into his sleeve, 'now you intend to cheat me out of my money.'

'*Your* girlfriend? *Your* money? Tut, tut. I hardly think so, old love. I mean, really!'

'We had a gentleman's agreement, you and I. We had a verbal contract.'

'And, again, I don't need to tell *you*, a verbal contract is not worth the paper it's written on.'

'You're a thief and a liar!'

'Look, do calm down, you'll have a coronary. It's no big deal. Some you win, some you lose.' Giles got out of his chair and came across to lay a paternal hand on Jamie's shoulder. 'Put it down to experience, what?'

'Get your hands off me.'

'Oh, pish, tush! Temper, temper.'

'I set the whole thing up for you; I let you in. I could make things very difficult for you, de Lannoy-Hunt.' Jamie covered his eyes with his forearm. Why couldn't people have straightforward names? Names like Smith, or Jones, or Rawlings. ('Giles is quite a mouthful, aren't you darling?' Lucinda's words came back to haunt him.) All at once he had a crashing, blinding, mind-numbing headache.

'You could? Do tell?'

'Just think what a stink I could raise if I chose to.' He flung out his arm, and a lustre jar went flying, to smash on the pocked wood floor. 'You have your reputation to protect. Which must be worth more than the money to you. What d'you need it for, anyway? You're as rich as Croesus.' Then, 'My mother's in the print,' he could not prevent himself from adding.

'Who steals my purse steals trash, is that it? But he that filches from me my good name robs me of that which not enriches him, and makes me poor indeed.'

'That's about the size of it,' Jamie confirmed, and he could not – the thought occurred to him – have put it better himself.

'Then what of *your* reputation, James Rawlings, estate agent? What is that worth to you? Because it is you, not I, who have behaved so unprofessionally, so – dare I say? – criminally. It is you who have undervalued a dear little old lady's house. All I did . . .' Giles touched the fingertips of both hands to his chest. 'All *I* did was to buy at the price you recommended.'

'And sold on for a packet.'

'And sold on for a packet. As was my prerogative.'

'You're a crook, that's what.'

'A clear instance, a textbook case, if you ask me, of the pot and the jolly old kettle.'

'What do you get out of this, huh? I mean, apart from the money?'

'Apart from the money?' Giles followed the retreating Jamie to the door. 'Absolutely nothing, please be assured. The money was quite sufficient. Now, I'll tell you what I'll do to show my good faith. I'll not charge you for the lustre jar, how's that? Well, cheeri-bye. It's been nice. I'll give your love to juicy Lucy shall I? Don't be a stranger. If ever you're passing do drop in.'

'I'll get you for this, Lannoy-Hunt.' Jamie stormed out on to the pavement, turned to wave a fist, 'I'll get even.' Then, barging aside a young woman who approached him and would press upon him the *Big Issue*, the magazine sold in aid of the capital's homeless, he flung himself into his car and went steaming down the road, leaving in his wake, in the hot, still air, a thin blue trail of exhaust.

———— • ————

Dee Rawlings sat in her cool, grey workplace, and gave Laura in Notting Hill extremely short shrift. Laura had been stealing from the chemist's where she worked, she had taken lipstick, tights, shampoo, mascara, goods to a total value of perhaps a hundred pounds. Now she was so beset by guilt, she could not sleep at night. Or, when she did, she dreamed of dreadful retribution. She longed to set matters straight with her boss, but he was a hard and unforgiving man, and would be sure to call in the police.

Reading between the lines, Dee perceived very clearly what this artful girl was after: she was asking for a free pardon. Dee, was supposed to say, 'now now', to say 'there there', to deliver the kindly advice that Laura must put it all behind her. It was amazing, really, how transparent these people could be.

We-ell . . . A smart slap on the wrist would do her more good in the long run than a kindly pat on the head. And, indeed, Dee took a dim view of this sort of petty pilfering. It was, in her book, scarcely better than grand larceny, the difference being only one of scale. A thief, after all, was a thief was a thief. (We have established what you are: it is only the amount that is in question.)

So, confession, she advised, was good for the soul. Laura should make a clean breast to her boss, she should tell the truth and shame the devil. She should throw herself upon his mercy, offer to pay back all the money, since only when she had made restitution might she be redeemed.

Having penned this austere advice, she slid her reply into the file for typing and took it out to Nancy, who, feeling deeply for Laura, would take it upon herself to soften the response. (Now that she dealt with the bulk of the mail, she figured she was sort of entitled to do this, and Dee would never know about it, sign it though she might.)

'When you've done that,' said Dee, bending over her, 'I'd like you to type out my expenses, so they'll go through for next pay day.'

'All right,' Nancy dejectedly consented, for she had planned to go this lunchtime, to sit in the park with a book, to feel the sun on her face. She had conceived this treat for herself on the way to work, and she had been sort of saving it up all morning like a sweetie, a perfect little pleasure, in her imagination.

The weather was so super and, this early in the year, so unexpected, it would have been nice to be out in it once in a while, to experience it in the flesh, not merely to look upon it through the tinted windows of an air-conditioned office building, to see it always through a glass darkly.

It was only Tuesday, the week was not half through; the chances of the fine spell lasting until Saturday were slim. Still, perhaps if she hurried there would be time for a short break. She opened the file and began.

'Look, look, here.' Dee emerged a second time from her office, smelling strongly of perfume, of Estée Lauder's Knowing, with which she had just given herself a respray. 'I think, on reflection, you can put that aside. Do the exes for me first, if you will. Here are my receipts. They're all dated, as you see. You can put them in order. Remember to add service where it isn't shown. Fifteen per cent on top. And you can estimate the taxi fares there and back.'

Dee placed before her a small sheaf of restaurant bills.

'But I shall need to know who you lunched with,' Nancy objected, pressing her thumb against her cheekbone, her fingertips to her brow, peering at the woman bleakly through the cage of her hand.

'Well, listen, I don't have time . . . Use your initiative, hmm? You know the people I have to see in the course of my work, to keep them sweet, to pick their brains. Go through my contacts books, there's a darling. Put down my chum the gynaecologist, and whassername the social worker, and the woman from Relate. These are mere details, after all. It's perfectly above board. In fact . . .' Dee drew herself up, she breathed in deeply, inflating her bosom by four or five inches, before repeating the old, old chestnut. 'I don't make a penny on my expenses. If anything, I lose.'

'Of course.'

'Now, do you think you can cope? I'm sure you can. I'm off for a bite at the Blue Print Café. They have a marvellous terrace overlooking the river. Perfect on a day like this. I'm being treated by my agent. Bye bye.'

She whisked out, and was back in an instant, to dip into the stationery cupboard, to pick out a notebook, a couple of felt-tips, which were always so handy to have around the home.

Kayleigh lay on the lawn with her knees drawn up, with her head in the ring of her arm, and watched as a legion of tiny brown ants scurried around in the forest of grass, bearing aloft great weights of leaf and twig, moving with a busy single-mindedness which exasperated her.

They're born, she thought, and they die. And what happens in between is not important. It has no point on earth that I can see. It has no end product.

It was the same for people, in a way, of course, except that they had more in their lives to lend purpose. Love and all that stuff. Family. Sex. Music. Dance. Holidays. Oh, and books.

Beside her lay a paperback, its spine broken, its pages spilling out like a fan. She was reading more and more with every day, discovering undreamed-of sweetness, solace, satisfaction in the printed word. As obsessively as she had once watched television, she now felt drawn into novels, becoming far too involved with the creatures of fiction. Her jaw would ache with unshed tears at this or that cruel twist of fate. She would weep into her pillow till her face was raw for the living dead of literature. Or – as she had in the case of *Tess of the D'Urbervilles* – she would wander around the whole day in a haze of grief and moral outrage, causing Ivy Burston to wonder aloud if a spot of light housework might not be just the cure for the misery-mopes.

Jane Eyre and Mr Rochester, Emma and Mr Woodhouse, Holly Golightly, Lolita, Little Nell, poor Tess, all had more reality for Kayleigh than anyone in, say, *East Enders* or *Eldorado*.

If ever she did switch on the telly, it would fail to hold her. It was not that she was especially critical: it had nothing to do with standards. The medium just didn't speak to her as it used to – or she could not hear it. Like an old married couple they now sat together, she and the TV, in total, mutual indifference. And what little passed between them was quite without consequence. I've gone off it, she put it to herself, regretting this as one would a marriage that had run its course. It's just one of those things, she reasoned it away. For she was embarked upon a new, consuming love affair.

She wanted very much, at this moment, to catch up with Catherine Earnshaw, and with the young Heathcliff, a waif picked up from the streets of Liverpool, who had been nothing but trouble since he arrived at Wuthering Heights. But the sun was so bright; it bounced back off the white page and made her eyes tired. She had tried lying on her back, holding the book up an inch from her face like a small, steep-pitched roof, but in less than a minute her arms had felt the strain, and the light had come in anyway to dazzle her. She had then tried lying on her front, propped on her elbows, but the grass was too spiky, it had needled her bare midriff, so she couldn't get comfy. Eventually, reluctantly, she had given it up as a bad job.

She could go indoors, of course, and flop out on the sofa with a pillow under her head. But it was so glorious out here, and already, in a few fine days, she had begun to acquire a tan, for the sun had only to look at her, it seemed, to turn her golden brown.

A few feet away from her, beyond the reach of her outstretched hand, Ben played with his ark, which gave him such endless amusement. The animals no longer went in two by two – a diaspora was scattered around the house, down behind the cushions, under the bed, in the coal scuttle, at the back of the wardrobe – but a few of the original complement remained.

'Woof, woof,' said Ben, banging a lion about on the turf then throwing it with a clumsy overarm motion which took it whizzing past his ear, as far as he was able.

'Oy, pick that up now,' she scolded him mildly. 'You won't have none left. It's not a doggie, anyway, it's a lion. It goes grrrrrr.'

'Grrrrr.' He tried it out, looking to her for approval. He, too, had the beginnings of a suntan, and his nose was lightly speckled like a linnet's egg.

'That's it. Grrrrrrr-ah.'

'Grrrrrah. Grrrrr. Grrrrrrrrr-ah!'

'All right. No need to shout. Go on, do what you're told and fetch it, you hear?'

She sat up, hugged her knees and dropped her chin on to them, watching her child with the amused fondness which was among the finer emotions he inspired in her. 'Uncle Charlie made that for you.'

'Unker Charlie.'

Ben got up on sturdy legs and went, as he had been instructed, to retrieve the lion, bringing it right to her, making a present of it to her. 'A big lion,' he said, forcing his face into hers, gasping, stretching his eyes in a pretence of terror. 'Woof woof.'

'You're funny, you.' When she put her arm about him, he capitulated utterly to her, becoming languid, lumpish, floppy, imposing his weight upon her, collapsing into her, half sitting on her hip, going through the kind of transmutation of which children and small animals are capable. She pressed her cheek against his warm head, curled her fingers into the warm, damp crook of his knee.

This, then, was the view of them which greeted Jamie Rawlings as he stepped unannounced out through the French windows. He glimpsed something so pure, so innocent and exalted in this tableau of mother and child, it made his heart turn over. His eyes filled like rock pools with salty, sentimental tears.

'Unker Charlie!' Ben greeted him, suddenly galvanised, using his foot to launch himself off Kayleigh's thigh and out of her embrace.

'Charlie?' She turned to greet him with a smile that died on her lips. Then, 'Jamie,' she said, 'it's you.' Her hands travelled protectively up to her camisole, to her cleavage. 'What are you doing here?'

This was, he might have replied, his parents' house, his family's country residence. He could, he might have said, come here whenever he chose. It was she, he might have reminded her, who was the intruder. ('What are *you* doing here? That is the question.')

But he said no such thing, nor was he moved to do so. Instead, he replied lightly, 'I fancied a change of scene. A run out. Some country air.'

'Oh.' She got to her feet and began busily to brush herself down, to dust off the grass which clung to her. She was wearing an old pair of jeans, cut off at mid-thigh, a negligible broderie anglaise top, a necklace of daisies. Her feet were bare, so was her waist; her knees were clad in mud and thatch, her hair was streaked with sunshine, and her skin was gilded.

She had never looked more beautiful, to Jamie or to anyone. 'Also,' he told her truthfully (though with perhaps greater force than he might have done, moved as he was by the loveliness of her, unmanned by her sexuality), 'I came to see you.'

'Me?' she mouthed. Her hand went to her heart.

'Yes.' He tossed his jacket on to the ground with a carelessness hitherto unknown. 'I say, it's hot. Would you like a Pimm's?'

'What's that?'

'You've never had a Pimm's?' Oh, the charming ingenue! 'It's a delicious drink. Wait there. I'll fix you one.'

He went through the French windows with Ben at his heels. 'Finger dots,' said the little boy winningly, clutching at his trouser leg, holding up to him the delicate blue flowers.

'Forget-me-nots,' Jamie corrected him vaguely.

'Fuck-me-nots.'

'Yes, yes, that's right.' He shook the child off. 'Run along now and show them to your mummy.'

As he stood at the kitchen table sawing through a cucumber, as he breathed the wet pond smell of it, he began to feel his spirit, his inner being, his essential Jamieness returning to him.

His instincts had not misled him, he had been right to come here. He had gone to see Giles this morning with no expectation of a square deal, but to give him a piece of his mind. He had told the guy in no uncertain terms what he thought of him: he had called him a scumbag from hell. And he had left him, at last, to ponder his baseness, his turpitude, among his bric-à-brac, his junk-shop tat, among the smithereens of a lustre jar which, in a dramatic gesture, Jamie had swept off the shelf.

He had then driven west with no particular plan, but with an urgent desire to put distance between himself and that loathsome specimen, to be as many miles as he could from de Lannoy-Hunt. But, as he'd reached the M25, the motorway which orbits London, and had begun to travel south, the idea had come to him to head for Kent, for Ashcombe, and for Kayleigh.

It had been as if the scales had fallen from his eyes. The girl had appeared to him, suddenly, to be the very epitome of all he held dear. He had invested her with the qualities of simple goodness, honesty, constancy, courage, humility. Whatever virtues had been so conspicuously lacking in his erstwhile friends, he now foisted on to her, he awarded them like merit badges without discrimination.

He needed her, as it had seemed to him, more than he had

ever needed anyone. And she was here for him. She was his to have and to hold – most especially to have.

Out in the garden, Ben bumbled up to Kayleigh smiling amiably. He thrust the battered flowers into her face. 'Fuck-me-nots,' he announced with pride.

Slap. She laid her hand across his chubby calf. 'Ben! Don't never let me hear you talk like that again, or I'll break your fucking neck!'

———————— • ————————

'This was a brilliant idea of yours.' Colin lay on his back in a sea of bluebells, with his eyes closed, with his hands folded across his stomach, one leg slung across the other, a slack smile running down his face almost into his ears.

'I have them sometimes.' Sandie picked a stalk of frondy grass and trailed it under his nose in the hope that it would make him sneeze.

'Gerroff,' he said sleepily, swatting at it, 'I know that's you.'

'What? What's me?'

'That tickling sensation.'

'What tickling sensation? It's probably a fly.'

He opened one eye just a crack and regarded her sternly. 'You're a bad, bad woman, Alexandra Rawlings.'

'You just said I was brilliant.'

'I said you'd had one brilliant idea in your life, which is hardly the same. Besides, the two are not mutually exclusive, brilliance and badness. Rather the reverse. The words "evil" and "genius" are frequently linked. They go together like . . . Like two things that go very well together.'

'Like rhubarb and custard?'

'Those, for instance.'

'Or Abbot and Costello?'

'Them too.'

'Should I feed you some grapes?'

'No, certainly not. For one thing, I'm so stuffed, I doubt if I shall be able to get up off the ground for at least four hours. You may have to send for a crane. And, for another thing, no one can eat lying on his back. Anyone who has ever tried it will tell you that.'

'What happens?'

'I don't know. Nothing. It's just not possible.'

'Have it your own way.'

'Now, *that* is an offer I can't refuse.'

'Oh, honestly. You're mad.'

She brushed her own foot lightly with the blade of grass, the sole, the arch. 'It is odd, isn't it, that however ticklish you are, you can't tickle yourself? I mean, not with a feather or anything.'

'Not even with a tickling stick.'

'Not even with one of those.'

Groaning contentedly, he dragged himself up to a recumbent position. 'We should probably be getting back.'

'I suppose so,' she agreed lazily, but neither of them moved, anchored as they were in time and space by their complete happiness.

Presently, restlessness would work away in them. The perfect bliss, which would coalesce into a memory, would be relegated by other feelings – by discomfort, impatience, anxiety. Their skin would start to itch, their bodies would twitch to be moving. Lively impulses would shoot from their brains to their nerve-endings and fidget them. They would need the loo. Or they'd find ants in their underwear. 'I must' and 'I ought to' would get into their heads and go whining round like gnats. But not now. Not yet.

'Just think,' said Sandie, 'if we hadn't met again.'

'If it hadn't been for Anne Marshall.'

'Good old Anne Marshall! Or if I had been booked already for that night, if the Hoopers had got someone else.'

'And if *I* hadn't gone to the party. Because I did try, you know, to wriggle out of it. Only my mother said I ought to be there.'

'Then, for once, mother knew best.'

This was a subject they returned to often in a mood of deep complacency, a means to celebrate themselves. Now they sat, with the hubris of lovers everywhere, marvelling at divine providence, at the mysterious workings of the Almighty, at the intervention of the planets, or at the machinations of fate which had propelled them once more into each other's arms.

'It was meant,' said Sandie with simple – simply breathtaking – arrogance.

She was wearing, today, a sundress in shades of blue, red, purple – a sign that her life was no longer on hold. Her legs were bare. Her feet were thrust into leather flip-flops, revealing her long toes, her large, square toenails of which she was – absurdly, in his view – rather ashamed. Her skin was so white, Colin thought, it made her look peculiarly naked. When she drew her knees up he glimpsed a pale thigh, a flash of knickers, and felt almost faint with lust.

He had always had his own notions of what was sexy, informed not by the current fashion, by the photographs of anorexic models in Vogue whom ordinary women were persuaded to envy; or by the teasing, winking, pouting, puckering, pneumatic images that thrust themselves out of the pages of Penthouse and apparently inflamed other men's desires. These were not flesh and blood, they had no substance, they were fantasies. Give him any day a *real* woman – and you'd not find one more real than Sandie Rawlings, with her round face, and with her brown hair now falling in gentle waves down her back.

If he'd been asked to enumerate her most appealing features, he would have counted among them the breadth of her hips, the knobs of her pelvis, the loose folds of skin at her elbows, the soft down of her lip, the lobes of her ears, the spaces between her teeth, even those hated toenails. . .

He could think of nothing more amazing than to possess – to touch, feel, hold, lay claim to, get inside of – another human being. And it was in an elbow and an earlobe that such humanity resided.

'So what shall we do?' he asked her.

'Mmm?' she responded vaguely, drowsily, supposing he meant that she should drive him back to his work.

'I mean, shall we get married, or what?'

'And is *that* a proposal?'

'Yes, yes it is. Will it do?'

'I expect so. I've had better.'

'You have?'

'No, not really. I was kidding.'

'Then, what do you say?'

'I say yes. But.'

'But?'

338

'But not straight from your parents' home.'

'What are you telling me?'

'I'm telling you . . .' She began to walk about on her knees, to gather up the picnic things, scraping the plates into a Tupperware box and sealing it with its lid, stacking the crockery in the hamper. 'Do you want to finish up this drop of wine?'

'No, you have it. It's gone to my head already.'

'Mine too.' She tipped the dregs of the Verdicchio out of the slender green bottle into the bracken. 'Sheeesh, what a smell of alcohol. I say, Col?'

'Yes?'

'Was this really a brilliant idea?'

'A corker.'

'I just woke up this morning and saw the sun shining, and I thought, Wow!'

'Wow?'

'Yes, wow. Wow-wee. I thought, I know what I'll do, I'll make a picnic lunch. I'll drive over with it, meet Colin from work, and we'll go to the woods and –'

'And fuck like crazy?'

'No, that didn't figure in my plans.'

'So what about this wedding business?'

'Ah, yes, that.'

'What do you mean, "Ah, yes, that"? This is our future we're talking about, yours and mine. It's the rest of our lives. It's not a small item at the bottom of the agenda, to be discussed if the schedule permits.'

'No, I know that. I was just playing for time while I thought what I wanted to say.'

'And have you thought?'

'Yup.'

'Then say on.'

She sat back on her heels and spread her skirt around her in folds, like petals. 'Do you like this frock?' she asked, smoothing it fussily.

'I adore it. I want one just like it. Now, for pity's sake, explain.'

'You were serious, were you? It wasn't the wine talking? You didn't just ask because you're drunk.'

'I'm not drunk.'

339

'Well, you know, tipsy?'

'I'm not even tipsy.'

'Okay. Right. Well, I want you to go and live in a flat. A place of your own. I don't want to be your surrogate mother. To take the place of Shirley. I don't want to have a mollycoddled husband. Do you think that's reasonable?'

'Mollycoddled? I'll have you know, I do all my own washing.'

'Truly?'

'I wash my own hands. My own face. I brush my own teeth.'

'And your clothes? Your towels? Your bedlinen?'

'Clothes go in the washing-machine. Bedlinen to the laundry. Towels, ditto.' He counted them off on his fingers dismissively.

'Still, someone has to put them in the machine. Someone has to strip the sheets and pillowcases off, and fold them up and put them in the bag. Someone has to put the fresh ones on the bed.'

'I could do that if I had to. I'd be happy to. Listen, we can make a deal. We'll split all the housework down the middle. Share everything. What's yours is mine, including the dusting. When you've slaved all day cooking for other people, I shall bring you a light but appetising supper on a tray.'

'That sounds fair.'

'Can we shake on it, then?'

'Yes. But.'

'Another but?'

'But it's not only about housework. It isn't *even* about housework. It's about something rather more fundamental.'

'Such as?'

'You know I have this difficulty.' She found a stray blue thread, yanked it, and several inches of her hem came unsewn. 'I love you, Colin, more than I can tell you. I love you so much it hurts. But I find it bothers me no end that you still live at home. I think you should experience a bit of independent living before you even think of settling down with someone. I would respect you more if you did.'

'Oh.' He collapsed with dejection like a soufflé. His shoulders slumped.

'Have I offended you?'

'Of course.'

340

'I can't help the way I feel.'

'No, no, I realise. Thank you for being honest with me.'

She crawled on her hands and knees over to him, laid her hands on his shoulders, leaned on him, planted a kiss on his fuzzy cheek. He turned away, his mouth jinked at the corner; he gave several little shrugs of his shoulder. 'Gerroff,' he said for the second time. 'Unhand me, woman.'

'Do you love me?' she demanded, hanging on to him, moving her mouth against his face.

'No.'

'Aw, go on. Please.'

'Oh, well, all right then.'

Kneeling, facing each other, they embraced.

'Will you consider it at any rate?' she asked over his shoulder, her eye drawn along a path of sunlight off into the silvered woodland. This was a magical place. She would always remember it. It was there, she would say to herself in old age, that Colin asked her to be his bride and she said yes. Said yes, but.

'Okey-doke. Anything. I am crazy for you, Sandie.'

'Oh, goodie.'

They kissed, his hot breath disturbing the fine down on her lip which was among her most endearing features. He closed those brown eyes which were among his.

'Now,' he said, releasing her at last, 'let's finish packing up the picker-nick basket. I'll do the rest, to show good faith. Split the job down the middle.'

'Then I must rush you back to the office before you're missed.'

'Yes, the place will grind to a halt without me,' he joked self-deprecatingly.

'Don't knock yourself so much. I'm sure you're valuable,' she soothed him, though in truth it was another thing that worried her. If only he were not so bound up with his parents. If only he'd not been suckered into the family business, kept there on a promise of an inheritance ('One day, son, all these paperclips will be yours') when she sensed it did not truly fulfil him.

Turning from him, she picked up her handbag and fished in it for the car keys. 'I'll open the boot.'

'You do that. And Sandie . . .'

341

'Yes?' She had begun to walk away, stopped in her tracks, turned again to him.

'Don't worry. I know where you're coming from. I'll make everything all right, you'll see.'

'I'm glad.'

'It's not a problem. It isn't.'

'Good.'

Then, 'Can we talk about it tomorrow?' she implored him as she opened the boot and he heaved the hamper in. 'Will you think about it tonight? Will you come over tomorrow evening? I could make dinner?'

'No, I'll take you to a restaurant.'

'Do you mind? Is it convenient?'

'Sure. You bet.' He put his arm about her shoulders, squeezed, made her a promise. 'I shall be there with my hair in a braid. Rely upon it.'

———————— • ————————

It was afternoon. A softer, more reflective time of day. The shadows on the ceiling, the pattern of leaves which at first light had been sharp and black and vibrant, had ceased their giddy dance. Now they swashed around like waves, dilute, insubstantial, and washed down the walls to merge with the floral pattern of the paper.

The May Gold rose outside the open window nodded in the amiable breeze, releasing its poky scent into the sun-warmed air. A fat, black bee, so gilded with pollen it could barely fly, went dipping, buzzing, in and out among the floppy, unkempt blossoms.

Kayleigh, vacuously wondering how it was to be blind, let her eyelids droop, but still saw through them the fluid movements, the cunning interplay of light and shade.

On the small, round cushion of her belly, Jamie's head rested heavily, rising and falling with her every shallow breath.

Opening her eyes, she smiled down on him, studying the whorls and artful curlicues that were his ear, the soft brown hair, the pettish mouth, his dear face in repose. And she reminded herself to feel happy.

In some perverse part of herself, she willed the encounter to be over. For only afterwards, when she sat down in solitude and thought about it, would she be able to make something sensational of it. Only when she had done some work on it would it come to seem remotely real. Already she looked forward to hindsight, to the private and selective recollection of events.

They had sat in the garden, she and Jamie, amid the humming borders, drinking those swanky drinks. Then he had reached out, the way she had dreamed he would, to cover her shoulder with his hand, kneading with his thumb with bruising pressure, gazing full into her eyes. And he had said all the right things, said, 'You're quite, quite lovely', before sliding his hand down inside her top and cupping her breast, and shuddering with stifled passion.

He had gathered her up in his arms as if she were no more than a doll, and had borne her upstairs to lay her here on her bed. Clumsy with excitement, they had torn at each other's clothing, and with a groan he had rolled on top of her.

The next moment, 'Sorry,' he had said in anguish, flopping on to his back, clapping his hand to his brow. 'I'm so sorry, sorry.'

'S'all right,' she had told him gamely, untruthfully, as she felt his sperm trickle down the inside of her thigh. 'I don't mind.'

'I'm so *tired*, you see. There have been so many . . . So many problems.'

'Don't worry, it's okay, I understand.'

When she had smoothed the hair off his brow and smiled a smile of counterfeit patience and understanding, he had sighed with relief, turned on to his side, sunk down upon her, resting his head and falling at once into a profound and needy sleep.

Now, with nothing else to do but watch and wait, she set about the business of recasting, of unravelling events, and knitting them up again to a new pattern, in which her bitter disappointment, her cheated desires had no place.

She resisted the spasms of impatience, the uppitiness, the itching of her spirit which would have driven her out from under him. Yet she could not lie completely motionless, while all her functions were . . . well, functioning, with respiration, digestion, metabolism all going full tilt.

'Please,' she prayed, 'oh, God, please don't let my stomach rumble?' It didn't seem a lot to ask. The Lord had done this

343

much for her: he had delivered Jamie into her arms. Surely he would grant her a supplementary?

Gradually, her thoughts disengaged, and she drifted off into a confused and fitful doze, even as Jamie emerged to consciousness from his.

He, in his turn, lay like a stone, listening to the gurgling of her gastric juices. He too dwelt an instant on his poor performance, before exonerating himself entirely. He thought too much had been demanded of him. He told himself there would be other times. He even, in his weakened state, thought the two of them might have for ever.

He had been under so much strain. He had been to hell and back. But finally – oh, thank heaven! – the nightmare was over. Those monsters, Giles, Lucinda, Audrey Atkins, a house called Clovelly, were consigned to history.

He had lost much in money, love and self-esteem, but there had been compensatory gains, for he was stronger and he was wiser. He had learned what truly mattered in life – and what did not. He could feel superior to his former so-called friends who, for all their wealth and privilege, were at heart cheap and nasty.

Lucinda was welcome to Giles, and Giles to Lucinda. They were welcome, both of them, to the profit from Clovelly. He would actually have pulled out long ago, had Giles not coerced him. He would have given Audrey Atkins better counsel. They were sullied by the business, while he was clean. He had come up, it now seemed to him, smelling divinely, fragrantly of roses.

As for Kayleigh, dear, sweet Kayleigh, she would dote upon him, she would devote herself to him. And he, in return, would make of her a lady. He would dress her in designer clothes, he would teach her about food and wine, music, theatre, literature. He would show her how to hold her fork, and patiently admonish her when she said 'yeah' or 'ain't' or 'innit'.

He would take her to live with him in a flat with a view of river or common, in Putney, maybe, or Wandsworth. She would sit beside him in the Porsche, and flip down the sun visor to study in the little square of mirror her beautifully made – beautifully made-up – face. And she would turn to smile at him a smile of love and trust and absolute dependence.

He was so entranced by his fantasy, he could see no flaw whatever in it. But, of course, there was one minor detail he had overlooked. Both of them, indeed, had overlooked it.

Ben had been happy enough, alone outside in the sunshine, with so much to hold his attention, a veritable blitz on the senses. For an hour he had sat taking in the scene, interpreting the world as he must through close study, touch and taste.

Beetles and bogeys, worm casts, his own willy, the wasp which crawled round and round his leg, a caterpillar on a leaf which was far less delicious than it looked, a small cigar of dried cat shit turning white and powdery, all were endlessly absorbing to him.

His earliest memory would be, not of the Wavertree estate, not of E block, not of flight upon flight of clattery concrete stairs, or of the unlandscaped grounds, the sparse and wind-bent grass, but of an English garden on a sublime early summer's day. He would breathe the ripe scent of roses, and a riot of impressions and emotions would come bursting in through the backdoor of his mind. (Where was that, he would wonder, and when? And he would experience that woozy, disoriented feeling, the *petit mal* which attends upon such assaults by the subconscious.)

Soon he would learn the word 'lonely', and the sensation which it described, but as yet he was content with his own company. Picture stories unfolded divertingly in his head, complete with soundtrack – with a baa baa here, and a woof woof there, with words from his increasing stock. Horsy. Lion. Mummy. Fish. He was not a stupid child, or backward. He could have spoken up sooner, but he'd bided his time.

'Grrrrrah,' he said now to Oedipuss, who had come to sit at a carefully judged distance, not too near, not too far from him, and who drove his claws into the turf to sharpen them, or in preparation for flight.

Ben made no great distinction between the society of bees and bugs, and black-and-white toms, and human beings. Confident of their friendship, he was pleased to converse with any of them. He was, indeed, as near to Eden at that hour as any of us will ever be.

'Meeeow,' said Oedipuss.

'Grrrrrrah,' responded Ben, slapping his hand down to make the animal start.

But the cat merely stared at him, blinked its glassy eyes, threw back its head and yawned, revealing two neat rows of teeth as sharp as needles. It licked in a desultory way around its shoulders, then hauled itself up, stretched its forelegs, and its hind ones, strolled over to the border, sniffed the lupins delicately, before bucketing over the wall into the lane.

'Woof woof.'

Ben stood up – a clumsy process which involved going first on to his knees, then struggling on to hands and feet, with bottom in the air, before finally achieving a rocky vertical – and toddled after him. He stood for a few seconds, gazing up, swaying, unbalanced by the weight of his own head. 'Lion.' He went to the side gate, casually unlatched it, as if this were something he had done a thousand times before, and slipped out.

'Oh, there you are!' Ann Horscroft greeted her eldest son with obvious relief, clutching at her hair, bunching it, looking faintly distrait and, in her jeans and bandeau top, almost like a teenager. 'I'm sorry to call you from your work.'

'That's all right. I was finishing up, anyway. I'd have been here sooner, only the van's in for a service. Where is he, then? What's all this about?'

'Come.' Ann led him through to the front room, where the child sat in an armchair with his legs straight out in front of him, a picture book spread open on his lap.

'Unker Charlie,' Ben said, beaming, striking one bare foot against the other, scuffing his sole in his excitement, drumming his heels. And, touchingly, he reached out, demanding to be picked up.

'Hello, young Benjamin, how're you doing?' Charlie scooped him out of the chair, held him up to the ceiling, then gathered him in and rubbed noses with him, until the child went boss-eyed.

'I found him wandering in the road,' Ann explained. 'All on his own. Well, I mean, I dread to think . . .' For a moment she gave herself over to the dreaded thinking, to visions of what might have been. 'You read such terrible things.'

'But he's all right, aren't you, mister?'

346

'I took him straight back to the house, naturally. But no one answered when I knocked.'

'Could be she was out the back,' Charlie suggested. 'Maybe she was in the garden and didn't hear the bell. She could have thought Ben was safe upstairs in bed. She could have put him down for a nap.' He crimped his brow as he offered this explanation. It was the best he could come up with, and it failed to satisfy even him.

'That's possible,' Ann agreed sceptically.

'I'll take him back there now, shall I? Because she may be going frantic. Ouch!' he exclaimed as Ben head-butted him. 'Mind what you're doing, mate.' He carried him out on to the red-tiled front step, with Ann at his elbow. 'You don't suppose . . . ?' He turned to her.

'What?'

'You don't suppose anything's happened to Kayleigh?'

Now it was he who dreaded to think – and who thought the more for dreading it. 'I'll go quickly. I'll run.' He thrust the bewildered Ben on to her. 'Have you got him? Keep him. Hold him. That'll be best. Till we find out what's going on.'

'Take my bike,' Ann called after him, as he began to sprint.

He was almost out of earshot, but he stopped to windmill an arm and to shout back to her, 'No, no, I'll run. I'll be just as quick. You phone the house, will you? See if you can raise her.'

He tore across the green, then along the main road and down the lane to Foxholes, where he hammered on the door in controlled panic. He had a feeling of such terrible foreboding that, in spite of the heat and the half-mile dash, in spite of his exertions, the sweat that ran off him felt icy.

'Kayleigh.' He walked backwards down the brick path, cupping his hand round his mouth as he called her name, shielding his eyes, craning to peer at the upper windows, which stared blankly, disdainfully down at him.

He hared round to the side of the house to find the gate swinging open. When he barged through it, a small flock of birds took flight with a great snapping of wings. A teasing stillness settled on the garden, a thrumming silence. Listening, he heard something and nothing. The sight of the French windows standing open increased his alarm. Anyone, *anyone* could have walked right in there. And the sound of the telephone, ringing, ringing, ringing, seemed to confirm his worst fears.

He was pledged to look after Kayleigh. That had been his promise to himself. He would be her guardian angel. But he was sure now that he had failed her. She had met some terrible end.

He closed his eyes, drew breath, prepared himself then went determinedly inside, as the telephone on the table fell silent with a disappointed little brr. A second later it rang again. Charlie picked it up.

'Hello,' said Ann.

'Hello.'

'It's you?'

'Yes.'

'Is all well?'

'I can't say.'

'Is she there?'

'I don't know. There's no sign. Look, I'll buzz you back.' And he hung up.

The sitting-room was pristine, as Ivy had left it, with everything done and dusted. The place had not been burgled, then.

'Kay-*leigh*.' He wandered into the hall.

'What's going on?' She appeared suddenly on the stairs in her baggy T-shirt, and hung on to the banister rail very tightly. The criss-cross imprint of creased linen on her cheek somehow enlivened her look of sheer ill temper. 'What the fucking hell do *you* want?'

'I thought . . .' He felt first very foolish, then incandescent with rage, although only by a twitch of the cheek did he betray it. God, the girl was irresponsible! Had she no sense? What was she thinking, to let her child wander while she lay around sleeping her head off?

When he folded his arms across his chest his biceps bulged with his lean strength. His jaw jutted at her accusingly. 'Where's Ben?' he asked her in a low, even, deceptively amiable voice.

'In the garden.'

'You think so?'

'I know so.' This, somewhat shakily, without conviction, for she was squirming inwardly under his scrutiny. (Oh, those eyes, those bloody eyes of his!) She took a step down, revealing one slim thigh almost to the top. 'Why?'

The idea came to him that she was naked beneath her T-shirt. Momentarily distracted, he did not reply. He looked away while he dealt with his emotions, with his need for her, which he must suppress, and he ground his fist into his forehead.

'What's all this knocking and ringing and yelling blue murder?' She tried to seize the advantage, to accuse him before he accused her. And she came jerkily down another four steps.

'You heard the door? You heard the phone?' He focused on the wall behind her, momentarily sparing her the glare of his regard, fixing on a precise point somewhere above her shoulder. 'Yet you didn't answer?'

'I was otherwise engaged,' she said with assumed hauteur, then giggled foolishly behind her hand and shook her hair about. She would have grabbed up the phone, if truth be told. Left to herself, she would have gone to the door, for she was never quite able to resist.

She had always had this feeling, deep, deep down, that she was destined for better things. A mistake had been made when they handed out good fortune: she had somehow been overlooked, but not for all time. One day would come the call to change her life. ('Miss Roth? We are solicitors representing your long lost uncle . . .' 'Kayleigh Roth, this is the pools people . . .' 'Kayleigh, you have been chosen out of a thousand hopefuls, to be the Revlon Girl of 1993' . . .). Debt collectors, social security snoopers, the man to cut off the electric, beating a path to her door, would find it opened at the first ring, they would be greeted with her look of eager expectation, which would give way rapidly to suspicion, then to hostility . . . then slam!

So, 'I must answer,' she had pleaded with Jamie.

But, 'Leave it,' he had ordered her, touching his finger to her nose and squashing it. 'No one else matters. There is only you and me. The rest of the world can go hang.'

'Ben is with my mum,' Charlie informed her acidly, as she came all the way down, as he came to the foot of the stairs to confront her. 'She found him roaming around in the lane. She brought him to the front door, she knocked, but no one came.'

When he raised his arm, she actually flinched in instinctive self-protection, she shrank back from him as if he might strike her.

He felt sheer disgust then, with her, with himself, he felt profound disaffection. Her insolence was one thing; her abjectness quite another. 'I was worried about you,' he told her bleakly, setting his face against her. 'I thought you might have had an accident.'

'Well, I haven't, as you see,' she told him with a show of bravado, a cockiness she did not feel, sensing how irremediably she had insulted him, reacting badly to her own offence. And she spread her hands, as if to exhibit herself, and performed a little twirl. What was it about Charlie that set her so on edge? He was too bloody good, he was too *right* all the time. Or, as she expressed it to herself, he 'put her in the wrong'.

'Look, just get some proper clothes on,' he commanded, 'and come with me to fetch him.'

'What's all this noise? What's the problem?' There now appeared at the head of the stairs, the supercilious Jamie, wearing a hand towel as a loin cloth, holding it at the hip. 'Is this guy bothering you, darling? Are you bothering her, chum? Then I think you should get out before I throw you out.'

'No.' Kayleigh stood, knock-kneed, clutching the hem of her T-shirt, wringing it with her two hands. 'No, Jamie,' she interceded, 'he's not bothering me. It's all right. It's only Charlie.'

Well, that did it! That just about put the tin lid on it! The sight of the creepy Jamie, his big sedentary body with its hard-won and tenuous muscle tone, his state of lewd undress, the realisation of what he had blundered into, would have been enough for Charlie Horscroft. Kayleigh shying from him had been more than enough. But 'It's only Charlie'! This was more than he could endure. 'My mum will bring Ben round to you,' he told Kayleigh with such scorching contempt that she made as if to back off, lost her balance and sat down hard on the stairs. Then, ignoring the hand she reached out to him, her imploring gaze, he turned abruptly, and went out the way he'd come in.

'Bloody gippo,' said Jamie. 'Good riddance.'

———————— • ————————

In the Magazines UK building, in *Mia*'s editor's office, Clare

Constantine turned from her window, from moody contemplation of the fading afternoon, and repaired to her desk, to her work-load.

She signed some page layouts which had been passed through for her approval. She okayed some cover lines for August. Then she ventured upon her in tray, her constantly replenished pile of readers' letters, complaints, queries, story ideas from freelance journalists, memoranda from members of staff.

She scribbed 'No!!!' on an unsolicited manuscript from an aspiring writer, and tossed it into her out tray ('Very much regret . . .' her secretary would write on her behalf, 'not quite suitable . . . wish you luck in placing it elsewhere.')

'Tell her yes,' she scrawled on a holiday request from Kristina.

'Absolutely not!' she appended to a note from Juliette Smart, proposing that they buy in a short story from American *Cosmo*.

When she picked up a memo from the managing director, she exposed a clutch of pink expenses forms. She drew them towards her and went through them briskly, signing the first three automatically. On the fourth, however, she paused. *Ah-hah*. She went through it once, quickly, then again more slowly, running her pencil down the page, subjecting each item to minute scrutiny, her exquisitely shaped scarlet lips moving as she read.

The room was silent except for the low hum of the air-conditioning. In the aquarium by the door, the six black mollies went tirelessly about the slippery business of seeing off evil influences.

Finally, Clare slapped her pencil down. She seized the pink form and flurried it in triumph. She even, with uncharacteristic lack of poise and restraint, sprang up off her chair and danced round the room.

'That's it!' she exulted. 'Gotcha!'

———————— • ————————

Jamie had gone back to London and left her.

'Don't,' Kayleigh had pleaded, clutching at him. 'Stay with me. Now that you're here, stay.'

'I have to go,' he'd argued, fending her off, smiling affectionately. 'I must.'

351

'But it's only six o'clock. At least spend the evening with me. I'll do us a fried egg,' she'd offered recklessly.

'I can't. You know I'd love to, but it isn't possible. I have some paperwork to do, and I must be out early in the morning. Besides, there are things that need sorting.'

'What things? To do with me?'

'Yes, in a way. Listen. Don't worry,' he had promised, holding her wrists, clamping her hands to her sides, courting her eyes with his, the better to impress upon her his sincerity, his noble intent. 'I will come for you, I will take you away with me. That I swear.'

'Soon? You'll come soon?'

'On my mother's life. The moment I'm able. Now, don't you fear.' And he had drawn her to him, to crush her in his powerful embrace. 'No sulks, eh? No tantrums? No scenes? I can't stand scenes. Look at me, Kayleigh. Give me a smile. That's my girl. And one last kiss.'

So she was alone again with Ben, but it was a new kind of aloneness, at once more and less isolating, and it would deepen with the night.

She experienced his departure as a sudden pain; he had torn himself off her like a sticking plaster, leaving her raw and sore and exposed to the scouring air. Yet it gave her space to think. She could run through her memories like a video, freezing this frame and that, fast forwarding, rewinding, cutting and splicing. . .

When, yet again, the doorbell rang, her first thought was that it must be Jamie ('After all, I couldn't tear myself away. I couldn't be one night without you').

Then she thought it might be Charlie, come to say sorry for his really gross behaviour (neatly, so neatly, and with what sleight of hand she had inverted the situation!). She quite hoped it was him, but would not tell herself why.

Pausing only to pretty herself, to ruffle her hair in front of the mirror, she went to open up.

'I don't have my key,' said Eric. 'Well, are you going to ask me in, or what?'

Well, everyone said it was too good to last. They said it would
break by the weekend. At bus stops, stranger turned to stranger
to voice this gloomy prediction. Cab drivers and their passengers,
if they could not agree about the fastest route from Hackney to
Holborn, were at least of one mind in the matter of the weather.
It would all be over by Saturday.

But no one had guessed just how sudden would be the change.
It was as if, at dead of night, under the cover of darkness, the
scene shifters had been in to replace not just the backdrop but
the props. The Magazines UK building, which had yesterday
gleamed bleached white against a hyacinth sky, was this Wednesday
restored to its former, familiar weepy cement grey. The London it
overlooked had lost its sparkle.

Cloud covered the capital like the lid of a pressure cooker,
and everywhere the population stewed. Passengers squabbled and
barged each other in bus queues. Taxi drivers slammed their
communicating windows upon carping customers. Café owners
cranked back their coloured awnings. Tables and chairs, so recently
pitched out on to the pavements, were stacked and dragged inside.
People tipped back their heads, they wrinkled their noses and
screwed up their eyes as they scanned the heavens for rain which,
though it seemed inevitable, still did not fall.

A less ebullient character than Dee Rawlings, gazing down

from her office window, might have been depressed by the view. But was she downhearted? Not on your life! She would not entertain a negative thought, while all was going so very well for her.

In two days' time the *Superwoman* programme would be beamed into homes the length of the country. Her perfect life would be public property. Her fame would be consolidated. Her position as Britain's best known, best loved agony aunt would be assured. She would stand alone.

'Thank you my sweet,' she said absently, hearing the tinkle of a teaspoon in a saucer behind her, and she turned to favour Nancy with a somewhat distant smile, for her mind was turned inward upon herself.

'You remember you have a lunch today?' Nancy reminded her, placing a cup of coffee on the desk, careful lest it slop.

'Mmm? I'm sorry. What did you say? I was miles away.'

'A lunch. With Jane Fox. She wants to interview you for "A Life in the Day".'

'Ah, yes, yes. That's this lunchtime, is it? I *am* in demand at the moment!' This with a winsome, self-parodying smile, to show that, of course, it was not seriously meant. 'Will you book me a chauffeured car, there's my girl? Tell them to charge it to the company account. What time is my appointment? One-fifteen? Than I shall expect it to come for me at one o'clock sharp.'

'You know there's a bit of a freeze on,' Nancy demurred, standing on one sandalled foot, scratching her ankle with the other. 'There was a memo round about expenses. It said to use ordinary cabs because they're cheaper.'

'Ah, yes, but . . .' A ripple of exasperation disturbed the serene Rawlings countenance. 'I do not think', Dee said grandly, sententiously, tugging and twisting her wedding ring, which seemed unaccountably to have shrunk, 'that this applies to senior executives such as I.' It would be a black day, she told herself, when this company could not run to a chauffeured car for its leading light.

'Oh,' said Nancy. 'All right. Sorry.' And she went out, closing the door softly behind her.

'How are we today?' enquired Edie of her, meaning, naturally, how was Dee.

'Fine.' Nancy frowned. 'I think, fine.'

'But . . .?'

'But, she's asked me to book her a chauffeured car.'

'So?'

'So. I thought they were only for the top brass.'

'Among whose exalted ranks she no doubt counts herself. Remember, we are on the brink of mega-stardom. You watch. When this programme goes out on Friday night she'll really be on a roll. There'll be Dee Rawlings the movie. There'll be the book of the film. The T-shirts, the videos. Dee Rawlings dollies. The ice dance version. Why wouldn't she want to ride in a Bentley?'

'Please, please.' Nancy, laughing, held up one hand to fend off this barrage of absurdities, while with the other she picked up the phone. 'I'm just not sure', she said as she raised it to her ear, 'that she has the authority for this.' And, as she punched the buttons, 'The memo stated quite distinctly, no one below the rank of editor.'

'You imagine Dee regards herself as more lowly than an editor? Particularly, than our editor? Look, it's not your problem. She asked you to fix it, so fix it.'

'There could be a hell of a stink. Clare won't like it, for a start. Ah, hello. Executive Express? It's *Mia* magazine here. I'd like to organise a car for one o'clock . . .'

'Never mind about Clare,' Edie continued, as Nancy hung up. 'This thing's between the two of them. When it comes to the clash of the Titians, Dee can do her own fighting. You and I stay well below the parapet, you understand?'

'Oh, I don't think it will come to a real showdown. In fact, I sometimes think that, secretly, Clare rather likes Dee. She shows an awful lot of interest in her. She always asks about her when she drops in for a chat.'

'Asks what, for instance?'

'Ooh, all sorts.'

Edie yanked open her top drawer. It was so empty, so innocent of clutter, that a tube of Polos ran all the way to the back and she had to reach in for them. Ye gods, she said privately to herself, there's dirty work afoot. But to Nancy she said only, 'Want one of these?'

'So, anyway . . .' said Francine, standing over the photocopier, resting her hand on the machine, craning sideways to watch as it spat a dozen sheets into the tray.

'So, anyway, what?' prompted Jamie, glancing up from his advertisement copy. But this was apparently sum and substance of it. No thought had preceded it; none would follow. She was, after all, just talking herself through her work, chivvying herself, urging herself on, as was her way. 'Do that next,' she would instruct herself. 'Make Mr Mabey's tea, then frank the mail.' 'Nip to the loo, then take dictation.' 'So, anyway . . .' It was a kind of verbal punctuation, the stops and commas, the ellipses and dashes with which she made sense of her day.

'It's the first sign, you know,' Jamie told her, smiling almost fondly.

'What is?' She scooped the copies from the tray, slipped them into a wallet folder and filed them. 'Nice one,' she commended herself.

'What?' For his mind was off on a ramble.

'What is the first sign? The first sign of what?'

'Talking to yourself. It's the first sign of madness.'

'Really? What's the second?'

'How should I know? Working in a dump like this, I dare say, when there's a whole, big wide world out there to be explored.'

'It's not that bad here,' she said reasonably. 'It's better than working in an abattoir.'

'If that were the choice, yes. But I want to go places. I want to do people.'

'You're in a larky mood this morning.'

'I'm in a larky mood every morning.'

'That you are not. You've been like a bear with a sore head for weeks and weeks. So what's happened? Your sex life looking up a bit, is it?'

'You could say that.' He rested his chin on his left hand, while noting down a list of superlatives, of mix-and-match adjectives to describe a half-dozen indifferent variations on the bricks-and-mortar theme. 'Superb', he wrote with reckless subjectivity, in devil-may-care mood. 'Splendid'. 'Elegant'. 'Exceptional'. He doodled a sun with a smiley face then put a hat on it, a jaunty trilby affair. He drew a sickle moon. A five-point star. Then, 'Randy', he wrote. 'Nice tits'. 'Neat little bum'. 'Pushover'.

'You still seeing that posh bird?'

'Who? Lucinda?' He gave a careless, a care*free* laugh. 'Good grief, no, I finished with her aeons ago.'

'So who is it now?'

'No one you know.'

'And is it *lurve*?'

'Could be,' he confessed. Then, under his breath, to himself, 'Could *be*.'

He had left Foxholes, left Kayleigh yesterday evening, in order to put some distance between them, to make space in which to think, to probe his own emotions, to find out what he truly felt. He could have stayed to enjoy a night of passion, but had needed more than anything to get his head together.

So much had happened so fast. This urchin, this scruff, had been anathema to him, representing, as she did, all that he despised. Now he was overwhelmed with desire and tenderness for her. Could this be real? Could he trust his own heart? Was he losing his grip? Losing his reason?

This much he knew for sure: he was, as Francine had remarked, in almost reckless high spirits. He had a sense that, if he moved from his anchorage, he might go floating up to the ceiling and bob around there like a helium balloon. (Perhaps he should tie a length of string around his ankle so they could haul him down, he mused facetiously.)

Much of this was indeed to do with Kayleigh, but much of it also related to Giles, to Lucinda, to Audrey Atkins and Clovelly, to that unholy mess which he had got himself into and, now, finally, thankfully, out of.

It seemed to him that he had turned a page, that the story of his life had at last moved on, and he was poised to begin a whole new chapter.

'Here, this can't be right.' Francine was reading a page of details. 'There must be a mistake. One nought too many. That can't be the real price.'

'Let me see.' Jamie held out his hand, crooked his fingers, signalling to her to bring it to him.

'It must be a typing error,' she said, not budging. 'Probably that temp you had in when I was off the other week. She must have been useless. I couldn't put my hand on anything when I got back.'

'Well, come here and I'll let you put your hand on something.'

'Oh, very comical. You've got a dirty mind, you have. Anyway, I'm not your slave. If you want to have a look, you come here.' She shot him a seductive glance which made him laugh aloud.

He stood up carefully, resting his hands upon the desk, edging his way around it, fearful of his own levity. Then, when he did not actually leave the ground but remained firmly earthbound, subject to gravity, he walked across to stand at her elbow, to read over her shoulder. 'You're right,' he said. 'Well spotted. Of course it should be seventy-five thousand, not seven-hundred-and-fifty.' His eyes travelled from the page in her hand to her cleavage. He could just discern, down the V of her blouse, the lacy edging of the Gossard Wonder Bra which gave her such impressive uplift.

'Well, I never typed that.' Her breast swelled and separated with indignation.

'No one's saying you did.' He placed a kindly hand on her shoulder. Out of the corner of his eye he saw a small and slightly shambolic old woman come into the shop. 'Please take a seat,' he invited her, gesturing with his free hand, sparing her barely a glance. 'I'll be with you in a tick.'

'I should hope you would be,' said Audrey Atkins darkly.

———————— ● ————————

Eric Rawlings sat with his head bowed, with his knees spread, with his hands resting limply on them, in an instinctive attitude of meditation, and talked himself through his condition.

I am an abject failure, he decided. 'Abject'? He liked that. It said so much more than 'failure' alone, unqualified, unamplified, ever could. It shouted of weakness, of inadequacy, of a life gone tragically to waste. It quite exactly described how he saw himself.

He was, as Kayleigh had told him, pathetic. Or 'paffetic'. He liked that, also. Why be second rate when, with practice, you could be third or even fourth rate? Why make a bit of a fool of yourself when you could be a complete fucking arsehole? Why be a mere nonentity, when you could be as the lowly worm and crawl on your belly in the slime? If a thing was worth doing, it was worth doing properly, he always said.

He didn't know what had possessed him. Yes he did. If he was honest, he did. And he was trying, for a change, for his sanity's sake, to be honest.

Drink had possessed him, that was what. He had been five parts pissed when he'd taken a notion to go to see her. With several large whiskies in his system, and with wild, ambitious schemes pumping out of his head, speeding his pulse, he had driven to Kent, to Kayleigh, to declare his undying love for her, to beg her to come away with him, to be his for evermore.

'Huh?' she had responded, wrinkling her nose in the way that so maddened and enthralled him.

Then, 'You're a dirty old man.' 'You're a creep.' 'You're useless.' 'You're hen-pecked.' 'Your whole life is a lie.' 'You're Dee's puppet.' 'You would never have the guts to leave her, while she pulls the strings.'

Thus she had hit him with a left, with a right, with a left, right, left, raining blows upon his ego.

'I would cherish you,' he had implored. 'I would care for you. I would make you secure. I'd look after your child. You would learn to love me.'

'Oh, yeah? And how would you propose to keep me?'

'I'd open a garden centre.' Now, where had that come from? Surely not from his conscious, since he had never knowingly entertained such a thought. The idea had just sort of popped up like toast, all ready cooked and hot for spreading.

Now he seized upon it. He would do it, he *would*, albeit not with Kayleigh's support, since she so frankly, unequivocally abominated him. He was familiar with the genre of fiction in which the heroine, against the dictates of her pounding heart, denounced the hero as a beastly rotter. He knew that 'no' did, indeed, at times, mean 'yes'; that sexual attraction could manifest itself as anger; that lust could be antagonistic; that the course of true love never ran smooth, but he also knew that none of this applied.

If he had had any lingering delusions, she would have dispelled them when she sneered at him, 'I wouldn't live with you if you were the last man on earth.' And, with endearing inconsistency, 'In any case, I've had a better offer.'

'You have? Who is it, then?' For some reason he'd pictured Charlie Horscroft – he had had a fleeting image of a well-wrought face, of flowing hair, of the dark intelligence of those eyes – and had felt almost faint with envy for the fortunate, fortunate guy.

Then, 'Jamie,' she had spat at him. 'It's Jamie if you must know. Your own son. He was here not an hour ago, making love to me. So you can put that in your pipe and smoke it!'

This had, of course, been insupportable, the thought of Kayleigh in the arms of that young toad, that spoilt, self-seeking mother's boy, that lout. And it had borne in on Eric how absolute was his humiliation, how thoroughly he'd been trounced.

In his own eyes, now, he was as nothing. He was shipwrecked. Sunk. But, curiously, at the same time he felt liberated, he felt empowered. He had a sense of resting on the bottom, fathoms deep, looking up, up, up, and seeing, very faintly, the light.

He might present a spectacle of utter defeat, as he sat there collapsed over his own misery. But inwardly he was gathering strength, he was gaining new resolve.

He would move out on Dee, her home, her influence. Perhaps for the first time, he would be his own man. He felt no love for her, never had. Nor, he suspected, did she feel love for him (at least, not of the pure, unselfish, unconditional quality which we all, against reason, believe we deserve).

You can get too close up to the truth, so you're caught up in the blur. And unless you stand off, stand back, you cannot hope to see it clearly. Eric had spent half his life with his nose to the broad canvas, fixating on a detail, and it had taken Kayleigh, an outsider, standing off, standing back, to offer him a true perspective. He had known that his marriage was something of a sham, but he had failed to see it for the travesty it was.

'She walks all over you,' Kayleigh had said. 'You know what she's done? She's . . .' She had screwed up her eyes as she sought for the word 'emasculated', screwed up her fists and banged them together, then had settled for 'cut off your balls'.

Well, no more. He would find a flat. He would take a job to begin with, in a nursery, he would work at the business till he knew it inside out. Then he would go to the bank to talk finance.

Eric Rawlings would be puppet no more.

There it was again, that weightless sensation. Jamie Rawlings touched his fingers to his temple as he felt himself drift. The room seemed to sway. 'Francine,' he said loudly, officiously, 'weren't you supposed to slip out for some teabags? We're down to our last one, and I know this good lady would like a cuppa. This is Audrey Atkins, by the way. We found her a lovely new home just before Christmas. What a delight to see you, Audrey. You must be well and truly settled in by now. Come along, Francine, do as you're told. *Subito*, eh? Chop chop. And while you're about it, we've no Sellotape.'

'Yes we have. We've got plenty.'

'I mean staples.'

'We've got –'

'For the small stapler. My baby one. You'll have to go to Ryman's. And,' he extemporised wildly, 'get some gummed labels. And some of those sticky ring things – the ones that look like corn plasters – for reinforcing punched holes.'

'I haven't got the key to petty cash.'

'Never mind, never mind.' Recklessly he extracted his wallet and counted out ten, twenty, thirty pounds.

Francine gave him a look which plainly enquired if he had gone clean off his rocker. 'There will be some change, I dare say,' she told him coolly, before flouncing through the door, then strutting past the window with her nose in the air, wiggling her bottom huffily, pausing momentarily to shoot him a glare of suspicion.

'So-o, Audrey, Audrey, to what do we owe the pleasure? Is this a social call? Or are you on the move again? Ha-ha.'

Jamie groped for his desk, his seat, sat down heavily opposite her, clasped his hands in front of him, summoned a smile of sorts.

'Not social,' she said, 'no.'

He had forgotten how deeply he detested her. That querulous voice, that trembling lip, the occasional flash of obduracy which made him want to punch her.

Christ, look at her sitting there in her shabby old coat (on this sweaty, sultry day, a coat!), with a funny cloche hat, like an upturned flower pot, jammed on her head. 'Well, then,' he went on, relentlessly jolly, 'what can I do you for?'

Grunting, she bent over and heaved on to her knee a tatty tartan shopping-bag, which she nursed there for a moment like a smelly old lap dog before drawing from it a back issue of the *South London Press*. 'It's in there,' she told him. 'My house.'

'Your . . .? I don't quite foll . . .'

'See, here.' She pointed to the ad in the property section, which she had ringed in biro.

'Well I'm blowed!' was all that Jamie could think to say. (Still, in the circs, on the spur of the moment, he told himself, he wasn't doing too badly.) 'Of course, they'll never sell. Not at that price.'

'They've sold.'

She was wearing, he now observed, pinky pearl earrings. For several seconds he sat fixated on them, and on the long and flaccid, curiously dead-looking lobes.

'Impossible,' he said distantly, and his vision blurred.

'I called the agents. They said it had gone.'

'But when? What?' He propped his elbow on the desk and gagged covertly into his hand. Then he reached into his pocket for a handkerchief and blew his nose. His thoughts bolted. How in hell was he going to explain this away? A sudden, aberrant upturn in the market? A blip? Would she believe it?

'I didn't see it until just the other day when I was lining my drawers.'

Jamie blinked away an unappealing image of giant silk bloomers.

'I always keep the old papers, see?' she said, as if she owed him this explanation.

'Very prudent. Very, er, ecologically sound.'

'And there it was.' She sat back and played an agitated little game of handy-pandy, laying her right hand on her left hand, withdrawing the left, laying it on the right, examining her wedding ring, her gnarled knuckles for a few seconds, then effecting another swap. 'I feel', she said woodenly, 'that I've been cheated.'

'But by whom? Not by us, I do assure you. And I cannot conceive . . . An astronomical price. It just doesn't seem . . . Mrs Atkins. Audrey. I valued your property in the best of good faith, when the market was at an all-time low. And if you remember, I did advise you that selling was a gamble. I said you might choose to wait until the market picked up. It was *you*, I now recall, who were so insistent that you must proceed.'

'I want to see the manager,' she said stubbornly.

'I am the manager,' Jamie lied in desperation, casting an anxious glance over his shoulder at Richard Mabey's office door. 'In fact, I own the business. There is only me.'

What did the wretched woman want? Christ! Would she never be satisfied? She had a nice little home, simply perfect for her needs. She had cash in the bank, enough to see her out (he gave her, conservatively, no more than five years). She had probably never had it so good. People these days were so bloody greedy. It was all grab, grab, grab with them. Everyone wanted to make a fast buck.

In an eminently reasonable tone he put it to her, 'It is not in our interests to undervalue . . . I mean, our commission . . . Not in our interests at all. Now, if we had been the selling agents, if that was our advertisement, I would say you had some grounds for complaint. But the fact that a competitor has hiked the price . . .'

'They sold it.'

'But not at that price. Oh, no, most definitely not! Mark my words, they didn't. This is some kind of mistake. A misprint. Ah, yes! These things can all too easily happen. In fact, just a moment before you looked in, I spotted one in our own literature. I was pointing it out to our typist. There! I'm so glad we got to the bottom of the mystery. I'd hate to think you were losing sleep over nothing.'

He was crazed, now, to be rid of her. He stood up, came round the desk to her, and gallantly he offered her his arm. 'I'll see you to the door. Do mind how you go. How's Cyril, by the way? Keeping well? It was quite a trip you made to see me here. You should have phoned. Always phone. It was fortunate that you found me in. I'm out and about a great deal as you can imagine.'

As he talked he steered her, jibbing, resistant, to the door. Her head in its silly hat was just about level with his shoulder. 'They got the asking price.' Her flat, sullen voice issued from under the brim. And, as he leaned past her to tug at the door handle, as he virtually turfed her on to the street, 'I shall take this to a higher authority,' she threatened. Then, meaninglessly, as people will who feel themselves to be impotent, 'I shall fight it through every court in the land. You haven't heard the last of this. Good day.'

———————————— • ————————————

Dee Rawlings was having a simply splendid time, she was in her element.

'Of course,' she announced, 'I do most of the cooking. Eric, poor lamb, can't so much as boil an egg.' And she smiled conspiratorially. 'Men!' her expression plainly said. 'What would you do with 'em?'

'That's great,' said Jane Fox, fiddling with her tape machine, adjusting the recording level, turning it down another notch, as she confirmed with a covert glance that everyone in the restaurant was audience to this conversation. She was beginning to wish she'd not accepted the commission. The things we struggling freelances must do to earn a crust, she told herself ruefully.

She would have preferred to conduct the interview in the subject's home, as was the norm, but Dee had insisted upon lunch ('so much more relaxing, so much more *fun*'), and really, Jane hadn't liked to insist.

'He's the mainstay of my life,' Dee broadcast. And then, lest the couple in the far corner had not quite got that, she said it again, 'The mainstay of my life. My rock and my comforter.'

'What does he, er, do?'

'Do? For a living? At the moment, nothing. Like so many small businessmen, he is a victim of recession. But he has enormous flair, *enormous* flair, he's a true entrepreneur, so I'm quite sure he'll come up with something.'

'Does it cause any problems between you?'

'My being the breadwinner, you mean? My being in a high-powered job while he is unemployed? My being famous when he isn't? Good gracious, no! We have an absolutely solid marriage. A perfect understanding.' She picked up her wine glass and waved it around. 'We are as happy together, and as much in love after thirty years, as we were on our wedding day.'

'That's terrific.'

364

Jane Fox ducked her head to meet her fork, to take a mouthful of risotto. Dee sawed through her steak with vigour and eyed the empty carafe meaningly.

'Would you like some more to drink?' asked Jane Fox dutifully, though it occurred to her that her companion had already had quite enough.

'Mmmm. Yes. Let's be devils, shall we?' Dee winked to draw the hapless, abstemious Jane into a drinkers' conspiracy. 'It slips down rather well, doesn't it? Oh, look, I say!' She signalled with her knife for the handsome young man, the resting actor, who was waiting at tables until his big break should come, and who had showed her rather less than due deference, rather minimal solicitude thus far. 'This steak isn't cooked,' she boomed at him.

He came at once to the table and bent over her, to remind her in an undertone, 'You asked for it rare.'

'There is rare,' she told him, creaking back in her seat, 'and there is rare. No human being could eat this.'

'I shall ask chef to show it the pan again.' With an air of long-suffering, he reached to take the plate from her. Silly bitch, his demeanour implied.

'No. Don't do that.' To detain him she hung on to the plate, engaging him in an undignified tug-of-war. 'I shan't fancy it. I'll have the fish instead. I'll have the turbot.'

'I'm afraid the turbot's finished.'

'Then the mullet.'

'Very well. Red mullet. But we'll still have to charge you for the steak,' he said adamantly, unapologetically.

'That's all right,' Jane Fox put in quickly, peering up from under her hand, hating this frightful scene. 'Yes, that's reasonable. That's fine.'

'It is *not* all right.' Dee's voice reached a painful new pitch. Her face was suffused with colour, as though the red wine ran just below the skin. 'It is neither reasonable nor fine. Do you know who I am?' she challenged the undaunted waiter. And, 'I', she declaimed, 'am Dee Rawlings.'

'Madam,' he informed her laconically, camping it up for the amusement of other diners (and there was nothing she could have taught him about voice projection), 'I don't care if you're the Queen of Sheba. That is prime quality steak, cooked rare as ordered. A noble Aberdeen Angus laid down his life to provide it for you. There are children starving in Africa. You should be made to sit there till you *do* eat it, and you are certainly going to pay for it.'

Jane Fox dabbed her brow with her starched white napkin, dropped it on to the table and reached for the off-switch on her tape recorder.

Meanwhile, at the next table, a man in a crumpled suit, smirking hugely, took a used manilla envelope from his pocket and made a hastily scribbled note.

———————— • ————————

Jamie changed into navy sweat shorts and a crisp white T-shirt. He sat on the bench and doubled over to fumble with the laces of his cross-trainers, to fold down the tops of his snowy sports socks. Then, hesitating only to check in the mirror that his head was on straight, he went through to the gym to work out.

There hadn't seemed much point in going to the health club when one's life was effectively over. On the other hand, there hadn't seemed much point in *not*. The way he regarded it, he could hang around waiting, in agonies of uncertainty, for all hell to break loose, or he could do fifty sit-ups, fifty lat-pulls, a punishing stint on a fixed bike, and twenty torturous minutes on the rowing machine.

If he was going to lose his job, as seemed certain, he would have ample leisure to build on the biceps and triceps, the quads and pecs and abs so formed.

If he was going to get banged up, as seemed possible . . . No, no, that was unthinkable. He could be accused of incompetence, but not of dishonesty, not of sharp practice, for – and wasn't this the bitter irony? – he had not made a brass farthing for himself. Giles de Lannoy-Hunt had done very nicely, thank you, he had cleaned up beautifully, while poor old Jamie was landed in it up to his neck.

Of course, if anyone were to dig deeper, they would turn up a neat conspiracy. If they put two and two together, if they linked his name with Giles's, they would both be in the proverbial doo-doo. Then they might both go down for their crimes. But that possibility was pretty remote . . . wasn't it?

Jamie Rawlings, who had often been heard to liken Her Majesty's prisons to holiday camps, was no longer so convinced. And, in any event, he was not a holiday camp person.

He would start with the exercise bike, he decided. But first he should do a few bends and stretches.

'Ouch!' he said, flinching at the mere word 'stretch', and a beautiful redhead paused in mid-plié at the barre, raised a finely arched eyebrow and smiled in a restrained and utterly self-possessed manner.

Jamie smiled back and his heart quickened. She was so gorgeous! He had seen her before here a few times, and had been forcefully struck by her fluency and grace. She had skin like porcelain, a smooth, supple body, long, sloping thighs, sculptural shoulders, a slender neck, while something of her gait, her swaying walk, her poise, suggested to him a dancer. Perhaps she was in the music business? Or on the stage? She might be a prima ballerina, or a singer.

Had he been less preoccupied he might have ventured a word with her, offered to buy her a fresh orange juice, or an Aqua Libra, but he was not really up to flirtation. Still, he drew consolation from her flash of interest in him. And he was more than ever glad that he had joined this gym.

He had cancelled his membership at the old place after his soppy sister Sandie had showed up there. It hadn't been the same for him from that day on, as he had been constantly on the alert, on the look-out for her.

This new club was more pricey, more exclusive, and was probably beyond Sandra's means. It was also more central and thus less convenient. He could rarely make it there in the lunch hour, and had taken to coming in the early evening, a time also favoured, apparently, by the flame-haired dancer (as he now apperceived her).

He went through his warm-up routine in an almost mechanical fashion, for he was jerky with tension, then adjusted a bike for himself, raising the saddle before mounting.

The rhythmic movement of the pedals, the whirr of the wheel, the sheer exertion began at last to soothe him. For a while he was conscious of nothing but the effort he must expend. Then, gradually, deliberately, he began to introduce thoughts, as one might introduce food in convalescence, with the emphasis on the light and the palatable.

Very deliberately he turned his mind to Kayleigh, to the plans he had made for her, the future he had sketched for himself. He concentrated hard on this, in order to exclude less pleasant speculation. He tried to visualise her face, but could only really see her hair. He tried to recall her growly voice, but, like a weak radio signal, it came and went.

Eventually Kayleigh was displaced entirely in his head by images, not of Audrey Atkins or of dole queues or of prison bars, but of the dancer. He threw a glance across the room and caught her eye as she moved among the Nautilus machines, a towel draped around her neck. She raised her hand as if to wave, but then, teasingly, used it to tuck her floppy hair behind her ear. Her interest in him was undoubted, yet how coolly she communicated it.

She had such style, such refinement. Kayleigh, poor poppet, seemed by contrast terribly gauche and coarse. He would have his work cut out if he was to make of her a lady. A part of him relished the challenge, the notion of being her Svengali, or, as it might be, her Professor Higgins. But another part of him questioned the wisdom of such an investment. Might it not, after all, be more sensible to go for what he termed to himself 'the real thing'? Why not, for instance, make a play for the dancing dolly?

In the end he came up with a no-lose solution (proof that the brilliant Rawlings brain was still on form). If, by some miracle, this Clovelly business blew over, leaving him free in his mind and with energy to spare for such diversions, he would make a play for this superb, splendid, elegant, exceptional female. Then, if he was successful in his bid, if she came across as he expected, he would drop Kayleigh out, not brutally, like a hot brick, but with delicacy, with sympathy, with heartfelt sighs and expressions of deep regret.

That was settled then! He stopped pedalling for a second while he adjusted the controls, increasing his effort level, and then he was off again, hell for leather.

•

Shirley Clarke considered herself a good plain cook. This was what she said to Colin: 'I consider myself a good plain cook.'

368

She made no reference to mango and cilantro vinaigrette, as she set before her son an evening meal of steak-and-kidney pie with buttered cabbage. She did not invoke stuffed courgette flowers or vegetable compôte with dry *zabaione*. She said not one word against Sandie. But this was about Sandie, of course.

'Aren't you having anything?' Colin asked her.

'No. Not just now. I'm not hungry.'

'You ought to eat.'

'I might have a bite when your father gets back from his snooker.'

'Oh. Right.'

But she sat at the table anyway, 'to keep him company', watched his every mouthful. And, of course, he knew better than to leave so much as a morsel. 'You used to love steak-and-kidney,' she would say accusingly, if he did. Then, with a sigh, 'But I suppose you are acquiring more exotic tastes these days.' He polished the lot off quickly, not really tasting it, so discomposed was he by her scrutiny, and he pushed his plate away.

'A little more?'

'No, thanks. I'm full.' He rocked back in the chair, puffed out his cheeks and patted his belly to prove it.

'I confess, it's not very exciting.' When she sniffed her whole face seemed gathered at the nose. 'There's only queen of puddings to follow.'

'Mum, I *adore* queen of puddings. I'll have it in a minute, if I may. First, there's something I have to tell you.'

'You find it a bit mundane, I dare say,' she said captiously. 'But I'm afraid I can't run to tiramisù. My repertoire is, after all, rather narrow.'

'For heaven's sake, Mum, I thrive on your cooking. I could eat it till it came out of my ears. Now, will you please listen. I have something to say. I'm thinking of getting a flat.'

There! Already he'd blown it! He'd not put it strongly enough. What he *ought* to have said was, 'I'm getting a flat.' No humming, no hahing, no equivocation.

'Whatever for?' She laughed incredulously, shook her head and touched her fingertips to her temple.

'It's time I did. I'm too old to be living at home. I should be independent.'

'You're not happy here with us?'

'Yes, yes, I am. That's not the point.'

'We're cramping your style, perhaps?' This with heavy innuendo.

'You aren't. At least . . . Look, it's just . . . what I say. I have to get out there on my own. I have to learn to do my own dusting and ironing.'

'I fail to see why,' she replied with asperity. 'I am perfectly happy to do these things for you. And one day, when you meet a nice girl and settle down, I am sure she will be as happy as I.'

'Times change, Mum. Women today want more equality. They expect men to do the dishes.' Oh, it was coming out all wrong! He was making it sound as if . . . 'I'm not saying I don't agree with that, because I do. I think it's great. More equal partnerships.'

'It's that Sandra, isn't it?' she queried. 'She's behind this.'

'No. Yes. I mean to say . . .' He gripped the edge of the table and swayed forward, as if to hammer home his message with his head. 'I am going to live on my own for perhaps a year. And then I'm going to marry Sandie.'

'She's turned you against us, I see. She's filled your head with ideas.'

'My head was already full of ideas. My *own* ideas. I'm not some kind of cipher.'

'Suddenly, we're doing it all wrong. Suddenly, our way of life is not for you. And you tell me she hasn't put these thoughts in your mind?' Shirley buried her face in her hands and forced a sob through her fingers.

'I wish you wouldn't make such difficulties,' Colin told her wearily. 'I'm a big boy, now, you realise? I'm not a baby any more.'

'Sometimes I wonder.'

'Well, I'm *not.*'

'We'll turn your room into a bedsitter,' she proposed, brightening, dropping her hands, raising her head to fix him with her avid gaze. 'How would that be? You can have your friends up there, and your records, and your meals on a tray. You can entertain who you like, come and go as you please. I shan't trouble you.'

'Mum, I'm not fourteen. Besides, it wouldn't be the same.'

'It will be so very much better. No rent to pay, no slot meter for the gas. Have you any idea what these greedy landlords charge?

You'd be throwing a fortune down the drain when you could be saving up for the marital home. If Sandie's so sensible, I'm sure she'll see that.'

'It's no use, Mum,' he insisted. 'I'm sorry. I'm set upon this plan.'

But, as the tears welled in her eyes, as she bunched a lace handkerchief under her nose, he felt his resolve weaken. This would be the first of many painful scenes. He wondered, frankly, if he had the stomach for it. And he felt obscurely, irrationally resentful of Sandie, for forcing the issue as she was doing.

———————— • ————————

Jamie dined alone that night, for he could not face home, where he must endure his mother's chatter. He perched on a stool at the counter in a tapas bar, staying his emotions with food and drink, working his way stolidly through serial dishes of plump, garlicky prawns, of tiny broad beans with bacon, a wedge of Spanish omelette, cubes of chicken in turmeric, saffron rice, baby artichokes, new potatoes in tomato and chilli, the lot washed down with a tolerable bottle of Rioja.

So tolerable was the wine, indeed, that he called for another glass. Outside, the long-awaited rain was shooting up off the pavement. When people barged laughing, stomping through the door, they brought it in with them on their coats, on their shoes, on their sparkling hair. Little pools formed around the umbrellas which leaned tipsily against the walls, the bar, the stocky legs of tables. Somehow the damp teased out the intoxicating scents of wood stain, resin, alcohol. The windows misted, isolating the merry drinkers in this haven. And there stole upon Jamie a sense of absolute security. He would stay here for ever, and no ill could betide him.

He would take a job serving snacks from the heated display, where small sardines and slices of serrano ham sat crisping, curling under the lamps. He would change his name to Pedro, dye his hair black, grow a moustache, live over the shop, have his evil way with the voluptuous barmaid, grow enormously fat, and the world would hear no more of Jamie Rawlings.

He ordered another glass of wine, then another, but it tasted like bile on his blackened tongue, and all at once he wanted his bed. 'A 'good night's sleep,' he prescribed for himself, as Dee always used to do, her panacea. And, 'Everything will seem better in the morning,' he promised himself, as he wove his way across the room and out into the street.

The rain had stopped as suddenly as it had started, and the tarmac had a polished appearance. The Porsche, bathed in golden light, had an almost preternatural gleam to it. Nothing, on this strange night, was quite as it should be.

For a few minutes he sat at the wheel of his car, blowing through his lips, making pom-pom-pom sounds, listening to the swish and splash of passing traffic, the rushing water in the gutters, the gagging of the drains, as he wondered what to do for the best. It came to him that he should drive round to see Audrey Atkins, to persuade her to back off. He would knock at her door and she would ask him in, and he would drink her peely-wally tea out of 'Dad' and make his peace with her. 'You've done wonders with this apartment,' he would tell her, gazing around him in frank appreciation. 'So homey. So harmonious. You have an eye for interior design, my dear.' The old Rawlings charm, the Rawlings chat, the Rawlings smile would not fail him.

It was . . . what? He peered in the darkness at the illuminated dashboard display. Ten-fifteen. Too late to pay a social call? Surely not, but he ought to get a move on . . . With a heavy hand and a heavy foot, he started the engine, let the clutch out. Then, with one bound, he was off.

Audrey had had a thoroughly pleasant evening. She had been to her whist club at the church hall, where she had won a prize in the raffle, a bottle of sparkling cider. The party had been on the point of breaking up when the heavens had opened, so they'd stayed there waiting for the rain to stop, laughing and chatting for an hour, talking of something called 'the old days', which meant quite different things to different people, but which had been, by common consensus, altogether better.

Now, she made her way home clutching the cider to her chest, through the deserted streets of her nice, quiet, residential neighbourhood.

It had been a big day for her all round. Fuelled by righteous indignation, by the certain knowledge that she had been diddled, she had hastened to the agents' and, with a fluttery feeling in her chest, had willed herself inside. From somewhere she had summoned the courage to give that patronising, supercilious, smooth-talking young man a piece of her mind.

She chuckled, now, to think how she had faced him down, how she had threatened him with the full might of the law. She had given him, she felt sure, the fright of his life. But, of course, she would never follow through. She was too tired in her bones for a fight. The mere thought of it made her hands tremble, made her legs go wobbly beneath her. The upset would probably do for her, she told herself, as, with a sense of sweet relief, she released herself from her perceived obligation, her duty as a citizen to see justice done. I am not a vindictive person, she decided with a glow of warmth and pride, misrepresenting to herself her frailty, her faintness of heart, fancying that she exercised mercy and forbearance when dire retribution was within her power.

She passed almost no one on her short journey – just a couple too deep in love to notice her, and a man in a sheepskin coat, walking briskly with a high-stepping poodle on a jingling lead.

Through net curtains she saw the blue flicker of television sets. The ground-floor bay window of one house was suddenly blanked; then the upper floor bloomed with electric light. For sensible folk, it was time for bye-byes.

Distracted, undiscerning, Audrey halted at the kerb, she raised her eyes to the buildings opposite – to the select estate of retirement apartments which was so much home to her now, it was as if all the years at Clovelly had never been. Then glancing neither to right nor to left, taking no account of the sleek red car which was at that instant nosing around the corner, she stepped into the road.

———————— ● ————————

Afterwards, Jamie would ask himself over and over whether or not it was a genuine accident – but he could never supply the answer.

It was just possible – well, *wasn't* it? – that, in a moment of crisis, he had stepped on the accelerator when he had intended to slam on the brake. He had, after all, had a glass or two. He'd been ever so slightly squiffy, his reactions had been slow.

373

Against this, drunk or sober, he was an experienced driver, it was the kind of error he would not normally make. And there was this . . . not exactly a memory, it was far too diffuse to be so described, but there was an elusive impression of himself at the point of no return.

He would vividly recall how he'd recognised Audrey as she stood there dithering in the beam of the headlamps. He would remember thinking that he had a choice. It had, indeed, seemed somehow above choice: it had seemed that he was being tested. 'Here you are,' a voice in his head had taunted, 'here's your chance. Go for it if you dare.'

Had he, though? Had he gone for it? Had he exercised choice? Had he dared? Or had he simply panicked, and in his panic lost control?

Whatever the truth, he would be haunted for the rest of his life by the sight of Audrey seeming to lunge at him through the windscreen as she slid gracefully up the bonnet. He would only have to close his eyes to see again her expression of almost comic surprise in the split second before she disappeared over the roof, to land in the road behind him with an audible thud.

Oh, Jesus, God, what had he done? He had slid to a halt, flung open the door, swung himself out, and stood there peering wildly up and down. No one, thank goodness, had witnessed the scene. No good Samaritans had come rushing. He would cover Audrey with his jacket, he had decided, then sprint to the nearest house and ring the bell. She had just stepped out in front of him, he would protest, wild-eyed, distraught, appealing for sympathy. He hadn't seen her in the shadow. There had been no time to avoid her. He hadn't stood a chance.

Or he could drive away.

This option had been almost irresistible. He could get back in the motor and drive like the devil to Kent, to Kayleigh, to safety. 'I spent the evening with my girlfriend, officer. She will be happy to support my alibi. And, no, I had nothing to drink.'

Suppose Mrs Atkins were dead?

Suppose she *weren't*?

Could she possibly have survived such an impact?

His scalp had prickled as he tiptoed back to take a peek at her. He had pressed his face into the crook of his elbow and, with a kind of revolted fascination, smelt his own underarm, the sudden sweat, the secretions of fear.

Audrey had been lying in a heap like so much old washing. At his feet had been her flower-pot hat. With a sort of gallant sweeping, bowing gesture, Jamie had scooped it up and pressed it to his thundering heart. He had inclined over her, convinced that her injuries were mortal, and had been petrified to find himself gazing full into her sightless eyes. . .

I should call the police, call an ambulance he told himself now, as he cruised down the Tonbridge by-pass. An anonymous tip-off, that style of thing.

But suppose they could trace the call to his mobile? It would, after all, be logged by the computer. He must stop at the next phone box. No, no, it was too late for that. By now they would have found the . . . Found Audrey. By now she would be receiving help – or she would be beyond it.

He had committed himself to a course of action the moment he leapt back into his car and went crunching over the shards of a shattered cider bottle. There was nothing he could do except to lie low. He must talk and act as if nothing had happened. And maybe, after all, his problems would be solved.

Angie Burston sat on a complaining basketwork commode, reading by the light of a small table-lamp, turning the pages of a hospital romance, while in the bed in the corner old Mrs Lycett lay with her face to the wall, resisting the cold sleep of death, but dying all the same.

In a minute, thought Angie comfortably, I shall make us both a cup of tea. She did not, however, stir herself, so gripped was she by the story. And she sighed to think that the headstrong Eloise should deny to the last her love for the brilliant but irascible Dr Broderick.

Angie, herself a trained nurse, these days did only occasional community work, sitting through the long night with terminally ill patients while their exhausted families snatched some rest. She was temperamentally well suited to the job, being placid, amiable and quite without imagination. She was cheerfully reconciled to the system in which the elderly and frail should pass over, slip away, succumb and breathe their last, and was wilfully oblivious of the violent struggle in which so many of them engaged. 'He had a good innings,' she would say serenely. 'She was a ripe old age.' 'It was very peaceful at the last.' And she frankly failed to feel connected with such people, to see their predicament as her own.

She had no sense of common humanity, always felt distinctly separate from and deeply other than her charges, and took none of their fear or pain upon herself. She fussed around them with a professional kindness which was itself a cruelty, saw them off to their final resting place as if tidying them away, and went home in time to fix her family's breakfast before turning in for a nap.

Life went on. It was for the living. Time was a great healer. Angie had a small, sustaining store of platitudes on which she drew to stave off despair.

'I could fancy a nice drop of Guinness,' said Mrs Lycett unexpectedly.

'A hot cuppa', Angie told her, 'would be better for you.' She stood up and went to smooth the sheets, to plump the feather pillows. 'I'll make us one, shall I? Are you warm enough? Would you like the heating on?'

'I'd prefer a Guinness.'

'Not a good idea, my love, when you're on your medication.'

Turning, Angie peered out of the window. 'The rain has stopped,' she reported. 'The sky's quite clear. Oh, do look! D'you see? What a lovely silver moon!'

'Yes,' agreed Mrs Lycett, as the moon swam in tears before her tired eyes. 'Yes, I see it.'

'And now, here comes a car. Who can it be at nearly midnight? It's stopped outside Foxholes. A smart red sports model. I say, it's the Rawlings son.' Angie folded her arms in front of her, she rested her bosom on the sill. Her forehead bumped against the cold pane of glass, knocking askew her starched white cap. 'The two of them, alone together,' she mused aloud. 'Jamie Rawlings and the young girl, Kayleigh. Well, I'm never one to gossip, but my mum does for Mrs Rawlings, as you know, and I can tell you she's no angel, let's just put it like that. The girl, I mean,' she added fatuously, 'not Mrs Rawlings.'

With impatient fingers Mrs Lycett twitched at the sheet. 'Are you getting us tea, then, or aren't you?'

'Yes, in a minute. Oh, I say! He's just thrown something into the hedge. Well, I ask you.' Tutting, clucking, Angie turned and made for the bedroom door. 'Here we are, hoping to win Best Kept Village, and these yobbos come from town and chuck their litter. Disgraceful. Now, you'll be okay, will you, while I nip downstairs. I shan't be two ticks.'

Not until he drew up at the cottage gate had Jamie noticed, on the seat beside him, Audrey's ridiculous flower-pot hat. The sight of it had arrested him, for it had seemed like a portent, stiff with menace. '*J'accuse*,' it had as good as said.

Get rid of the bloody thing, he'd told himself, grabbing it, sending it spinning, Frisbee fashion, into the sodden undergrowth, where, with any luck, it would lie and rot away.

There had – praise the Lord! – been no one about, for it was approaching midnight, and all the village slumbered.

Having disposed of the beastly bonnet, he went quickly up the front path of Foxholes, to tug at the iron bell-pull and to rap at the studded oak door.

'What?' said Kayleigh crossly, hanging out of an upper window. 'What's all the noise about? Who the hell . . .? Oh, Jamie, it's you.'

'I had to come,' he told her truthfully. And, 'To see you', his tone dishonestly implied.

'Hang on a sec.' She slammed the window, then, in seconds, he heard her beyond the door, fiddling with chains and bolts and latches.

'What are you doing here?' she wanted to know as he crossed the threshold and scuffed his feet on the mat. She was wearing the inevitable outsize T-shirt. Her head hung, heavy with unresolved dreams, her face was puffy with sleep.

'I was missing you.' He reached out to stroke her tangled hair. 'I decided to give you a surprise.'

Some impulse moved them along to the kitchen, where he sank down at the table with a groan.

'What's up?' Kayleigh plonked herself on his lap in a peculiar, perfunctory manner, as if he were an old sofa. She hooked an arm around his neck, planted a kiss in his ear.

377

'Nothing. Nothing really.' He wrapped his arms about her waist, rested his cheek against her breast. His breath felt hot enough to bring her out in blisters. 'I guess I'm shattered.'

'You've been working too hard,' she decided. Overwork, to her, was a very real, identifiable concept. 'Take some time off,' she offered as a remedy. 'You owe it to yourself.'

'I'm sure you're right.'

'Can I get you something? A drink? Or have you had enough?' She sniffed. 'You reek of booze and, yeeuck, of garlic.'

'Sorry. Yes, yes, I've had enough. I only want to lie with you, to hold you in my arms and feel at peace.'

'Huh?' She gazed at him in disbelief. What was the sense in simply lying, cuddling, when you could be doing the business?

'I'm just so very . . . So very tired.'

'Oh. All right,' she conceded with a shrug.

'And here with you, away from . . . Here I can be tranquil.'

'Ah.'

'You soothe my very soul, Kayleigh. You give me solace.'

'Well . . .' Well if he put it like that. She slipped off his knee and extended a hand. 'Come, then. Come upstairs.'

'If anyone asks you . . .' he ventured, stumbling at her heels.

'Yeah?'

'If anyone asks you – not, of course, that they're likely to, but if they do – please tell them I was here with you all evening. Will you do that for me? And will you not question me?'

'If you like,' she agreed without a qualm. 'Anything, Jamie. Anything.'

'That's my girl.' He gave her hand a squeeze. 'I love you. You know that, don't you?'

'Sure,' she told him happily, openly. 'And I love you.'

———————— • ————————

'I've plunged it and I've plunged it,' related Ivy Burston, 'but the water still won't run away.' She sat up very straight, like the Queen, in the front of the van, gazing ahead of her as the village sped by, gripping with her two hands her handbag on her knee. And, 'Oh! Stop! Shoo!' she shrieked in protest, hunching her shoulder to her ear when Polly poked her head over from the back, to nudge her with a cold, wet nose, to rasp her cheek with a sandpaper tongue.

'Don't worry. I'll fix it,' Charlie assured her, shifting down a gear, blinking the morning sun from his eyes. 'It won't take five minutes. Stop that, now, Pol, and behave.'

'You're a good lad.'

'It's no bother, Ivy.'

'Now, what's the betting we find that idle girl still in her bed?' She invited him, with a sly sideways look, to join in her vituperation. By his silence, he eloquently declined.

'D'you know, I believe she could sleep the clock around,' Ivy continued, only slightly discouraged. 'I never met such a lazybones.' Then she took in Charlie's angry profile, saw how his brow bunched with irritation, and let the matter drop.

The next moment, however, as Foxholes loomed before them, she was at it again. 'Well, well, well. So the car's still here. You know, Angie was telling me, Jamie arrived in the middle of last night. I don't know what that young man can be thinking of. I can't imagine what his poor mum would say.' Not that Dee's finer feelings were her concern, but they were, when all was said and done, both mothers; this much at least they had in common.

'Hmm,' responded Charlie noncommittally, sparing the most cursory of glances for the swanky red Porsche parked so offensively at Foxholes' gate.

'And you know how people are. How they talk.'

'I certainly do.'

'I mean, I'm not old-fashioned, but it isn't on, it really isn't. Now, I suppose, I shall have to run around after the pair of them.'

'I don't see why. It's not your problem.' When Charlie switched off the ignition, the engine ran on for several seconds, lumpily, like an old cart-horse out of control. 'It's not your business, either.'

'Ooh!' protested Ivy, taking umbrage. 'I was only saying –' And she tucked her mouth reproachfully away.

But the driver's door gaped. Charlie was already around at the rear of the van. When he unlocked it and reached in for his tools, Polly debouched on to the road and ran along the border, to anoint the steep embankment, the clustered ferns, the ropes of bramble, with a fine yellow drizzle of urine, before crashing off into the undergrowth.

The day was warm and tremulously bright. Breathing deeply

379

– sighing, really – Charlie filled his lungs with the savour of the countryside, of young grass and sodden earth.

'Nobody up, by the look of things,' Ivy muttered, more to herself than to Charlie as she preceded him up the path. She turned her key in the latch, then she surprised him by bending double to scoop up the mail from the mat, presenting him with her tightly rounded backside.

'Oops,' he said, barging her, 'sorry.'

'Not so fast. You'll be sending me flying.'

Once over the threshold she paused to shuffle the letters, to make a close study of the envelopes. Charlie pushed the front door to, leaving it slightly ajar for Polly. The interior had a cared-for smell: the scents of wax polish and warmed cotton conspired to create an impression of modest luxury. It was very still within after the boisterous birdiness without, but the silence was not of the kind that pervades an empty house.

'Nothing of interest,' Ivy reported with a sniff, stacking the mail on the small hall table. 'Come along. Come through and see to this. Look. Would you look? Completely blocked with god alone knows what.'

When she peered into the sink, it failed to return her steely glare, silted as it was with the residue of scummy water, a thin, unappetising gruel. 'If you ask me,' she pronounced, unlikely as this proposition was, 'it's her that's done it. She'll have tipped some bacon fat down the plughole, no doubt.'

'Did you try caustic soda? Well, of course. Okay. Leave it to me. Let me at it. Have you got a bucket? That old washing-up bowl will do. Can you pass it? Ta.'

He slid the bowl under the waste and began to wrench at the trap, whistling as he did so, unconsciously punning, 'Oh, Danny boy, the pipes, the pipes are . . .', then mentally searching for a rhyme for 'calling'. (Stalling, he thought. Galling. Appalling.)

Polly came trotting into the kitchen at the same instant as Oedipuss oiled through the cat flap. There was, to put it at its mildest, a frost between the two. Cat regarded dog with cold hauteur – as a snooty lady might regard her social inferior at a ball, on finding they were wearing the same dress – before electing to skip breakfast and making a dignified withdrawal.

'What *have* you got there? What *have* you brought?' Kayleigh would have recognised the scolding voice ('Don't get your knickers in a twist,' she would probably have retorted). But it was to Polly that Ivy addressed herself. 'Put it down at once. You don't know where it's been.'

'What's that?' Charlie crawled from under the sink and stood to take delivery from the dog's mouth of a quaint old flower-pot hat. 'Where did you find that, eh? You may be a retriever, Polly Perkins, but I do wish you would learn that there are some things best left unretrieved.'

He inverted the hat and peered inside it, as if in search of a name tag or identifying mark. Finding none, he set the thing aside, placing it on the draining-board, then went down on hands and knees again to finish unscrewing the trap. Probing with a length of wire, he dislodged a lovely hairy mess of matchsticks, Kirby grips, spaghetti hoops. . . The sink puked its contents into the bowl.

'Would you believe it?' tutted Ivy with distaste. 'Well, I think you've earned yourself a cup of coffee, Charlie. Now, hand me up that bowl, that's my boy. I'll just take it out of your way.'

'Don't –' he cautioned as he passed it up to her, but too late, for she had tipped the water down the plug-hole, treating him to a greasy shower. 'Why do people always do that?' he wondered with a shake of the head, for it seemed to him to conform to some immutable law of human behaviour.

'Did someone mention coffee?' asked a jocular male voice.

Charlie marked the plodding progress of a pair of fat feet, he focused on the sturdy calves of Jamie Rawlings which protruded from beneath a towelling robe. He noted, in more detail than he cared to, the fuzz of hair, the jutting of an ankle bone, the blue snaking of a vein, the corrugated skin of an instep, the white rind and horny nail of a big toe.

'Oh, hello there,' said Jamie, talking down to him, 'what have we here? A little plumbing problem?' Charlie himself, he seemed to suggest, and not the blocked waste, was the 'little problem'.

'He sorts out the sink for me,' related Ivy, more in glee than in contrition, jabbing Jamie with an elbow, sharing the joke with him, 'and what do I do? I soak him.' This minor domestic disaster had invigorated her no end.

'Yes, there is something of the drowned rat about him,' Jamie, drawling, agreed.

Supercilious shit, thought Charlie, gritting his teeth as he clamped the trap into place. He felt sorely disadvantaged, grubbing around on the floor before his arch rival, and he quickly raised himself up to confront him.

He had Jamie Rawlings' number, never you worry. He had the measure of the man. But, as he squared up to the big fellow, expecting to be met with a look of insufferable complacency, he was disconcerted to find him distrait, haggard, with a distinctly unhealthy pallor, and a mad gleam in his eye.

Jamie opened and closed his mouth like a fish. He made a vague gesture, an ambiguous hand signal. 'Where . . .' he asked with a pretence of nonchalance, and with none of his customary assurance. 'Where did you get that hat?'

This struck Charlie Horscroft as richly amusing. At least as funny as a drenching in bilge water. 'Why?' he asked, slapping his palm with a spanner. 'Is it yours? I shouldn't have thought it was your style. But then, we are way behind the times out here in the sticks. It could be they're all the rage in the great metropolis.' And he began to hum and whistle to himself. 'Where did you get that hat? Where *did* you get that hat? Isn't it a lovely one? I'd like one just like that.'

'Good grief, no. I never saw it before. It's just, it looks so, ah . . . I just wondered, that's all.'

The familiar kitchen seemed suddenly to Jamie an unfriendly, a hostile place. He saw nothing but hooks and points and blades, sharp corners, hard edges. Groping for a chair, he sat down heavily. His throat felt closed; his face was washed with heat. Last night's Rioja returned to rebuke him, backed up with garlic and chilli. Then, when Ivy spoke, she set up a piercing ringing in his ears.

'My Angie saw you last night,' she informed him with deceptive lightness, with a coded message, an implicit menace, he supposed, for him alone. 'She asked me to tell you,' Ivy went mercilessly on. 'She said to remember her to you.'

'Oh,' responded Jamie, with his head in his hands. And he laughed a hollow, humourless laugh. 'Oh, is that how it is? I see.'

16

'You see,' said Clare, and the sweetness of her tone this Thursday morning had a brittle, caramel edge, 'you really have no choice.' She sat back in her chair, crossed one slender leg over the other, made a minute adjustment to her skirt, smoothed the hemline, and smiled at her editorial director across his leather-inlaid desk, a smile so malicious, it scared the living daylights out of him.

'But . . .' Bob Tanner protested hopelessly. He spread his fingers and pronged his temple with them. 'But . . .' he tried again.

He was an agreeable man with crinkle-cut hair dyed an implausible black. Years of intemperance had written their own rubric upon his face. He had the livid complexion, the brandy-stained eyes of a boozer. A meal without wine, he was fond of saying, was like a day without sunshine. But in truth he drank now to feel 'normal', having long ago lost touch with any true normality, never mind with sunshine. Alcohol, in other words was a part of him. He was twenty per cent proof by volume.

He had scant education, of which he was perversely proud: it was his boast that he had come so far in life despite, not because of, his background. Instinct, nous, native wisdom must be thanked for his success. He wore ill-cut suits, insufficiently cleaned, the lapels dusted with cigar ash. He was also a kind man, and a fair one, with a need to be liked. He was everything Clare Constantine despised.

'She's got to go, you must agree. You compromise yourself if you protect her.'

'It's not as if . . .' Those drink-discoloured eyes began to travel the room in search of some excuse, compelling argument or inspiration. Instinct, nous, native wisdom seemed to have deserted him today.

'You must be guided by precedent,' Clare insisted. 'You cannot have one law for the minions and another for your personal favourite. If an employee is found to be on the fiddle, whether she be a cleaner or a contributing editor, she is sacked.'

'But Dee is such a great asset. Such a feather in our corporate cap.'

'She's an albatross around our corporate neck.' Clare mimed the wincing sensitivity of a princess who feels, beneath a dozen mattresses, the intolerable presence of a pea. 'It's not just the expenses racket. Look at the adverse publicity she attracts.' She leaned forward avidly, to tap, tap, tap with an imperious finger, the latest issue of *Private Eye*, which lay open on the desk before him, and which carried, on its 'Street of Shame' page, the story of how Dee Rawlings, cruelly characterised as Tweedle Dee, had last week thrown a tantrum in a restaurant, and how she had been bested by the waiter. 'Tired and emotional' was how her condition was described. Meaning, of course, drunk as a fiddler's bitch. 'Face it, the woman's had her day. She's become a liability, nothing more.'

'She does an excellent job.'

'Does she?' Clare got up and crossed to the window, where she stood fiddling with the blind cord, playing with the plastic toggle, opening and closing the metal slats, so the sunlight fell in stripes upon the carpet. '*Is* she?' she asked challengingly a second time.

'Well, I . . . I think so. Yes, indeed.'

'You do not, however, know so. You don't know the half, if I may say. To be frank, her department would run very well without her. It already does.'

'Now, that's absurd.' He was forced to swivel in his chair to confront her. 'That's simply preposterous.'

'The situation is preposterous, but the accusation is just. We could rid ourselves of Dee at no cost in redundancy, make up her assistant to her job at a mere fraction of the salary. She already deals with most of the mail. She's pretty, she's personable, she has a charming, fresh, girl-next-door quality which would be eminently marketable.'

'You mean Edie?' he asked, incredulous.

'Not Edie, no. Good heavens, not her.' Clare's tinkling laugh expressed, as always, something other than mirth. 'I'm speaking of Dee's secretary, Nancy Wilkins.'

'I know. I think I know. Attractive little . . .' For a moment, only, he appeared to be caught up in the plan. Then, remembering the crisis, he was chapfallen. 'And you're sure about the expenses? There's no misunderstanding? No mistake?'

'As I told you, I'm quite certain. Dee claims to have had a business lunch with a PR, Helen Streeter, on the very day I met with Helen to discuss a skin-care advertorial. She claims to have had lunch with Dr Gillespie on the day he was holding a press conference on breast screening which I myself attended. I've made a few phone calls, checked out her stories; half of them prove to be sheer fiction.'

'We-ell . . .' Which of us, Bob Tanner had been about to ask, does not at some time bend the truth a tiny bit? Which of us has never had a social dinner, then passed off the bill as a legitimate lunch? Fortunately, one glance at Clare, at the ice maiden, dissuaded him from such loose talk.

'Call them up here,' Clare now urged him. 'Edie. Nancy. Ring down and summon them. Let us have this all out in the open.'

'Maybe . . . sleep on it . . .'

'If it were done when 'tis done, 'twere well it were done quickly. You must seize the opportunity, before Dee bowls in. She's gone to the hairdresser this morning.' And, 'In company time, I need not add,' she needlessly added.

'We do expect her to be presentable,' Bob Tanner, Dee's old buddy, loyal to the last, defended her.

'Your secretary will buzz down for them.'

'But . . .'

But he did it. Exhausted, defeated, he reached for the phone.

'That's funny,' said Nancy, holding the receiver in front of her face, examining the earpiece as if for clues.

385

what is?

'I just had Lynne on the line from upstairs.' Nancy finally hung up. 'We're to go and see Bob Tanner. Both of us. Without delay.'

'Very rum,' Edie agreed.

'It will mean leaving the office unmanned.'

'Unwomanned.'

'Unwomanned, yes. What do you suppose they want?'

'Oh, I expect there'll be merit rises all round,' Edie told her cynically, raising her eyebrows, twitching her glasses up her nose. 'A vote of thanks from the directors. Company cars for thee and me. A nice, fat bonus. Or . . .'

'Or?'

'Redundo. They may have a shrewd suspicion that our jobs could as well be done by two chimpanzees and a typewriter. Which in a sense, of course, they could.'

'That isn't true.' Nancy flushed defensively. 'They most certainly could not.'

'You don't think so? Ach, you could be right. But I sometimes wonder if anything we say can make a jot or tittle of difference.'

'It does. Of course it does.' Nancy slid a hand under the neck of her T-shirt to haul in her bra strap. 'You don't really suppose . . . ?' She stood up and tugged the T-shirt down over her waist-band, for all at once she felt under-dressed. 'What you said about redundancy. You don't imagine . . . ?'

'Only my fun,' Edie reassured her dourly. 'I should be so lucky as to be given a pay-off!'

'In which case, what?'

'Well, in which case, we'll have to go and find out.'

'Ah, come in Edie. Come in Nancy.' Bob Tanner did his utmost to be avuncular, though to Edie he had the look of a man in extreme physical distress. 'Please take a seat. We need to have, uhm, er, a brief chat.' He made a steeple of his hands, pressing palm to palm. 'There's a small matter we must clear up.'

When Nancy dithered, Edie jabbed a finger in her back to spur her on.

'That's right. Make yourselves comfortable. We have a rather delicate problem to discuss.'

'Fire away,' Edie prompted. She sat with her legs stretched and flexed her feet. 'You've come to the right department. Problems are right up our alley, after all.'

'It's about Dee,' Clare put in tartly. She flashed a cool smile at Nancy who was far too apprehensive, too busy knitting her fingers, to return it. 'For some time I've been concerned that she doesn't pull her weight.' Her *considerable* weight, she had been tempted to say, but that would, of course, have been unworthy, it would have been a bitch too far. 'I have been unhappy with her performance. I have wondered if she was quite in tune with our readership.'

'Yes, yes, yes,' cut in Bob impatiently. 'The nub of the matter is . . .'

'The nub is, we have evidence of gross dishonesty. Untruths have been told. Expense claims trumped up.'

Roses blossomed fetchingly in Nancy's cheeks. She ducked her head to hide her shame. Her ponytail bobbed. It's the sack for me, she told herself woefully. I'm an accessory after the facts.

'Nancy,' Clare commanded. 'Look at me. It's imperative that you tell us all you know.'

'I . . .' Nancy picked at a thread on her skirt. She could not raise her eyes to face her editor. She begged her conscience for some ruling in this matter, but it delivered none. She could not have fibbed to save her own skin, but should she fib to save Dee's, and in so doing, incidentally, spare herself?

She had jolly well better tell, Edie privately decided, seeing the girl's dilemma. Or if she doesn't, I shall, for this farce has gone on long enough. She sat forward slightly, clasped her hands around her knees, drew breath, prepared to make her statement.

Then, suddenly, Nancy had her answer. She had it, indeed, ironically, from the horse's mouth. For she had read an article, not so many weeks ago, written by Dee herself, saying quite unequivocally and not a little high-mindedly that no secretary need lie for her superior. The piece had envisaged philandering male bosses, whose wives must, for instance, be fobbed off when they phoned. But surely, in the present circumstances, the same principle held good?

'Sometimes,' she confessed then, softly but distinctly, 'if Dee was very busy, she would give me her receipts, and I would have to . . . I mean, she had genuine expenses. It was simply that the details . . . I would fudge it a bit. To save time.'

'And why would Dee be pushed for time?' Clare sat up very straight, held herself rigid, she raised her chin, she smiled minimally. 'Considering you do most of her work, why should she be busy?'

'I don't . . . It's what I'm paid to do, after all. To cope with a share of the letters.'

'And what share would you say you do these days? With what proportion do you cope?'

Nancy could not, or would not respond.

'I'll tell you what . . .' Edie removed her glasses, she held them at arm's length and inspected the lenses. The effect on her face was disconcerting. Everyone waited tensely for her to replace them on her nose. This she did after a studied pause, and eyed Clare beadily through them. 'If I take care of, let's say, thirty per cent of the correspondence, then Nancy does a good sixty-five per cent, and Dee handles the odds and sods.'

'And of the letters that are published?'

Edie shrugged. She played with the strap of her mannish sandal, adjusted the buckle. 'Nancy's, mainly,' she revealed in her matter-of-fact way.

There followed an expectant silence of which Bob Tanner was the focus. He slapped a hand down on the table as a loser might slap down his cards. He scrutinised his fingers, his knuckles. He shook his head. His shoulders slumped. Eventually, he reached for the telephone. 'Lynne. Be a love. Buzz down to Dee Rawlings. See if she's in yet. Get her to pop up. We have to have a word.'

'Better send for a black plastic sack,' suggested Clare without compunction, *la belle dame sans merci*.

Dee had been having, as she mentally expressed it with no sense of self-parody, a whale of a time. The *Superwoman* programme had been screened a week ago, to rapturous reviews – from her friends, if from no one else. Her latest 'Lifelines' book was now completed, and had been well received by her publishers. Her own life was as full, as fulfilling as ever. Physically, psychologically, she was on tip-top form.

This morning she had had her roots done, and the girl, the

colourist had insisted that she wasn't – she *couldn't be* – fifty-three years old. ('I would have put you round about the forty mark,' she had said, for which solicitude, dear child, she had earned herself a nice, big tip.)

Dee's agent was to give her lunch, and with this in prospect, she breezed in to work, thinking to make a couple of phone calls – to the bank, to the building society, to John Lewis about the new carpets – before ordering a chauffeured car to whisk her to the restaurant.

There was, however, one small blight on her happiness. The blasted Kayleigh was going to have to go. It was not just that her lack of any sense of obligation or appreciation, her scowls and sulks, were no longer tolerable. In all the months that Dee had given her shelter, she had made not the slightest effort to advance herself, to sort herself out. And she had, with her bad behaviour, quite wrecked last weekend. She had seemed rude and unstable, had been openly despising of Eric, scratchy and argumentative with Dee, but, then, they were used to this.

What was new was a dangerous delusion: the girl had taken a notion that Jamie had a thing for her. Incredibly, absurdly, she had claimed he was her lover. 'Ask him,' she'd shouted in fury. 'If you don't believe me, just you ask him.' But, of course, Jamie had not been there to answer, he had not been there to deny her wild contention.

It was terribly sad, actually. Kayleigh was plainly deranged. She was the victim of erotomania; she was in the grip of an obsession. One had to feel sorry for her. But while she sympathised, Dee could not indulge this fixation. It was altogether too destructive, it would wreak emotional havoc. It was a real-life *Fatal Attraction*, it suggested the poor kid had lost her reason (they'd come home one day and find she'd boiled the cat).

'I'm not good enough for him, am I?' Kayleigh, red-faced, had accused. 'That's what you think, isn't it?'

And, 'My dear child,' Dee had responded soothingly, 'that has nothing whatever to do with it. Now, if you calm down and think about this rationally, you will see that it's all in your imagination.'

So, Dee reluctantly concluded now, she must follow the kindest, the fairest, the most responsible course: she must send her young house guest to a hostel.

Edie, or perhaps the more willing, more tractable Nancy, must be charged with the job of finding somewhere. One or other would be set to work on it this very afternoon.

She was more than slightly surprised, therefore, as she made her entrance, expecting to see her team, her two busy bees, hard at it, to find neither at her desk. 'Very curious,' she said aloud to the empty room, which had a strange desolate air, reminiscent of the *Marie Celeste*, as if abruptly, unaccountably, the occupants had simply downed tools and dived overboard. There was a such a sense of time transfixed, that Dee actually checked her watch.

Then the telephone rang.

'Hello, hello, hello. Yes, Lynne, this is Dee. Now, you mean? This minute? Most certainly. But what is this about? How frightfully mysterious. Right you are.'

It would be one of Bob's little wheezes, she decided, smiling to herself as she waited for the lift to bear her aloft. He'd have had some new idea for the page. His enthusiasm touched her, rather, the way he liked to get involved. Every so often he had some bright idea for her, some new proposal for her section of the magazine. She would listen to him attentively, smiling encouragement, she would hear him out before explaining, gently, firmly, just why his suggestion would not work.

She stepped in the lift car, pressed the button, and spent the twenty-second journey checking hair and make-up in the mirror, performing a twirl to admire the effect of her navy spot-print flares and platform sandals. 'I would have put you round about the forty mark.' Oh, yes, indeed!

It was thus in ebullient mood that she entered the director's office. 'I've arrived,' she jokily announced, 'and to prove it . . . I'm here.' A momentary hesitation, a mere hiccup, was her reaction to the presence of Clare Constantine, who sat sucking in her cheeks, biting on the inside of her face. She wondered crossly, What's *she* doing here? For the agony input on *Mia* was not, in her view, any business of the editor.

'Close the door,' said Bob grimly. 'Pull up a chair.'

While everyone waited, he took a ribbed gold fountain pen from his top pocket, uncapped it, and made some notes on his jotter. Gazing around her, Dee saw how Nancy hung her head, saw how Edie sat with arms folded and stared stonily in front of her, while Clare seemed to roll something round on her tongue (tasting, had Dee but known it, the pure, honeyed sweetness of her triumph).

With a deep breath, Bob Tanner embarked upon a long, meandering narrative, the story of his career to date, his meteoric rise from post-room messenger to editorial top brass. Pausing, he capped, uncapped, recapped, uncapped his fountain pen. He made another note, pressing too hard so the nib crossed, depositing an ink splodge on the page.

Where might this be leading, Dee asked herself, listening indulgently, nodding her encouragement, though she had heard it all before. Bob Tanner must be about to resign. Yes, that would be it. Perhaps there had been some sort of boardroom coup. Well, she for one would be sorry to see him go. Still, it was probably no bad thing. Management badly needed an infusion of new blood. This would leave the way clear for a younger man. And it would be a first-class excuse for a party.

She did not for one second guess where Bob was headed. In fact, though he was now a little lost in his preamble, he had set out to make a relevant point. The burdens of office, he had intended to say, were often heavy. On occasion they were scarcely tolerable. Unhappy duty . . . Deepest regret . . . Uneasy lies the head that wears the whatsit.

Then Clare uncrossed her legs, she swayed forward, she shot him a glare which plainly said to stop this silly filibuster and to get the bloody thing over.

She was right, he realised. He could not stave off for ever the evil deed. How had she put it to him? Rather well, as he remembered (she could obviously turn a neat phrase). If it were done, 'twere best done sharpish. Or words to that effect.

'The thing is,' he said to Dee, at last dispensing with the dressing, 'you're going to have to go. That is, I mean, you're fired.'

Dee's laugh of incredulity rang out like a gunshot. 'What?' she exploded. '*What?*'

'I shall explain.'

Which he did, with some force and with mounting anger, as it seemed to dawn on him how badly he had been betrayed. He acquitted himself well, in Clare's estimation. He might have gone further. She wished he had. He might have given Dee, say, fifteen minutes to clear her desk. He might have called Security to escort her off the premises. But, what the hell? She could be magnanimous in victory. And he had seen it through.

So the charges were laid before Dee Rawlings, who had no answer to them. The witnesses were cited – Edie, Nancy. Their loss, Dee decided bitterly, will be greater than mine.

She got to her feet. She turned to her assistants, to fix first one, then the other, with a long, hard stare.

To Nancy she said, with a shake of the head, more in sorrow than in anger, *'J'accuse.'* Then, like a holed liner making for safe harbour, she sailed slowly from the room, rode the lift down to her office, and with aplomb which even Clare might grudgingly admire, picked up the phone and commanded a chauffeured car to take her, this one last time, home to Clapham.

———————— • ————————

'Nice one,' Francine commended herself, bringing mugs of instant from the kitchen, one for Jamie, one for herself. 'So, anyway . . .' she said as she set his mug on the desk before him. And then, when he failed by so much as a nod to acknowledge her kindness, 'Thank you Francine, you really shouldn't have. I don't know what I'd do without you.'

'Thank you Francine,' responded Jamie in muffled tones, declining to look up, 'you really shouldn't have. I don't know what I'd do without you.'

'What are you up to?' she demanded to know.

'Riding my unicycle, singing a medley of sea shanties, while balancing a ball on my nose. What does it look like I'm up to?'

'It looks like you're reading the paper.'

'Precisely so.'

She perched on his desk, sipped the dark-flecked coffee and grimaced. 'Eeeugh. Too strong. Been doing a lot of reading lately, haven't you?'

He raised his heavy head from the trestle of his hands, to regard her briefly, balefully. 'I'm improving my mind,' he told her.

'You'll not do that, reading them things.'

'Well, then, I'm keeping abreast . . .'

She rolled on her hip and reached across him to edge the paper towards her, treating him in the process to an unasked-for glimpse of her preposterous cleavage. 'Keeping abreast of world events – among other things.'

'There's not a lot about the big wide world in the *South London Press*.'

'Buzz off, can't you.' He slapped her hand away. For a deeply stupid person, he told himself, she could be annoyingly acute.

'You'll ruin your eyes. You'll do your head in.' She glanced at his waste bin which was stuffed with rolled dailies, tabloids, broadsheets.

'As I said to you, I'm keeping up with current affairs. Now push off and give me some space.'

'Ooh, you are an old grumble-sticks this week. Are you expecting your period or what?'

'I expect nothing around here.' His tone was martyred. 'But I ask, I merely *ask* for peace and quiet.'

'Suit yourself.'

He did not watch, but visualised her strutting like a chicken back to her own desk. He heard a drawer open and close, heard the busy scrape of an emery board, heard her huff and puff to blow the nail filings from her clothing.

'Who'd have thought it?' she said finally, for perhaps the twentieth time. 'I mean, you of all people. You're a dark horse, you really are.'

It would be wisest, Jamie reckoned, not to answer her. She would only start on if he did, with her 'Who'd have thought it?' With her 'You of all people.' 'Dee Rawlings' son,' she would marvel. 'You never said. How come you never said? I couldn't believe it when I saw you on the telly. I told my mum, "Christ, that's my Jamie!".'

It was the possessive pronoun that most irked him. How dare she lay claim to him? He cursed himself for ever having agreed to appear on film, rued the day when he was suckered in. At the time it had seemed so very remote, it was as if it might never happen. But it had happened, of course, a week ago today, and he wondered now if he was ever going to hear the last of it.

393

'Could we simply forget it? It's terribly tedious. I mean, it's not as if my mother is really famous.'

'She's very big in our house,' Francine insisted.

'She's very big in *our* house, but that still doesn't make her famous.'

'Your own mum. How can you be so rotten?'

'Years of practice.'

'Besides,' said Francine charitably, 'she's not *that* fat.'

'No.' Jamie closed the paper, folded it, crammed it in the bin with the others. Nothing, he thought hopelessly, furiously. Absolutely bloody nothing.

Every day since the dreadful accident (as he now chose to term it), he had scoured the papers, the news pages, the small ads, for mention of it, for the story of an old lady killed by a hit-and-run driver, or for notification of her funeral ('Dearly beloved wife of Cyril . . . no flowers, by request'). And what had been said about her death? Not a dickie-bird. It was deplorable, when you came to think of it.

If, indeed, she were dead. And how, but through the media, could he ever hope to know? There was no other channel, no other source of information to be tapped. He could scarcely call up the police, could he? He could scarcely get in touch with the hospital. 'Oh, hello there, Rawlings is the name. Just wondering what became of some bewildered old granny whom I mowed down with my Porsche last Wednesday night.'

He had once on an impulse tried dialling her home number, had hung on in a phone box, in agonies of uncertainty, the sweat beading his upper lip, while at the other end it rang and rang and rang. But he had emerged, at last, none the wiser.

The uncertainty is killing me, he told himself self-pityingly.
· She must be dead. She may not be. Oh, God, I hope she is. I mean, I hope she isn't.

He felt like poor old Damocles, over whose head a sword had hung on a silken thread. If ever he were to meet the guy, he reflected gloomily, they'd have an awful lot to talk about.

'Want a sarnie?' Francine asked him.

'All right.'

'Yes *please*.'

'Yes please, Mummy.' And, throwing caution to the wind, 'I'll have a brie and walnut on granary.'

'They smell like old socks.'

'Who cares?'

'I do. I have to live with it.'

'All right, all right. I'll tell you what, forget the granary. Just get them to slap the filling between two Odor Eaters.'

'You're mental.'

'So you're always saying.'

'Well, you are.'

'Maybe you're right,' he was disposed to agree, for it seemed to him, in his anguished state, after eight nightmare days, eight sleepless nights, that she had never been closer to the truth.

———————————— • ————————————

'If you closed your eyes,' said Colin, mopping up taramasalata with a strip of pitta bread, swabbing the plate clean of the fishy pink paste, 'you could almost imagine you were on Mykonos.'

'Oh, hardly.' Sandie smiled lazily, contentedly. 'Athens, perhaps, at a pinch.' For the warm air was heavy, not with the scents of lemon, of wild garlic, fennel or thyme, but with grit and exhaust grease which combined with charcoal smoke to clog the pores, to irritate the skin, and which dressed the hair with a layer of grime, dulling and darkening it. Nor was the roaring in her ears that of the blue Aegean, but of sooty London traffic. Whenever a car passed close by their pavement table, the draught ruffled the scalloped petticoat edges of the paper cloth, revealing splotched red gingham beneath. Just the same, she felt wildly, absurdly happy and in holiday mood.

'All right, Athens,' Colin cheerfully conceded. He was just talking, anyway, from sheer exuberance, filling the space between them with words.

'Where I've never been, have you?' She raised a Duralex beaker to her cheek and squinted at the contents – at wine the colour of old straw, which tasted as it smelt, of disinfectant, and which, yet, was somehow so very delicious. 'I just love retsina, don't you?'

'No. Yes.' He helped himself to a wizened black olive, worked

395

it over, spat the stone neatly into his hand and palmed it into the ashtray. 'Yes, I love retsina. No, I haven't been to Athens. I hear the nightlife is great.'

'In what way?'

'I don't know. I imagine everyone stays up till all hours drinking ouzo and smashing china and dancing as fast as they can.'

'I'm more of a morning person, myself, to be honest.'

'Me too.'

'I like my bed.'

'I like your bed.'

'Oh, *you.*'

She helped herself to a stuffed vine leaf, which she cut up primly into bite-size pieces, sawing through the stringy veins.

'We should go away somewhere, you and I,' he said. 'We should have a holiday.'

'We should,' she agreed, 'and yet I can't imagine being happier anywhere on earth than I am here at this moment.'

'Me too. I'm glad I thought of it.'

'*Who* thought of it.'

'All right, I'm glad *you* thought of it as usual. You have all the best ideas.'

'I've an appointment in town in the morning,' he had told her on the telephone last night. 'I'm going to see a client.' Then, 'We could meet when you're through,' she had proposed. 'We could have lunch, if it's sunny, in Charlotte Street. In a Greek place. Sit outside. Eat mezedes.' 'Mercedes?' 'No, you nut, mezedes. Mezze. A mixture of little dishes.' And, 'Smart thinking,' he had agreed.

He unwound his long legs, now, kicking her ankle sharply, inadvertently, under the small square of table. She shifted her rickety chair on the concrete. 'Sorry,' they each apologised.

'That looks interesting,' he enthused, as a waiter in his shirt-sleeves brought more bread in a basket, and a dish of baby octopus, glistening green with oil. 'What is it?'

'It's squid,' Sandie hazarded.

'I asked what it was,' Colin joked, spooning some on to his plate, 'not how much it cost.'

'Eeek,' she protested.

'You know . . .' He swayed back to take a longer view of her. 'I would never have guessed.'

'Guessed what? About my mother? Colin, for pity's sake, don't start on that again.'

'I can't help it. I can't get over it.' He shook his head in honest incredulity. 'You're the daughter of a famous agony aunt, and you never breathe a word of it to me.'

'She's not that famous actually.'

'Well, my mother has heard of her. She's an avid reader of the magazine. She couldn't believe it when she saw you on the television. You could have knocked her down with a feather, she said.'

'She did?'

'She did.' He took a swig of retsina. 'Funny stuff, this.'

'Two seconds ago you were claiming to love it.'

'I do, I do. It's to die for. But it's funny stuff for all that.'

'So Shirley was surprised, was she? About Mum?'

'Gobsmacked.'

'And impressed?' Momentarily, Sandie entertained a wild hope? Was it possible that this increased her standing with Mrs Clarke?

'Up to a point,' he responded cautiously, helping himself to an oblong of pitta, tossing it from hand to hand, blowing on his fingertips, then ripping it apart. 'Ouch. Wow, that's hot. To be perfectly honest, she had her reservations. Ooh, I say, what's he bringing us now?'

'It looks like fasoulia.'

'Which is . . . ?'

'It's bean stew,' she explained. And then, catching Colin's eye, recognising the wicked glint, anticipating another of his excruciating jokes, 'No, no, no, spare me,' she headed him off. 'Please don't say it.'

'Don't say what?'

'Don't say "I don't care what it's been; what is it now?"'

'I wasn't going to,' he fibbed indignantly.

'Bet you were.'

'And I just bet I wasn't.'

'So, anyway . . .'

'So?'

'So Shirley had her reservations, did she?'

'Well, you know what she's like.'

'Yes, I do. I sure do. And what were they?'

397

'What were what?'

'Her, er, reservations.'

'Ah, you know. The usual stuff. No one could call her narrow-minded.' He took upon himself a hoity-toity aspect, dabbed fastidiously at the corners of his mouth with a napkin, made of his features a kind of posy, gathered his whole face at the nose and sniffed as if he caught a whiff of something not quite nice.

'Perish the thought,' Sandie giggled behind her hand at this wicked parody, thinking only that Colin had Shirley off to a T. Rather stupidly, she failed to apprehend how wretched it made him feel to mock his own mother – a practice as irresistible to him as it was unworthy, much like the squeezing of a spot or the picking of a scab, which can leave one, afterwards, with a vague sense of self-disgust.

'I mean, Live And Let Live, that's the Clarke family motto.'

'Ah-hah.' She beamed encouragingly.

'Laissez faire and let laissez faire.'

'Absolutely.'

'Anything goes.'

'It does?'

'Almost anything. But one does have to draw the line.'

'Mm.' She slapped her arm, squelching a tiny fly, and was immediately remorseful. Nothing now remained of a life extinguished, but a damp black smear on her fair skin. 'Oh, dear. It took me a fleeting instant to kill that insect, but if I had a hundred years I could never make one.'

'Why would you want to?' he blinked at her. 'No one in their right mind would make flies.'

'But it's the principle. Now, what were we saying? One has to draw a line. Certain things are just beyond the pale, are they?'

'They are.'

'Certain behaviour cannot be countenanced?'

'It cannot.'

'Some things are simply not on?'

'That's about the size of it. For instance, extra-marital you-know-what. Any kind of experimentation, any irregularity. Mixed-race marriage. Living in sin. Schoolgirls on the pill. Cross-dressing. The love that dare not speak its name . . .'

'All of which, of course, are the stock-in-trade of agony columns.'

'Yes. Dee Rawlings should, we feel, understand a little less, and condemn a little more. She should not be seen to condone unnatural practices. If she does not say that she is for these unsuitable things, she does not say, either, that she is agin them.'

'She can be, actually. She can be agin all sorts when the mood takes her. She can be horribly judgmental.'

'But we feel . . . Mum feels . . .' Colin could not sustain the send-up for one moment longer. 'If she were answering those readers' letters, she'd adopt a strong line. She'd be telling them all to take a cold shower or to read improving books. She'd say "It will make you blind, your hair will fall out, you will catch some ghastly disease and go completely insane." Almost everyone would be too young, too old, or in some other way disqualified from having S-E-X. Whereas, from what I can gather, *your* mother takes an indulgent view of teenage lovers, urging only that they exercise precautions, while also believing that senior citizens should be at it like rabbits.'

'I guess you could say she is fairly unshockable,' Sandie allowed. 'So, far from enhancing my status, it seems, my association with the great Dee Rawlings makes me . . .'

'Well, you know, in one way Mum's rather tickled. She says "Fancy that Sandra being on the box." But, in another way, it confirms her worst fears. She has long suspected there was something of the bohemian in your background.'

'Which there isn't. Not remotely.'

'It's all relative, of course.'

'Of course.'

'Anyway. . .' Sandie, sighing, helped herself to a spoonful of houmus, scooping it up on a square of bread. 'If she doesn't approve of me, then she doesn't approve. It's simply too bad. But the sooner you're out of there and into a flat of your own, away from her influence, the happier I shall feel.'

'Yes,' replied Colin in apparent agreement, but when she sought his eyes and they evaded hers, sliding away from her gaze, she sensed that he was full of trouble.

'You have told her, haven't you, that that is what you plan to do?'

'Oh, I've told her all right.'

'And have you started to look? To check the local paper? To read the small ads? Have you tried any agencies?'

'Listen . . .' He speared a flabby piece of octopus with his fork. His tone was truculent. 'Don't get on to me, okay? I said I'd find a flat and I will.'

'I'm not getting on to you.' She was dismayed to hear, in her own voice, an unappealing whining note.

They were both in ill humour, suddenly, and set against each other like snappish dogs.

'You don't half nag,' he accused.

'And you. You're useless,' she retorted nastily. 'You're a complete and utter mummy's boy. Excuse me a minute, will you, I must go to the loo.' She dumped her napkin on the table, peeled her damp thighs from the PVC cushion, shoved the spindly chair back and made for the interior.

She was wearing big, box-pleated navy shorts, a high-necked white T-shirt so new it still bore the creases of its packaging, and, on her feet, a pair of slip-on, slip-sloppy plimsolls. She appeared to him extraordinarily chaste, like an overgrown schoolgirl, in the fashion of an Enid Blyton heroine, a stalwart of the Famous Five. Her face was slightly flushed, though whether it was touched by temper or by retsina or the sun he was not sure. She was strong-limbed, sturdy, and could somehow only have been English. He found something extremely poignant about the broad backs of her knees. When she went inside, his heart followed her, all the way down to the basement, to the ladies' lavatory, two rudimentary cubicles in a stuffy tiled room redolent of Airwick.

I must stop this, Sandie told herself, scowling at her smarting face in the speckled mirror. I must give him a break. I don't want to be a scold.

I must get a bloody flat, thought Colin. In a slightly self-conscious dramatic gesture, he tossed wine down his throat, and immediately coughed it back up. An alcoholic trickle ran down his nose. She's right. Sandie's right. It's essential that I do it. It will be good for me.

But an image of Shirley, pink with dismay, moist-eyed and pleading, made his stomach muscles seize.

Women! Who needed them.

The sun, at that moment, disappeared behind a cloud. The

sudden withdrawal of warmth and light was reminiscent of a power cut.

'Difficult,' muttered Colin, as, with greater circumspection, he sipped his drink. 'Bloody, bloody difficult.'

———————— • ————————

He had packed, with his customary neatness, only such items as were indisputably his. His clothes, ironed with care, his toothbrush, his shaver were stowed in a bulging canvas hold-all, a sports bag with stitched leather handles dating from those days of higher optimism or of deeper vanity, when he'd played a passable game of squash, when physical fitness had seemed a goal worth pursuing, and a beer with the lads on the way home a reasonable male aspiration. Once upon a time, then, he had lived out there in the world. But he had been in retreat for so many years, he had become holed up inside himself.

For more than a week he had planned his departure: it was that cold-blooded. He would, he had resolved, take nothing away to which Dee might lay claim. He would travel exceedingly light.

In this, he told himself, he was showing admirable scruple, but perhaps, in truth, he was merely contriving to hurt her more exquisitely, to refine the emotional torture, to reject her more utterly, to revenge himself more absolutely. Besides, he had a romantic fancy for straitened circumstances, and there would be space for few possessions in his new accommodation, under the roof of a certain Mrs Briggs, in a dismal rented room in Maidstone.

His new landlady was an awesome woman with white hair permed tight like a cauliflower. He was pleased to think how she would mark his comings and goings, watching beady-eyed and increasingly intrigued from the hall as he made his way up- or downstairs, in or out of the door. ('Mr Rawlings? I don't know nothing about him. A bit of a mystery man, to tell you the truth. Keeps himself to himself. But he's tidy, I will give him that, and always pays his rent nice and prompt. I can only speak as I find.')

The house in Clapham and all its contents, furniture, records, books, ornaments, the car in which he'd chauffeured his wife . . . He was leaving all behind.

He meant also to leave a note. This, he had decided, would be fairest. There were some men – and you read of them from time to time in newspapers – who simply disappeared. They came down to breakfast as normal, drank their usual cup of coffee, munched their usual triangles of toast with Oxford marmalade, scowled as always at the morning mail, muttered about the size of the phone bill, pecked their wives' cheeks, said 'See you tonight', said 'Have a good day', then walked out of the door, never to be heard of again.

He had himself considered such an exit, but while the method had much to commend it, being both dignified and enigmatic in the style of Captain Oates, it would commit him to a fugitive existence, and would deny him the chance to explain.

By 'explain' he of course meant 'justify'. He meant 'vindicate', and, indeed, 'recriminate'. He wanted to lay the blame where it belonged, to say 'I'm leaving you for ever, and it's *all your fault*'.

Last night, while Dee slept beside him, rolled as usual in the duvet, exposing him to piercing draughts, he had lain wakeful, sick with resentment, editing his acrimonious sentiments, composing his farewell message, his final 'Dear Dee'.

The prospect of freedom appalled and excited him; he was damp with sweat under his hair; his forehead gleamed. He had cleaned out his building society account, he had about enough to last him till he found a job. He imagined the stock of his life boiled down to a rich reduction, thick in consistency, strong in flavour. He saw himself rather as a character in a play, acting out a fantasy. And, at the same time, paradoxically, he saw himself at long last getting real.

'I am going to find myself,' he said to the empty sitting-room. This would be the main thrust of his letter, the cut of his jolly old jib. He paced up and down, to the window, to the sofa, to the bureau. 'I shall be my own person once more – whatever that means. I shall rediscover who and what I am.' All of which sounded very fine in his head, but lost much in the utterance, since his voice was reedy with nerves.

He sat down and drew out a sheet of headed notepaper. For the last time, he would write from this smart London address. Henceforth it would be The Lindens, it would be number twenty-eight, it would be c/o the estimable Mrs Briggs.

Once he was settled in, as soon as he was established, he

would make contact with his children, or at any rate with Sandie. He would ask her round to his humble lodgings and cook her spaghetti on his two-ring hob. They would open a large bottle of execrable plonk, get hideously, howling drunk, weep, laugh, commiserate like a couple of students, and she of all people would sympathise, she would be on his side.

Sometimes he would spend an evening in the pub, playing dominoes with the local characters, or chatting to a comely barmaid. 'I'm divorced,' he would reveal to her. 'I walked out of my marriage.' And, with a wryness, a dry wit to crack her up, 'The problem was, you see, that my wife understood me.'

The truth of this struck him now with force. Dee did understand, or at least apprehend him. She saw where he was coming from, she saw where he was going, and she thwarted him.

His mind ran on to better things, to his own thriving horticultural business, his own splendid house, his own car, his independence, his autonomy. It might take years, but he would make it, he was set upon it. He would no longer be a shadow, but would be someone in his own right.

'Dear Dee,' he wrote in haste, in an effort to outrun his shaking hand. His tongue clove to the roof of his mouth. His throat felt occluded, he could not swallow.

A car drew up outside. He heard the engine running, running, ticking over in the quiet of the street, then someone must have climbed out, for the door clunked shut.

'By the time you read this letter I'll be gone from here.'

Hurried footsteps on the front path. The rattle of the key in the latch.

'I have to go away to find myself.'

A familiar tread in the hallway. Then there she was, in the room with him, staring across at him in a dazed, unseeing way.

He opened his mouth to speak, but made no sound. By what black magic, what diabolism came she here? Was she after all a witch, possessed of some demonic power? How had she foreseen this, how had she *known*?

It was worse than he had feared. It was far more serious. It was one thing for her to read his body language, his expression, his humour. It was one thing to catch his eye or to remark his movements and to guess at his intentions. It was one thing to know, empirically, how he would behave in given circumstances. But to have intuited at such a distance his innermost secrets, to have come here at speed from the office to intercept him, was altogether more sinister. It was as if she had hacked into his very brain.

Dee sat down heavily, even by her own standards, and made a collar for herself with her hands. The blood crept up under the skin and turned her face puce. 'Something terrible has happened,' she managed eventually to reveal, in a strange, choked voice, so different from her usual confident boom. 'Something unspeakable. I . . .'

He laid aside his pen, rose from the bureau and turned to stare at her, flexing and curling his fingers. This had nothing to do with him, he now perceived. She'd had no notion of his leaving. Indeed, she barely seemed to notice him, and could as well have been addressing the table, the television, the tall blue vase of irises on the hearth, so much was he part of her furniture.

'She's done for me. Clare Constantine has done for me, the scheming little bitch.'

'I don't . . .' ventured Eric futilely.

For the first time his wife seemed to focus on him, properly to acknowledge his presence. 'Pour me a drink,' she commanded. 'A whisky. A large one.'

He did not much care for her tone, but obeyed without question, tiptoeing warily around her, as if she were a stranger of uncertain temper (which, in her present state, in a way, she was).

She reached up and clawed in the cut crystal glass which he proffered, pressing it to her bosom. She seemed almost literally to have come apart, as if power now devolved upon her hands, her feet, her face, with no part of her subject to central governance. Her eyes rolled maniacally in her head; her mouth hung slackly.

'I lost my job, you see,' she said in a very different, a lisping little girl voice, and she looked up at him with an unspoken appeal, arousing pity and disgust in equal measure.

'I . . .' Once more he tried, and once more failed to respond. Lost her job? Lost her job? But she *is* her job, he told himself. Her whole identity, it seemed to him, was bound up in it, even as his own identity had somehow, much against his will, become bound up in hers.

With a self-indulgence that appalled him, Dee began to cry. It was a noisy and undignified performance involving rocking and moaning, great gusty sobs and hiccups, and a welter of tears. Her face fell in on itself. She was a travesty.

It is said that rats will always leave a sinking ship. And Dee Rawlings at this moment resembled nothing so much as the *Titanic*.

Thus Eric did the only thing he could: he left.

———————— • ————————

It had not, after all, been hard to find her, to run her to earth at Foxholes, as he put it to himself with no intent to pun.

First off, he had thought the task would be beyond him. Needles and haystacks had suggested themselves, tiny filaments of metal buried in steaming great scratchy bales. But he had slept on it, and slept on it, and he had awoken yesterday morning determined to seek her out, to tour the area, to ask the locals, to identify the village with its Norman church, with a pub called the Hare and Hounds, and with a big old half-timbered gaff.

What had happened was this. There he'd been, sat in front of the telly last Thursday night, watching and not watching, if you follow, with only half an eye on the action. Then, all of a sudden, there had been Kayleigh, *his* Kayleigh, on the screen, sitting down to a meal with the Rawlings family in their charming house, as the commentary would have it, near Tunbridge Wells in the Weald of Kent. 'A new daughter', Dee had accounted mysteriously for her presence. 'Unmarried mother . . . Domestic violence . . . Nowhere to go . . . Took her in . . . Staying with us till she's sorted out.'

Well, what would you expect? He'd had to come after her, hadn't he? Her and the nipper. He'd had to come to take her home where she belonged.

He had considered for a matter of hours the possibility of calling in at the magazine, facing down Dee Rawlings, thumping the desk, demanding the return of his girlfriend and child, whom he regarded as hostages in need of rescue. (Kayleigh had, he imagined, been enticed into that family, as into a religious sect, she had been brainwashed by the Rawlings woman – and he was not entirely wrong, at that.) But he had not, in the end, had the courage to confront her.

No one could call him coward. Ask who you like. Ask anyone. He had never bottled out of a fight. But the world of offices, of long, carpeted corridors, of desks and filing cabinets and trilling telephones and snooty secretaries in crisp white blouses, was altogether alien and threatening to him. As a motorcycle messenger, he had access only to front of house, to brisk receptionists whom he addressed in surly manner from under his raised visor; he did not go behind the scenes, nor ever wished to do so.

Besides, he had reasoned, this Dee character was hardly going to help him, was she? She was hardly going to lead him straight to Kayleigh. More probably she would call the security guards, she would have him thrown out on his earhole, then where would he be? He'd be nowhere.

Better, surely, on reflection, to go straight to Kayleigh, wherever the hell she was.

Surprise would be of the essence. If these people had so much as a hint that he was on to them, they would be sure to spirit her away. So, sooner than check in to headquarters, he had zipped himself into his leathers, rammed his crash-helmet on his head, then mounted his bike and set off at speed for the countryside, for the Weald, whatever a weald was when it was at home.

Now, wasn't it amazing what you could do if you set your mind to it. He'd gone roaring up and down leafy lanes, following signposts, visiting this village and that, asking anyone he saw, and within an hour he had found himself outside the Hare and Hounds.

He had considered stopping in for a pint, a reward for his exertions, but then he'd seen, across the road, this big old sort with a little girl. He'd called out to her, did she know anyone name of Rawlings, and she'd said oh, yes, most definitely she did, seeing as how her own mother worked for the family. She had come across to him, to explain where he should go, and had even drawn it for him on the back of her shopping list. So, here, at last, was the place. You bloody reeker!

He had been feeling pretty pleased with himself, pretty bucked by his success as a detective. I mean, cunning or what? But now, as he stood on the front step and waited for her to answer his knock, he felt the first creeping misgivings.

406

Suppose she was out? Or had moved on already? Suppose he were mistaken, and she'd never been here? What if she had changed so much he did not even know her – or, worse, that she did not know him?

When she opened the door, however, she took him in with a glance. 'Oh, it's you,' she said – just that, 'oh, it's you' – with a kind of weary acceptance, as though she'd been expecting him, as though the question for her had been not if but when he would come.

'Yeah, it's me. Going to invite me inside, are you? Or am I to be left hanging about like a spare prick?'

'Huh?'

'I've come all this way, you know. I've come to find you.'

'Well, so you've found me. So what? All right, come through. We can't discuss our business out here, can we, for all the world to see?'

'No,' he agreed, although quite who she meant by 'all the world', he couldn't guess, since the road in both directions was deserted. This was a dead-and-alive hole and no mistake, he decided irritably.

She led him through the hall to the sitting-room. 'Fell on your feet, then, didn't you?' he remarked accusingly, placing his helmet carefully on the coffee table, pulling off his gauntlets, thwacking them together, laying them down. 'Nice house, eh?'

'Very nice house,' she agreed without animation. She crossed to the open French windows and stood there with her back to him, with her arms folded and her hips tilted, staring out. He thought with a pang how beautiful she appeared, and how fragile. It made him want to shake her.

'Like something out of *Homes and Gardens*,' he pressed on awkwardly, conversationally, as if they were strangers at a cocktail party, stiffly polite, constrained to make small-talk, and he looked around him with a faintly disparaging eye. 'It wouldn't be my choice, mind you. It's not really my taste. I'd go for something more in the modern style.'

'Yeah.'

'Still,' he conceded in a spirit of enlightened generosity, 'it takes all sorts to make a world, I suppose.'

'I guess so. What is it you want, Greg? What brings you?'

'I've come to fetch you back.'

'On the bike?' she scoffed. 'The three of us? I should cocoa.'

He hadn"t thought of that. 'I've thought of that,' he told her smartly, 'never you worry. I dare say there are trains.'

'I dare say.'

An unfriendly pause. And then, 'Any beer in the house?' he asked.

'No. Though I guess I could make you a Pimm's.'

'A who?'

'It's a cocktail.'

'I'm not a great one for cocktails. Great big Nellie drinks with paper sunshades. Although Malibu and pineapple, that's nice and refreshing.'

'Suit yourself.' She shrugged. Then, 'Come into the garden,' she proposed.

'Maud.'

'Huh?'

'It's some kind of song, isn't it?'

'Is it?'

'Sure it is.'

'I wouldn't know.'

They found Ben playing on the lawn with the hose. 'Water,' he crowed, spinning round to shower them, creating for an instant, a dazzling rainbow. He was naked and bonny and brown from the sun, but his state of undress, the little tassle of his baby penis, was an obscure affront to Greg who averted his gaze. 'Didn't you ought to put something on him?' he asked her crossly.

'Why? What would be the point? He's fine as he is.'

'He might get burnt. Or stung or something. He might get bitten by a wasp.' Greg, in his tight skin – his skin-tight – trousers, sat down with some difficulty on the margin of the lawn. The leather creaked and strained at the knees. 'Hello, then, my son,' he ventured, extending a hand, 'how're you doing?'

'He won't remember you,' said Kayleigh, the unfeeling cow, with a dismissive toss of the head. 'He doesn't know you from a bar of soap.'

'Of course he knows me, don't you boy? You know your Daddy don't you?'

'Unker Charlie,' tendered Ben, frowning, uncertain, anxious to please.

'He calls all men Unker Charlie,' Kayleigh explained. 'Didn't I just tell you, Greg. Sorry and all that, but he doesn't know you from Adam.'

'He will though, won't he? Get to know me? When you bring him home?'

'Home?' She snorted at the very proposition. 'You call that dump home?'

'Not good enough for you any more, is it? Now that you move in better circles? Now that you're in the lap of luxury?'

'It's not good enough for me or for you or for anybody else. It's a dustbin.'

'But it's ours,' he romanticised implausibly. 'It's our own space, our little nest, and we've been happy there.'

'Have we bollocks!'

'We *have*. We were. I mean, be fair. We used to have some great times.' He cast around desperately for some lure or inducement, one single thing to entice her back to Wavertree and to him. The Ninja Tanto, finely crafted though it might be, and richly embellished, and certified authentic, did not somehow seem to meet the case. 'You're asking for a smack in the mouth, you are,' he said at last, but in a defeated sort of way, without menace, so she laughed at him.

'It's too late, Greg. I'm sorry. You don't frighten me. And besides, I've found someone else.'

'You have?'

He peered at her suspiciously from beneath his hand.

'I have.'

'And who's that, then?'

'None of your business. I'm not saying.'

'The famous Charlie, hm? Is that it?' It was hot out here in the garden. He had begun to perspire profusely.

'No.' She seemed for a moment to be trying to eat her nether lip. Then, 'Not Charlie,' she said finally and, as it seemed to him, regretfully. 'Not him.'

She stepped on to the flower-bed, trampling some tiny seedlings, and measured herself against a hollyhock, which stood a foot taller than she. 'This guy . . . I won't say his name. But he's brilliant and successful and rolling in money.' She clasped one of the bell flowers, pulled it down, over her face like an oxygen mask. When she released it it sprang back, leaving a black smudge on her nose. The pollen it must have been, a touch of hay fever, that caused her eyes to fill with tears. 'He wants to marry me,' she added desolately.

It was a week now since she last saw him, and in all that time she'd had no word from him. She had been driven for months by her desire for him, for a brief spell she had believed that she had him, now she felt only a kind of dull despair. Her reserves of optimism were all used up. Emotionally, she was running on empty.

'Got any smokes?' Greg asked her.

'I gave up.'

'You never!' He whistled, impressed.

'For New Year. My resolution.'

'That must save you a few bob.'

'Yeah.'

She stooped to pick a marigold, to snap the stem, and proceeded idly to strip it of its petals, reciting pointlessly, barely audibly, 'He loves me, he loves me not.'

'I love you Kayleigh,' Greg insisted. 'Why else would I come chasing half way across the sodding country? Stone the bleeding crows.'

'What you feel isn't love. Not true love. You wouldn't recognise it, Greg, if it jumped up and bit you. What you're talking of is ownership.'

'Say you don't know.'

'But I do. I do know. I lived with you, remember?'

'And you will again. You will come back. You need me, Kayleigh, and I need you. We're a team.'

'We are not. We never were. It won't work.'

'Well, look . . .' He flopped down on his back and flung his arm across his face. He felt exhausted, spent, as if from some terrible ordeal. He was too tired to bandy words. 'At least promise that you'll think about it, will you?'

'I already did,' she said sadly, because she already had. For a full two minutes she had considered it. We're two of a kind, she had reasoned. He's the father of my child. He's not so bad.

He has his good points. And it's not as if Jamie . . . Well, does he? It's not as if Jamie gives a damn about me.

But it was only with a sense of obligation that she had run these arguments through her mind. She had come too far now to return. The only way was onward, though to what fresh hell she could not guess. 'I'm sorry,' she told him humbly.

'That's all right,' he said blankly. 'At least now I see where I stand.'

'At least you do. Listen, Greg, I'll write you sometimes. I'll let you have the news of Ben. Photos and that.'

'Yes, okay.'

'And I'll tell him about you. He will know who you are.'

'Whatever you think best.'

'Have you seen my mum?'

'Not lately. Well, it's not as if I'm welcome . . .'

'Give her my best, will you, if you do. Say I'll be in touch. I'll come and visit.'

'And should I give her this address? Yes or no? Which?'

'You can give her what you like.' When she sighed, Kayleigh's shoulders rose and fell. 'I shan't be here much longer, I'll be moving on.'

'To where? Where will you go? With this rich geezer?'

'I haven't quite decided.' She rolled her head around to relieve a stiffness in her neck. She looked at the sky, the borders, the house, the grass. 'I haven't got a clue, to be honest. I haven't got an earthly.'

——————— • ———————

Two things Jamie noticed the instant he came in early from work: first, that, unusually, his father wasn't around; second, that, unusually, his mother was. For all the stress he'd been under, then, his powers of observation were undiminished.

Dee was sitting on the sofa in what appeared to be a kind of trance. And so mere, so preoccupied was her response to his hello, he supposed she must be miles away.

'Phew, goodness, I'm knackered,' he confided, flopping out in an armchair. When he whistled through his teeth, she said harshly, 'Don't', but that was all.

'Sorry, sorry. It's been one of those weeks,' he continued, patting a yawn with his fingertips, as if to shoo it back into his mouth and down again into his lungs. 'I've just about had it with Mabey's, I can tell you. I'm just about up to here with it.' Although up to where, precisely, he did not indicate.

'Mm,' said Dee. Or maybe she didn't. Maybe it was just one of those fugitive sounds that escape a daydreamer, loosed from the body in a moment of abstraction and immediately disowned.

'God, I'm starving. I had to skip lunch.' Thus he rewrote his day, deleting from it one brie and walnut sandwich. 'What's for supper, Mother?'

'What?' She seemed to be moulding something between her palms. Or she might have been applying handcream, massaging it into the skin. Still, she did not spare him so much as a glance, he pettishly remarked, but was thoroughly wrapped up in herself.

'Supper,' he prompted. 'What are we having? I'm ravenous.'

'Ah, supper.' She nodded over the word. Then, rousing herself fleetingly with a shake of the shoulders, 'Nothing. I'm sorry. I've not shopped.'

'It doesn't matter,' he decided. 'Not to worry. I'm not bothered. I can always go out. I can grab myself a snack at the club.' Yes, that was what he ought to do, to work out for an hour, then look into the juice bar for a salad. If the flame-haired dancer, the leotard-clad siren, was there he would invite her to join him. He could take her, indeed, to a proper restaurant, he could dine with her by candlelight. Or something more casual, more spur-of-the-moment? They could nip down the road for tapas. Oh, heavens, no, not tapas! At the very notion of it, the events of last Wednesday night repeated on him, memories welled in his throat till he retched.

He was going to have to get himself together. At times he feared he was heading for a breakdown, for total nervous collapse. Physically, he was all over the place, his hands shook, his voice woofed and tweeted, or it deserted him altogether, and he could not order his thoughts.

He had tried to persuade himself that feelings were optional, that by some effort of will you could banish guilt, fear, remorse. But the harder he had tried to discipline his emotions, the more clamorous and unruly they had become till they ran riot throughout his system.

He needed to talk to someone, to confess. He had toyed with the possibility of calling the Samaritans, but had quickly dismissed their agency, which existed, in his mind, for the socially inadequate, for real no-hopers, rather than for thrusting professionals, for go-getting businessmen like himself.

Then, hey, here was an answer! He had his own Samaritan, his own counsellor, not a million miles from him, a woman so devoted to him she could be relied upon to support him right or wrong.

He should seize the opportunity, while he had her to himself, to pour out his troubles to his mother. He would relate how he'd been pressured and coerced by Giles. He would explain about Lucinda. And about the accident, about his panic. He might even mention Kayleigh, poor, dear, common little Kayleigh, whom he had resolved, in fairness, to set free.

He would not deny his own responsibility, though he would modify it, even as he had modified it to himself. 'I've done wrong,' he would say manfully. 'I've been foolish.' And Dee would kiss and comfort him, she would advise and console him, she would rock him in her arms, relieve him of his burden and reprieve him.

Swiftly, impulsively, he transferred himself to the sofa, to her side. He wrapped his arms around himself, then wrapped himself around his arms, doubled over to stare down at the carpet. 'Mummy,' he said, addressing his two feet, his buckskin shoes. And, recalling a childish endearment, 'Mumps. I have something to tell you. I've been terribly stupid. I've done wrong.'

'Mm.' That sound again, almost a whimper, a meaningless squeak.

'I could be in very serious trouble. If I'm found out, I could even go to . . . I need to discuss it. To have it out in the open. I need you to tell me what I should do. Mummy? Mummy?' For there issued from her no gentle prompt, no encouraging reply.

Sitting up, sitting back, pressing himself against the sofa cushion, he regarded her curiously, and belatedly it dawned upon him that all was not well with her. There was about her none of the usual complacency; no smile played on her lips, and the light in her eyes had been extinguished. 'Are you hearing me?' he asked, brusque in his alarm. Fear fed his anger, anger his fear. 'Are you paying attention. For Christ's sake wake up! I'm pleading with you, Mummy, as your only son. You help everyone else in the goddamn world. Now, for once in your fat life, help me.'

'*Help* you?' She regarded him levelly, but with those strange unlit eyes. 'Help *you*? But Jamie, my dear, I cannot even help myself.'

'What? What are you saying? I implore you, please, to listen to me. You have to tell me what to do.'

'I? To tell you what to do?' She fanned her fingers in front of her face and peered through them as through bars. Dee Rawlings, this was, who had all the answers. Dee Rawlings, who had made her name by setting the world to rights. 'How should *I* know what you should do? How should I advise you? Don't come to me with your problems, Jamie. I don't have any magic solutions.'

'Well, you're in a peculiar mood, I must say.' He stood up and stretched till a shirt button popped. He took a series of deep breaths in a futile effort to calm himself. His heart was battering in his chest. Oh, God, he couldn't handle this! He had enough troubles, thank you very much, without his own mother turning funny. He had enough to cope with as it was without her going doolally on him.

'Look, cheer up,' he cajoled her, suppressing his desperation, endeavouring to lighten up, to sound normal, 'it can't be that bad, whatever it is. Nothing a good night's sleep won't cure, as you yourself would say. Okay, okay, I'm off to my club. I need the exercise. I shan't be late back. We'll chat then if you want. Be seeing you. Bye-bye.'

And he ran – or almost – from the room, out through the front door, down the tiled path to the road, to leap into his bright red, rampant killing machine.

———————— • ————————

'Media types', proclaimed Shirley Clarke, 'are notoriously unreliable.' She was perched on her fluffy stool at her dressing-table, cleansing and feeding her complexion in preparation for an early night. Twenty-something years ago she had embarked upon the Pond's Seven Day Beauty Plan, and she had been following it slavishly ever since. The sweet, cloying smell of the moisturising cream was for Roy the smell of his wife. Her essence was contained, like a genie, in that opaque white jar.

'It isn't fair to generalise,' he told her with none of his usual good humour, from the bed where he lay propped up on pillows, buttoned into his pyjamas to the neck. His own relentless cheeriness increasingly enervated him; his reserves of patience and of bonhomie were not after all inexhaustible. There had been days, recently, when he'd let his smile slip for minutes at a time. 'People are individuals, not types. Besides, what has Sandie to do with the media? Just because her mother writes an agony column, it doesn't mean –'

'It's a matter of upbringing, isn't it? Of family values. Sandra has been raised in an atmosphere of what can only be called libertarianism. Her moral education has been lax. I'm not small-minded, you'll agree, but a climate in which divorce, adultery, promiscuity are the order of the day, is not in my view a healthy one. Oh, certainly not. It augurs very ill indeed, if you ask me.'

Roy closed his eyes and let her talk wash over him like a shower. But, as in the shower, his ears clogged up, they were awash with words like 'libertarianism', 'moral education', 'lax'.

'I do wish', he said, suppressing a sudden flash of temper, 'that you would stop this nonsense. I am beginning to worry that you're obsessed.'

"Obsessed? Of course I'm not obsessed.' Shirley dabbed around her nose with a wad of cotton wool and inspected with grim satisfaction the make-up traces that adhered to it. 'I am simply concerned with your son's well-being, a subject which seems to exercise you scarcely at all.'

Something inside him finally snapped. He heard it go boi-oing. 'Whose son? *My* son?' he recklessly demanded, from behind his eyelids, from the darkness, the relative safety of the inside of his head. All the same, he dared not to so much as peep to see how Shirley might react to this, and anyway her sudden stillness, the silence, fraught with things unsaid, was reproach enough. He imagined her sitting there, rigid with shock and hurt and mortification. How could he, she'd be thinking, how *could* he bring this up?

'How could you?' There were tears in her voice when at last she replied. 'How could you be so callous as to bring that up?'

'I'm sorry, Shirl, old girl, but you will keep on and on.' He pressed his wrist to his brow. 'I'm sick to death of it, to tell the truth. I'm sick to death of hearing about this unsuitable girl. She's a nice lass. Colin loves her. Just give them your blessing, let him go his own way, and give us all a break.'

But now she was crying, really sobbing, burrowing her cleansed and shining face into the crook of her arm. 'Am I never to be allowed to forget it?' she asked in a throttled tone. 'Must I be punished for as long as I live? As if my own shame were not punishment enough!'

'Hey, hey, hey,' he protested hotly, 'That's hardly fair. I've never mentioned . . . Not from that day to this. It hasn't been an issue between us.'

But, of course, he had to go to her then, to place his hands on her shoulders, to apply a gentle, reassuring pressure, rotating his thumbs, till she swivelled on the stool and clung weeping to his waist.

'You swore,' she rebuked him tearfully. 'You absolutely swore we wouldn't speak of it.'

'Nor have we. And I'm sorry to do so. To have to do so. But I'll tell you this . . .' It would cost him, he was aware, to make this speech, it would tear at his heart, yet make it he must. 'If you don't lay off Colin, if you don't let go your hold on him, I shall tell him the whole truth.'

Roy was not, nor had he ever been, the kind of chap who got a kick from pulling the wings off flies, or from tying tin cans to cats' tails. He would never, for sport, put out the eyes of puppy dogs or throw lighted fireworks fizzing under horses' hooves. But none of these imagined cruelties was more obscene to him than this one, exercised upon the woman he loved.

Because he did love her. Always had. He had proposed marriage to her, not out of nobility, or in a spirit of uncommon chivalry, but opportunistically, because she charmed him with her femininity, because the chance had arisen to snap her up. She had been so pink and white and sugary, in her shiny patent shoes with kitten heels, her flared skirt and her frilly blouse. She had been the very epitome of giggly girlishness. She had also been, to her unutterable dismay, ever so slightly pregnant.

Shirley's attitude to sex, then as now, had been less than robust, and her condition had seemed to her the more intolerable for the cause of which it was effect. Had babies been something one caught, like influenza, had it been a case of mere innocent infection, she could have borne up bravely. She could have retired to the couch for the length of her confinement, taking a little nourishment, picking at grapes, smiling gamely.

As it was, she had succumbed at the tennis-club dance when, under the pernicious influence of vodka and orange, she had consented, unsuspecting, to step outside with the club heart-throb. He was called Terry Gent, but he hadn't been. He had definitely not been a gent.

Quite what had happened on that sultry summer's night, she could never afterwards recall, still less cared to imagine. She had woken next morning with a sick foreboding, and with nettle stings all over her bottom, unable to account for an hour of her life for which, perversely, she had been accounting ever since.

'You wouldn't,' she begged. 'Roy, you *wouldn't* tell Colin. You mustn't.'

'Only if . . .'

He wouldn't, of course. Not even if . . . Because he loved the boy as though he were his own. Because he adored his wife to the depths of his soul.

But, to persuade her, he was forced to pretend. So he left it at that. 'Only if . . .' And she, in recriminatory silence, with head bowed, finally, bitterly acquiesced. And the bugger of it was – as he put it to himself – that, while Colin could get on with his life, while he could be happy for ever with Sandie, his own precious marriage to Shirley would never now be quite the same again.

CHAPTER

————— • —————

17

For the second morning, Superwoman Dee Rawlings awoke in a thundering panic, on the wrong side of the bed, and drew the duvet up over her head to exclude a Saturday which bore down upon her, bringing with it no prospects, no possibilities, no husband, no hope.

She seemed to hurt in every cell of her being. She was one big blob of pain and affront. She was rage and indignation incarnate. Not just her heart but her whole body ached with it. There was also, today, a terrifying sense of physical disintegrating, of the flesh running off her bones. I am falling apart, she decided, and nobody can save me.

She who had done so much for so many, who had offered succour to her readership, who had reached out and touched all those in need, was denied in her darkest hour anyone to whom she might turn. She had given of herself, to her parents, to her partner, to her children, to friends, to complete strangers for Pete's sake, one hundred and one per cent, and she had received in return a stone.

She had taken into her home a child from the slums who had repaid her by turning her husband's head. She had taken into her office an inexperienced schoolgirl who had repaid her by stealing her job.

A laugh flew from her, black as a bat, and went flapping round the room. Bastards, she thought bitterly. Treacherous, scheming, bloody bastards.

Well, she would show the lot of them. She would make them sorry. She would remain here, inert, with her face to the wall, as night followed day followed night; she would refuse to speak, or to swallow so much as a morsel, and would simply waste away.

A sympathetic biographer would at once be commissioned by her publishers. Her tragic story, titled, tellingly, *The Final Agony*, or, in affectionate tribute, *Dear Dee*, would be serialised in a major Sunday newspaper, with TV and radio promotion. It would be in its third reprint before it even hit the bookstands. It would expose the perfidy of those in whom she had placed her trust. Public opinion would be outraged. People would write in their thousands, acknowledging their debt of gratitude to Dee Rawlings. Her name would be sanctified. Oh, what a shame that she would not be there to see it!

For several minutes she lay supine, embellishing the fantasy, plotting her elaborate revenge, her dignified withdrawal from this cruel world – until the call of nature, the insistence of her bladder, drove her from beneath the covers to her bathroom.

So beguiled was she by her own imagining, so fast did her mind run ahead of her, that she pictured herself already wraithlike and wan. The wounded bull elephant that went blundering past her full-length mirror could not, then, have been Dee.

There might be no disowning, however, the blotched and swollen face in the glass above the basin, which reciprocated her look of abject self-pity as she stood and dabbled her hands. There might be no denying that this ludicrous middle-aged woman with a pinched little mouth and sagging jowls and a shock of unnaturally red hair was indeed hers truly.

Groaning, she clung to the cold porcelain, squeezed her eyes shut, wrung out her face like a rag till more tears trickled down her pouchy cheeks. They've all gone, she told herself in desolation. They've pissed off. Deserted me.

She had seen or spoken to no one since Thursday night. Jamie had left the house early yesterday, and had returned very late. She had waited and waited for him to come home in the evening, but he had not shown up or called to say he wouldn't. His supper – had she cooked him one – would certainly have been ruined, yet he had not even bothered to telephone her.

At some time around midnight she had heard his key in the latch, heard footsteps on the stairs, heard him out on the darkened landing going whisper-whisper-whisper to a mystery companion – to some fancy piece whom he must have picked up God alone knew where.

Such advantage he took of his mother! So much did he impose upon her good nature! Yet when it came to giving something back, when it came to being there for her, he was conspicuous by his absence.

But, already she was forgetting, losing track. Yesterday had of course been Friday. Jamie must have expected her to be away with Eric in Kent. He would have been surprised to find the car still parked outside; to see the thin seam of light beneath her bedroom door, behind which, for all he knew, the pair of them, Dee and Eric, still slept as man and wife. Had he had any inkling of her distress, he would certainly have rallied round, he would have given her his full support. If she had no one else, she had her children. Jamie, Alexandra, she could surely count on them.

This realisation consoled her somewhat. It's not the end, she assured herself. It is merely a new beginning. It was time, in any case, that I moved on. I had quite outgrown *Mia* magazine. I shall be snapped up by the opposition for sure. My readers will follow me. Meanwhile, no one will give any credence to a flibbertigibbet like Nancy Wilkins. *Mia* will go under. Clare Constantine will be discredited. The last laugh shall be mine.

By now the news of her abrupt departure would have spread around the Magazines UK building. The announcement would have been pinned on noticeboards: Dee Rawlings had left to concentrate on her freelance career. (Writers, editors, were never sacked, they just 'went freelance'. As politicians will now and then leave office to spend more time with their families, so journalists will leave to spend more time with their word-processors. Everybody knows that there has been some unpleasantness, but its precise nature is a matter of mere conjecture.)

Well, thank goodness that she had a freelance career on which to concentrate. Thank goodness she still had her books, her television work. She was even now a household name, with a huge, devoted following. She was not finished. Good gracious, no!

As for Eric, the poor man had plainly suffered some kind of breakdown. His mid-life crisis must be more profound than she had guessed. He would come to his senses in due course and return to her. Everything would be much as it had always been, it would be *better*.

Meanwhile, appearances must be maintained. She should run herself a nice hot bath, she should make up her poor face, smile though her heart was breaking.

She must keep up her strength, too, this was essential. She must force herself to eat breakfast, a slice of bread, a couple of rashers, perhaps one or two of those delicious new Pop Tarts. . .

Dee Rawlings had not spent the best part of her adult life treating other people to pep talks, without being able to give herself pep. She was a woman of resilience and resource. She had vast stores of homespun wisdom on which to draw in times of trouble, and she drew on them now to the dregs.

It had all been taken care of, Jamie was positive of it. He felt it in his bones and in his water. Somehow his problems had been sorted out. He was free to get on with his life and not to fret.

He was thankful now that he had not given in to impulse, had not in a moment of weakness discussed with his mother the unpleasant little matter of Audrey Atkins. How fortunate that Dee had been too preoccupied or too poorly (going down with a bug, perhaps) to hear him out! If he never told another living soul about what happened, it would come to seem in time that nothing had.

Jamie Rawlings was not a great one for religion, for worship, for hymns and hallelujahs. He did not go in for genuflection, for oblation, for propitiation, for dreary recitations from the Book of Common Prayer or murmured confessions behind velvet curtains. He would, however, in emergencies, try to strike all kinds of deals with the Almighty, whose ear he rather fancied he had.

He was possessed of an infantile sense of his own importance. He had a sneaking suspicion that he was singularly favoured, a spoilt-childish conviction that the world revolved around him. If he believed in anything above all else, he believed in Jamie Rawlings.

People would, he had noticed, take the most perverse, pre-posterous things upon themselves. They would organise garden parties, paint their front porches, polish their cars, hang out their weekly washing, leave their umbrellas at home, and then, laughing with a kind of sham self-deprecation, would claim full responsibility for an ensuing downpour. But they were ridiculously deluded. If it rained it did so for quite other reasons, since the weather did nothing without reference to him.

If he arranged to spend the weekend in the country, he could more or less count on glorious sunshine. If he desired to be excused from some onerous duty – a visit to his grandparents, an errand for his mother – he had every hope of being snowed in, fog bound, or by some other means exempted. If he was late for a train or plane, it would be delayed. Once, at school, when he'd been honour bound to fight some ugly brute who had threatened to punch his lights out, the Lord had visited upon his adversary, a boy named Osborne, a very nasty case of conjunctivitis and the fixture had had to be scratched.

On the rare occasion when things failed to go his way, there would always be some reason which would later make itself apparent. The plane he missed would develop engine trouble and turn back for Heathrow. The train he missed would be derailed at Crewe. Once, sheltering in a shop doorway from the torrential rain which had scotched his plans for a day at the races, he had met a gorgeous girl with marmalade eyes and long, flowing curls like Botticelli's Venus. (It was chucking it down, she had solemnly assured him, because she had just washed her hair. Jamie, however, knowing better, and offering up his silent thanks, had taken her home and fucked her bandy.)

Divine intervention, then, and not sheer chance, had doubtless delivered Audrey Atkins to him, propelling her into the path of his speeding Porsche. His sense, at the time, of being challenged, had not been misplaced. He had done what he'd had to do, and there was an end to it.

If Audrey was dead, as dead she must be, it was because some higher power had decreed it. Someone, watching over him, had rescued him from his ordeal.

There had been no witnesses, nor was there a shred of evidence to link him to the crime. Nobody on earth – least of all fat, lethargic

Angie Burston – would connect him to it. No one would identify the soppy hat.

He stretched with satisfaction, clasped his hands behind his head, and gazed indulgently upon his sleeping companion. What more proof could he want of God's belief in him? For here, in his bed beside him, drowsing, replete with love, was the gorgeous girl from the club.

He had nipped over to the gym last night, straight from the office, just knowing he would meet her there. He had chosen his moment to smile at her as she stood balanced on one braced leg, with a heel resting on the barre, with her arms raised above her head, stretching and bending at the waist in delicious contortion. 'Hello,' he had mouthed at her, his eyes drawn to the inner aspect of one lean thigh, to her crotch concealed by a wisp of black material. And 'Hello,' she had mouthed, returning his smile in a languid, lingering fashion.

Later, she had come into the bar, with that swaying walk of hers, with a sweatshirt knotted around her hips, and with the looseness of someone who has been thoroughly extended. He had signalled to her, offered her a drink, and she had hopped on to the stool next to his, lowering her eyes, lifting to her luscious lips a glass of purple plum juice, as privately he exulted in her loveliness.

She was truly sublime, possessed of peerless, priceless, patrician beauty. She was quite without flaw. Her skin was so satin-smooth, her hair so glossy, her eyes so clear, her physique so finely wrought, she was so manifestly, radiantly healthy, that beside her the braying Lucinda Blackstock would look shoddy, second-rate – while with silly little Kayleigh Roth there might, of course, be no comparison.

In an Italian restaurant where Jamie had taken her to dinner, she had eaten sparingly of salad and shellfish, sipping at still mineral water. She had answered in an enigmatic fashion, and in soft, mellifluous tones, the questions he had fired at her. And, though a teasing smile had now and then tweaked at her mouth, she had not once honked with laughter, or tipped back the wine and called for more, or sworn like a trooper, told him for fuck's sake not to be so witless.

'I'm in property,' he had bragged to her, bending the truth

423

very slightly. 'And you? No, don't tell me. Let me guess. You're a dancer.'

To which she had replied neither yea nor nay, though she had seemed by the mischievous sparkle of her eyes, as she bit through a prawn with her strong white teeth, to offer him ample confirmation.

'I guessed. I could tell. I somehow knew. Your poise, your grace . . . You simply had to be . . .'

To know her (to know, as in to become acquainted with) would not be easy, for there was something of the sphinx about her, mysterious, secretive, elusive. Yet to know her in the biblical sense, to have his way with her, had been simply a matter of asking. 'Would you . . . ?' he had ventured. 'That is, will you come back to my place?' And she, by an enchanting pout, by a narrowing of the eyes, had consented. Then, what joy, what delight, what delirious pleasure he had had in her!

Naked, she was somehow extraordinarily unified, the perfect sum of her parts, with no unsightly lumps or bumps, with nothing surplus, and with everything sweetly proportioned. He had never set eyes on a body so cared for, so firmed and pared and pampered. Her legs, her underarms, her pubes had been stripped of hair, a discovery which aroused him mightily. She had the small, high breasts, the tiny waist, the muscularity of an adolescent gymnast. And, boy, did she go for it! She had been insatiable. Unstoppable. She'd been on him, she'd been under him, she'd been absolutely all over him. She was dynamite, he told himself in self-congratulation, meaning, of course, that with *him* she was dynamite, that the two of them together had gone with a tremendous bang.

The word 'nymphomaniac' suggested itself to him. He had heard it said that no such creature exists outside the male imagination, and had been disposed to believe it until this moment. For no one, after knowing – after *knowing* knowing – this woman, could for one instant doubt it.

He was drifting back into a deep, contented sleep, when her hand closed upon his flaccid penis and coaxed it once more into life. 'No,' he protested feebly, as the whole of him seemed to impact around his own desire.

But, 'Yes,' she whispered, close to his ear, 'Oh, yes, Jamie, yes, yes, yes.'

Freedom, if you can believe the song, is just another word for nothing left to lose. And by this reckoning Eric was free as a bird. He sat stark naked at the foot of the bed to pull on his socks, then got up to fill the kettle, set it on the hob and lit the gas under it with a Swan Vesta, all the while delighting in his unaccustomed liberty.

No doubt this small room would come in time to oppress him, for it was poky and dingy and undeniably grim, but for now it infused him with perverse delight.

The carpet design might have been inspired by a bout of projectile vomiting brought on by the injudicious consumption of lager and a chicken biriani. A drop-leaf table under the window was scratched and chipped and dulled with use. It had a small drawer crammed with short lengths of string, and with old carrier-bags – blue-and-white from Tesco, brown paper, beige – all neatly folded, saved by some conscientious former tenant.

The one deceptively 'easy' chair, with its bent wooden arms, was fiendishly uncomfortable and precarious: under the prickly bouclé cushion, telltale strips of rubber webbing hung down. Siege Perilous, Eric had already dubbed the piece, and he was mindful never to sit down too hard or in haste upon it, lest he fall right through it.

The skittish single bed, teetering on thin black legs, animated by castors and draped in mauve candlewick, appeared vaguely institutional, recalling an old people's home run by some well-meaning but cash-starved local authority. Above it hung, at staggered heights, three small framed prints of anaemic watercolour roses.

The view, too, was pretty dismal. His first-floor window overlooked a square of crazy paving on which gaudy French marigolds and floppy petunias bloomed in polystyrene urns. A rockery sported a beard of alyssum. A hose snaked around and around before disappearing in a clump of aubretia. A plastic patio set, white tables and chairs, had been herded into the far corner. A motorbike lurked beneath tarpaulin.

A mirror image of this house gazed balefully across the creosoted rear fence. Peering, Eric half expected to see, in the identical window to his own, a small and balding man much like himself, with pale, tired skin and pale, tired eyes and a two-day growth of beard.

Yet, withal, he was happy and excited. Everything was so fantastically novel, so fearfully strange, so bizarre. He hadn't done anything this daring since, as a boy, he had slept out in the garden in a tent of his own devising, and on that occasion he had fled indoors in panic in the early hours.

He had taken control of his life. He was empowered. He had become, as Dee would term it, pro-active. He was his own man finally.

Beneath him, outside the kitchen, the drain bloomed suddenly with iridescent foam. Then Mrs B (as he liked to think of her), in a blue nylon overall, emerged to shake out a coconut doormat. He gazed down at her thick white frizz of hair until, sensing his presence, she glanced up at him, took in his naked torso, visibly tut-tutted, and turned impatiently, irritably, away. She had so far displayed very few of the characteristics of the archetypal landlady. She had shown not the slightest curiosity about him or his circumstances. To arouse in her a glimmer of interest, he suspected, he would have to do somewhat more than simply keep himself to himself.

He flung open the wardrobe, dragged out the first clothes to come to hand, dressed himself haphazardly. Later, when he'd made a trip to the shared bathroom, he would spruce himself up. For the moment, what the hell, he'd be scruffy.

When the kettle came wheezing to the boil, he made himself tea and carried it to the table. There he sat with the steaming mug before him, alternately sucking on a biro and whistling through his teeth, as he considered the wording of a card for the newsagent's window. He meant to offer his services as a jobbing gardener to generate a small income until he felt ready to put into effect his plans for a flower nursery.

His needs for the present would be modest. So long as he could meet the weekly rent, so long as he had the price of a pint, enough for a fish-and-chip supper or a takeaway Chinese dinner, he would be well satisfied.

He expected to be lonely. But, then, when had he not been?

He had spent so many interminable days looming around the house in Clapham, vainly searching for tasks to occupy his hands and to engage his idling brain. He envisaged for himself, now, a better quality of loneliness, austere, deep, dignified, and decidedly short-lived, since any day he could meet someone new and fall hopelessly in love.

She would not be a young girl such as Kayleigh (he quite saw how foolish, how headstrong, how deluded he had been over her), but a nice, warm, humorous lady of much his own age. He pictured smile lines, crinkly eyes, rouged cheeks and loose yellow curls; he pictured shapely legs, pictured straining blouse buttons, a big, high, jaunty bust. He had her sat up at the bar smoking menthol cigarettes, enjoying a saucy joke with the lads. He had her in clerical work, filing and suchlike, or at the supermarket check-out, nothing too high powered. He had her as unlike Deirdre Crabtree as she could conceivably be.

In spite of himself, he began to wonder what Dee would make of his situation. She would not, of course, begin to comprehend. Here was her problem, the poor old love: she might be long on the theory of human emotion, but she was woefully short on insight. She didn't know, nor would she ever, what made a person tick.

Right now, he supposed, she would be wondering how soon he would come crawling home. She would have explained away his behaviour as pure aberration, would have attributed it to depression, to breakdown, to hormonal turbulence. She would doubtless, even now, be working out the punishing terms upon which she would receive him back.

Well, he wasn't *going* back. Not today, not tomorrow, not ever. And you could forget about breakdown, forget depression, forget hormones. He could frankly not remember when he'd felt more larky.

———————————— • ————————————

This was a bit bloody weird, wasn't it? It was a bit of a bleeding mystery.

Kayleigh buttered a slice of bread and handed it to Ben, who slapped it over his face like a compress. 'You're a funny boy, you,' she told him fondly, indulgently, stirring his hair with the tip of her finger, tapping on his skull. 'Now, you eat that nicely, you hear me?'

She subsided into a chair, rested her elbows on the table and made a pediment for her face with her hands, narrowing the focus of her gaze, fixing on a knot in the pine which took upon itself distinct human characteristics then aged horrifically before her eyes.

The silence of the house sank in through her skin, and with it a new and awful realism. She had told herself such pretty lies these past few weeks, she had charmed herself with her fancies, she had quite turned her own head with sweet self-deception. But there was something ruthless in her make-up, a need, at least sometimes, to deal in fact, to subdue her wayward heart, to discipline her emotions, to grapple with the truth – whatever that might be, and however painful.

Besides, she was committed. She had entered into solemn compact with herself and could not now renegotiate the terms. Had Jamie come to her before today, or had he called to speak to her, she would not have abandoned hope as now she must. This had been her test for him, which he had so signally failed. (If I don't see him or hear from him by Saturday, she had decided, I shan't see him ever again.) Therefore, it was over – or, perhaps, had never been. Nothing could excuse, nothing explain away his negligence. Simply, he did not care enough. He did not care at all.

She had set a certain standard by which he must be judged. If he had loved as deeply as she, if he had been as hopelessly embroiled, he would have done as she would do. And he hadn't, so he didn't, and there, sad to say, was an end to it.

But here was the most peculiar thing: it was not only Jamie who had gone missing from her life. For where were Dee and Eric this weekend? Where was Sandie? Kayleigh had spent yesterday evening in a mood of drear anticipation, which had given way, contrarily – as eight, nine, ten o'clock came and went – to disappointment. Little as she had relished seeing Dee with her overbearing, self-opinionated manner, or Eric with his attitude of injured vanity, his sneaky glances of reproach, she was profoundly disconcerted and ever so slightly miffed by their non-appearance.

The place had never seemed more empty, never looked more strange since first she came here. Over the months, familiarity had blurred her perception of it. She had ceased to see with any clarity the scene to which she had become inured.

Yet, this morning everything was once again distinct. With a kind of ghastly ostentation the expensive carpets, curtains and upholstery declared themselves to her. Furniture flaunted itself. All was somehow exhibition and spectacle. Foxholes had the aspect of a swanky show house, or a series of room sets, in which nobody, after all, had ever lived or ever would.

'They might have had the courtesy to telephone,' she said to Ben. And, 'Don't do that. Yuck. Christ! You'll make yourself all sticky.'

What had been accomplished by her stay here? More than she would acknowledge. By her own creative accounting, she was in some ways much the poorer. She had been used by Dee to some obscure purpose. She had been used by Jamie, whose purpose, in hindsight, was only too clear. She had been got at by Eric, she had been sexually harassed. Sandie, alone of all the Rawlings family, had been a genuine friend. But Kayleigh had also changed inwardly, she had grown spiritually. She had distanced herself from her life, the better to examine it. She had enjoyed the benefits of a retreat.

'Come outside, Ben. Yes, bring the bread with you if you want. You can eat it on the grass. We'll have a picnic.'

The garden was so very, very lovely. The ancient walls dripped with wisteria. The borders overran with big, fat, blood-red peonies, pink arabis, daphne and phlox. Fuck-me-nots spattered the lawn, over which the house cast a long, black shadow, for it was barely half past eight and the sun had still to climb above the steep, tiled rooftop.

Picking her child up for a warming hug, Kayleigh nuzzled his downy cheek. 'You'll be happy,' she promised him earnestly as he beamed with pleasure. Then, peering into his impossibly blue eyes, 'I'm sorry I've made such a mess of it all, but it's going to come good, you wait and see.'

———————————— • ————————————

'So are you coming with me or what?' asked Colin breezily.

'What,' responded Sandie, her voice thick still with sleep,

her eyes tight shut, and she snatched wildly at the sheet which he hauled off her to expose her to the faintly chilly morning air.

'What?'

'You said, was I coming with you or what, so I said "what".'

'You're not coming, you mean?'

'Well, all right.'

'Just all right?'

'Yes, of course I'm flipping coming. You know I am.' She shook herself properly awake. 'You try and stop me. This flat, I have got to see.'

'It sounds all right, doesn't it?' he queried in a falsely modest, an it-was-nothing-really sort of voice.

'Mm. It sounds tremendous.' She rolled on to her stomach, hung her head over the edge of the mattress, and read again with bleary eyes, from the newspaper on the floor, the small ad around which he had inked a border of spidery stars. 'Barnes, eh? Nice.'

'We could have lunch at a pub if you liked.'

'I would like.'

'Saturday's the nicest day, isn't it, San? Of the entire week.'

'Yes, it's the best.'

A rivulet of sunlight, washing through the dormer window of her attic bedroom, lapped around her where she lay prone reciting out loud from the paper. 'Lge ktchn/dnr,' she said. 'One rcpt. Two dble bdrms. Bthrm.'

'Not to mention sep WC.'

'And sep WC.'

'I said not to mention sep WC.'

'Oh, sorry.'

'That's all right.' He slapped her jovially on the backside. 'Don't do it again.'

'I'll try not to.'

He smiled down on her, entranced as always by her sturdy back, her broad waist, her flattened buttocks, her strong, uncompromising build, her coarse and tousled hair. Moving closer, he slid his hand between her legs and probed around to make her wriggle with desire. 'Don't,' she protested happily. 'Where's the sheet? Please cover me up.'

'Why should I?'

'I feel fat.'

'Don't be daft.'

'But I am.'

'What, daft?'

'No, fat.'

'You are not.'

'I don't look it? Not to you?'

'Not a bit of it. You're splendiferous.'

'But my thighs,' she persisted, fishing for reassurance. 'I hate my thighs. They make me want to weep.'

'I can't think why. You know what they say?'

'What do they say?'

'Thighs doesn't matter.'

'Listen, don't you believe it, buddy.'

'No?'

'No. That's one of the three big lies. Along with "I love you".'

'I love you,' he assured her.

'And "the cheque is in the post." '

'The cheque is in the post.' Flopping on top of her he skewered her from behind.

'Not that you need concern yourself,' she mumbled, 'in the matter of size.' And, with a wail of disappointment, as the telephone began to ring, 'Oh, no-o!'

'Ignore it.'

'I can't.' She began to struggle out from under him. 'It'll be Mrs Sturgess. She promised to call to confirm numbers for Monday night.'

'She can talk to the machine.'

'But the machine isn't on. Let me out. Let me up. Ooh, quick, quick.'

'Hurry on back, now, you hear?' he called after her as she went bounding to pick up the receiver. But, in the event, she was gone for some while.

Lying there in lazy contentment, as his erection subsided, he wondered at the change he had perceived in Shirley. 'I've seen a flat advertised,' he had told her yesterday evening as, sick at heart, he had anticipated her bleating response. 'I'm going to look at it tomorrow.' Then, 'That's nice,' she had replied in a faintly distrait manner, as though her mind were elsewhere, as though it mattered not a jot to her either way. 'If it's suitable I shall move in.' 'You will?

Right.' 'As soon as possible.' 'Very well. Whatever you want.' 'And I'm going to get engaged to Sandie,' he'd informed her, pushing his luck to the limit. But, 'That's nice,' was all she'd said.

It was a real break. It was tremendous. He was profoundly thankful and relieved by this lightening in her attitude, this apparent letting go, this new acceptance. And yet he was puzzled. There was something rather odd about. . .

'That was my mother,' said Sandra, her shadow falling across the bed. He raised his eyes to see her standing there with her arms across the soft swell of her belly, hugging herself, frowning.

'Something up?'

'Nothing really. Only . . .'

'Mm?'

'Well, you know, she sounded . . . How can I put it? Not quite herself.'

'Explain.'

'I'm not sure that I can.' She knelt with one knee on the bed. 'She said how was I and what was I doing with myself, all the usual mumsy stuff.'

'And . . .?'

'And then she said she wanted to see me.' She sat down heavily. 'She said, "It would be nice to see you, Sandie."'

'And that's odd?'

'Yes, it is, actually. Oh, I know it doesn't *sound* odd. But there was something kind of . . . something needy in her tone. And something . . . Something fond.'

'Is that not normal?'

'Not exactly. I mean, I'm sure she loves me in her fashion, I'm not saying she doesn't. And I am occasionally summoned to the presence. She likes to gather her family around her from time to time.'

'But . . . ?'

'But there was a note in her voice that I never heard before. As if it mattered terribly that I should go round there.'

'Are you going?'

'*We* are going. Tonight, if that's okay. I said "I'm with Colin. For the whole of today. The whole weekend." And she said, "It's high time I met this Colin." So I said we'd come for supper, and she said that would be lovely. That's all right, isn't it? You don't

432

mind, do you?'

'Mind? Not in the least. She's right, it's time we met.'

'She can be a trifle . . . overbearing.'

'I shall brace myself to be overborne. Hey, hey, Sandie, what's the problem? Has she upset you?'

'Upset me? No.' She frowned and scratched her eyebrows. 'To tell the truth, I'm gratified. It was always Jamie, you see. He was the blue-eyed boy. I never had much sense of being important to her. I was always a sort of . . . sideshow.'

'Well, I'll tell you, that has its advantages. It's a bit of a strain to be the main event.'

'Which you are for your mum.'

'Her little ray of sunshine.'

'The light of her life.'

'Precisely.' He opened his arms and she sank down gratefully into them. 'Mothers! What can you say about them?'

'Nothing really.'

'They're all bonkers.'

'All of them?'

'Most of them.'

'Shall I be? When I'm a mother?'

'Mad as a hatter, I have no doubt. But are you going to be one?'

'Am I? What do you reckon? Should I be?'

'In the fullness of time.' He kissed her on the tip of her nose. 'Once we're good and married I shall get you banged up, big with child, Mrs Clarke.'

———————— • ————————

Charlie Horscroft faced the facts, not head on so they could dazzle him, but slightly asquint. As he stood, narrow-eyed, over the frying-pan, as he flipped his egg then flopped it between two buttered slices, he made a frank admission to himself: he was good on his own, but not great. He needed somebody. The company of his dog, delightful though it might be, was no substitute for the company of another human being. He was not, after all, one of nature's loners. He was not temperamentally single. He was not Tom Jenner's like, his natural heir, his successor. Providence Cottage would never be the home he had envisaged, unless he

433

found a mate with whom to share it.

There, now. He'd said it. He had confessed it to himself. He was lonely. He was creaking with loneliness.

He had been in such ill humour for the past couple of weeks, his ladies, his customers, must surely have noticed. He had gone about his tasks without a song, without a whistle. He had sat at their kitchen tables, eating their crumbly fruitcake, drinking their tea, with scarcely a civil word for any of them. Each job had seemed too big, or too small, or too tedious. He had skimped, if not on his work, on his commitment to it.

God, he was low. He could not remember ever being more so. Because – here was another unpalatable truth, a sad reflection on his character – he was sick with jealousy of Jamie Rawlings, he was eaten up and wormy with ignoble thoughts about the guy. Because of course he was in love with Kayleigh. Because he didn't want just *anyone* to share his life. He wanted her, and he wanted her child, for whom he had made in his heart such huge, such generous accommodation.

He lounged against the sink, drummed his heels against the cupboard door, a brooding figure in torn jeans and singlet, as he ate the sandwich he had so carelessly slapped together. His sense of his own sufficiency was horribly undermined. He did not know what to do, how to manage the feelings within him. He was so choked up with emotions, he could scarcely swallow. He crammed the bread down in the vague belief that he must eat, that in burning up calories he would also mysteriously burn off some of his ire.

One day, for sure, there would be someone else for him. A girl would come into his life and take her place. Then he would try, by way of mental exercise, to call to his mind little Kayleigh Roth, and, amusingly, he would find himself quite unable to reconstitute her.

But that could be years and years away, and in the meantime there was just this dismal, hateful, hollow sensation, and his life, always so vivid, had been drained of colour.

Disgusted with himself, with his weakness and despair, he chucked the half-eaten egg sandwich into the pedal bin.

Saturday. He would dig over the garden, he decided, and sweat out his ill humour. He would exhaust his body and, at last, his mind. He would push himself through the barrier to a place beyond pain.

434

But then he couldn't move, he absolutely couldn't move a muscle.

When the bell rang, he ignored it. He had no wish to see anyone just now. He hated everybody.

It rang again, long and insistently.

'What the bloody hell . . . ?' he muttered as he went at last and yanked the door open.

She stood there with her bags, with her baby, with her buggy, in an attitude at once bold and diffident. She tossed her head, and the sun, riding higher now in the morning sky, seemed to torch her hair so it incandesced.

'Can we come in?' said Kayleigh in that growly voice of hers.

———————— • ————————

When she opened her eyes there were lilies, pale and pink-tinged, with furly, curly petals and golden stamens, there were daisies with bright yellow eyes. It was all a bit swimmy. A figure came towards her, amorphous, blue and white.

She wondered for a while where she was. She wondered *who* she was. She had her sense of self, of course, she had some kind of continuity, unbroken and unbreakable, with the old her. But if you'd asked her her name she might have hesitated. She might have said, 'Er . . . well now . . .', she might have been forced to confess herself at somewhat of a loss.

Then the blue-and-white shape coalesced, it took on human form, it took on uniform. A face smiled rosily down on her. 'Ah, so you've woken up at last. Doctor will be pleased to hear it.'

She must, then, be in hospital. She must be ill. A stiff-necked glance to right and left confirmed it. But what in heaven's name had brought her to this place?

'I . . .' she said, but her mouth was quite dry. She waved her hand around to signal her distress.

The nurse bent over her, professionally attentive. 'A lovely bouquet from your friends at the club. People have been most concerned. Now, don't you fuss yourself. You're on the mend.'

When she closed her eyes again it came to her, in every detail, with great suddenness, as if someone had switched on the light inside her skull.

She knew who she was, and that she had nearly died. She knew that at some point she had had a choice, and that she had chosen to survive. The young in their arrogance imagine that our hold on life becomes more tenuous with the years. Seldom is it so. We hang on in.

So she was back in the land of the living. She was returned to consciousness. 'Now . . .'

'Yes, dear.' the nurse frowned at a fob watch as she took her pulse.

'Now I remember everything,' said Audrey Atkins.

———————— ● ————————

Jamie lay back, lickerish, oily with lust, with his arms wrapped around his head, and watched as she emerged from the bathroom, dauntingly brisk and businesslike.

'You're beautiful,' he told her, hoping to retard her, to slow the pace of her departure, though the word seemed woefully inadequate, a pathetic apology for an adjective. 'You're more than beautiful, you're . . .' Then there wasn't another word – at any rate not one that he could think of – so he was forced to let it pass.

However, she nodded, either in acceptance or agreement, she took the compliment as she found it. No false modesty for her. Beautiful, she seemed to indicate, would do.

As he watched, she stood before him, in knickers and suspenders, combing her red hair till it crackled. Then, turning, she picked up a stocking, a whisper of silk, gathered it in her two hands, slipped it over her toe, rolled it over her foot and up her leg then snapped shut the suspenders. Jamie was entranced by the elegance, the efficiency, the sheer femininity of the performance.

But then, 'Yesterday's clothes,' she said with a little moue, a look of distaste, more to herself than to him. 'This is always the worst part.'

Always?

He couldn't bear to pursue it, for it was all too imaginable, its implications too dismaying. It opened up a line of questioning which could only lead to trouble. ('You do this a lot?' he might have asked. 'You make a habit of it?' 'You get off on one-night stands?' 'It's just a means to feed your vanity?' 'You took advantage of me?') And sooner than enquire he let it pass.

He needed to think this thing was very special, he needed to think it was love. He needed to believe he was, if not a first, at any rate the best. Not least, he needed to believe she was what he fussily termed 'clean'. He had heard it said, very graphically, in the matter of disease, that when you slept with someone, you slept with all their former sexual partners too. Well, he wasn't entertaining every Tom, Dick and Harry in his bed, thank you very much! He wasn't sharing this delightful creature with every Tom's and Harry's dick. So he banished the legions of others from his mind.

'I want you to meet my folks,' he told her casually, suppressing a note of fierce possession, affecting a yawn.

This was how proud he was with, how utterly thrilled by, his conquest. He was keen to parade her before his parents, to bask in his mother's approval.

Because of course this was what he craved above all else: Dee's blessing, her approbation. He wanted her to see, to understand, to acknowledge his manifest success. He wanted to be her best boy.

He had shrunk from introducing Lucinda to her, principally because she would have frowned upon her. In the end it had been her scorn and not Lucinda's he had dreaded.

Then, if she'd known about Kayleigh she would of course have hit the roof.

As for his father, he'd be pig sick when he saw this flame-haired lovely, he'd be green with envy of Jamie's good fortune. Oh, what sport! What an absolute hoot! What a triumph!

'Normally they'd not be here on a Saturday,' he boasted. 'We'd have the place to ourselves. Because they go to the country, you know.' He got up, staggered under the weight of a sudden secret anxiety, pulled on his blue silk robe and knotted the sash. 'So I guess they must have had a change of plan.'

'Mm,' she responded indifferently.

'And I expect you'd like some tea? Some coffee? No?'

'No. I'd like some water, though.'

'That can be arranged. Whatever. Come.'

437

When they stepped on to the landing he smelt bacon and felt ravenous. Then he glimpsed the fastidious crinkle of her nose, and his appetite deserted him. 'Bit much,' he muttered, 'a fry-up at this time of the morning.'

Following the scent, he led the way downstairs, along the hall to the kitchen, and put his head around the door.

His mother was sitting there in solitary splendour with a plate in front of her. She was eating that most indigestible of meals known in the hotel trade as the 'full English breakfast', she was shovelling it in. Her manner was strange to him, at once concentrated and distracted. 'Uhm,' he said, and cleared his throat.

'Ah, Jamie.' She spared him the briefest of glances as she speared an egg. The yolk ran yellow.

Perhaps this was not, after all, such a great idea, but there might be no going back. So, 'I want you to meet someone,' he said awkwardly, and he cleared his throat a second time. 'The new love of my life,' he added in inverted commas, with earnestness disguised as self-parody.

'Yes?' Dee raised her eyebrows in polite enquiry as she plied her fork.

Then the door swung back and Dee Rawlings found herself gazing, with sheer incredulity, into the cool, green eyes of Clare Constantine.